The Simple Stage

Recent Titles in
Contributions in Drama and Theatre Studies

THE SIMPLE STAGE

Its Origins in the
Modern American Theater

ARTHUR FEINSOD

Contributions in Drama and Theatre Studies, Number 38

GREENWOOD PRESS
New York • Westport, Connecticut • London

Library of Congress Cataloging-in-Publication Data

PN
2091
.S8
F43
1992

Feinsod, Arthur.
  The simple stage : its origins in the modern American theater /
Arthur Feinsod.
    p. cm.—(Contributions in drama and theatre studies, ISSN
0163-3821 ; no. 38)
  Includes bibliographical references and index.
  ISBN 0-313-25715-9 (alk. paper)
  1. Theaters—United States—Stage-setting and scenery—
History—20th century. 2. Theater—United States—History—20th
century. I. Title. II. Series.
PN2091.S8F43 1992
792'.025'09730904—dc20   90-25222

British Library Cataloguing in Publication Data is available.

Library of Congress Catalog Card Number: 90-25222
ISBN: 0-313-25715-9
ISSN: 0163-3821

First published in 1992

Greenwood Press, 88 Post Road West, Westport, CT 06881
An imprint of Greenwood Publishing Group, Inc.

Printed in the United States of America

The paper used in this book complies with the
Permanent Paper Standard issued by the National
Information Standards Organization (Z39.48-1984).

10 9 8 7 6 5 4 3 2 1

Copyright Acknowledgments

Grateful acknowledgment is given for permission to excerpt from the
following sources:

From *The Dramatic Imagination* by Robert Edmond Jones. By permission
of the publisher, Routledge, Chapman & Hall, Inc.

From *Inspiration and Rhythm, 1914-1916* by Maurice Browne. By
permission of The Ellen Van Volkenburg/Maurice Browne Papers,
Department of Rare Books and Special Collections, The University of
Michigan Library.

Every reasonable effort has been made to trace the owners of copyright
materials in this book, but in some instances this has proven impossible.
The author and publisher will be glad to receive information leading to
more complete acknowledgments in subsequent printings of the book and in
the meantime extend their apologies for any omissions.

For my parents, Robert and Kalma Feinsod, who have been a constant support over the years. This book is written with love and gratitude for the example they have set.

CONTENTS

ILLUSTRATIONS

Chapter 6. Robert Edmond Jones and Arthur Hopkins

Chapter 7. Lee Simonson, Theodore Komisarjevsky, and *The Tidings Brought to Mary*

Chapter 8. Thornton Wilder and the Playwright's Initiative

ACKNOWLEDGMENTS

This book was made possible by the generous gift of time and funding from the National Endowment of the Humanities and the Faculty Research Committee of Trinity College.

I am also indebted to my two mentors, Professors Michael Kirby of New York University and Dunbar Ogden of the University of California at Berkeley. Their integrity and excellence as teachers and scholars have been a constant source of inspiration to my life and work.

I particularly want to express my gratitude to six people who read portions of the manuscript and served this book by not letting me off easy: Trinity Professors Hugh Ogden, Judy Dworin, Ellison Findly, and Patricia Eakins; Faculty Grants Director Naomi Amos; painter Sheffield Van Buren; and my dear friend Andrew Davis.

I want to thank former and present colleagues at Trinity who were always willing to listen, react, and, in other ways, contribute to the development of this work: Professors Carter McAdams, Nusha Martynuk, Katharine Power, Andre Gribou, Joshua Karter, Mohammad Ghaffari, Lenora Champagne, Mardges Bacon, Dori Katz, Eugene Leach, and Dan Lloyd. I also would like to thank Dean of the Faculty Jan Cohn and Associate Academic Dean Jack Waggett for the release time and financial support that made this book possible.

Colleagues from other institutions offering warm counsel were: Len Berkman of Smith College, Barbara Kirshenblatt-Gimblett and Brooks McNamara of NYU, Michael Yurieff of Norwich University, Ralph Swentzell from St. John's College (Santa Fe), Cheng Pei Kai of Pace University, and Greg Leaming, Associate Artistic Director of the Hartford Stage Company.

Over the period during which I have worked on the present book, I have been fortunate to receive strong personal support from family and friends. In addition to my parents, to whom this book is dedicated, they include: Mary

Kramer, Lincoln and Simon Peterson, Fred Feinsod and Buffy McDevitt, Ellen and Jerry Jacobs, Ruth, Allen, and Melissa Wertzel, Cheryl Stidolph, John and Kelly Magill, Arthur Brown, Martha Burtt, and Carol Wolf Holtzman. I also would like for this book to help remember family members no longer present whose blessings at the early phases of this project continued to provide inspiration through to its completion: Gertrude Shapiro, Mira Jacobs, and Larry Stidolph.

I am also indebted to those who supplied technical assistance: David Stidolph, who generously shared with me his computer expertise; Marilyn Brownstein, Maureen Melino, and Lisa Reichbach from the Greenwood Publishing Group; Paul Stern for design and typesetting; and, from Trinity College, Philip Duffy in the Audio-Visual Department, Austin Arts Secretary Lynn Morrissey, and Theater/Dance Department Secretary Mary Sheppard-Earon.

I would also extend my gratitude to those who granted me free and unimpeded passage through their library collections, gave permission to use photographs, quotations from their work, or otherwise supplied useful information on subject matter pertaining to this book: Jane Booth and the San Diego Historical Society; R. K. Mater and the Theosophical Society; William Roberts of the Bancroft Library, UC Berkeley; Dr. Robert Bradley; Joanne Vallas of Henry Holt and Company; Dr. Bettina Knapp, author of *The Reign of the Theatrical Director* published by Whitston Publishing Co., Troy, New York; Former Director MaLin Wilson and Tiska Blankenship, Jonson Gallery, University of New Mexico, Albuquerque; Kathryn L. Beam, Manuscript Librarian, Harlan Hatcher Graduate Library, University of Michigan; Dr. Bernard F. Dukore, Virginia Tech; Jonathan Dodd of Dodd, Mead & Company; Seth Denbo and the Routledge, Chapman and Hall; Nancy Roberts, MIT Press Journals Permissions Manager; Patricia Willis, Curator of American Literature, Beinecke Rare Book and Manuscript Library, Yale University; Thornton Wilder's executor Donald C. Gallup and Wilder's sister, Isabel Wilder; Kathryn Mets of the Museum of the City of New York; G. Cohen from the Bibliothèque Nationale in Paris; Richard M. Buck, Assistant to the Chief, Performing Arts Research Center, Astor Lenox and Tilden Foundations, Billy Rose Theatre Collection, the New York Public Library at Lincoln Center; and Ralph Emerick and the staff of the Trinity College Library. And special thanks to Edith Golub of the Macmillan Publishing Company.

INTRODUCTION

Since the Italian Renaissance, filling the stage has been a persistent temptation in Western theater. This book is about American theater artists—mostly directors and designers—who resisted that temptation, preferring the evocations of a simple stage.

Today in the American theater we take the simple stage for granted. Artists working in professional, community, and academic theaters—by aesthetic choice, financial necessity, or both—are always discovering or rediscovering ways to create imaginative more with material less. But between 1912 and 1922, when several influential directors and designers were consistently exercising extreme restraint in the number and complexity of visual elements they put on stage, their experiments were controversial, applauded as visionary and poetic by some, and dismissed as drab, monotonous, or austere by others.

This book examines the thought and practice of stage designers, directors, and, finally, a playwright who dared to be simple, who shunned detailed naturalism and showy spectacle in favor of essential stage images. Between 1912 and 1938, these artists created simple stages through economy of means, self-imposed aesthetic restraint, and reduction to bare elements. Their work disdained decoration and elaborately detailed literalness, both of which signaled to them a lessening in substantive value. They subscribed, explicitly or implicitly, to the aesthetic paradoxes that less can create more, that adding takes away, that rich display somehow impoverishes, and poor theater (to borrow Jerzy Grotowski's term) can be imaginatively or spiritually rich. Statements of these and related paradoxes are forever appearing in their writings and implied in their practice.

Whether the initiative for stage simplicity came from producer, director, designer, or playwright, it was most clearly evident in what the audience saw on stage—the *mise-en-scène*. Therefore stage designers played a pivotal role in simplifying the stage. They sought many ways to economize aesthetically, i.e., allow few things to stand for multiple realities. They created "permanent settings," i.e. designs consisting of one constantly visible scenic element often representing many places. They designed "unit sets," i.e. rearrangements from scene to scene or play to play of the same few neutral flats, cubes, platforms, step units, or pylons, to stand for a wide range of contexts. They achieved even greater aesthetic economy with "architectural stages" whereby the architecture of the stages themselves, not scenery, would be the primary visual factor for all productions in those spaces—as in the Ancient Greek theaters.

Set designers imposed various special kinds of limitations on themselves which resulted in simple stages. One was in the area of color. They restricted themselves to one or two colors in their settings. This color simplicity was especially noticeable when the designers stayed within low color saturations such as the black-to-white spectrum or to shades of brown.

Another self-imposed restriction was in the size of the performance space designers chose. This could entail opting for a small stage over a large one or using only a fraction of the stage space that was available. Following precedents already set in the European theater, American stage designers in the 1910s and 1920s sometimes employed the "relief stage," where actors performed on so narrow a stage that they appeared like figures in a bas-relief. In other instances set designers flattened their stage picture by eschewing painted and architected perspective, deliberately choosing instead compositions that were static and undynamic.

Designers could not simplify the stage without the cooperation of their collaborators, especially the director, who at times initiated the choice of stage simplification, at other times merely followed the stage designer's lead. The director simplified the stage by finding ways to curtail stage business and elaborate movement, composing blocking that minimized the need for literal objects and detailed activity. Oftentimes the director found ways to depersonalize the characters so that they became essentialized human figures moving through space rather than highly individualized people surrounded by all the paraphernalia necessary to locate them in a specific time and place. Sometimes the directors imposed severe voice and movement limitations, deliberately keeping vocal inflections flat and monotone or severely restricting movement to only one part of the body.

Eventually the decision to simplify filtered down to the actor, who was given less to do. Faced with fewer properties and thus fewer possibilities for stage business, the actor had to rely more on voice, simple movements and gestures, and mime skills. The art of acting became the art of suggestion and evocation rather than detailed depiction by way of multiple and minute activities in concrete literal contexts.

Once the playwright took up the cause, stage simplicity could become a more permanent part of theater tradition. The simple-stage playwright's stage directions could direct designers, directors, and actors toward choices not requiring a lot of things or busyness. For instance, the playwright called for bare or neutral stages and for mimed or suggested activity from the actors. Shorter, sparer, and more elliptical plays were written, employing concise dialogue and stage silence and avoiding sound effects, background music, and embroidered language.

In general, the simple-stage artists, through aesthetic economy, sought to convey immediate impressions through bare minimum means. They preferred few elements over many, one over few, and nothing over one. Stripping down to an overall impression of singleness or even zero-ness would be a primary objective of artists for a simple stage.

While reducing down to bare essentials, the simplifiers often discovered the potential impact of a single element—a single setting to serve for many different places, a single character to represent many, or a single property to be endowed with many meanings or uses. Purity—handling individual theatrical variables so that they disappeared into one uniform entity—was favored over a display of parts or complex combinations.

The simplifiers also looked positively at qualities like repetitiveness and sameness which, in the illusionistic theater, might be dismissed as monotonous. The simplifiers recognized how repeated images, movements, and sounds could help create stylistic or thematic unity, while differentiated changing ones often resulted in a dismaying complexity. A stage picture with visual factors repeating in a given moment (e.g. identical arches, pillars, trees) or from scene to scene (as with a permanent, skeletal, or architectural stage) more easily conveyed a singleness of impression. Music that continually repeated a single phrase or theme also accomplished this. A director or playwright's decision to have many characters look alike, talk alike, and move alike simplified the stage by turning many elements into one.

The logical next step in the paring-down process was to reduce to zero, i.e., images conveying a sense of nothingness. The simplifiers, in other words, were as interested in more of nothing as less of something. They were attracted to the aesthetic possibilities in skillfully manipulating empty space (visual nothingness), silence (auditory nothingness), and stillness (kinetic nothingness). Creating stages composed of minimal elements isolated in a void and extensively using still or silent actors provided the kind of focus and power they saw lacking in filled, well-decorated stages with many physically active performers. If empty space, silence, and stillness were attractive in themselves, then visual representation, dialogue, music, and stage movement could be added only when absolutely essential to the artist's intent. In terms of the visual picture, the simplifiers tended to design stages that gave particular emphasis to empty space. They created "space stages," for instance, consisting of combinations of platforms and step-units surrounded by black curtains and other features to suggest a black void. They also designed sets composed of undecorated walls, columns, pillars, towers, curtains, or screens. The dominating presence of massive or long uninterrupted vertical lines (achieving a sense of monumentality), horizontal lines, and undecorated planes called attention both to the bareness of the lines and planes themselves as well as to the great volumes of empty space surrounding them.

Related to the notion of nothingness is stage neutrality i.e., placing on stage that which provides no time or place definition by itself. Directors and designers created neutral stages by stripping them bare or utilizing any combination of simple scenic cubes, screens, platforms, step-units, unparticularized costumes, and actors not yet defined as specific characters. It awaited the spoken text, the addition of simple properties, or the actor's activities to specify it, temporarily, until the next redefinition. Fluid and malleable, the neutral stage provided the simplifiers with the possibility of multiple contexts for theatrical action that appeared and disappeared through collaboration between the imaginations of creators able to suggest and spectators willing to fill in. The neutral bare platform made the stage available to the limitless imagination.

This book is about those who were leaders in simplifying the modern American stage: their application of the aforementioned principles to their own productions and their writings which testified to their commitments to the values of stage simplicity. The theater practitioners to be discussed include director Margaret Anglin and Livingston Platt; director Maurice Browne and designer Raymond Jonson of the Chicago Little Theatre; director George Cram Cook, founder of the Provincetown Players; director/producer Lyman Gale of the Boston Toy Theatre; Samuel Hume of the Arts and Crafts Theater of Detroit; director Arthur Hopkins and his collaborator, designer Robert Edmond Jones; designer Lee Simonson; and playwright Thornton Wilder. Foreign artists who influenced the simplification of the American stage will also be examined, especially English designer Edward Gordon Craig, Russian director Theodore Komisarjevsky, and French director Jacques Copeau.

These theater artists did not belong to a movement or a school, did not adopt an "ism." Even if they influenced one another's work, they still were mavericks, defying easy classification. They were not symbolists or expressionists, though these tags were occasionally foisted upon them during their careers or afterwards. One could pick up on the catchphrase less-is-more and their passion for simplicity and neutrality and identify them as proto-minimalists. Various scholars and critics have so identified some of their contemporaries, such as sculptor Constantin Brancusi,[1] painters Kasimir Malevich and Marcel Duchamp,[2] and stage designer Adolphe Appia.[3] Or the stage simplifiers could be classified as part of a minimalist aesthetic reaching back before the minimalist movement to the early years of the century and including artists in other fields such as architect Ludwig Mies van der Rohe, composer Erik Satie, poet Ezra Pound, mime Etienne Decroux, as well as Brancusi and Malevich.[4]

The simple-stage theater artists could also be referred to as revivalists. Thornton Wilder, for instance, characterized himself not as an innovator but as a rediscoverer of forgotten goods.[5] Each of these artists had his or her own favorite influence from among the simpler stage traditions originating before illusionistic conventions came to dominate Western theater. Some held up as models the Ancient Greek theater, others the platform stage of the itinerant players in the Middle Ages and Renaissance. Some focused on the neutral stages used in public performances in the Medieval, Elizabethan, and Spanish "Golden Age" periods. Still others mentioned the precedents of the traditional Chinese and Japanese theaters. Whatever the preferred antecedent, the simplifiers were looking for guidance from stage traditions before the illusionism of the Italianate and naturalistic stages began to dominate Western theater practice. They were drawn toward stages in which imaginations of actors, playwrights, and audiences could fill in where materiality left off. They were hoping to re-establish the power of the stage as stage rather than as something dressed up for an occasion.

Programs and philosophies advocating aesthetic restraint and simpler, sparer forms of artistic expression have appeared throughout the history of the arts. Under the influence of Taoism and Ch'an Buddhism in China and Zen Buddhism in Japan, East Asian artists developed monochromatic landscape painting, *haiku* poetry, elegantly spare stone-and-flower gardens, and Noh theater—arts characterized by simplicity and the eloquence of severe artistic restraint. Itinerant players throughout the history of theater have always minimized their accessories out of logistical necessity. In the seventeenth century, the French Academy shackled dramatists with the unities of time, place, and action which necessitated certain kinds of dramaturgical and production simplicities, especially relative to the extravagant elements utilized by their predecessors. Molière, one of those writing within the restraints of Neo-Classical norms, articulated that all one needs for theater is a few boards and a passion—the epitome of simple-stage thinking.

Even though the past served at least as a precedent, often as a guide, for their theory and practice, the twentieth-century theater simplifiers were not so connected to any one particular historical stage practice (as was, for instance, William Poel to the Elizabethan revival in England) that they could only be associated with that one tradition. Nor were they just eclectic revivalists, merely making their own combinations from among all the old solutions. They also discovered—or were influenced by contemporaries who discovered—new approaches to stage simplification. They had something their theatrical ancestors lacked: electricity and a more controllable system of lighting than sun and weather would allow (all the major simple stages before the twentieth century were outdoors). Now deftly controlled light, half-light, and shadow could replace the need for things. And once the stage could be pried loose from the proscenium arch and illusionistic thinking, then new experiments in simplicity could be tried along with new syntheses between these discoveries and historical stage traditions.

The modern simple stage originated not in the United States but in Europe. Before it appeared in America around 1912, a new simplified stage had already appeared abroad, in theoretical writings, sketches, and in actual productions, under the leadership of stage designers Adolphe Appia and Edward Gordon Craig, director Georg Fuchs, and, in the second decade, French director Jacques Copeau and the Irish Players at the Abbey Theatre. By 1912, Fuchs had already experimented with a relief stage, Copeau with an architectural stage, Craig and the Irish Players with movable screens (a form of unit settings), Appia with his "rhythmic spaces" (a form of permanent settings). Individual productions by the above directors and designers and by others like Max Reinhardt (most notably, his relief-stage production of *Sumurun*) offered models for various kinds of simplified stages. The work of these simplifiers, under the rubric the "New Stagecraft," influenced the American simplifiers directly or indirectly mostly through trans-Atlantic visits in both directions between 1911 and 1924. The simplifications of expressionism came to the attention of American theater artists during the 1920s when the Americans saw European productions in this style not only by Reinhardt but also by directors Jurgen Fehling and Leopold Jessner and their designers Hans Strobach and Emil Pirchan.

At home, the American simplifiers were also seeing many productions weighted down by elaborately illusionistic and decorative stages and the endless demands for stage business that this "stuff" required of actors and directors. To the simplifiers, all this distracted from actor and text. And they identified American producer and director David Belasco—artist of the "little things"—as their chief target. Advocating the ceaseless occupation of the eye, Belasco came to epitomize the tendency to overuse literal detail in the American theater. With his production of *The Governor's Lady* in 1912, which boasted a facsimile Child's Restaurant for the final scene (authentic to the last cup and saucer), illusionistic thinking seemed to have gone as far as it could go. The simplifiers were poised for rebellion.

But Belasco was at the center of a much broader target. Ultimately the simplifiers were protesting the proliferation of people, objects, technology, and wealth resulting from the Industrial and Scientific Revolutions and the manifestation of that explosion in works of art. Abundance seemed to be the measure of all things in the nineteenth-century Euro-American society, and that abundance reflected itself in the arts. Middle-class taste demanded accumulation and an ornate display of things, and that ostentation found its way into the arts which they patronized. Extravagance permeated artistic expression throughout the century: Romantic writing and music were emotionally extravagant and florid, especially by twentieth-century standards; Victorian architecture was extravagant in decorative detail; naturalist painting and literature were extravagant in depicting details of everyday life; and the visual arts in certain late nineteenth-century art movements (e.g. Art Nouveau, the more ornate wing of symbolism, the so-called decadents, and the secessionists) exhibited a new but no less ornamental extravagance. In addition, the same technology that brought the simplifying powers of electric light on dimmers also brought new forms of visual complexity, including spectacular stage effects such as facsimile house fires, live horse and chariot races, and, later, the cinema.

Like their contemporaries in other arts, certain theater artists sought refuge in simplicity. For them, cutting away and self-limiting in their work offered sanctuary from the excesses and bewildering complexities of life and art, promising purification and a kind of spiritual cleansing. Just as Henry David Thoreau found solace in his simple way of life on Walden Pond, the theater simplifiers discovered a way of doing their art which offered peace from plenty.

There also was an economic motive for simplicity. Directors of the so-called little theaters (where the simple stage flourished), such as Maurice Browne, Lyman Gale, and George Cram Cook, began producing plays in small theaters because they could not afford to rent or buy large ones. Shunning what they viewed as the crass entertainment values of mainstream theater, they promoted plays that generally appealed to a relatively small part of the theater-going population—the intellectuals and the artists—many of whom could not afford high ticket prices. Few seats and low ticket prices meant little revenue and, in the 1910s, there was no government support for theater. The inevitable consequence for all of them was austere production budgets. These directors had no choice but to find imaginative and cost-effective ways to create a lot with a little and find designers who were capable of being creative within severe financial limitations.

At some early point in the careers of these theater simplifiers who might have initially begun simplifying for financial reasons, economic necessity turned into aesthetic preference. Once they witnessed the power of stage simplicity, they did not want to abandon it. For even when many of the simplifiers were more established and had access to substantial financial resources, they still held to an aesthetic philosophy of less-is-more. The principles of a simple stage and the ideal of an empty stage can be discerned in their aesthetic choices long after they had left the financial stringencies of the little theaters where their careers had begun.

An example of this is Robert Edmond Jones who, by 1947, was the king of American stage design and could command large resources for his work. In that year Julian Beck and Judith Malina went to Jones to solicit his help. When Jones heard that they had $6000 to start a theater (which would eventually become the Living Theatre), he was dismayed. Beck quotes Jones as saying the following:

> I wish you had no money, no money at all, perhaps then you
> would create the new theatre, make your theatre out of string and
> sofa cushions, make it in studios and living rooms. Forget the big
> theatres, he said, and the paid admissions, nothing is happening
> there, nothing can happen there that is not stultifying, nothing
> will ever come out of it.[6]

It was within the context of this kind of rebellious and pragmatic thinking that the little theater movement began in 1912, led by Maurice Browne's

Chicago Little Theatre and Lyman Gale's Toy Theatre of Boston. Their experiments inspired others, until a thriving little theater scene existed by 1916, one that reveled in a spirit of economy of means. And similar pioneering efforts entered the professional theaters, so that by 1914 Sheldon Cheney could observe a "revolutionary gospel of simplicity" sweeping through the American theater.[7]

This continued in many guises over the next decade. By the early 1920s, directors and designers had extensively explored the simple stage. Little theaters and professional mainstream theaters alike were featuring relief stages, space stages, permanent settings, unit sets, and architectural stages. They also were using another kind of simple stage, one that proved an effective compromise with the elaborately realistic settings popular at the time. Led by Robert Edmond Jones, Lee Simonson, and Raymond Jonson and their directing partners, this new kind of setting entailed stripping a literal set (usually an interior) to only its most essential walls, furniture, decorations, and properties. This style, variously called "simplified realism," "suggestive realism," and "symbolic realism," was first utilized in the little theaters but was soon picked up by the big professional theaters as well. By the middle 1920s, it was often employed in major theaters, perhaps more for its cost-saving features than for its aesthetic appeal. In December 1922 the Theatre Guild presentation of Paul Claudel's *The Tidings Brought to Mary*, designed by Lee Simonson and staged by Russian director Theodore Komisarjevsky, brought the simple stage about as far as a professional designer and director would take it, even though stage simplification in its various guises would remain in the province of director/designer teams throughout the rest of the 1920s and 1930s.

But the simple-stage revolution would not become fully realized until a major playwright joined the fray. There were plays by little-known playwrights writing for the little theaters that called for simple settings and few properties, but it took more than a decade after the heyday of the little theater movement for a major playwright to write multiple plays that called for stripped-bare stages. This occurred in the American theater when Thornton Wilder wrote a series of one-acts in 1931 and a full-length play, *Our Town*, in 1938. Finally the simple stage had become embraced by the theater artist who could preserve it by building it into the plays themselves.

To trace the journey undertaken by the stage simplifiers, we will look at precedents and influences of the modern simple stage in Part One and the thought and practice of the leading American theater simplifiers in Part Two. In so doing, we will examine the work of those who helped educate American audiences in a vocabulary of basic forms, bare surfaces, still figures, and empty silent spaces. The success of these pioneering simplifiers paved the way for future theater artists to eschew bountiful display and elaborate depiction and risk choosing the way of simplicity.

NOTES

[1] Scott Burton, "My Brancusi," *Art in America*, (March 1990), p. 149. Burton discusses how Pontus Hulten's 1983 essay on Brancusi "reiterates the now old case for Brancusi as the first minimalist."

[2] Barbara Rose, "ABC Art," in Gregory Battcock, *Minimal Art: A Critical Anthology* (New York: E. P. Dutton, 1968), pp. 274-297. In this article, Rose claims that Kasimir Malevich and Marcel Duchamp are two beginning points—one mystical, the other rationalist—of minimal art.

[3] John Rockwell, "The Death and Life of Minimalism," *New York Times*, December 21, 1986, p. 29. Among other precedents, Rockwell sees the roots of minimalism in Adolphe Appia's "grandly simple, archetypal staging ideas."

[4] I take this position and argue it in my dissertation, "The Origins of the Minimalist *Mise-en-Scène* in the United States" (NYU 1986) and in my response to Orville Larson's letter to the editor, *The Drama Review*, Winter 1986, (T-112), p. 9. To draw the connection between the simple stage and the minimalist aesthetic that extends throughout the twentieth century would require a more thorough-going theoretical and historical argument than is possible in the scope of this book. To argue it here would prove tangential to the main direction of this study.

[5] Thornton Wilder, Preface to *Three Plays* (New York: Avon Books, 1976), p. xii.

[6] Quoted in Julian Beck, *The Life of the Theatre* (San Francisco: City Lights Books, 1972), section 9, n. p.

[7] Sheldon Cheney, *The New Movement in the Theatre* (New York: Mitchell Kennerley, 1914), p. 169.

PART ONE:

PRECEDENTS AND INFLUENCES

1

The Greek and Elizabethan Revivals

The simplified *mise-en-scène* came about in part as a reaction against the visually busy stages of the realist tradition that took hold in the nineteenth century. But these stages would not have seemed so busy and complex if audiences, scholars, critics, and other theater artists did not have something with which to compare it. As scholars and critics looked back at the Greek and Elizabethan stages, they found conventions that directly opposed—and provided alternatives to—the naturalist stage conventions of the day.

The passion to achieve photographic accuracy in productions first swept through the European theater and eventually made its way to the United States. By the middle of the nineteenth century, three related aspects of a realistic production tradition were already present in the United States: (1) Realistic interiors (typically living rooms) mostly for contemporary plays featuring middle-class characters; (2) spectacular effects such as onstage representations of fires, storms, and horse races; and (3) historical authenticism in production of classical plays, especially those by Shakespeare.

The rise of middle-class drama demanded a kind of scenography to allow for its fullest representation. The need to present realistic interiors led to the invention of the box set usually credited to English producer Madame Vestris. Edwin Booth helped establish its use in the American theater. After 1869, he regularly employed the box set, complete with decoration and bric-a-brac.

Presentation of the minutiae of everday life continued to exercise a strong influence on the imaginations of American producers after the box set was a firmly established tradition, though it was not until David Belasco's meticulous handling of the "little things" in the first two decades of the twentieth century that this part of the realistic tradition reached its fullest realization. Robert Nordvold summarizes some of the most famous examples of Belasco's meticulous concern for naturalist detail and authenticity:

> to depict the all night vigil of Cho-Cho-San in *Madame Butterfly* (1900) he devised a sunset-to-sunrise lighting sequence that lasted nearly a quarter of an hour; for *Du Barry* (1901) he imported authentic Louis XV furniture and tons of fine silks and velvets from France; for *The Easiest Way* (1908) he bought and transferred to the stage the entire furnishings, including the wallpaper, of a dingy New York boardinghouse room; for *The Return of Peter Grimm* (1911) he completely furnished an off-stage room that was visible only when a door was opened; and for *The Governor's Lady* (1912) he built a fully operant replica of a portion of a Childs' Restaurant in which food was cooked and consumed during the performance.[1]

The most notable leaders of the second aspect of realistic depiction on stage—spectacular effects—were Augustin Daly and Steele MacKaye. Between 1869 and 1892, Daly accomplished startling feats such as presenting a hero tied to the tracks with the obligatory on-rushing train and a heroine locked in a room on a burning steamboat. Not to be outdone, Steele MacKaye's Madison Square Theatre, which opened in 1879, boasted technologically advanced features which enabled him to create a realistic cyclone and stampede. Once these sorts of spectacular effects were successfully represented in the theater, producers competed to out-do each other, so that productions in the last quarter of the nineteenth century dazzled with explosions of fireworks factories, chariot races with real horses, and other daring technological achievements.

The initiative toward historical authenticity came from England. Visiting the United States in 1846, English actor/manager Charles Kean demonstrated for New York audiences the virtues of highly detailed historical accuracy in his watershed production of Shakespeare's *King John*. An American producer to follow Kean's example was William E. Burton who, between 1848 to 1856, endowed his Shakespeare productions at New York's Chambers Street Theatre with historically accurate and colorful settings and costumes. From around 1869 to 1873, this kind of historical correctness continued under the leadership of Edwin Booth, who combined painted flats of the Italianate tradition with the three-dimensional constructed scenery to be used more regularly as the century progressed. Illusionistic thinking continued to dominate Shakespearean performance for the next fifty years, even showing signs of vitality as late as

1922, the year of David Belasco's only Shakespeare venture, his production of *The Merchant of Venice*.

Ironically, the interest in historicism led not only to an attempt to illustrate the times and places of Shakespeare's plays, but also to a desire to find out how his plays (and those written in other eras) were actually produced. The idea of reproducing production conditions of other times became almost as alluring as reproducing historical periods called for in plays. And once scholars and then actor/managers learned about and began replicating Greek and Elizabethan stage conditions, they found that those conditions offered a viable alternative to literal settings and the massive production needs dictated by naturalistic convention.

THE GREEK REVIVAL

At the pinnacle of its glory in the fifth century, Greek theater performances were presented on the simplest and sparest of stages, so that any revivalist intention to recall that glory could not help but rediscover those qualities. In building the funnel-shaped *theatron* into the side of a small hill, the Athenian audiences looked down onto a large dancing circle *(orkestra)*, empty but for a simple stone altar, and a stone facade *(skene)* with high vertical lines from its front columns. There they saw the diminutive actors backed by a vast countryside or the edifices of their *polis*. Few properties or scenic elements were employed, and those that were used did not distract from the overall grandeur of the theater architecture.

The Greek chorus, placed on this great stage, was treated more as a single unit than as individuals. Chorus members moved and chanted mostly in unison and were costumed alike, often in loosely-fitted white *chitons*, which tended to de-individualize the twelve or fifteen members. Modern directors have often handled a stage grouping in a manner reminiscent of Ancient Greek practice, i.e., by treating them not as highly specified individuals in accordance with the bias of the naturalists, but, like the Greek chorus, as a group that looks, talks, and moves alike. Marjorie Hoover, in her book on Russian director Vsevolod Meyerhold, calls this "multiple uniformity" and, as treated in the modern context, usually entails a statement about conformity, not a representation of a specific societal sub-group, as in the Ancient Greek theater.

Between 1881 and 1928 a Greek revival did occur in the United States, bringing with it these and other simplified features of fifth-century performance. Not only did this movement result from a fascination with historical authenticity pervasive in nineteenth-century theater, the Greek revival movement also emerged from an academic interest. Classical studies at the university would inevitably lead scholars and students to inquire how the great plays of Aeschylus, Sophocles, Euripides, and Aristophanes were first performed.

One can trace the Greek revival in the United States to the 1881 production of *Oedipus Tyrannus* in Sanders Theatre at Harvard University. It is estimated that over six thousand people attended the five performances. Producer Daniel Frohman was so impressed with the production and its response that he organized a professional production of the same play and presented it in an English translation for two weeks in Boston and New York.

The impulse to revive Greek dramas and production methods quickly spread through the academic world, gathering momentum between 1904 to 1914. Domis Plugge cites statistics showing that there were fifteen Greek revivals in American colleges between 1881 and 1892, thirty-four between 1893 and 1903, and sixty-one between 1904 and 1914—an indisputable upsurge from earlier periods.[2]

Many of the most notable Greek productions in the first three decades of the twentieth century were presented in outdoor theaters, usually Greek theaters. Writing in 1913, Huntly Carter links outdoor performances with the new spirit of reform in the theater, including stage simplification.[3] Sheldon Cheney also draws the connection between the two, explaining how the large open-air Greek theaters, by their very natures, demand a kind of simplicity in performance:

> The Greek Theatre, with its immense stage and imposing architectural background, is uncompromising in its demands of simplicity and largeness in action and staging. The rapid volleying of question and answer, the timid voice, the delicate facial expression, all these are lost in the immensity of space. The plays that really succeed here are... the Greek tragedies, with the beauty of their simple stately action and their rigid economy of means reflected in the dignified, almost severe beauty of the towering background.[4]

Production in outdoor Greek theaters, Cheney goes on to say, must be "of a certain largeness and simplicity,"[5] the properties must be few, all scenic elements massive.[6] Arthur Krows, author of *Play Production in America*, agrees, contending that out-of-doors performance offers "relief from the oppressive conventions of indoor staging—an infinite sky above, and nature itself all about."[7]

Carter, Cheney, and Krows surely had two specific outdoor Greek theaters in mind, built two years apart and both in California. In 1901, under the aegis of the International Theosophical Society, a Greek theater was built at Point Loma under the supervision of Katherine Tingley (photo 1.1). The theater, "a chaste little temple in pure Greek architecture"[8] with no less than the great Pacific Ocean as its backdrop, became the site of many of Tingley's Greek revival productions. She won acclaim for her simple-stage production of Aeschylus's *The Eumenides*, which came to Point Loma after achieving success in New

1.1 Greek Theatre at Point Loma 1912. Built under aegis of International Theosophical Society in 1901. Copyright Archives, The Theosophical Society, Pasadena, California.

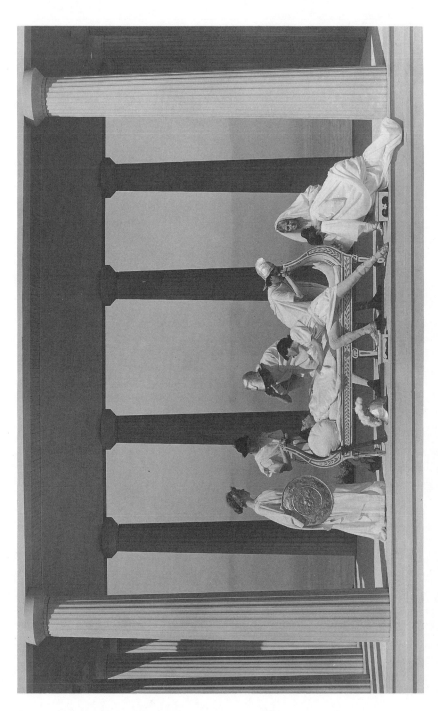

1.2 Thetis bringing the armor to Achilles from *The Aroma of Athens* in production directed by Katherine Tingley at Point Loma Greek Theatre. Copyright Archives, The Theosophical Society, Pasadena, California.

York. Harmonious classical simplicity and purity also characterized the Tingley production of *The Aroma of Athens* in 1911. This is evident in the white costumes, the formal, balanced and clean-lined blocking, the few properties, and the lack of any other scenery besides the theater itself and the open space beyond (photo 1.2).

Two years after the Greek Theater at Point Loma was constructed, the University of California at Berkeley opened its Hearst Greek Theatre. Designed by John Galen Howard, the Hearst Theatre soon surpassed Point Loma in the number and quality of Greek productions presented. The Hearst Theatre is not an accurate reconstruction of a fifth-century Greek theater; it includes certain features of Hellenistic and Roman theaters, too.[9] It has the full dancing circle, the spare Greek columns on the *skene*, and the overall harmonious grandeur associated with fifth- and fourth-century Greek theaters (photo 1.3).

Professors and students were the first to work in the space. A three-day festival of Greek plays inaugurated the theater's opening, and, over the next ten years, the Greek Department at the University of California attempted to recreate fifth-century performance there, doing productions of Sophocles' *Ajax*, Aeschylus's *The Eumenides*, Aristophanes' *The Birds* in Greek, and Sophocles' *Oedipus Rex* in English.

Sheldon Cheney's 1914 book, *The New Movement in the Theatre*, which aggressively promotes the values of stage simplicity over naturalist stagecraft, opens with a photograph of the *Ajax* production in the Hearst Theater. He offers an explanation as to how that picture "provides a text for the entire book"[10] (photo 1.4). He bases his conclusion on the "simple, almost bare, setting," the lack of the "artificial scenery and crowded naturalistic properties that clutter up the commercial theatre stages," and the fact that this production is "reaching backward and forward to the real essential beauties of dramatic art."[11] Even the amateur spirit is viewed as a refreshing change from the artificial sophistications of the "over-stuffed" professional theater.

Eventually professional producers came to realize the potential of the space and began to adopt it for their own purposes. During the first three decades of the new century, the most celebrated Greek productions at the Hearst Greek Theatre were those by actress/manager Margaret Anglin, who was also a key figure in the Elizabethan revival movement in America. Between 1910 and 1928, Anglin produced and appeared in fifteen critically acclaimed productions of Greek tragedy, seven of which were presented in the Hearst Theater.[12] Of those presented in the Berkeley theater, Cheney cites *Antigone* (1910) and Sophocles' *Electra* (1913 and 1915), her sparest Greek productions, as the "most nearly perfect productions" ever presented in the space,[13] and scholar Gordon Arnold Johnson considers Anglin's *Antigone* the first artistic success among Greek productions in the United States.[14]

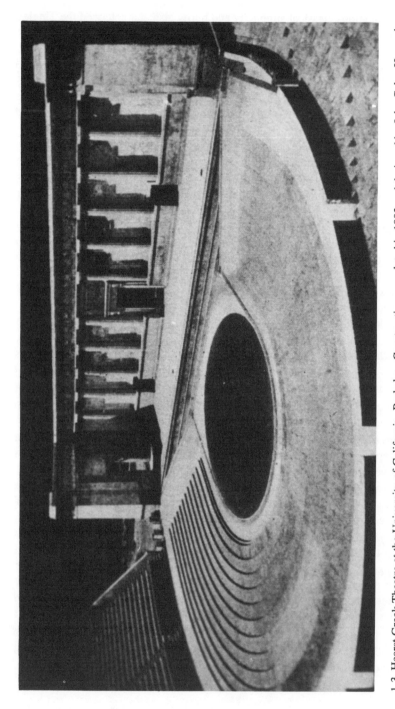

1.3 Hearst Greek Theatre at the University of California, Berkeley. Construction completed in 1903 and designed by John Galen Howard. Site of several Margaret Anglin Greek productions. Courtesy of The Bancroft Library.

Anglin was conscientious about simplifying most aspects of her Greek productions. Gordon Johnson summarizes from various Anglin writings her view that simplicity should be the keynote for a Greek production. Johnson begins by quoting Anglin that the spirit of the Ancient Greek world should be transmitted to today's audience through a "clear lens":[15]

> This clear lens would be a beautiful yet austere mounting and presentation. Beauty and simplicity of form and design coupled with good taste, she thought, would make Greek revivals effective. Nothing that smacked of cheap theatricalism would be allowed to creep into her production. The settings and properties would be simple and unobtrusive, the music... dignified and appropriate,... the choral movements... plastic yet stately, the costumes... fitting and tasteful, the acting... spirited yet exalted—the whole production would be austere, majestic and beautiful.[16]

1.4 Student production of Sophocles' *Ajax* in Hearst Greek Theatre, the University of California, Berkeley. Courtesy of The Bancroft Library.

Her simplified approach began with an appreciation for the simple grandeur of the Greek theater itself. According to Cheney, one can attribute some measure of Anglin's success to her frank acceptance of:

> conventions which the immensity of the stage and the lack of a
> curtain imposed; she triumphed by fitting the play to the stage,
> instead of attempting futilely to bring the setting into conformity
> with what is commonly considered modern stage art.[17]

She emphasized the simple monumental beauty of the Greek theater, not allowing it to become obscured by mere accessories. She opposed the naturalist habit of dressing up the stage, preferring the naked beauty of the Greek stage.

Cheney contrasts Anglin's successful productions with one in the same theater by actress/manager Maude Adams, another important figure in the revivalist movement. Adams, argues Cheney, resorted to illusionistic thinking with *As You Like It* by transplanting a forest to create Arden and blocking out the theater's facade with thousands of yards of blue cheesecloth. Anglin's productions, in comparison, were highly simplified with few accessories and, rather than trying to block out the theater's *skene*, Anglin used it as the principal scenic element.

Cheney identifies Anglin as one of the "first to revolt against the inartistic naturalism of the average American production."[18] And her approach was not just reviving old solutions; she knew about and became an early advocate of the new simple stages in Europe. She synthesized what she knew about the ancient Greek and Elizabethan production conventions with the new ideas and images from Edward Gordon Craig and Max Reinhardt in her effort to translate the spirit of the Greeks and Shakespeare classics for modern audiences. In 1911 she witnessed Max Reinhardt's production of *Oedipus Rex* in Europe and learned from him not only how to do that particular play, but also aspects of how to modernize the classics while maintaining their essential spirit.[19]

To help her fulfill her goal of a simple stage, she elicited help from Livingston Platt, who designed all but two of Anglin's fifteen Greek productions. His philosophy of stage simplification matched hers. He wrote: "Too much detail often ruins a play because it distracts attention from the action of the drama itself."[20] He would apply this philosophy to his Greek and Elizabethan revivals performed under Anglin's direction.

His acquaintanceship with the new stage simplicity in Europe predated Anglin's. Even before he created sets for the Boston Toy Theatre in 1912 and later for John Craig's Castle Square Stock Company (also in Boston), he had come into contact with new art movements while studying the visual arts in Europe. He worked at the Royal Opera House in Bruges and was one of the first American designers to become familiar with the designs of Edward Gordon Craig. In Belgium he organized a small touring company of English actors with whom he began to apply ideas and images that are associated primarily with the European New Stagecraft. Indeed Anglin hired Platt to do her settings partly because of his knowledge of these new ideas. The resulting Anglin/Platt collaborations effectively combined revivalist and New-Stagecraft sensibilities.

Being the star performer and director, Anglin was in a position to carry ideals of simplicity into her own performance and encourage it in her fellow actors. Johnson quotes Anglin that all roles in Greek tragedy should be "interpreted in a simple and in a human manner to reach the pure spirit of the character."[21] Anglin applied this principle to her own acting. She tended to move on stage in a stately, slow-moving fashion, often "speaking her lines without much change in the inflection of her stirring voice."[22] Paraphrasing from various reviews, Johnson provides samples of critical appraisals of Anglin's simple acting style:

> As Clytemnestra [in *Iphigenia in Aulis*], she gave a performance which was... simple as well as forceful. Her performance of Medea had a simple clarity and purity of conception. In *Antigone*, she assumed noble stature... by being extremely simple and restrained in her acting. A stirring simplicity was noticed in the role of Electra, the greatness of subdued power. [Brooks] Atkinson considered her acting in *Electra* simple, restrained and moderate.[23]

One critic, writing in 1915, sums it up this way: "The economy of Miss Anglin's manner and the reticence of her art are the imperial signs of her genius."[24]

Two productions that implemented her ideals of stage simplicity more thoroughly than any others were Sophocles' *Antigone* (1910) and her various productions of Sophocles' *Electra*, especially those in 1913 and 1915 in the Hearst Theater and the 1918 *Electra* performed in Carnegie Hall. The production of *Antigone* was characterized in general as "austere" and "severe," and these qualities were in evidence, not only in Anglin's acting as discussed above, but also in her handling of the chorus. She lined up the chorus members along the back wall of the Hearst Theater stage, creating the effect of a Greek bas-relief coming to life.[25] For the set, Anglin devised a scheme to emphasize the architecture of the Hearst Theater while finding shrewd ways to focus the action on so immense a stage. She positioned on either side of the stage thirty cypress trees twenty to twenty-five feet tall, which narrowed the stage from 133 feet to 80 feet in length. She installed oak doors in the center opening along with a platform in front which extended ten feet downstage and had two descending steps.[26] Thus Anglin created a performance area before great palace doors surrounded by trees and the awe-inspiring Greek architecture.

With Livingston Platt working with her on the *Electra* designs, Anglin was able to carry the same basic set idea to a level of greater sophistication and power than the one for *Antigone*. In the *Electra* production, she used the large dancing circle rather than confining the actors to the raised stage. In the center of the dancing circle was placed an altar. Platt built ten wide pyramidic steps descending from the stage so that they overlapped the orchestra for a few feet. The cypresses were again used on either end of the stage but this time he enclosed them with six-foot walls. The central portal was again plugged with oak doors. On either side of the doors stood giant busts of two Greek gods. As in her *Antigone* production, Anglin positioned a platform in front of the doors. She also placed two benches about ten feet equidistant from stage center.[27] Anglin's increased use of platforms and steps attests to the influence of Reinhardt's *Oedipus* which she saw between her *Antigone* and first *Electra* production.

The basic stage elements were kept fairly constant for all the *Electra* productions: the busts, the platforms, the stairs. The first indoor production in 1918 required certain modifications, but still the overall image, described as a radical treatment of the original Greek stage, was spare and simplified. One change from the original outdoor production was in having a "limitless space at back" rather than a Greek theater as a background.[28] Having that space behind made for a more severe outline but simple nevertheless.[29] Platt's 1927 setting for *Electra* incorporated a massive facade similar to the one used in Anglin's *Medea* production; the words to describe it could have suited any of the *Electra* settings: "vast and sombre."[30]

The lighting for both *Antigone* and *Electra* accentuated the point that Greek plays took place in one day. Both productions began in virtual darkness. Then came the dawn light, followed by ever brightening daylight, ending with a darkening toward dusk and night.[31] This unremitting brightening to darkening lent a kind of classical purity to the simple steady build in the actions of these two plays.

In general, Anglin and Platt were not restrained in their use of color in the costuming, even though most Greek productions before theirs employed white *chitons*. They veered away from simplicity, toward extravagant color display. While this was certainly true of the *Antigone* costumes, the *Electra* costumes were more subdued than those of Anglin's other productions. Johnson describes Electra's costume as "a tight-fitting dark blue garment that on stage looked almost black. The costume was unadorned, almost peasant-like."[32] The chorus reflected Electra's somber mood by wearing various shades of grey and dark brown. Clytemnestra was arrayed in scarlet- and gold-colored robes with rich accessories and jewelry; her attendants also wore colorful costumes.

As the attributes of these costumes suggest, practical and aesthetic considerations often overrode Anglin's interest in simplifying the stage. She sometimes preferred colorful pageantry to more subdued images. For instance, she generally chose not to go with the plain white *chitons* of Periclean Athens, but rather preferred the far more colorful costumes of the pre-Hellenic or Homeric period.[33] And she directed her chorus away from the more simplified choice of unison chanting and monotone delivery, adopting instead the practice of breaking up the lines among individuals and orchestrating them with far more vocal variety than the original Greek choruses. In this case she went the way of naturalism rather than the way of singleness and simplicity.

Sometimes whole plays were produced more in the direction of pageantry. For her productions of Euripides's *Iphigenia in Aulis* (1915) and *Hippolytus* (1923), for instance, she opted for scenic splendor, large casts, and spectacular effects, prompting one critic to admonish Anglin's *Hippolytus* production with the words: "The accessories don't help."[34] Her earlier *Iphigenia* production boasted participation from 500 Berkeley students and was replete with marching soldiers, panoplied chariot arrivals, and a lavish bridal procession.[35]

But these productions were more the exceptions than the rule, at least in the eyes of her critics. Anglin's simplified productions of *Antigone, Electra,* and Euripides' *Medea* determined her reputation for Greek productions as exhibiting austere beauty and restraint in presentation of the *mise-en-scène.*

1.5 Performance of Euripides' *The Trojan Women* in New York City, 1915. Directed by Harley Granville-Barker.

Next to Margaret Anglin's revivals, the most famous were those by visiting English director Harley Granville-Barker. Between May 15, 1915 and June 12, 1915, Granville-Barker presented six performances of Gilbert Murray's translation of *Iphigenia in Tauris* and five of *The Trojan Women,* the latter play having a highly praised performance at the Adolf Lewisohn Stadium in New

York City in May 1915 (photo 1.5). One cannot help but notice the high vertical lines, the bare surfaces on the columns and facade, and the dwarfed, somewhat depersonalized, human figures below. Attempting to capture the grand but spare qualities of the original performances, this production—along with *Iphigenia in Tauris* performed in the stadia at Harvard, Yale, Princeton, and the College of the City of New York—were more in keeping with actual production practices of the Ancient Greeks than those by Anglin. His productions were frequently compared (often to Anglin's advantage), and the press continually portrayed the two directors as rivals. But Anglin's style of presentation was already well in place by the time Granville-Barker visited and remained virtually unchanged after his departure so that, if there was a rivalry, it was short-lived and lines of influence cannot be detected between the two.

The only other Greek revival group of note was the Coburn Players. In November 1910, Charles Coburn and his players presented a production of Euripides' *Electra* at the Hudson Theater in New York to bad reviews, especially with regard to the acting. But they still managed to stay alive for another four years, touring Greek productions mostly to college audiences. The importance to the simple stage is that their productions were performed without scenery or music, and with little stage activity. But their amateurish acting detracted from their accomplishment, especially when compared to Granville-Barker and Anglin. Like Granville-Barker and Anglin, Coburn also devoted much of his energies to reviving Shakespeare on simple stages out-of-doors, making him a part of the American Elizabethan revival, too.

THE ELIZABETHAN REVIVAL

Like the Greek revival, the Elizabethan revival in the United States began in the universities from scholarly interest and then spread to the professional theater which contributed higher-quality acting and new ideas of stage simplification coming out of Europe. The Elizabethan revival had a much larger scope than the Greek one for several reasons. First of all, the plays were in English and constituted part of an Anglo-American literary tradition. Second, the nineteenth-century Romantics (e.g. Coleridge, Hazlitt, and Carlyle) deified Shakespeare, a hero-worship that was sustained by scholars and critics in the twentieth century. Inevitably, scholars would want to examine how the great Elizabethan's plays were performed.

The discovery of the Johannes de Witt drawing of the Elizabethan Swan Theatre in the 1880s fueled interest in studying Elizabethan theaters and performance techniques. Like the revival movements in general, this discovery, which helped satisfy a passion for archaeological authenticity, would be used as a basis for opposing historically accurate Shakespearean productions, common since the days of Charles Kean.

The Elizabethan platform stage, when emulated, would ineluctably lead a

director or designer toward a simplified stage design. Public outdoor stages in
the Elizabethan era began as a simple platform or thrust jutting out into a
courtyard, with spectators viewing the action from three sides. This arrangement
became formalized with the introduction of permanent theater structures. Scenes
were changed rapidly and in full view of the spectator; consequently, only a bare
minimum of properties and scenic elements were used. Shakespeare and his
contemporaries writing for the public stage tended to incorporate into the text
itself allusions to time and place so that the spectator's imagination would fill in
where the few properties left off.

Many of Shakespeare's plays, written before 1608 for the outdoor
circumstances of The Globe, could best realize themselves when produced in the
kind of elemental stage conditions he faced writing for the Globe. Arthur Krows
makes this point in *Play Production in America*:

> These plays, with their colorful costumes, their descriptive
> passages, and their generally decorative qualities, are splendidly
> fitted for stages where the background is simple and unobtrusive,
> where there is no necessity of a curtain to shut off the scene, and
> mechanical illusions are out of place.[36]

A fuller understanding of the simplicity and economy of Elizabethan stage
conditions added to discontent among scholars and critics in the early part of the
twentieth century with the contemporaneous naturalist stage. The Elizabethan
platform stage presented an especially attractive alternative to an anonymous
critic writing in *The Living Age* (1910). The essay, entitled "The Limits of Stage
Illusion," broadly attacks the detailed stage, while proposing a return to old stage
traditions. The writer despairs how "the weight of the trappings, to which the
last thirty years have accustomed us, has crushed the spirit of the theater."[37] The
writer deems the Elizabethan stage far superior to the cluttered contemporary
stage:

> Burbage and his colleagues were set a task that was all the more
> difficult on account of its simplicity. They had nothing else to
> rely upon for their effect than dignity of bearing and perfection of
> speech. If they failed at elocution, they had no furniture to
> distract the attention of the house; they had no limelight to dazzle
> the eye and dull the ear of the spectator. Their speech must be
> noble, their gesture grand in its restraint, or they failed utterly.[38]

Not only is the author blaming overly elaborate sets, but he more subtly brings
in other potentially distracting elements of the production as well: the dazzling
limelight, the furniture, and unrestrained gesture.

Critics like Walter Prichard Eaton portrayed David Belasco as the antagonist to the Elizabethan simple stage. When reviewing two Shakespearean revivals in 1910, he let loose a barb at the naturalist director: "Let us rejoice that he [Shakespeare] did not possess scenery, that there was no Belasco in Elizabethan England!"[39]

William Poel in England was beginning to revive Shakespeare productions in the Elizabethan manner even before the discovery of the de Witt drawing. As early as 1881, he staged a first-quarto version of *Hamlet* on a bare stage. With the new information from the drawing, he staged *Measure for Measure* in 1893 on a reconstructed Elizabethan public stage. From 1895 to 1905 he guided the Elizabethan Stage Society through facsimile Elizabethan productions of Shakespeare's plays.

Poel visited the United States during the 1916-1917 season on an invitation from Thomas Wood Stevens of the Carnegie Institute of Technology in Pittsburgh. He lectured there as well as in California and Chicago. He also directed a production of Ben Jonson's *The Poetaster* with student actors. The production was executed on a simple platform before black curtains parted to reveal a balcony above and with "gorgeous costumes," contributing to a "colorful stage picture."[40] Following the Elizabethan manner, the costumes supplied the color while the stage remained neutral both in color and in being stripped of defining characteristics. With only three performances, this production did not contribute much to the Elizabethan revival directly or to the evolution of the simple stage, although a thorough account of the production appeared in the widely-read *Theatre Arts Magazine*.

One of Poel's associates in the Elizabethan Stage Society was Ben Greet. After working with Poel for several years, Greet came to the United States where he performed revivals similar to the ones Poel was doing in England. From 1903 to 1914, Greet toured the United States, performing in gardens, courtyards, and other open-air locations, demonstrating for mostly academic and community audiences how, supposedly, the Elizabethans actually did Shakespeare—on simple outdoor stages. He also presented a production of *Everyman* and thus provided impetus to a Medieval revival which carried with it some of the same neutral-stage traditions as the Elizabethan revival. But Greet's reputation and potential influence, as with the Coburn Players who also performed open-air Shakespeare, was diminished by amateur acting.

The more critics and scholars watched or read about productions in the Elizabethan manner and the more they saw the standard naturalist productions, the more they saw the limitations of stage illusion. The contrast between the two approaches became more and more apparent as American audiences were exposed to the scenic elaboration of theater artists like English actor/manager Henry Irving, who visited the United States with trainloads of scenery, and their own Augustin Daly. Writing in the *Atlantic Monthly* in 1899, Norman Hapgood complained how Irving's Macbeth was "smothered in Sir Henry's magnificent adornments."[41] Hapgood asserted how "scenery should be a background, hardly noticed, to take the place of stage directions and explanatory dialogue, not an independent attraction" and hopes that the overly elaborate stage will die from the cost of its own excess.[42] What is needed, argues Hapgood in his book *The Stage in America: 1897-1900*, is a return to stage simplification.[43]

In 1899, John Corbin, writer, director, and literary manager for the New Theatre in New York, wrote about Poel's 1898 production of *The Merchant of Venice*, favorably comparing it to a more elaborate production by Augustin Daly. In the Elizabethan Stage Society version, "the stage was as bare as the stages of old on the Bankside... If we are to get at the pith of a play like *The Merchant*, we must guard against an elaboration of scenery that clogs the action...".[44]

Over the years, Corbin kept reiterating the need to return to Elizabethan stage techniques when performing plays of that era. In 1906, he was still voicing reservations about the conventional production methods for doing Elizabethan and Jacobean plays when he wrote against Irving's production of *Macbeth*. He quarrelled with Irving's approach on the basis of economy. It would be aesthetically uneconomic to describe something and then show it. Besides, illustrating steals from the imagination:

> The attempt to make a locality which Shakespeare has been at pains to define more real by means of the trivial art of the scene-painter is, to say the least, to produce the deadening effect of redundancy. When the curtain rises, as, for example, on Macbeth's castle as Irving represented it, the eye takes in the whole at a glance. Then Banquo speaks those marvelous lines. Instead of perceiving the inner vision Shakespeare intended... the result is to dispell the dreams of poetry. Instead of reinforcing this moment of beauty and foreboding, the redundant illustration kills it.[45]

In an article in *The Atlantic Monthly*, Corbin brought up the related issue of economy in terms of efficient use of financial resources. Not only does an Elizabethan Shakespeare performance benefit the play artistically by allowing the action to flow swiftly and fluidly, but it also saves money. Corbin asserted that doing plays as Shakespeare performed them enabled less money to go a lot further.[46]

Other scholars and critics voiced their dissatisfaction with literal stagecraft based on the economy factor. One was Clayton Hamilton, professor of literature at Columbia University and critic for *The Bookman*. Hamilton reminds us how "it cost Shakespeare nothing to make his audience imagine a moon-rise at the opening of the last act of *The Merchant of Venice*."[47] Hamilton also alludes to the issue of aesthetic economy when he explains how a dextrously handled few can incite the imagination to envision many:

> There is no advantage in setting half of Rome upon the boards to
> listen to Marc Anthony's oration if, with a mere handful of
> supernumeraries, the stage-director can make the audience
> imagine that half of Rome is present.[48]

Corbin had the opportunity to exercise his influence as literary manager of
the New Theatre to turn principles of economy into stage reality. In 1910, the
New Theatre hired Louis Calvert to direct a bare-stage Elizabethan-facsimile
production of *A Winter's Tale*. Calvert had firsthand exposure to simplified
stages acting for Granville-Barker at the Royal Court Theatre in London. A
critic from *The Outlook* describes the Elizabethan stage Calvert fashioned:

> The stage was extended into the auditorium by flooring over the
> space generally assigned to the orchestra, a gallery ran around the
> back of the stage, and beneath the gallery... was a small alcove,
> or inner stage in which the use of properties or bits of scenery
> indicated the location of the action....*The Winter's Tale* loses
> nothing in reality and verisimiltude, and gains much in the
> rapidity of the action.[49]

The only accessories to this production, besides the few properties needed to
indicate time and place for individual scenes, were sumptuous costumes and
medieval tapestries for backgrounds. Even though these features manifest a
complexity in terms of color and detail, the other aspects of the production
evidence an inclination toward stage simplification.

Walter Prichard Eaton comments on some of these other aspects of Calvert's
mise-en-scène. Eaton praises the show's acting for its overall simplicity and
restraint. He specifically picks out Edith Matthison's Hermione for its simplicity
and Rose Coghlan's Paulina for its "suggestion of power in reserve."[50] It is clear
that Calvert and his actors were attempting to match simplicity in acting to the
restraint of the stripped stage.

Despite the costumes and tapestries, this production's spare qualities led
Eaton to rhapsodize on the values of stage simplicity. He closes a review of the
production with words that recall Corbin's own strong preference for
Shakespearean performance with scenographic restraint: "To a spectator with
imagination... Shakespeare's pen was more potent than any scene painter's
brush."[51]

In 1916, Corbin returned to his mission of bringing back bare-stage
Shakespeare, when he himself directed *The Tempest* without scenery at the
Century Theatre. Corbin constructed a platform stage with an inner alcove built
under a balcony—just as deWitt displays the Swan-Theatre stage in his famous
sketch. The inner alcove served first as Corbin's ship cabin and later as

Prospero's cave. Eaton enthusiastically describes how the bare boards became Shakespeare's magic island and how two box trees in a pot sufficed to create a tangled forest.[52] Eaton was so moved by Corbin's success at recapturing the Elizabethan performance style that he even proposes that at least one Shakespeare play a year be produced in this simple way, arguing that it would be "a splendid stimulus to our pampered imaginations."[53] Clearly Eaton here is referring indirectly to an issue that concerned Corbin himself: the deleterious effect overly literal stagecraft has had on the imaginative powers of the American spectator.

From 1908 to 1920, two actress/managers were displaying simple stages in reviving Shakespeare's original performance conditions: Maude Adams, who, before becoming a director of Shakespeare, had already become a cult figure in the title role of J.M. Barrie's *Peter Pan*, and Margaret Anglin who, as we have seen, had already become well known for her Greek revivals. Shakespearean studies, like classical studies, found a happy home in the American university, so it is not surprising that key productions of the Elizabethan revival would occur in a college setting.

In 1908, the Harvard English Department invited Maude Adams to campus to present a Shakespearean comedy in the Elizabethan manner. Originally they planned to perform *As You Like It*, but they later changed to *Twelfth Night*, with Adams as Viola. It was presented in Harvard's Sanders Theater on a facsimile Elizabethan stage. Writing in 1910, Eaton recalls the Adams *Twelfth Night*, criticizing it for being too bare and stark. Adams built a protruding thrust and placed boxes on stage for audience members. Other scenic accessories were kept to a bare minimum. Eaton contends that the production fell short, partly because the acting was as "barren" as the stage. Eaton also admits his preference for Corbin's *A Winter's Tale* (which he reviews in the same article) because it captured, with its sumptuous costumes and tapestries, the Elizabethan love for "bright and beautiful things," whereas Adams's production (and Ben Greet's revivals) were altogether too drab.

Adams's stage was not so bare as to avoid illusionistic touches altogether. In order to recreate the outdoor Elizabethan theater inside Sanders Theater, an indoor theater, Adams and her Harvard counterparts painted a blue sky with clouds and hung it over the stage. The same illusionistic tendencies evident in her *As You Like It* production in the Hearst Greek Theatre reappeared in this one. Evidently she had not yet freed herself from the illusionistic and painterly traditions she inherited.

The most highly regarded Shakespeare revivals were those of actress/manager Margaret Anglin and her designer Livingston Platt. Anglin's first exposure to Platt's work occurred when she saw his *Comedy of Errors* set, created for John Craig at the Castle Square Stock Company in Boston (photo 1.6). This was one of four Shakespeare productions that Platt designed for Craig. Anglin was so impressed with Platt's work that she hired him to design productions of *As You Like It, The Taming of the Shrew, Twelfth Night*, and *Antony and Cleopatra* which toured sixty-five cities. All but *Antony and Cleopatra* were presented at the Hudson Theater in New York City in March 1914.

1.6 Watercolor of priory scene in *Comedy of Errors*, designed by Livingston Platt.

Just as they combined Greek stage conventions with the new stage ideas in their Greek revivals, Anglin and Platt began to synthesize the simple features of the Elizabethan stage with the bold new images of stage simplicity coming onto the American scene from the European New Stagecraft which Platt had already been exposed to in Bruges. For the four Shakespeare productions, Anglin and Platt combined the Elizabethan virtually bare platform stage with suggestive lighting in the style of New Stagecraft designers Craig and Appia. Anglin and Platt also employed the expedient of a double proscenium which allowed for quick changes and unimpeded fluidity in the flow of action.

The palace setting for *Twelfth Night* was typical of settings in the three productions presented in New York. Robert Harlow Bradley describes the evident restraint in the set: "Simplification was the keynote. The palace... had three arched windows and through them the deep blue sky could be seen, while in the room itself were only two pieces of furniture."[54]

Like Corbin's *Winter's Tale* production and their own Greek revivals discussed earlier, the three Anglin/Platt Shakespeare revivals in New York were not restrained in the area of color. Platt brought a wide range of color not only to the costumes but also to the settings. But his way of bringing lots of color to the settings was not through adding material things but through the simplifying effects of "painting with light," i.e., using light to take the place of different color flats, drops, and additional onstage objects. Arthur Krows writes that, in Anglin's New York production of *Twelfth Night*, swaying opalescent curtains were contrived almost exclusively by light. He also notes, in the Anglin/Platt *As You Like It* production, that they used a simple drop showing a river winding its way across the stage from side to side and that the scene was virtually painted anew by changing the lighting color on the two banks and illuminating the river—a transparency—with white lights from behind.[55]

Another method of painting with light that Platt utilized was the so-called "pointillistic" technique, credited to another famous American stage designer, Joseph Urban. Platt applied this method not only in his Shakespeare productions but four years later in his 1918 indoor productions of *Medea* and *Electra* productions as well. Rather than painting many different settings in many different hues, much of the colorfulness of the Anglin/Platt Shakespeare productions resulted from painting the same settings with primary colors in a pointillistic or stippled manner such that the settings were covered with dots—like a Seurat painting—of all the colors that the designer would want to use in the course of the show. By reflecting back whatever color light was projected onto it, the same setting could reveal a wide assortment of colors and textures, depending on which color of light was projected onto it. This method, which is now part of common usage in scene shops, was new in 1914 and provided the set designer with the capacity of changing atmosphere and the color of settings by merely changing which color light hits the flat, not changing the flats themselves. Through these various methods Platt created a lot of color with minimal material means.

Thus, Platt was able to achieve lots of color and visual effects not by relying exclusively on Shakespeare's poetry inflaming the spectator's imagination (the Elizabethan way) nor by resorting to construction of a lot of scenery that would clutter the stage as in the Italianate and naturalistic traditions. He found a compromise solution whereby the new sophisticated indoor lighting in combination with minimal decor could imaginatively suggest a lot with little.

Beginning in 1910, Anglin and Platt and others who revived aspects of Greek and Elizabethan productions achieved a simple stage primarily by looking backwards but also by incorporating ideas and images for a new simplicity coming out of Europe. Between 1912 and 1919, the American theater community witnessed this simplicity themselves when key European theater artists came to visit.

NOTES

[1] Robert Nordvold, "Showcase for the New Stagecraft: The Scenic Designs of the Washington Square Players and the Theatre Guild," (Diss., Indiana University, 1973), pp. 9-10.

[2] Domis Plugge, *History of Greek Play Production* (New York: Bureau of Publications, Columbia University Teacher's College, 1938), p. 147.

[3] Huntly Carter, *The New Spirit in Drama and Art* (New York: Mitchell Kennerley, 1913), p. 189.

[4] Sheldon Cheney, *The New Movement in the Theatre* (New York: Benjamin Bloom, 1914), p. 197.

[5] Ibid., p. 198.

[6] Ibid., p. 199.

[7] Arthur Edwin Krows, *Play Production in America* (New York: Henry Holt and Company, 1916), p. 364.

[8] Cheney, *The Open-Air Theatre* (New York: Mitchell Kennerley, 1971), p. 36.

[9] It is probably closest in style to the Theater of Epidaurus, a Hellenistic Greek theater in Epidaurus, Greece.

[10] Cheney, *The New Movement*, frontispiece.

[11] Ibid., frontispiece.

[12] Gordon Arnold Johnson, "The Greek Productions of Margaret Anglin." (Diss., Case Western Reserve University, 1971), p. 4.

[13] Cheney, *Open-Air*, p. 34.

[14] Johnson, p. 17.

[15] Margaret Anglin, "Playing Greek Tragedy," *Hearst's International Magazine* 28 (July 1915), p. 44, quoted in Johnson, p. 92.

[16] Ibid., pp. 92-93.

[17] Cheney, *Open-Air*, p. 34.

[18] Cheney, *The New Movement*, p. 171.

[19] Ada Patterson, "The Greek Theatre and Margaret Anglin," *Harper's Bazaar*, 50 (June 1915), p. 24, quoted in Johnson, p. 87.

[20] Quoted in Gerald Bordman, *The Concise Oxford Companion to American Theatre* (New York: Oxford University Press, 1987), p. 337.

[21] Ibid., p. 78.

[22] A. S. "Anglin Cheered in *Electra*," *American* (New York, December 2, 1927), quoted in Johnson, p. 124.

[23] Johnson, p. 121.

[24] Walter Anthony, "Margaret Anglin Stages Euripides," *Chicago Evening Post*, August 26, 1915, quoted in Johnson, p. 122.

[25] Johnson, p. 114.

[26] Ibid., p. 230.

[27] Ibid., p. 231.

[28] Ibid., p. 147.

[29] Ibid., p. 147.

[30] Vreeland, *Evening Telegram*, May 4, 1927, quoted in Johnson, p. 148.

[31] Ibid., pp. 240-241.

[32] Ibid., p. 245.

[33] Patterson, "A Beautiful Adventure in the Drama," *Cosmopolitan*, 59 (August 1915), p. 358, quoted in Johnson, p. 241.

[34] John Barry, "Ways of the World," *San Francisco Call*, June 11, 1923, quoted in Johnson, p. 107.

[35] Johnson, p. 106.

[36] Arthur Krows, p. 364.

[37] "The Limits of Stage Illusion," *The Living Age*, 268 (December 3, 1910), p. 589.

[38] Ibid., p. 588.

[39] Eaton, *At the New Theatre and Others* (Boston: Small, Maynard & Co., 1910) p. 82.

[40] Stephen Allard, "William Poel in America," *Theatre Arts Magazine* (November 1916), p. 25.

[41] Norman Hapgood, "The Upbuilding of the Theatre," *The Atlantic Monthly*, 82 (March 1899), p. 423, as quoted in Robert Harlow Bradley, "Proposals for the Reform of the Art of the Theatre as Expressed in General American Periodicals, 1900-1915," (Diss., U of Illinois at Urbana-Champaigne, 1957), p. 77-78.

[42] Norman Hapgood, "Upbuilding," p. 422-423, as quoted in Bradley, p. 77-78.

[43] Norman Hapgood, *The Stage in America: 1897-1900* (New York: The Macmillan Co., 1901), pp. 140-141.

[44] John Corbin, "This is the Jew that Shakespeare Drew," *Harper's Weekly*, 62 (January 14, 1899), p. 35, as quoted in Bradley, p. 96.

[45] John Corbin, "Shakespeare and the Plastic Stage," *The Atlantic Monthly*, 97 (March 1906), pp. 380-381, as quoted in Bradley, p. 95.

[46] Corbin, "Plastic Stage," p. 383.

[47] Clayton Hamilton, "The New Art of Stage Direction," *Bookman*, 35 (July 1912), p. 486.

[48] Ibid., p. 486.

[49] "In the Manner of Shakespeare's Time," *The Outlook*, 44 (April 9, 1910), pp. 784-785, as quoted in Bradley, p. 97.

[50] Eaton, *New Theatre*, p. 85.

[51] Ibid., p. 83.

[52] Walter Prichard Eaton, *Plays and Players: Leaves from a Critic's Notebook* (New York: Appleton, 1916), p. 245.

[53] Ibid., p. 245.

[54] Bradley, "Proposals for Reform," p. 99.

[55] Krows, p. 215.

2

New Simple Stages from Europe

In July 1911 Walter Prichard Eaton declared war in an article appearing in the *American Magazine*. But in his essay, entitled "The Theatre: The Question of Scenery," he distanced himself from the chorus of critics who had opposed the naturalistic *mise-en-scène* in the name of superior stages of the past. He called for something new:

> We can no more go back to the Elizabethan theatre than to the Elizabethan stagecoach or Elizabethan surgery. But we can experiment with our modern scenic settings to discover if there is not some way of simplifying it, of making it a more effective aid to the drama as well as a less costly one, of making it more suggestive....[1]

Eaton identifies three American non-Shakespearean production settings utilizing, albeit in primitive ways, greater suggestiveness and less literal detail: Charles Frohman's "illusive" *Chantecler* designed by John Alexander and J. Monroe Hewlett for the actress/manager Maude Adams; Hamilton Bell's depiction of a spare convent for *Sister Beatrice* for the New Theatre; and the New Theatre's *The Blue Bird*, also designed by Bell. In the case of the *The Blue Bird* (1910), the New Theatre stumbled upon stage simplification. The production began in a large theater, then moved to the smaller Majestic Theatre stage, for which designer Bell had to cut down its scenery. Due to popular demand, the show returned to its original home, but now Bell, needing to fill the gaps, suspended long, graceful hangings of gauzy material. According to Eaton, these hangings created a hazy expanse of empty space, within which the setting seemed to float. This was the approach that Platt chose to take with his indoor productions of Shakespeare and the Greeks.

By the turn of the century, ideas and images for stage simplicity were already being born in Europe. But it was not until 1911 that the new simple stages appeared on American shores. When they did arrive, they received strong support from several influential scholar/critics[2] who, like Eaton, were dissatisfied with the stages they associated with David Belasco. They were scholars who were writing books on contemporary theater production and were professors at major universities. They were also theater critics for influential magazines and newspapers. From these vantage points, they wielded significant influence in the American theater community. Walter Prichard Eaton, Clayton Hamilton, Sheldon Cheney, Kenneth Macgowan, Arthur Krows, and Hiram Moderwell wrote extensively of their preference for simplified stages and provided a welcoming environment for the arrival of the European New Stagecraft and an increasingly hostile one for the American naturalistic theater artists.

Clayton Hamilton, the theater critic for *The Bookman*, was the one most directly in battle with "Belascoism." In July 1912, he launched an offensive against Belasco's productions on the grounds that his meticulous naturalism: (1) disperses and distracts audience attention; (2) is unnecessarily costly; and (3) is unimaginative and hence inartistic.[3] Hamilton took issue with Belasco's comment that a set should provide "ceaseless occupation for the eye."[4] Hamilton proposes that it is more economic and a finer art to present mood, time, and place in a single impression:

> His [Belasco's] only error is a tendency to diseconomize attention
> by forcing the spectator to look at several hundred interesting
> details, instead of summarizing these details in an impressionistic
> picture that should suggest... in a single glance, the mood of the
> action... exhibited.[5]

Hamilton's battle with "Belascoism" became overt, even nasty, in 1917 when Belasco wrote a vicious attack on the little theaters and the ethos of simplicity sweeping across America. With the bold-faced headlines "DAVID BELASCO SEES A MENACE TO TRUE ART IN TOY PLAYHOUSES AND LITTLE REPERTORY THEATRES," Belasco condemned the new art movement as incompetent, a mere "flash in the pan of experience."[6]

Hamilton retaliated, reminding Belasco he had been using the very ideas of suggestiveness and simplified imagery condemned in his January 7th article.

Hamilton also asserted that productions in the little theaters had been superior to Belasco's in every respect, except the acting.

Others entered the fray, but Belasco and Hamilton remained the two major antagonists. They continued to raise the same issues years after their first confrontation. Belasco was still fighting as late as 1920, expanding the battleground to his book *The Theatre Through the Stage Door* and his article "Stage Art Old and New," which appeared January 16, 1920 in the *Saturday Evening Post*. But now stage simplification was solidly in place; Belasco could not hope to dislodge it.

Eaton and Hamilton's views against the Belasco method won the support of other scholar/critics. Sheldon Cheney's *Theatre Arts Magazine*, which began publication in 1916, continually ran laudatory articles on simple stages in the United States and Europe. In the magazine as well as in his books, Cheney proved himself a determined advocate of simplifiers like Maurice Browne and the Chicago Little Theatre, Sam Hume and the Arts and Crafts Theatre of Detroit, Jacques Copeau, Edward Gordon Craig, and Adolphe Appia. Two of Cheney's frequent contributors, Kenneth Macgowan and Hiram Moderwell, were especially vocal in their support. Macgowan elaborated his point of view in *Theatre of Tomorrow* and *Continental Stagecraft*, as did Hiram Moderwell in *Theatre of To-day*. They overtly praised stage simplicity in general and the work of stage designers Robert Edmond Jones and Lee Simonson, specifically.

By 1911, these champions of stage simplicity had access to many models from Europe rather than relying on past theater traditions. Under the rubric of the "New Stagecraft" and the "New Art of the Theater," a new look had appeared on European stages. The main contributions came from the writings and designs of Adolphe Appia, Edward Gordon Craig, and Georg Fuchs, all of whom, in their own ways, conceived stages that were shorn of literal detail and rich in suggestiveness. For the three of them, the evocative qualities of light constituted a major element in their determination and ability to simplify. As for settings, Appia stripped stages to one essential image, oftentimes to platforms and step-units going in different directions. These were his "rhythmic spaces." Edward Gordon Craig conceived a system of screens and other modular units. And Georg Fuchs, founder of the Munich Art Theatre in 1907, wrote about and, with designer Fritz Erler, worked on a narrow "relief stage" where action was restricted to horizontal patterns and the actor's bodies stood out from the background the way figures stand out in bas-reliefs.

Their simplified stage ideas influenced directors and designers throughout the first three decades of the century. Vsevolod Meyerhold's stages in St. Petersburg around 1906 featured shallow stages and essentialized characters and settings as well as cases of synchronous movement of multiple characters. Austrian director Max Reinhardt, the most eclectic of all European directors, continually experimented with many kinds of stages, including simplified ones, especially during the first two decades of the century. French director Jacques Copeau and the Vieux Colombier were responsible for the most consistent and complete stage simplifications. William Butler Yeats and his fellow Irish Players were advocating a simpler stage and putting Craig's screens into practice and experimenting with simplified realism. By the late teens, the earliest expressionists in Germany—including director/designer teams Leopold Jessner and Emil Pirchan as well as Jurgen Fehling and Hans Strobach—were stripping the stage, often to black voids and permanent settings, some dominated by steps or skewed set pieces.

Not all European pioneers of the simple stage contributed in equal degrees to the simplification of the American *mise-en-scène*. The writings of Appia and Fuchs were not accessible to most American directors and designers, and the symbolist experiments at Paul Fort's Theatre d'Art and Lugne-Poe's Theatre de l'Oeuvre in Paris and Meyerhold's in St. Petersburg barely reached the American theatrical consciousness. By far, the most influential were Craig, the Irish Players, Reinhardt, and Copeau—either through their visits to the United States or through the travels of American theater simplifiers to Europe. Throughout the second and third decades, Livingston Platt, Sam Hume, Maurice Browne, Arthur Hopkins, Robert Edmond Jones, and Lee Simonson went abroad and returned with vivid accounts of what they saw.

In the crucial first few years that New Stagecraft ideas and images were entering the American theater world, the predominant sources were Edward Gordon Craig's book *On the Art of the Theatre* (published in America in 1911), the productions of the Irish Players which first toured the United States in 1911, and Max Reinhardt's *Sumurun*, which came to the Casino Theatre in January 1912. The first ongoing program of simplified productions on the professional stage came five years later when Jacques Copeau began the first of his two seasons at the Garrick Theatre. One can find a smattering of other influences in these early years, but these four had the largest impact on the American directors and designers who went on to simplify the American stage.

Some of the impact on American theater practitioners from these sources resulted from direct encounters; much came second-hand. Many learned about Craig's ideas not directly from his book, but from what others had to say about it; knowledge about the Irish Players' and Reinhardt's productions not always resulted from attendance, but also by reading accounts in theater journals, newspapers, and general magazines. Exhibitions of stage designs also provided indirect access to the ideas and stage images of Craig and Reinhardt, most notably Sam Hume's celebrated Exhibition of the New Stagecraft, which toured Boston, New York, Chicago, and Detroit from 1914 to 1915 and was written about in journals. The simple stage had many proponents and many varied examples from which to choose.

THE IRISH PLAYERS

The Irish Players began their American tour in September 1911 in Boston, where they were seen by Robert Edmond Jones and the Boston Toy Theatre's founder, Mrs. Lyman Gale. The Players went to New York in November and later travelled to Chicago, where Maurice Browne attended performances and was inspired to start the Chicago Little Theatre. The Irish Players showed American directors and designers the possibilities of a highly simplified realism in settings, acting, and directing.

Being away from the Abbey Theatre—their homebase in Dublin—the company had to travel light and cheaply, so its settings were kept to a bare minimum. But this was done not only out of practical necessity, but also from aesthetic preference. This fact was made clear in William Butler Yeats's Harvard lectures on Edward Gordon Craig and the Players, which were presented in coordination with the Players' Boston tour. Those who could not hear Yeats directly were given access to his thoughts through *Harper's Weekly*, which published the complete text of his address. In the lectures, Yeats expressed support for simplified, symbolic stagecraft, like the kind used by the Irish Players.

Clayton Hamilton attended some of the Irish Players's performances and witnessed their simplified staging. In his theater column for *The Bookman*, he notes, for instance, how the Players found the secret of doing so much with so little and how they, among other advantages, enjoyed significant financial savings. Hamilton's vivid descriptions also show how the Irish Players presented the first models for two types of simplified realism that would become standard on the American stage: relief-stage simplified realism and space-stage simplified realism.

Hamilton provides us with a vivid description for T. C Murray's *Birthright*, an example of simplified realism of the relief-stage kind:

> *Birthright*... is set in a homely cottage, with only a few necessary bits of furniture and scarcely any properties. There is a fireplace... and a staircase leading off-stage... The set is very shallow. The back discloses a blank, bare wall, interrupted only by a window and a door. Not a single picture is hung upon this surface of dingy plaster... The stage is lighted only by the firelight, a candle on the table and unindicated illumination in the flies. The result is that the actors, as they move about, cast huge and varying shadows over the bare surface of the wall and decorate it continuously with fluctuating and impressive designs.[7]

The stark and shallow stage, the bare walls with few visual interruptions, the lighting from few sources, the few properties on stage, and the shadows exhibit stage simplicity, even if the "fluctuating" shadows seem to indicate something more visually active and complex. The *mise-en-scène* also embodies many of the same elements that will later be seen in productions of simplified realism by director Maurice Browne at the Chicago Little Theatre and Robert Edmond Jones in the professional New York theater. Both of these artists acknowledged that they were influenced by the simple stages of the Irish Players' American tour. Jones movingly writes about his recollection of the *Birthright* set in *The Dramatic Imagination*, as we shall see in Chapter Six.

The *mise-en-scène* of Lady Gregory's *The Rising of the Moon* exemplified a kind of space-stage simplified realism Americans would later witness at the Theatre Guild. According to Eaton, the setting consisted merely of a large keg, the suggested outline of the quay, and rays of moonlight which threw shadows by coming in from only one side of the stage.[8] Hamilton, who also was impressed by this scene, recalls it this way:

> the stage is lighted only by two streams of apparent moonlight which come to a focus at a large barrel in the centre, on which the two most important actors seat themselves,—while the wharf and the water in the background are merely imagined in a darkness that is inscrutable and alluringly mysterious.[9]

Besides the relatively empty stage, three features typical of the simplified *mise-en-scène* are evident in this description. First, the high-angle lighting creating pools of light in a surrounding darkness are hallmarks of the "space stage." Second, there were no more than two sources of stage light, both untinted, and from only one direction. And third, the use of a "suggested outline of the quay" indicates that the Irish Players were utilizing fragmentary scenery—another common attribute of what would later be called simplified or selective realism.

Nothing in Hamilton and Eaton's accounts reveal simplified acting and directing, but we do see references to it in other descriptions. Cheney quotes Yeats's words of praise for the Irish Players' acting: "It was the first performance I had seen... in which the actors kept still enough to give poetical writing its full effect upon the stage."[10] As we will see in the next chapter, Maurice Browne was deeply affected by the Irish Players' relative stillness on stage and their ability to sustain long periods of stage silence.

Lack of movement was only one aspect of an overall simplicity in their acting. Thomas Dickinson, author of *The Insurgent Theater*, one of the many books describing the New Stagecraft in Europe and the United States, takes the position that the Irish Players taught Americans simplicity and naturalness in all aspects of acting.[11] Another commentator observes how critics and actors faulted the Irish Players for merely walking through their parts because audiences in the early 1910s were so accustomed to the embroidered acting style of the American theater.[12]

ON THE ART OF THE THEATRE BY EDWARD GORDON CRAIG

Edward Gordon Craig's ideas and design style had more influence on the modern American *mise-en-scène* than that of any other designer or theoretician. Calling Craig's influence in America as "greater than any other one man's,"[13] Moderwell holds Craig up as the "father of them all,"[14] contending that "all the advanced European theaters... acknowledge his artistic paternity of their work."[15] Cheney agrees, referring to Craig as "the most important figure in the new theater"[16] because his ideas impregnated the imaginations of others with the desire to create.[17]

Much of that influence can be traced to Craig's *On the Art of the Theatre*, published by Brown's Bookstore of Chicago in December 1911, followed by a second impression in January 1912. The book had a wide circulation in the American theater community, and, as it was the first work by Craig to be published in this country, it received the most attention and registered the strongest impact. All the major theater simplifiers read it or were exposed to its principles indirectly through other directors, designers, scholars, or critics who had read it and then wrote or spoke about it.

From the beginning of the book, Craig lays out his artistic preferences as a designer and creator of theatrical performances. He is after "the large and sweeping impression" and "general and broad effects,"[18] not meticulous detail. To create a cliff, for example, Craig would have us concentrate on the lines and their direction, rather than the cliff itself. Go as high as you want, he tells the reader; you cannot go too high. These words were encouraging designs toward monumentality, the trait that virtually identifies a Craig or Craig-influenced stage design.

The goal is to capture the soul of an image—its essentiality—rather than linger on its outward characteristics. The designer and the director (or stage manager, as Craig calls him) must confine themselves to only what is absolutely necessary. They must seek the essential line and rhythm, the essential gesture and action—not waste time with the random, haphazard, and insignificant details of everyday life.[19] To Craig, the main enemy is literal detail. Craig recounts how, as a young man, he tried to design Shakespeare's *Henry IV* with countless true-to-life properties and scenery and how he only achieved something interesting once he got rid of all those "stupid restless details."[20]

The director who is portraying a crowd should not differentiate each individual as the realists do, but rather treat them as a mass of figures and shapes: "Masses must be treated as masses... Detail has nothing to do with the mass... Detail is made to form a mass only by those people who love the elaborate."[21] This idea also applies to group costumes. "It is the mistake of all theatrical producers that they consider the costumes of the mass individually."[22] Craig is here advocating "multiple uniformity" and the traits of uninterrupted and repetitive movement and imagery.

Craig admits that complicated and subtle movements in nature have little appeal to him as a designer; he prefers "the plainest, barest, and simplest movements."[23] And if action on stage cannot be kept simple and basic, then it is better not to have movement at all. Craig quotes Rimbaud in this regard, that "action is a way of spoiling something."[24] His ideal stage is one that is silent and still, one that will "unveil thought to our eyes, silently... in visions."[25]

The ideal is not the supple, willful actor, but the controllable marionette—not the manic puppet one sees in the fairground, but rather the über-marionette, who moves with his "stamp of reserve."[26] He would move not the way humans move in their lives, but like the "body in trance," with its aura of stillness, quietude, and other-worldliness. He seeks the "calm and cool whisper of life in trance."[27]

The desire for an über-marionette to replace the actor is symptomatic of Craig's predisposition toward a depersonalized stage. He wants shapes, shadows, and shades, not differentiated human personalities. "Shades—spirits seem to be more beautiful, and filled with more vitality than men and women."[28] And when these anonymous figures are placed on a stage with towering vertical lines around them, an even greater sense of depersonalization can be achieved.

Not only does Craig reject literal detail, but also decorative abstraction. He advocates aesthetic moderation and restraint over flamboyance. To him, reserve is a capital law of art.[29] The designer must be "in the service of simple truths,"[30] in harmony with the spirit or sense of the play. Since the designer must be guided by "the sound of the verse or prose as by the sense or spirit," he must suggest not decorate, pare away not elaborate.

Craig urges that color be applied with great restraint. He recommends mono- and duo-chromatic designs over multicolored ones. As an example, he describes an ideal scene for *Macbeth*, consisting of only two colors: "one for the rock, the man; one for the mist, the spirit." He warns the designer to avoid additional colors in set and costumes "yet forget not that each color contains many variations."[31] And the two colors he suggests—brown rock and gray mist[32]—are neutral-tone; he prefers them to colors with greater saturation. He is encouraging stage designers to create within a limited palette.

Craig also advises the director/designer to employ an economy of means and apply the principles of suggestion, whether creating crowds or environments:

> you must be able to increase the impression of your numbers
> without actually adding another man to your forty or fifty. You
> must not, therefore, waste a single man, nor place him in such a

> position that an inch of him is lost.... By means of suggestion
> you may bring on the stage a sense of all things—the rain, the
> sun, the wind, the snow, the hail, the intense heat —[33]

In *On the Art of the Theatre*, Craig backs up these aesthetic ideas with illustrations. American theater directors and designers reading this book sometime after December 1911 would have seen Craig's sketches for an *Electra* with what he himself called a "vast and forbidding doorway... the best background for any tragedy."[34] (photo 2.1) They also would have leafed through sketches of *Macbeth* (photo 2.2) and *Hamlet* (photo 2.3) for which Craig, taking the cue from Belgian playwright Maurice Maeterlinck, sought to suggest "the murmur of eternity on the horizon"[35] rather than depict the plays with full historical detail. Even if the American simplifiers had not read a word of Craig's book, the sketches themselves would have presented an enticing alternative to the traditional Italianate and naturalistic *mise-en-scènes*.

With its American publication, *On the Art of the Theatre* helped prepare the ground for American theater simplifiers. They read about and viewed sketches illustrating Craig's theater of essentials, one that is restrained, spare, monumental, with limited palette—a theater of austere but dignified shapes, lines, and masses. They could not miss Craig's forecast that this simplicity was an idea whose time had come:

> He [the modern theater manager] scents a grave danger in simple
> and good work; he sees that there is a body of people who are
> opposed to these lavish decorations; he knows that there has been
> a distinct movement in Europe against this display, it having been
> claimed that the great plays gained when represented in front of
> the plainest background. This movement can be proved to be a
> powerful one.[36]

THE REINHARDT/STERN *SUMURUN*

At about the time that Craig's book reached the first ready hands of American theater artists, Max Reinhardt's production of *Sumurun* came to New York's Casino Theatre, providing another stunning example of European stage simplicity. Opening on January 16, 1912, *Sumurun* was to be seen by virtually every leader of the New Stagecraft in the United States. Scholar/critics Walter Prichard Eaton, Clayton Hamilton, Hiram Moderwell, Sheldon Cheney, and Kenneth Macgowan saw and wrote about it. Maurice Browne, Sam Hume, Robert Edmond Jones, Arthur Hopkins, and Lee Simonson were also there to

2.1 Edward Gordon Craig's sketch for *Electra* as it appeared in the 1911 American publication of *On the Art of the Theatre*.

2.2 Edward Gordon Craig's sketch for *Macbeth* as it appeared in the 1911 American publication of *On the Art of the Theatre.*

2.3 Edward Gordon Craig's sketch for *Hamlet* as it appeared in the 1911 American publication of *On the Art of the Theatre*.

witness what many regard as the beginning of the New Stagecraft in America. Designed by Ernst Stern, this production reinforced principles laid out by Craig.

In *My Life, My Stage*, Stern writes that the *Sumurun* production proved himself a designer, if one accepts the old proverb that "'it's easy enough to cook with the best of materials, but the real cook is the cook who can cook with next to nothing.'"[37] The impetus for simplifying this production, as Stern points out, was financial, but once done, there was a strong aesthetic commitment to its simplicity.

2.4 Scene before the harem in Reinhardt/Stern production of *Sumurun*. Performed in New York City at Casino Theater in 1912.

This is evident in Stern's anecdote on the London production. Asked to replicate the Berlin sets, the London sponsor Sir Oswald Stoll followed it precisely, except that he painted the sets in reds, golds, yellows, and blues to accommodate what he perceived as English taste and understanding of the Orient. With only twelve hours before the London debut, Reinhardt ordered a return to the original colors, arguing that "motley was the enemy of color, and that the white background was an essential feature of the production."[38] When this story leaked out to the London Press, Stern was nicknamed "Mr. Black-and-White."[39]

The settings in *Sumurun* were generally white and gray; the stage and the draperies were black. In only one scene was the background other than white. Stern painted the outer wall of the palace pink, which contrasted nicely with the green-faced eunuchs who were standing guard before it (photo 2.4). Except for this scene, Stern limited himself to settings in the black-to-white spectrum, with lots of bare surfaces. Restraint in color was one of the most obvious traits of the set, even if the costumes and that one scene remained colorful. But Hamilton states that even when vivid colors were used, the surfaces were left plain and undetailed.

An even more obvious self-imposed limitation in the *Sumurun* production was that it was a pantomime, i.e. performed without words. Thus, audiences encountered a bold directorial choice to do a performance within a severe auditory restriction. There was music playing throughout the production but it tended to be "leading motifs" associated with individual characters and hence was deliberately kept repetitious rather than constantly changing.

American audiences were exposed to a shallow "relief" stage. The black-to-white color spectrum of most of the settings enabled the players and their colorful costumes to stand out in bold relief. In the procession scene, the flat background, designed without perspective, and the shallow foreground forced the figures of the performers to emerge from the backdrop like figures in a bas-relief. Hamilton notes how this "stopped the eye, instead of luring it onward by perspective lines."[40] Because of the restricted space of the shallow stage, the actors' movements had to flow in horizontal patterns. All of these factors tended to keep the eye still. In addition, Reinhardt often moved groups of characters in unison—which fixed the spectator's eye through contributing a singleness of impression.

Many American observers commented on Reinhardt's suppression of details and emphasis on a general mood over literal depiction. Huntly Carter, who wrote the first book on Max Reinhardt to be published in the United States, characterized the scenery as having an "almost austere simplicity."[41] Eaton, who saw the London production before it came to New York, quoted a London newspaper's description of the third scene:

> a backcloth painted with a flat black silhouette of an Oriental town, with minarets, bulb-shaped cupolas, and flat roofs against a luminous, sapphire moonlit sky and the plain surface of an earth-colored wall extending right across the stage. Nothing could be more unreal, more demonstratively conventional, more boldly simplified—nothing more in accord with the spirit of the East.[42] (photo 2.5)

The town is depicted not explicitly, but rather as a flat-black silhouette against blue; as Carter points out, "one simple mass against another."[43] As one can see, the wall had a plain surface, devoid of literal or decorative detail. Eaton sums up the impression with the less-is-more paradox: "with just a backdrop, a wall and a manipulation of lights to shroud the rest of the stage in darkness... conveyed the atmosphere of the Orient more than a whole stage littered with 'real' properties."[44] Kenneth Macgowan also alludes to the less-is-more idea with the following description of the *Sumurun* set: "A touch or two of Eastern decoration on a flat wall summoned more of the Orient than acres of carved filigree."[45]

Reinhardt and Stern had succeeded in creating a generic "Orient"—the spirit of the Orient—rather than a specific place in Asia. Stern notes that he created a pastiche "Orient" combining elements from Roumania, Turkey, India, Malaya, China, and Japan. But in other respects, Reinhardt and Stern succeeded in blotting out a sense of place altogether, arranging entrances and exits "to suggest the coming of persons from nowhere in particular."[46] In other words, they succeeded in creating a kind of neutral space.

2.5 Ernst Stern's sketch of scene three of Reinhardt/Stern production of *Sumurun*.

The lighting in the production, as Hamilton points out, was simple. In the Sheik's bed-chamber scene, for instance, Reinhardt only employed two light-values: "a lantern at the head of the stairway and a streaming light cast down funnel-wise over the bed of the Sheik."[47] In another article, Hamilton notes the economy in Reinhardt's lighting of the scene inside the theatre of the Hunchback.[48]

This kind of theater was revolutionary and contrasted dramatically with a production such as Belasco's *The Governor's Lady* presented that same year. Belasco's production showed New York audiences a world so literal and, in the case of the Childs Restaurant epilogue, so authentic that it left nothing to the imagination; Reinhardt's world introduced the bold alternative of a simple, evocative stage.

JACQUES COPEAU'S THEATRE DU VIEUX COLOMBIER

Before Copeau took up the task of creating in New York a "new French theater,"[49] he had already developed and articulated his aesthetic of stage simplification in his native France. As a drama critic for the *La Grande Revue* between 1907 and 1910, he was already voicing this ideal. In 1913 he founded the Theatre du Vieux Colombier and laid the theoretical groundwork for the company in an article entitled "Un Essai de renovation dramatique: Le Theatre du Vieux Colombier." There he set down how he hoped to strip away so as to regain "the soul of the theatre."[50] Copeau maintained this ideal throughout his career.

Copeau housed his young company at the Athenee Saint-Germain, a former music hall, after having thoroughly remodeled it by removing all ornamentation. The refurbished theater, with a black proscenium arch amid an otherwise neutral gray interior, and the simplified productions he presented for the 1913/1914 season, were so austere that one of Copeau's detractors stigmatized him and his company as the "Calvinist Follies."[51] But he also won for himself and his company a reputation for excellence that spread throughout the West.

Unfortunately, the war cut Copeau's plans short after only one prolific season. With many of his actors called to the front, Copeau embarked on a journey to meet and study the work of like-minded stage simplifiers. In September and October 1915, Copeau paid a visit to Edward Gordon Craig's "School for the Art of the Theatre" in Florence as well as to Adolphe Appia and Emile-Jacques Dalcroze in Switzerland. He found in them brethren spirits who shared common aesthetic goals.

Appia and Dalcroze helped Copeau in different but related ways. Dalcroze's system of "eurythmics" and the concept of a depersonalized, essentialized mover became the basis for the physical training of Copeau's actors. From Appia, Copeau learned specific ways of viewing the *mise-en-scène* as an integrated whole—the plastic attributes of moving actors responding to music on platforms and step-units in a three-dimensional "rhythmic space," lit so as to accentuate their sculptural qualities. From this follows, Copeau writes in his notebook, "the banishing from the stage of all inanimate decorations, all painted cloths" and a corresponding emphasis on the "practical and active role of light."[52]

Although put off by Craig's character and "meglomania," Copeau was intrigued by Craig's neutral screens and geometric cubes. In fact, these neutral scenic elements had so strong an impact on Copeau that he kept writing about them to Louis Jouvet in the trenches of World War I. During this same moratorium period between theatrical enterprises, Copeau spent months developing a similar system of screens and adaptable neutral cubes—like giant storable children's building blocks—with the help of painter Theor van Rysselberghe in pursuit of what Frederick Brown has labeled a "proto-minimalist vision of the 'objective' stage."[53] A modified version of these ideas came to the United States with Copeau.

From February 1 to May 31, 1917 Copeau lectured throughout the United States as a cultural ambassador for the French government. His six lectures at Winthrop Ames's Little Theatre not only spelled out fully his program for the theater (one lecture was devoted exclusively to the simplification of the *mise-en-scène*), but also won him an invitation to set up a theater of his own in New York City under the patronage of a wealthy banker, Otto Kahn, and other New York benefactors. In November 1917, Copeau presented his first bill at New York's Garrick Theatre. For two seasons—1917-1918 and 1918-1919—Copeau gave to New York its first look at a professional company with a consistent ongoing program of stage simplicity, from its decor to its directing and acting style.

Copeau had already sown the ground for his new efforts through his ambassadorial lectures as well as essays and interviews which appeared in theater and popular journals and newspapers before and during his first season in New York City. One can extract from these sources a body of theory supporting the austere stage, economical stage scenery, and the essentialized style of acting and directing he was bringing to the Garrick.

Throughout these sources were calls for a theater of bare essentials, always implying an intimate connection between the ideal of beauty and simplification of means.[54] By simplicity, Copeau seems to mean creating in a selfless spirit of self-abnegation and restraint and foreswearing extravagance even when it parades under the guise of originality.[55] Fundamental to the spirit of the Vieux Colombier, Copeau asserts, is the spirit of austerity.[56]

He prefers an art of allusion rather than illusion. Quoted by Henri Pierre Roche of *The New York Times* on the eve of his Garrick Theatre debut, Copeau explains that his ambition is to "suggest things, not to reproduce them."[57] One must therefore strip away and exercise disciplined restraint: "If you want to build up, you must suppress."[58]

As Grotowski would echo decades later, Copeau championed a poor theater: "What you need is poverty. Real poverty." He alludes to the paradox of wealth in poverty and poverty in wealth: "You as a country are much too wealthy. If you knew what can be done with two boards and three good actors minus paint you would know the real poverty of over-decoration and greed."[59] In an essay written for *The Drama*, Copeau bemoans the consequences of external indulgence: "It is disastrous for dramatic art to be surrounded by a great many exterior contrivances which enervate and diffuse its power."[60]

To strip to essentials, Copeau claims he is not innovating but renovating: "We are invited to turn to the past,"[61] not only the Greek and Elizabethan stage to which so many English and American simplifiers had already looked back as a source, but also to his own country's heritage: "This is what the theatre should be—a few boards thrown across two trestles as in the time of Molière, with superb indifference to effect."[62]

The consequences of overemphasis on externals are most blatant in elaborate stage decoration. He berates the American theater scene with these harsh words: "you blunder by placing too much faith in scenery and color schemes and too little on the simplicity of real art."[63] Certainly stage decor produces an illusion, but "it is not the illusion of drama."[64] Do not mistake "scenic form for dramatic form,"[65] warns Copeau; stripping the former will expose the contours of the latter.

Thus concern for trappings takes attention away from where it belongs—on the text and the acting. Copeau explains the effect of excessive scenery on the play: "We have had enough of that absurd wealth of scenery and stage setting that draws the attention away from the play itself and stifles its spirit."[66] He frames his argument more positively in the program for the first season at the Garrick. There he states his overall objective: "to release the spirit of the poet from the text of the play" through "absolute simplification, even the suppression of scenery."[67]

In the *Boston Transcript* he emphasizes more the quarrel between stage decoration and the actor. Reminding theatergoers that "scenery is merely a background for acting,"[68] Copeau challenges the actor to step boldly forth and, without the crutch of properties and scenery, show his talent. Copeau emphasized this point at a lecture he gave at Harvard in April 1917:

> The barer the stage, the more can action give birth to its wonders.
> The greater the austerity and rigidity, the freer the play of the
> imagination... The actor must realize everything, extract
> everything from himself, on this arid stage.[69]

Copeau asks only for what it takes to create pure theater: "Give me real comedians and, on a platform of plain rough-hewn boards, I will promise to produce real comedy."[70] Months before his first Garrick Theatre production, Copeau enlists a strong metaphor to drive home his point, declaring that concern for the stage picture over actor and text is ultimately thinking "more of the color of the mouth than its wisdom."[71]

Thus simplicity is a means for bringing out the truth of a text and the actors' characterizations. And to allow those essential truths to emerge in their fullest clarity, the stage is best kept as neutral as possible. Copeau explains this principle in the *New Republic*:

> If I stretch a gray cloth on the stage instead of a decor it is not because I find it more beautiful, nor above all because I think I have discovered a new and definitive decorative formula. It is a radical remedy, a purgation. It is because I want the stage to be naked and neutral in order that every delicacy may appear there, in order that every fault may stand out; in order that the dramatic may have a chance in this neutral atmosphere to fashion that individual garment which it knows how to put on.[72]

Copeau recognized that not all simplicity succeeded in drawing attention to text and performer and therefore was to be encouraged. He makes the distinction between stage simplicity and "simplism,"[73] the latter being distinguished from the former in its tendency either "to draw attention to itself"[74] at the expense of play and players or to magnify through superficial stage effects what a poet is trying to say. Obvious lighting or stage devices to underline a symbol would fall into the category of simplism. Copeau warns how the simplicity craze, when artlessly pursued, can lead to cold aesthetic demonstration.[75]

His reasons for undertaking stage simplification at the Garrick were primarily aesthetic;[76] financial savings would serve merely as a happy by-product. This is not to say that financial as well as logistical considerations did not play a part in the development of his aesthetic. Making do with scarce resources was as much a part of his theatrical beginnings as those of other artists who later came to embrace simplicity as a good. Copeau explains in an article appearing in the *Boston Transcript*: "When I began in Paris I had very little money to spend on scenery and every setting had to be of the simplest character, but they all served the purpose."[77] Financial and logistical necessity only reinforced Copeau's own aesthetic principles which predated his work as a director.

In his theoretical pronouncements, Copeau also applies his ideal of stage simplicity to the actor's style of performance, sometimes stating it in terms of opposition to literal representation. Copeau proposes that "acting should be simple rather than natural,"[78] that gestures and stage movement should be pared down to essentials and economical forms of expression—line drawings rather than fleshed out portraitures. The minute details of everyday activity are not artful; essences are.

To Copeau, two obstacles to simple acting were affectation and manner. Copeau continually proclaimed his animosity toward any form of affect, using the term "cabotinage" to identify it. As much as authorial pretensions were seen as contaminating texts, acting was ruined by mannerisms.[79] Strip acting of its "false coloring,"[80] strip it to its bones, to an athletic, supple, and versatile performer on a naked platform, he proclaimed, and the truth of the role would become visible and clear. This was his goal as he began the Vieux Colombier in Paris in 1913 and, armed with new methods of stage simplification learned from Appia, Craig, and Dalcroze in the interim, it remained his goal as his first Garrick Theatre season was about to begin.

2.6 Sketch of Jacques Copeau's remodelled stage at the Garrick Theater with proscenium doors.

To keep the performer and text as uncontested focus, Copeau needed to renovate the Garrick Theatre as he had done years before in Paris. In consultation with Louis Jouvet, he stripped his theater of all ornament—made it as "simple, direct and unassuming as plain plaster can."[81] To help him accomplish this, he and Jouvet were aided by architect Antonin Raymond who supported their vision of a theater which, to quote Raymond directly, "would insure the reign of the poet and the actor in the theater."[82] Raymond and Copeau decided to eliminate the Garrick's gallery altogether, even if it meant reducing the seating capacity and thus losing potential audience. They built out a forestage beyond the proscenium. They also placed one door on each side of the proscenium in a manner resembling eighteenth century theaters but tried something more innovative by adding little platforms in front of the doors with steps leading to them (photo 2.6). The side platforms and extended fore-stage were designed to lend greater sculptural value to the onstage figure, making the actor seem less of a flat, two-dimensional entity within a picture frame.

For the productions themselves, Copeau, under the influence of Craig, worked out a system of neutral cubes, screens, and platforms that could be set up and taken down at will and could be adapted according to the needs of any given play. Copeau and his chief designer Louis Jouvet (credited with designing twenty-three productions during the two New York seasons[83]) chose from among these screens, rectangular solids, cubes, columns, staircases, and platforms those which best suited a particular play, i.e., its most minimal set and property requirements. With Jouvet, Copeau also developed a versatile system of electric lighting to allow for many combinations of angles and levels to maximize possible ways of lighting actors on this "naked stage."[84] Thus Copeau and his company could create very different looks from varying configurations of shapes and lights and with a minimum of representation and a maximum of suggestion. The actor's mimetic abilities and the text itself would then define the context and meaning of each setting as traveling troupes had been doing for centuries.

The tone for Copeau's New York radically simple *mise-en-scène* was set at the very beginning of his New York engagement in the double-bill of Molière's *Les Fourberies de Scapin* and *L'Impromptu du Vieux Colombier*, a take-off on Molière conceived by Copeau himself. The stage for the first production, aptly described by Bettina Knapp as a virtual "gray desert," was a neutral gray; on it stood a small platform stage—what Antonin Raymond identifies as a *"treteau* of the ancient village players"[85]—with removable step units leading up to this "stage on a stage" from all sides. Between the two front staircases leading to this three-by-sixteen foot platform, Copeau placed neutral cubes joined together, which, when sat on, suggested a bench. Copeau called on this basic structure, with minor variations, for many productions in his first season—so many that this *treteau nu* can be considered part of the architectural stage created at the Garrick (photo 2.7). In this particular double-bill he added a semicircular orange velvet cyclorama draped enough to the rear of the stage to allow actors's figures on the platform to stand out in their fullest three-dimensionality. When the curtain was up, the fixed upstage balcony—part of the architectural stage at the Garrick—was exposed for use.[86]

Properties for *Les Fourberies de Scapin* were employed far more economically than New York audiences were used to. For instance, Copeau gave the character Geronte (played by Louis Jouvet) a parasol instead of the traditional cane and, like the fan of the Noh theater, the parasol had multiple meanings. How he handled it helped reveal character, as when he struck the ground with it or dragged it behind as he walked. Besides protecting him from the sun, it at times became a weapon. All of this "stood out in sharp relief on the bare platform."[87]

2.7 Jacques Copeau's stage at the Garrick Theater with *treateau nu* in place.

Copeau's company also exhibited restraint in the costuming. Arthur
Hornblow, a critic for the *Theatre Magazine*, commented how the costumes for
the inaugural double-bill lacked "the richness and variety that we are
accustomed to see in American theatres."[88] Copeau's costuming, however, did
not stay so restrained. Many critical comments on later productions indicate use
of a more varied and colorful palette.

The critical reaction to the austere *mise-en-scène* in this first double-bill was
quite divergent, from those who applauded it, as did the writer for the *Literary
Digest* who felt that Copeau was proving that it is possible for even the most
jaded to "find new sensations" in the theater "by simplicity rather than
complexity,"[89] to those opposing it, like Hornblow who described the stage as
"bare and attractive as a barn."[90] Critic George Jean Nathan was even more
dismissive of Copeau based on the opening productions. Nathan, already
disappointed by Copeau's work in Paris years before and put off by the high-
minded tone of the anticipatory hoopla in preparation for Copeau's visit,
condemned the first bill as showing "little of novelty, nothing of distinction,
little done better than has been done." Getting more specific, Nathan summarily
writes off Copeau as disclosing: "nothing more than a transcript of staging

methods long ago made familiar by Reinhardt and, since Reinhardt, made further familiar by Granville-Barker and others." Copeau's approach is ultimately counterproductive to the theatrical experience, concludes Nathan, because his stage is simplified "to the point where it actually interposes a barrier to imagination instead of encouraging imagination."[91] This kind of wide range in opinion regarding Copeau's design aesthetic would trail him not only through the rest of his New York engagement but also throughout his career.[92]

The rest of Copeau's program in New York followed these principles of stage simplicity. The Molière productions tended to utilize the most elemental stagecraft, usually some variant of the bare center platform, step units, screens, drapes, and neutral cubes. Typical and yet distinctive of his spare, economic settings were his highly acclaimed productions of *Twelfth Night* and *The Brothers Karamazov*. One critic remembered how, in *Twelfth Night*, the same set was used for Olivia's salon, the Duke's garden, a kitchen, and a roadway. All it took to set the spectator's imagination to work were "three girls in sun hats, a wicker basket of oranges on a bench, a lantern throwing yellow lights along the ground." The same critic recalled how stripping to certain essential pieces of scenery went to the heart of the mood and meaning behind *The Brothers Karamazov*:

> Could there have been a more fitting background for the scene between Katrina and Ivan than the narrow blue room with its illumined window against which they showed in restless, shadowy silhouette? No setting seen in New York for years was more effective than the hall in old Karamazoff's house with the staircase leading to upper stories. They were real stairs, two long flights, up and down which the characters came and went, stealthy, reeling, vaulting in energetic leaps, creeping in sick fear. They were amazing stairs, mysterious and abominable carrying the current of the debased Karamazoff life, a pasageway for its accumulating horrors.[93]

The overall reception toward Copeau's program and ambitious two seasons was mixed; the first New York season seemed to elicit the most extreme responses, positive and negative. Those already positively predisposed toward stage simplification were consistently and sometimes effusively complimentary, while others were vociferously negative. Scholar/critic Clayton Hamilton, after the inaugural Garrick season, concluded that the Theatre du Vieux Colombier "deserves to be heralded as the most important theatre in America. In fact, there is no other institution in this country that can even be considered in the same class."[94] Rollo Peters, who designed several stunningly simple and evocative settings for the Washington Square Players and later for the Theatre Guild, wrote a public encomium to Jacques Copeau which appeared in the *Theatre Arts*

Magazine in February 1918.[95] Livington Platt, who designed a *Twelfth Night* for Margaret Anglin, was quoted publicly as having considered Copeau's *Twelfth Night* one of the finest productions he had ever seen.[96]

But that sort of praise was by no means universally echoed. Reactions to most productions in the first season were either mixed or hostile. And gradually the critics became less and less interested in the productions, so that reviews became fewer and more cursory in the second season. Attendance was never outstanding for various reasons, including the fact that the productions were presented in French, which discouraged a significant portion of the potential theatergoing population. Audience response improved somewhat over the second season as Copeau catered somewhat to popular taste but it never matched the levels achieved by mainstream commercial theaters.

As for the long-term reaction to Copeau's work in New York and the influence he wielded on the American theater in general, it is difficult to make sure assessments. Some theater historians argue that the influence was minuscule, others that it was enormous; some argue the influence was immediate and lasting, others that it was delayed but lasting. Albert Katz admits that references to Copeau's New York season in theater history books are meager, that when Copeau's work is mentioned and evaluated in terms of the evolution of the twentieth century *mise-en-scène*, it is usually the productions in Paris and the Vieux Colombier stage as remodeled by Louis Jouvet in 1919 that are shown. But Katz also argues that Copeau is the first theater practitioner in twentieth-century Western theater to call "conspicuous attention to the use of a permanent setting as a principle of *mise-en-scène*" and the "first to call conspicuous attention to symbolic scenery: the presentation of a key element to stand for a setting."[97] Thus, any use of permanent, architectural, and unit settings in the United States, argues Katz, may be traced directly or indirectly to Copeau— either to firsthand observations of productions in Paris or New York or through acquaintanceship with Copeau's ideas and practices as discussed or displayed in books and articles by scholar/critics Sheldon Cheney, Kenneth Macgowan, and Clayton Hamilton as well as by stage designers Lee Simonson and Robert Edmond Jones. According to Katz, there also is evidence of "imitation and influence" on Simonson and Jones in their own designs, especially their uses of permanent and unit settings in the 1920s.[98]

But it is hard to untangle influences and relative impacts from among the European theater artists visiting the United States between 1911 and 1920. Samuel Eliot, writing in January 1919, lends support to Copeau's preeminence among them, declaring that the enthusiasm generated by Copeau was greater than that generated by the Irish Players and Granville-Barker's production of *The Man Who Married a Dumb Wife* and at least equal to the reception to Reinhardt's *Sumurun*.[99] Still, one does have to keep in mind that Reinhardt, Craig, and the Irish Players's impact on the American theater predate Copeau's New York visit by at least five years. Copeau's architectural stage, unit settings, and simple stage ideas in general developed in part from his encounters in 1915 with Craig, Appia, and Dalcroze and in part from his understanding of theater traditions from the past—especially the stage of Shakespeare, Molière, and the Commedia dell' Arte troupes. By his own admission, Copeau was not an innovator but a renovator. But his renovations influenced American theater history directly through his own work as well as through his legacy of stage simplification continued by his disciples: Louis Jouvet, Jean-Louis Barrault, Etienne Decroux, Marcel Marceau, and Michel Saint-Denis.

Still ahead for Copeau and his company after leaving New York were some of their most celebrated productions in Paris on the fixed Vieux Colombier stage as redesigned by Jouvet. Also ahead lay the development of a school out of which emerged many great actors, directors, and mimes as well as a curriculum with Copeau's values of stage simplicity incorporated throughout. In the early 1920s, Copeau continued to experiment, including work with neutral masks and the Japanese Noh theater. And it is to the precedent and influence of East Asian theater traditions on the American simple stage that we now turn as a third factor in its origins and early development.

NOTES

[1] Walter Prichard Eaton, "The Theatre: The Question of Scenery," *The American Magazine*, 72 (July 1911), p. 374.

[2] For a more complete investigation of the role of scholars and critics calling for a simpler stage and attacking the established naturalist *mise-en-scène*, see my dissertation, "Origins of the Minimalist *Mise-en-Scène* in the United States," (NYU, 1986), pp. 80-98.

[3] Clayton Hamilton, "The New Art of Stage Direction," *Bookman*, 35 (July 1912), p. 485.

[4] David Belasco, "How I Stage My Plays," *Theatre Magazine*, 2 (December 1902), p. 32.

[5] Hamilton, "The New Art," p. 485.

[6] David Belasco, "David Belasco Sees A Menace to True Art in Toy Playhouses and Little Repertory Theatres," *New York Herald*, January 7, 1917, Drama Section, p. 1.

[7] Clayton Hamilton, "The New Art," 487.

[8] Walter Prichard Eaton, "The New Stagecraft," *American Magazine*, 74 (May 1912), p. 109.

[9] Hamilton, "The New Art," p. 487.

[10] Sheldon Cheney, *The Art Theatre* (New York: Alfred A. Knopf, 1917), p. 143.

[11] Thomas Dickinson, *The Insurgent Theatre* (New York: B.W. Huebsch, 1917), p. 60.

[12] Annie Nathan Meyer, "The Vanishing Actor: And After," *Atlantic Monthly*, 113 (January 1914), pp. 89-90.

[13] Moderwell, *Theatre of To-day* (New York: John Lane Co., 1914), p. 75.

[14] Ibid., p. 75.

[15] Hiram Kelley Moderwell, "The Modern Stage Movement in Europe and America," *Drama League of America Yearbook 1915/1916*, p. 71.

[16] Cheney, *The Art Theatre*, p. 42.

[17] Cheney, *The New Movement*, p. 303.

[18] Edward Gordon Craig, *On the Art of the Theatre* (Chicago: Browne's Bookshop, 1911), p. 21.

[19] Ibid., p. 35.

[20] Ibid., p. 29.

[21] Ibid., p. 34.

[22] Ibid., p. 33.

[23] Ibid., p. 51.

[24] Ibid., p. 36.

[25] Ibid., p. 123.

[26] Ibid., p. 83.

[27] Ibid., p. 89.

[28] Ibid., p. 74.

[29] Ibid., p. 85.

[30] Ibid., p. 87.

[31] Ibid., p. 23.

[32] Ibid., p. 26.

[33] Ibid., p. 26.

[34] Ibid., between pages xiv and xv, in front of *Electra* sketch.

[35] Ibid., p. 269. Craig quotes Maeterlinck but does not state the specific source.

[36] Ibid., pp. 79-80.

[37] Ernst Stern, *My Life, My Stage* (London: Victor Gollancz Ltd., 1951), p. 84.

[38] Ibid., p. 88.

[39] Ibid., p. 88.

[40] Hamilton, "The New Art," p. 486.

[41] Huntly Carter, *The Theatre of Max Reinhardt* (New York: Mitchell Kennerley, 1914), p. 207.

[42] Eaton, "Question of Scenery," pp. 375-376.

[43] Carter, *Max Reinhardt*, p. 207.

[44] Eaton, "Question of Scenery," p. 375.

[45] Kenneth Macgowan, "New Stage-craft in America," *Century*, 87 (January 1914), p. 418.

[46] Carter, *Max Reinhardt*, p. 209.

[47] Clayton Hamilton, "The Decorative Drama," *The Bookman*, 35 (April 1912), p. 168.

[48] Hamilton, "The New Art," pp. 486-487.

[49] Article in Program for First Season at Garrick Theater, November 1917, Billy Rose Collection, Lincoln Center Library for the Performing Arts.

[50] Jacques Copeau, "Un Essai de Renovation Dramatique," September 1, 1913, quoted in Walther Volbach, "Jacques Copeau, Appia's Finest Disciple." *Educational*

Theatre Journal, 7 (October 1965), p. 206.

51 Frederick Brown, *Theater and Revolution* (New York: Random House, 1989), p. 200.

52 Jacques Copeau, *Registres*, 1, p. 67, as quoted and translated in John Rudlin, *Jacques Copeau* (New York: Cambridge University Press, 1986), p. 58.

53 Frederick Brown, *Theater and Revolution*, p. 209.

54 Jacques Copeau, "The True Spirit of the Art of the Stage," *Vanity Fair*, (April 1917), in Billy Rose Collection, Lincoln Center, Robinson Locke Collection, vol. 84, p. 155.

55 Jacques Copeau, "The True Spirit of the Art of the Stage." Robinson Locke Collection, vol. 84, p. 155.

56 Jacques Copeau, in a lecture quoted in Elizabeth Shepley Sergeant, "A New French Theatre," *The New Republic*, 10 (April 21, 1917), p. 350.

57 Henri Pierre Roche. "Arch Rebel of French Theatre Coming Here," *New York Times*, January 28, 1917, in Billy Rose Collection, Lincoln Center Library for the Performing Arts, Stead Collection Scrapbook, p. 4.

58 Djuna Barnes, "Introducing Monsieur Copeau," *Evening Telegraph*, June 3, 1917, in Robinson Locke Collection, Vol. 84, p. 156.

59 Ibid., p. 157.

60 Jacques Copeau, "The Theatre du Vieux-Colombier," *The Drama*, 29 (February 1918), p. 72.

61 Copeau, "True Spirit," Robinson Locke, p. 155.

62 Barnes, "Introducing," Robinson Locke, p. 157.

63 Ibid., p. 156.

64 Jacques Copeau, "To Bring Back Actors to Fervor," *Boston Transcript*, December 19, 1917, p. 11.

65 Jacques Copeau, "Vieux-Colombier," *The Drama*, p. 72.

66 Copeau, "True Spirit," Robinson Locke, p. 155.

67 From an article in program for First Season at Garrick Theater, November 1917, Billy Rose Collection, Lincoln Center Library for the Performing Arts.

68 Jacques Copeau, "Bring Back Actors," p. 11.

69 Jacques Copeau, Lecture at Harvard University, April 1917, quoted in Bettina Knapp, *The Reign of the Theatrical Director* (Troy, New York: Whitston Publishing Co., 1988), p. 216.

70 Jacques Copeau, "True Spirit," p. 155.

71 Barnes, p. 157.

72 Sergeant, "New French Theatre," p. 351.

73 Antonin Raymond, "The Theatre du Vieux Colombier in New York," *Journal of the American Institute of Architects*, 5 (August 1917), p. 385.

74 Jacques Copeau, quoted in Russell Bryan Porter, "Copeau Says No 'Highbrow Ideas' Rule Vieux Colombier," *New York World*, January 13, 1918, in Robinson Locke Collection, vol. 347, p. 129.

75 Jacques Copeau, "The New School of Stage Scenery," *Vanity Fair*, (June 1917),

p. 36.

[76] Roche, "Arch Rebel," Stead Collection Scrapbook, p. 3.

[77] Jacques Copeau, "Bring Back Actors," p. 11.

[78] Ibid., p. 11.

[79] Copeau, "Vieux-Colombier," *The Drama*, p. 74.

[80] Ibid., p. 75.

[81] Raymond, "Vieux Colombier," p. 386.

[82] Ibid., p. 386.

[83] Albert Katz, "An Historical Study of Jacques Copeau and the Vieux Colombier Company at the Garrick Theater in New York City," (Diss., University of Michigan, 1966) p. 86.

[84] "Jacques Copeau and His Theatre," *Theatre Magazine*, 26 (December 1917), p. 342.

[85] Raymond, "Vieux Colombier," p. 386.

[86] Bettina Knapp, *Louis Jouvet: Man of the Theatre* (New York: Columbia University Press, 1957), p. 44.

[87] Bettina Knapp, *The Reign*, p. 211.

[88] Arthur Hornblow, "Mr. Hornblow Goes to the Play," *Theatre Magazine* 27 (January 1918), p. 21.

[89] "Theater of the Old Dove-Cote," *Literary Digest*, (December 15, 1917), p. 26.

[90] Hornblow, "Mr. Hornblow," p. 21.

[91] George Jean Nathan, "New York Letter," *Chicago Herald*, (December 16, 1917), in Robinson Locke Collection, vol. 347, p. 102.

[92] Later on in the season, even the production of *Twelfth Night* was criticized for its subdued design. A reviewer for *Vanity Fair* comments on the drabness of Copeau's design sense, attributing it to a larger phenomenon, "a disease now passing over decoration." ("Twelfth Night in French," June 1919). Long after Copeau left the United States, this kind of criticism pursued him, even by fellow simplifiers. For example, Samuel Hume condemns Copeau's architectural stage in 1928 in the book *Twentieth Century Stage Decoration*, calling the rigid construction of the Vieux Colombier architectural stage as "an unbearable monotony." Hume accused Copeau as contributing to the public's constant exposure to "drab Puritanism." (p. 41) Of course this echoes criticisms from 1913 when Copeau's company was branded the "Calvinist Follies."

[93] Geraldine Bonner, "M. Copeau's Players," *New York Times*, (March 17, 1918), in Billy Rose Collection, Lincoln Center, Robinson Locke Collection, vol. 347, p. 131.

[94] Clayton Hamilton, "Seen on the Stage," *Vogue* (December 1, 1918), n.p.

[95] Rollo Peters, "To Jacques Copeau," *Theatre Arts Magazine*, 2 (February 1918), p. 84.

[96] "Le Vieux Colombier," *Vogue*, (February 15, 1918), p. 53.

[97] Albert Katz, "Jacques Copeau: The American Reaction," *Players Magazine*, (February 1970), p. 134.

[98] Katz, "A Historical Study," p. 361.

[99] Samuel Eliot, "The Theatre du Vieux-Colombier," *Theatre Arts Magazine*, 3 (January 1919), p. 25.

3

The Chinese and Japanese Precedent

Many Western theater artists, emerging from four centuries where detailed representation and embroidery were dominant, developed, in reaction, a hunger for simplicity. In the last chapters we have seen how American theater artists looked to their pre- and early-Renaissance past and to the New Stagecraft developing in Europe. In looking toward simplicities of the European New Stagecraft, they were encountering East Asian theater methods and aesthetic values indirectly since they had already made an impact on Max Reinhardt in his *Sumurun* production; on the Irish Players through their association with William Butler Yeats who was inspired by the Japanese performing arts; on Edward Gordon Craig as evidenced by articles on Asian theater issues and techniques in his journal, *The Mask*; and on Jacques Copeau, who became acquainted with the Noh theater in the early twenties through the writings of Arthur Waley and the French scholar Noel Peri. American theater artists, in searching for models, also learned from East Asian techniques and values more directly. In looking to the arts and culture of East Asia for essential images and the aesthetics of empty space, stillness, and silence, they did not have to look far.

Fundamentally, East Asian artists and their Western counterparts have gone in very different aesthetic directions. Fritjof Capra, in his groundbreaking work *The Tao Of Physics*, makes a convincing argument that East and West were pursuing a common path in the sixth century B.C. as evidenced by strong similarities between the dialectical/mystical ideas of the Greek philosopher

Heraclitus and those of Lao Tsu[1], the Father of Taoism. But in the fifth century, when the Greek atomists Leucippus and Democritus made the separation between spirit and matter, contends Capra, the two paths split.[2] If we accept and extend Capra's line of thinking, we can compare the history of Western and East Asian art and trace the aesthetic consequences of this split, watching how Western artists, responding to a dualistic worldview dividing mind and matter as well as body and soul, turned off onto paths of detailed representation, embellishment of surface realities, or internal complexities, while East Asian artists remained on the original road. Nurtured by religious traditions sustaining the notion of a fundamental unity within and between the objective and subjective worlds wherein opposites are ultimately One, Chinese and Japanese artists have sought to call attention, directly or indirectly, to the Great Nothingness (the emptiness, the stillness, the silence) from whence all life begins and ends and where all truth and beauty reside in harmonious tranquility. Consequently, the East Asian artists have, over the centuries, generally sought ways to simplify and achieve essences rather than embellish or elaborate and have preferred an overall singleness of impression in their art.

Obviously not all East Asian art is simple and spare, nor is all Western art highly detailed and embroidered. One can find examples of East Asian artistic genres that are dynamic, busy, colorful, and dominated by lush surface detail, and Western art traditions that tend more toward simple, subdued colors and elemental forms—even before the coming together of Eastern and Western art traditions in the twentieth century. The Kabuki *mise-en-scène*, for example, is visually complex, dynamic, and detailed, as are many Japanese prints.[3]

But aspects of the East Asian theater *mise-en-scène* that seem very detailed and colorful at first glance may be viewed as having an underlying simplicity or singleness of impression. Arguing for the notion of "simplicity at a higher level," H. S. Hisamatsu, in looking at the colorful Noh costumes makes the point that they have a way of negating the color they show so brilliantly,[4] especially in combination with the dancing figure of the actor within them.[5] But even if we accept Hisamatsu's perception in the case of Noh costumes, it would be a mistake to force the issue and read into all East Asian art that is complex and colorful some form of underlying simplicity or singleness of impression.

Others have remarked on the two contrasting aesthetic traditions, albeit reluctantly. Noting the dangers of generalization, aesthetician Thomas Munro concedes that the qualities of suggestiveness, terseness, and economy are more "persistently" in Chinese and Japanese art than Western art;[6] Clay Lancaster has observed how Japanese architects tend to simplify while their Western counterparts tend to embellish;[7] and Hisamatsu, in his book *Zen and the Fine Arts*, even goes so far as to claim that Eastern culture "may be spoken of as the culture of Nothingness."[8]

The fact that simplicity and aesthetics centering around empty space, stillness, and silence have permeated the arts of China and Japan for centuries can be traced to the pervasive impact of Taoism and Ch'an or Zen Buddhism. Whether the primary role in simplifying the art and culture of East Asian countries is attributed to Zen or Taoism or a culturally braided combination of both, it is clear that these religious traditions are at least an indirect force behind virtually all the East Asian artists and art forms to which American theater artists were potentially exposed between 1900 and 1925.

The earliest writings in Taoism, beginning with Lao Tsu and his *Tao Te Ching* in the sixth century, are imbued with values calling for simplicity, moderation, and restraint. Lao Tsu implores his followers to "see the simplicity"[9] and to avoid "display."[10] He advises us to speak less and do less since "more words count less."[11] Frenzied activity after material things and goals of this world is wasted motion since the "Tao abides in non-action"[12] and, in the end, "stillness and tranquility set things in order in the universe."[13]

Lao Tsu conceived the Tao as the Nothing, the Great Emptiness from which all life is created and dies in an endless cycle of change. This void that is the Tao, which cannot be seen, cannot be heard, but is inexhaustible,[14] is viewed in a positive way as the source of movement in the great wheel of life: "Thirty spokes share the wheel's hub;/It is the center hole that makes it useful."[15]

In the fourth century B.C., as the philosophical ideas and aesthetic principles of the West were veering toward an interest in surface realities and psychological probing, Lao Tsu's principles were reinforced in the writings of another great Taoist philosopher, Chuang Tsu. Looking at the seven so-called "Inner Chapters" of his work—the ones scholars are confident he alone wrote—we note continual references to notions of simplicity, restraint, and the value of nothingness. To Chuang Tsu as to Lao Tsu, "the Tao abides in emptiness," that, from emptiness, "light is born."[16] Therefore the way to understanding the Tao is the way of few words and little display, for the "meaning of words is hidden by flowery rhetoric."[17] Chuang Tsu urges all to "wander in the pure and simple."[18]

Chinese artists, who have for centuries breathed the air of these values, have brought to the world an art noted for its simplicity, suggestion, and stillness. In the book *Creativity and Taoism*, Chang Chung-yuan makes the connection between Taoist philosophy and Chinese poetry and painting. He gives numerable examples of Tao-influenced poetry and painting that reflects *p'o*, the so-called "uncarved block," a work's "original simplicity."[19] The principle inherent in this term is that the value of a work lies partly in its overall simplicity and directness. He points to examples in Chinese painting where solitary images floating in a void, can turn empty space into the painting's protagonist.[20]

The art of suggestion follows naturally from the Taoist worldview. The artist, whether in theater, art, or poetry, suggests a totality through presentation of an essential part: "The petal of a blossom never comes forth alone, but unimpededly takes in all related parts of the blooming tree."[21] Fung Yu-lan, a contemporary Chinese philosopher/historian, contends that the art of suggestion "is the ideal of all Chinese art, whether... poetry, painting or anything else."[22]

Fung explains how in Chinese poetry, for instance, "the number of words is limited but the ideas it suggests are limitless."[23] One can clearly discern Taoist ideals.

One can trace the commingling of these ideals and the arts at least to the first half of the eighth century. Under Emperor Hsuan Tsung (referred to in English also as Yuen Tsung and Ming Huang) of the T'ang Dynasty, Taoism and the arts received royal sanction and patronage. Hsuan Tsung professed Taoist principles, especially at the beginning of his long reign (713-756). He bestowed degrees for excellence in the study and practice of the faith and, early in his reign, his Taoist values prompted him to set a tone for simplicity and austerity through decrees to rid the empire of extravagance. He prohibited the wearing of expensive garb and, to set an example, he publicly set fire to a large quantity of embroidered robes and jewelry.[24]

Hsuan Tsung also brought Chinese culture to what has been termed a Golden Age for the arts. He established an academy for training in music, theater, and literary and visual arts. This institution, known as the Hanlin Yuan (the "Forest of Pencils," i.e., Imperial Academy of Scholars), became a place where musicians, painters, poets, performers, and scholars were exposed to Taoist and Buddhist values while learning their respective disciplines. It was here that the Buddhist Wang Wei implemented the use of a monochrome ink-wash, described as a penetrating or breaking ink, with the intent of revealing directly what is within rather than supply details of external appearances,[25] setting in motion the monochromatic tradition of Chinese landscape painting that persists to the present day.[26] It was also here that Wang Hsia (Wu Tao-Tzu) developed his method of splashed or flung ink, which gives almost literal meaning to the notion of "single-gesture design"[27]—a phrase used to characterize designer Robert Edmond Jones's ideal for a simplified stage design. The "Pear Garden" of the Hanlin Yuan was where actors were trained, and the traditional Chinese theater is said to have been born.

A. E. Zucker suggests that the earliest performances—perhaps in the palace, perhaps in a courtyard in the Pear Garden itself—were presented on a platform erected at one end.[28] One can only hypothesize on the nature of that stage—how it was used and what was placed on it. One can surmise that it had the quality of what A. C. Scott calls "uncompromising austerity"[29] that we now associate with the traditional Chinese stage where from virtual nothingness an infinite number of realities could be created by the actor with few suggestive properties.

The bare and neutral Chinese stage with infinite imaginative possibilities may have been born in Hsuan Tsung's court or, like the Elizabethan theater, it also may have evolved over centuries of practical demands made on a rough popular theater where severe economy had to be the rule. Most likely, the Chinese stage came about from a mutual influencing combination of both. Taoist philosophy would certainly have informed its popular evolution as much as its development under Hsuan Tsung's reign.

It was in this bare, neutral state with infinite imaginative potential that the concept passed on into the origins of Peking Opera in the eighteenth century; audiences had already come to accept that the bare Chinese stage would begin as any place and any time and depend on the actor to define and continually redefine those coordinates. In having this quality, one can not help but draw the parallel with the Elizabethan stage[30] which evolved out of the *platea*, the neutral space used in Medieval Mystery and Morality Play performances. It, too, was the product of an evolution combining the religious and the practical necessities of a poor people's theater. On both the Elizabethan and traditional Chinese stages, theater happened through the collaboration between the actor's mimetic skills and an audience with a flexible imagination. Michel Saint-Denis's quotation of a traditional Chinese saying, that "it is not doors that are interesting, but what happens behind them: so why have doors?" applies as much to the Elizabethan stage as the near-empty stage of Chinese theater. Both stages, devoid of representational scenery and properties, thrived on the nothingness/infinity paradox traceable, in part, to their religious roots. As we shall see, American audiences witnessed the suggestive powers of the traditional Chinese stage upon viewing *The Yellow Jacket* in 1912.

A line to the American simple stage can also be traced from Zen Buddhism through its impact not only on the Noh theater, but also through other Japanese arts. The ideas of Zen Buddhism and the visual images they helped produce have circulated among artistic circles in the United States throughout the twentieth century. Evidence of their impact on the American arts can be seen in creations by several generations of artists, from the programs, tea-room decor, and production style in Maurice Browne's Chicago Little Theatre in the 1910s to the silent concerts in the early 1950s of pioneering composer John Cage who credits many of his experimental musical ideas to his exposure to Zen ideas from Daisetz T. Suzuki and Alan Watts.

D. T. Suzuki, in his book *Zen and Japanese Culture*, and H. S. Hisamatsu, in *Zen and the Fine Arts*, show how Zen principles are pervasively reflected in all the arts of East Asia, but especially in Japanese culture. As much as Taoist principles dominate Chinese art, Zen Buddhist principles prevail in Japan. Suzuki and Hisamatsu trace these principles in the origins and development of the Japanese arts traditions: *haiku* poetry; swordsmanship; flower arrangement; the tea ceremony; architecture; all the various crafts; the Noh theater; as well as various painting styles.

The Taoist ideal of simplicity made its way into Ch'an and Zen Buddhism, and that trait is evident as much in the Zen-inspired arts of Japan as those influenced by Taoism in China. Suzuki, who spent his long life studying and disseminating Zen ideas in the West, contends that "Zen has no taste for complexities that lie on the surface of life."[31] Suzuki takes the position that "direct simplicity is the soul of Zen"[32] and that "Zen is the keynote of Oriental culture."[33] In art, any form of embroidery takes away rather than adds: "As soon as there are signs of elaboration, a man is doomed."[34] In the book *Zen in Japanese Art*, Toshimitzu Hasumi presents simplicity as the second salient quality of Japanese art, the notion—ever-present among Japanese painters and poets—that "everything inessential must be eliminated."[35]

The preference for simplicity (*kanso*) is further investigated in Hisamatsu's study of Zen's influence on the fine arts where he lists it as one among seven Zen characteristics in Zen-inspired art of all varieties. Under the rubric of simplicity, Hisamatsu includes traits such as sparse and uncluttered design; little or unobtrusive color; and the presentation of a single thing that leads to all things.[36] This singleness of impression is key to Zen art. Hisamatsu explains and gives multiple examples of how Zen does not pursue minute detail but rather "grasps truth at once, and then expresses it directly and immediately," that the "whole is painted in one stroke—in one breath, as it were— without regard for the details."[37]

Suzuki uses two terms which are especially germane to Zen-influenced art and touch on the very core of Zen philosophy. The first is *wabi*, defined as meaning "poverty." In art, it has connotations of dryness or austerity, a shearing away of all extraneous parts and color such that only the bony essential remains.[38] A second term that Suzuki uses, *sabi*, means "loneliness" or "solitude." In art it refers to a single image floating in empty space, rendered with restraint. Suzuki states: "Aloneness indeed appeals to contemplation and does not lend itself to spectacular demonstration."[39] *Wabi* and *sabi* epitomize the spirit of Zen and, taken together or separately, call attention to the basic paradox behind Zen, "the One in the Many and the Many in the One."[40] There are other terms and concepts that Suzuki finds throughout Zen literature that are related to simplification in the arts. These include emptiness (*sunyata*), nothingness (*nasti*), quietude (*santi*), and no-thought (*acinta*). The term *sunyata* or emptiness is as key to Zen as it is to Taoism. Seeing into the emptiness constitutes a key step in the process of attaining enlightenment (*satori*), at least according to the twelfth century Chinese Buddhist Kakuan who sought to symbolize the ten-step process of *satori* with ten drawings in which a man is seeking and subduing a bull. Three steps in the process are informed by qualities of simplicity and *sunyata* or emptiness. Toshimitzu Hasumi sees in the first step—the seeking after truth—as demanding a "complete elimination of the inessential."[41] Hasumi interprets the sixth picture as meaning that "the further the understanding, the simpler things are."[42] And the eighth picture is an empty circle, when man transcends both himself and his quest.[43] Achieving this state of Nothingness is the common goal of Taoism and Zen Buddhism.

Like the sage, the Zen artist also must face the nothingness to achieve what Herrigel in *Zen in the Art of Archery* calls the "artless art," the point where will is transcended and the All can appear. When the Zen artist, like the sages in Taoism and Zen Buddhism, faces the Great Emptiness, he comes face to face with the unbroken truth, "the Truth beyond all truths, the formless Origin of origins, the Void which is the All."[44] The ultimate paradox of Taoism is also the underlying paradox of Zen Buddhism, and it can be seen and transcended by artists and sages of both religious traditions.

JAPANESE PRINTS

Taoist and Zen Buddhist ideas and the images they influenced streamed into the West throughout the nineteenth and twentieth centuries. Of most relevance to the cross-fertilization between East Asian and Western visual arts was the influence of Japanese prints on the Impressionists, in the United States most notably James Whistler and Mary Cassatt, beginning as early as the 1860s. Eastern influences on art before that time were sporadic and superficial. Impressionists became fascinated with the delicate, pure lines and muted colors of eighteenth-century prints by Suzuki Harunobu and Isoda Koryusai as well as the flat, unmodeled "spread-out surfaces for sea, sky, earth,"[45] in late eighteenth- and nineteenth-century prints by Hokusai and Hiroshige. Japanese prints helped lead Impressionists away from perspective, shading, and three-dimensional composition toward a new appreciation of empty space and simple lines.

Among the most influential prints by the more contemporary Japanese printmakers were the much reproduced series "Thirty-six Views of Mt. Fuji" by Hokusai and "Hundred Famous Views of Edo" by Hiroshige. While both of these series range from the highly complex and detailed to the severely austere, most of the prints follow in the Zen-influenced art tradition and feature huge expanses of a seemingly endless sky, perhaps with the figure of a lone mountain (and a corresponding feeling of monumentality) or a single bird or flock of birds within this isolation. The dominant mood of both series is solitude.

The prints gradually reached a broader audience, first in Europe, then across the Atlantic. During the last decade of the nineteenth century, a large Japanese migration into the United States occurred; with the new immigrants came books and artwork by Japanese artists. Massive quantities of prints flooded the art market, bringing this popular artform to wide public awareness in the West. Japanese art dealers capitalized on the growing interest in Japanese prints among Americans. The economic conditions in Japan during the late nineteenth and early twentieth centuries were ripe for a flourishing market abroad since the prints were both undervalued and plentiful in their native land. This situation greatly facilitated their wholesale shipment to dealers and auction houses in the West.[46]

The sparer aspects of the works seemed to have had the biggest impact, at least in the theater community. American artists found the spare qualities and limited color range of certain prints a refreshing change from the elaborately detailed realism so common in Euro-American art. Not only would these images affect the styles of painters, especially the Impressionists, but also the creators of the *mise-en-scène*. Director Maurice Browne and designers Robert Edmond Jones and Lee Simonson all acknowledged influence—or at least confirmation of their own aesthetic dispositions—from Japanese printmakers like Hiroshige, Hokusai, and Shunei on at least some of their productions. And as we shall see in later chapters, it was the more simplified aspects of the prints—the subdued colors, the stillness, the use of economy and suggestion, the spareness—that made the strongest impression on these theater artists.

KAWAKAMI OTOJIRO AND SADDA YAKKO

The presence of Japanese theater models in the mainstream American theater can be found as early as 1898, when Kawakami Otojiro and his wife Sadda Yakko arrived in San Francisco to begin a West-to-East "study tour" in route to the Paris Exposition of 1900. Kawakami and Sadda Yakko belonged to the *Shimpa*, a group of Japanese artists committed to synthesizing Kabuki conventions with Western theater styles, especially modern realism. Initially, Kawakami and Sadda Yakko traveled to the United States and Europe merely to augment their understanding of Western theater conventions. Yumito Kushibiki, a well-known merchant and proprietor of the Japanese tea gardens in San Francisco, convinced them to perform.

Billed respectively as the Henry Irving and Ellen Terry of Japan, Kawakami and Sadda Yakko opened at San Francisco's California Theatre in the summer of 1899, where they presented their own modernized versions of Kabuki dramas. Despite a shaky start (years later, Sadda Yakko commented in an interview that their company had not yet understood American taste), the pair left San Francisco after having finally achieved some positive recognition by the press and general public. Their appeal grew as they became more experienced before American audiences. After performing in Chicago, Kawakami and his actors came East and were especially popular in Boston and Washington D.C.; they were even invited to perform before President McKinley. By the time they arrived in New York's Berkeley Lyceum Theater in March 1900, their performances were being attended by "a number of well-known theatrical people,"[47] and the Japanese couple continued to be heralded as the finest performers in Japan. In April, their productions moved to Broadway's Bijou Theater. By their final New York performance on April 21, 1900, they had made a significant impact on the New York theater community.

Since they came to the United States to absorb the Italianate and naturalist traditions of the West, much of what Kawakami and Yakko presented were newly-learned Western theater customs modified by their own perspective and background. Accordingly, Kawakami and Yakko's settings seem to fit snugly into the Italianate tradition. In the setting for *The Geisha and the Knight*, their most popular piece, Sadda Yakko, who is credited with supervising the creation of the *mise-en-scène*, presented for one scene a street painted in perspective with street lamps disappearing in the distance and elaborately painted palace doors for another.[48] The perspective backdrop led the viewer's eye to move into the distance, thereby creating a dynamic rather than static effect. The costumes, which generally were traditional Japanese dress, were very colorful and detailed, receiving comment not for their simplicity, but for their resplendent, exotic qualities. The main characters in the scene before the palace doors were Buddhist monks who were all dressed alike, but this reflects traditional monasterial garb rather than a decision toward what we can identify as Zen-influenced simplification and sameness.

But other aspects of the *mise-en-scène*, especially the style of performance, showed a distinct tendency toward these values, especially those of silence and stillness. Critics noted, for instance, how Sadda Yakko's acting was exceptional in her ability to communicate so much in silence. Epes Sargent of *Metropolitan Magazine*, for instance, identified this element: "She has several scenes in which no word is spoken, and in which she fully succeeds in conveying to her audience the thoughts which are passing through her brain."[49]

American audiences were also impressed with the ability of the Japanese to create tableaux and maintain utter stillness for long periods of time. Sargent expressed it this way:

> In one other respect the Japanese players excel, and that is in reference to tableaux. Their control of muscles and features in that direction is little less than marvelous. In several scenes large numbers of stage characters remain perfectly motionless for fully a quarter of an hour.[50]

The performance style of Kawakami's company—especially Sadda Yakko's—was distinguished from standard American acting by virtue of the simplicity, economy, and restraint in movement, gesture, and vocal inflection. While some reviewers criticized her lack of variety in expression, others commented on her "light, simple movements" and her restrained death scenes, carried out "without contortions, without grimaces."[51]

The Japanese music and dance style that constituted part of the performance also showed signs of restraint and repetitiveness. It is difficult to know how the music sounded, but one critic condemned it for being "monotonous".[52] Another critic described Sadda Yakko's dancing as "subdued" and "very quiet."[53]

Whether the production decisions were viewed pejoratively as monotonous or positively as showing restraint and economy, they provide evidence of an aesthetic of self-imposed limitation, sameness, and simplification. It is difficult to piece out what came from Kawakami and Yakko's own unique performance values, what from their own Buddhist-based performance traditions, and what from their own perceptions of the Western Italianate and realistic traditions they wanted to emulate. What is clear is that they were helping guide Western artists toward a more simplified performance style, even if they were simultaneously borrowing the tired Italianate and the emerging realistic conventions from the West and carrying conventions from their own Kabuki theater—all of which often militated against but did not disguise their interest and inclination toward stage simplification.

Kawakami and Yakko's influence on stage simplicity in the United States, however, did not only occur directly from their visit, but also indirectly through their subsequent effect on Georg Fuchs in Munich and Vsevolod Meyerhold in Russia who in turn influenced directors and designers working in the United States between 1910 and 1925. Meyerhold, who saw Sadda Yakko during her 1902 Russian tour, was deeply affected by her "ability to economise with gestures."[54] Fuchs, in his influential book *The Stage of the Future*, praised Kawakami's settings as being "expressionless, a rhythmical monotone."[55]

Kawakami returned to Japan to do simplified productions of Western classics, including plays by Shakespeare and Ibsen. He was not alone. He was joined by other *Shimpa* theater artists as well as representatives of the *Shingeki*, successors to the *Shimpa*, who were also committed to bringing Western plays and production techniques to Japan. Two proponents of the *Shingeki*, Osanai Kaoru and Ichikawa Sadanji II, achieved distinction in their productions of Ibsen and other modern Western plays in Japan between 1909 and 1915. Like Kawakami, in trying to emulate Western realism, they combined it with their own tradition and ended up with a sparer, more simplified realism than the Western prototypes.

One description of these restrained, spare productions appeared in Sheldon Cheney's *The New Movement* in 1914:

> The most unobtrusive thing is the ordinary tasteful room stripped of its unessential details. The designer must keep the main wall spaces as unbroken as possible, so that the action will not be lost in the intricacy of the background; and he must not fall prey to the desire to add this touch or that just because it is "natural." Among the finest examples of settings of this kind are those used by Japanese actors in some recent productions of Ibsen in Tokio. It is interesting to see how the Japanese have... shown their realization of the value of bare spaces. Their achievement of absolutely simple but satisfying rooms is a fine contrast to the average Occidental parallel.[56]

The American theater community, in reading Cheney's book, was exposed to a positive assessment of the Japanese use of empty space and bare walls.

Several years later, American audiences would witness these spare Japanese interiors in Michio Ito's production of *Bushido* by the Washington Square Players and *The Faithful* at the Theatre Guild.

After the Kawakami tour, the American theater community had little direct exposure to Chinese or Japanese theater. Besides David Belasco's productions of *Madame Butterfly* (1900) and *Darling of the Gods* (1902), there was little in the theater manifesting Eastern stage aesthetics. But then in 1911, the Irish poet William Butler Yeats articulated in one of his lectures at Harvard his advocacy of simplification and suggestion in theater and drama, comparing his own predilection with that of Japanese artists: "Being a writer of poetic drama, and of tragic drama, desiring always pattern and convention, I would like to keep to suggestion, to symbolism, to pattern like the Japanese."[57]

But Yeats did not specify this Japanese tragic drama form. Information about the Noh drama to which he was alluding would not fully come to public attention in the United States for another five years, but soon to come was a performance that would mark the next major acquaintanceship for American audiences with stage techniques and aesthetic values of the East.

GEORGE HAZELTON/J. HARRY BENRIMO'S *THE YELLOW JACKET*

As we have already seen, the year 1912 can be viewed as a watershed for the simple-stage revolution in the American theater. Adding to the stream of simplified stage images and ideas that came with the Irish Players, Max Reinhardt, and Edward Gordon Craig was Winthrop Ames's production of George Hazelton and J. Harry Benrimo's *The Yellow Jacket* at the Fulton Theatre opening on November 4th. This highly acclaimed Broadway show introduced conventions of the Peking Opera[58] to a wide American audience.

To create this play and its production, the playwrights researched Chinese customs and theater conventions and discussed them with the actors for an entire week before beginning work on the play. By so doing, certain traditional elements of Peking Opera were incorporated into the presentation.

Benrimo and Hazelton recognized the similarity between the Peking Opera neutral stage and the traditional Elizabethan stage, for which revived interest was well underway in the United States by 1912. Knowledge of production techniques from Elizabethan times helped in recognizing production possibilities in a Chinese theater piece. In an interview appearing in the *New York Dramatic Mirror*, Benrimo credits his collaborator with having helped the production process by knowing Elizabethan drama as well as Chinese: "Mr. Hazelton brought... his intimate knowledge of the Elizabethan drama. That is akin to the Chinese drama in simplicity."[59]

The production borrowed many aspects of Peking Opera performance conventions. Like the prototype, certain elements in the New York production were complex, detailed, and colorful. The borders of the setting, which stayed constant throughout, were unabashedly decorative, with highly detailed arrangements of Chinese figures and dragons in bright and contrasting colors. The costumes also were notable for their vivid colors and ornamental detail.

But the neutral, near-empty stage with transformable properties also was present. American audiences had already been exposed to the economical Elizabethan stage, but this production demonstrated another way of creating a lot with a little, a way that was deeply imbedded in the traditions of East Asian theater, predating the birth of Peking Opera, conceivably stretching back as far as the eighth century. In the course of the evening, audiences watched as characters traversed mountains and rivers, even went to heaven, with no change in scenery and only a minimal change in properties. The different locales were indicated by simple rearrangements of chairs and boxes with only occasional contributions from other properties: blue cheesecloth held between two stagehands indicated a river, a small box placed on a chair to elevate the seat served as a throne, and a mountain was created merely by stacking tables and chairs.[60] Since the eighteenth century, this had been standard fare in Peking Opera in mainland China; at least since the beginning of the twentieth century, it was a widespread practice in performances presented in Asian-American communities in cities like San Francisco; but it was new to mainstream American theater audiences in 1912.

Of special significance was the use of the Propertyman, who indicated changes of scene and, at times, even became part of the scenography. He sat to one side of the stage with a box of properties by his side. He entered the action and changed scenes by adding, rearranging, or taking away simple properties. Thus, he indicated the successful execution of a beheading by holding a little red flag before the victim's face; he dusted chairs and tables, thereby redefining objects previously standing for elements of an exterior landscape as interior furniture and himself as a servant; he held a bare bamboo pole with a noose at the end to represent a weeping willow tree on which the hero was to be executed; and he created a snowstorm by sprinkling powder on the leading actor's head.[61] By carrying out these activities outside the play's action, he followed an East Asian performance tradition that goes beyond Peking Opera and includes Noh, Kabuki, and Bunraku. Even though the New York audiences took the Propertyman's involvement as quaint and sometimes comic, it introduced a new method for minimizing literal properties and scenery and acted as a precedent for Thornton Wilder's neutral Stage Manager figures in his plays of the 1930s.

The Winthrop Ames production also had a bare-essentials chorus consisting of one man named Chorus. Perhaps the playwrights borrowed this idea from Shakespeare's *Henry V*, wherein a single character represents a whole Chorus, or perhaps this device, too, had its origins in Chinese convention; regardless of its source, having a single factor stand for many exemplifies the principle of stage economy.

American exposure to *The Yellow Jacket* did not end with its original New York production. Afterwards it toured the United States for several years and then was revived in New York in 1916.[62] And yet it is difficult to trace direct and specific influences of the original production and its revivals. Performance conventions of Peking Opera like those in *The Yellow Jacket* do surface in highly simplified American productions between 1912 and 1922. Most notably, we witness it in the Komisarjevsky-Simonson production of *The Tidings Brought to Mary* at the Theatre Guild in 1922. But there is no concrete evidence that Komisarjevsky, Simonson, or other directors and designers attended *The Yellow Jacket*. Kenneth Macgowan, one of the most influential proponents of stage simplicity, mentions the production in his book *The Living Stage*[63] and Cheney, another advocate, makes reference to the Propertyman convention in *The Theatre: Three Thousand Years of Drama, Acting and Stagecraft*, which inclines one to think that the model was the Benrimo/Hazelton production.[64] It is even more probable that director Arthur Hopkins witnessed this production as evidenced by his reference to the Propertyman of Chinese drama in his book *How's Your Second Act?*. Thornton Wilder attributes his Stage Manager figure to Chinese stage convention, but it is unclear whether this production was the source.

In the case of one theater artist, no guesswork is necessary in identifying influence from *The Yellow Jacket*. The production had its biggest acknowledged impact on Ruth Draper, famous for her one-woman performances of her own scripts. This actress, whom John Gielgud called the greatest individual performer the United States ever produced,[65] was working on sketches before the Benrimo/Hazelton production, but it was this event, she claims, that awakened her to how much could be done without scenery and costumes through the art of suggestion.[66] From the experience of seeing this play in 1912 until her death in 1956, Ruth Draper presented solo shows on a stage bare but for neutral background curtains, a few chairs, a table, a property here or there, and a few hats and shawls. From these meager elements, she performed plays (usually around twenty minutes long) in which she would evoke a wide variety of situations and people—plays with as many as twenty-six characters, differentiated merely through a change in walk, gesture, attitude, voice, focus, hat, or shawl. She would suggest time and place by her imaginative treatment on a bare stage of the few stage accessories she chose to use. It is difficult to know exactly whom she in turn influenced, but we know she greatly impressed her friend Thornton Wilder who perhaps had her partly in mind when he wrote plays for a neutral stage in the 1930s. Thus the Benrimo/Hazelton production planted an important seed for the American simple stage.

THE NOH

East Asian influence also came to the American theater through introduction to the Noh theater. Even though President Ulysses S. Grant had attended a Noh performance as early as 1879, Leonard Pronko points out that before 1945, few Westerners had had the opportunity to see a live Noh performance.[67] Thus, initial contact with this art form was through descriptions in books and essays that became available after 1916 rather than exposure to live performances.

Amongst the Chinese and Japanese theater traditions with potential influence on the American theater community between 1900 and 1925, the Noh is the one most directly influenced by East Asian religious philosophies. Noh theater, the most aesthetically restrained East Asian theater form in almost every respect, was honed by the values of Zen Buddhism at its very origin in the fourteenth and fifteenth centuries. The Noh developed into its present-day form at the court of Ashigata Yoshimitsu after the Shogun brought Kannami and his young son Zeami there, offering them full protection and patronage. At the court, Zen Buddhist ideals were everywhere; not only were Yoshimitsu's warriors impressed by Zen Buddhist physical and mental discipline, but Yoshimitsu himself was expert in Zen Buddhist philosophy. Yoshimitsu was also a painter and an expert *tanka* poet, his poetry and painting reflecting Zen Buddhist simplicity and restraint. Yoshimitsu even abdicted the shogunate in 1394 to take Buddhist orders.

Zeami and Kannami's dramas and writings on the theory and practice of the Noh are at least "tinged" with Zen Buddhist metaphysical and aesthetic principles, as pointed out by Arthur Waley.[68] But these principles are even more pronounced in the writings and practice of Zeami's successor, his son-in-law Zenchiku, who was closer to Zen Buddhism than either Kannami or Zeami. In fact, Donald Keene contends that the overall look and feel of Noh performance today may owe more to Zenchiku's more austere worldview, especially:

> the bare stage, the insignificant props, the movements of the actors, recalling at once the Zen priest and warrior. The overpoweringly sombre tone of the plays certainly brings to mind not Zeami's 'flowers' but the gloom of a monochrome, flowerless world.[69]

And it is Zenchiku himself who perhaps has best articulated the aesthetic principle of Noh theater in terms of Zen values: "Everything redundant has been pruned, the beauty of the essential is wholly and fully cleansed. It is the inexpressible beauty of doing nothing."[70]

Leonard Pronko traces the Noh as having developed out of the Zen way of life and thus embodying "the virtues of restraint, austerity, quietness, suggestivity, [and] formality." Like Zen thought, Noh concerns itself with essences and suggesting "the core of a situation or event in the simplest terms, reducing the whole to a highly controlled experience within clearly defined artistic limits."[71]

Donald Keene also draws the connection between Zen and the Noh, tying the Noh in with its "sister arts," all of which developed in Yoshimitsu's court:

> Noh... shares much with other forms of expression during the period: it is bare, yet evocative, like the monochrome landscapes; beautiful, yet austere, like the temple gardens; ... The movements of the actors owe much to... the decorum expected of the Zen priest. The actors' distinctive walk, a bare lifting of the feet from the floor, occurs also in the tea ceremony.... These arts are all marked by an economy of means used to achieve a maximum effect, a preference for suggestion rather than representation.[72]

But little was known in the United States about this art form before 1916. In that year a volume containing Ernest Fenollosa and Ezra Pound's translations of Noh plays was published. Included in this work were introductory essays about Noh performance by both authors. The collection also contained an essay by William Butler Yeats detailing the influence of the Noh on the Irish poet's plays and their productions. The *Theater Arts Magazine* carried essays on the Noh theater beginning with a rave review of the Fenollosa/Pound book in December 1917, followed by articles on the Asian theater by Hermann Rosse in 1918 and 1919. In the January 1919 issue, W. B. Yeats's essay "Instead of a Theatre" credits the Noh for having influenced the stagecraft called for in his plays. In 1920, Arthur Waley published another set of Noh translations, with an introduction describing Zeami's theories of acting and stagecraft. Waley's book also contains an essay in which he discusses Zen Buddhism in relation to the Noh. From these sources, American theater practitioners began to learn about the stage conventions of the Noh, increasing its potential influence on American theatrical performance after 1916.

Information disseminated through the Fenollosa/Pound and Waley books as well as the essays in *Theatre Art Magazine* were reinforcing a fundamental aesthetic principle to which the American theater world had already been exposed through the New Stagecraft, Ruth Draper, and the production of *The Yellow Jacket*: art as allusion rather than illusion. This principle is reflected in three characteristics of the Noh, all of which are discussed throughout these books and essays: (1) the use of minimal scenery and properties; (2) the use of properties that are suggestive and capable of having multiple significances; (3) the transformability of the same properties from scene to scene; and (4) the art of acting as non-mimetic and symbolic rather than representational. Information about these traits could contribute to the simplification of the American *mise-en-scène*.

American theater audiences and practitioners reading these books and essays would have encountered how Yeats celebrates a performance tradition in which "few properties can be packed up in a box"[73] and in which players need only unroll a single mat in some Eastern garden.[74] Yeats credits the Noh for inspiring him to realize that his theater "must be the ancient theatre made by unrolling a carpet, or marking out a place with a stick, or setting a screen against a wall," wanting his theatre to be comprised of half a dozen players who can "bring all their properties in a cab."[75] Yeats traces to Japanese theater aesthetics his decision to simplify his scenery and describes how, in doing so, he achieved greater significance and eloquence:

> I have simplified scenery, having *The Hour Glass* for instance played now before green curtains, now among those ivory-colored screens invented by Gordon Craig. With every simplification the voice has recovered something of its importance....[76]

The essays and books gave many examples of how the few properties that are used in the Noh—like those in Peking Opera—are suggestive and symbolic rather than literal. Arthur Waley lists examples of how a part can stand for the whole with Noh stage properties: "An open framework represents a boat; another differing little from it, denotes a chariot. Palace, house, cottage, hovel are all represented by four posts covered with a roof."[77] Hermann Rosse's essay "Sketches of Oriental Theatres," appearing in the *Theatre Arts Magazine* in 1918, explains how "a forest in the Noh is indicated by a branch, a horse by a gesture."[78]

Fenollosa and Waley's essays also make reference to a third aspect of the Noh: the imaginative transformability of properties from scene to scene—another trait which New York audiences witnessed in the production of *The Yellow Jacket*. Both translators comment on how the same fan is variously used to represent a cup, paper, pen, sword, knife, or brush—depending on the context and how it is handled by the actor.[79] This calls attention to a potential economy factor in simplifying the *mise-en-scène*.

A fourth trait described in Zeami's treatises and relayed to the American public through Waley's introduction is symbolic and suggestive (rather than literal) acting. Waley conveys Zeami's warning against "irreverent realism," describing how excessive imitation actually impinges on the elevated reality of theater.[80] Pound explains that communication must be left incomplete and suggested, reminding us not to forget that Noh performers—in the words of Noh actor Umewaka Minoru—"work in pure spirit."[81]

Yeats relates a story traditional among Noh actors, which provides a model for a suggestive, non-imitative acting style. The story relates how a young actor followed a woman in the streets to learn her walk and tone of voice so he could play an old woman on the Noh stage. Yeats records her response:

> If he would become famous as a Noh player, she said, he must not observe life, nor put on an old voice and stint the music of his voice. He must know how to suggest an old woman and yet find it all in the heart.[82]

Yeats praises a performance tradition in which "for nearly three centuries invention has been making the human voice and the movements of the body seem always less expressive."[83] Remembering the April 1916 performance of his play *At the Hawk's Well* performed by dancer Michio Ito in a friend's drawing-room, Yeats expresses his debt to the lesson this experience taught him—that aesthetic retreat can produce tremendous theatrical power:

> My play is made possible by a Japanese dancer whom I have seen dance in a studio and in a drawing-room and on a very small stage lit by an excellent stage-light... There where no studied lighting, no stage-picture made an artifical world, he was able, as he rose from the floor, where he had been sitting cross-legged or as he threw out an arm, to recede from us into some powerful life.[84]

The aesthetic inclinations of East Asian artists, supported by their primary religious heritages, resulted in work that had traceable influence on the work of American theater simplifiers. The ideas and images of simplicity supplied by East Asian sources were joining with those from the European New Stagecraft and the Elizabethan revival. By January 1912, the air was already alive with precedents for simplifying the stage and yet no American theater artists had yet made it a major thrust of their work. Walter Prichard Eaton made that observation in an essay published in July 1911. His final question about simplifying the American stage rings out as a challenge: "What manager in America will be the first to attempt it?"[85] Six months later, Maurice Browne took the big step, as if heeding Eaton's call.

NOTES

[1] For this chapter, I will follow the Wade-Giles system for Chinese characters because most scholarship in the English-speaking West—past and present—still tends to prefer it to the Pinyin system and also because the Pinyin system was officially adopted

in 1958, long after the period of American theater history this book principally investigates.

2 Fritjof Capra, *The Tao of Physics* (New York: Bantam Books, 1988), p. 7.

3 See, for example, Utamaro's "Flower Festival at Yoshiwara," Hokusai's "Waterfalls," or his "Two Fishing Barks on a Swelling Sea."

4 H. S. Hisamatsu, *Zen and the Fine Arts*, trans. Gishin Tokiwa, (Kyoto, Japan: Kodansha International Ltd., 1971), p. 66.

5 Ibid., p. 56.

6 Thomas Munro, *Oriental Aesthetics* (Cleveland: The Press of Western Reserve University, 1965), p. 95.

7 Quoted in Munro, ibid., p. 48.

8 Hisamatsu, *Zen*, p. 53.

9 Lao Tsu, *Tao Te Ching*, trans. Gia-Gu Feng and Jane English, (New York: Random House, 1972), Book 19, Verse 4 (19.4). From now on, all citations will give the book number first and the verse number second.

10 Ibid., 22.2.

11 Ibid., 5.2.

12 Ibid., 37.1.

13 Ibid., 45.3.

14 Ibid., 35.2.

15 Ibid., 11.1.

16 Chuang Tsu, *Inner Chapters*, trans. Gia-Fu Feng and Jane English, (New York: Random House, 1974), Chapter Four, p. 68.

17 Ibid., Chapter Two, p. 26.

18 Ibid., Chapter Seven, p. 150.

19 Chang Chung-yuan, *Creativity and Taoism* (New York: Harper Colophon Books, 1963), p. 36.

20 Ibid., p. 12.

21 Ibid., p. 12.

22 Quoted in Munro, *Aesthetics*, p. 95.

23 Ibid., p. 95.

24 From William Stanton's "The Chinese Drama," quoted in A. E. Zucker, *The Chinese Theater* (Boston: Little, Brown and Company, 1925), pp. 4-5.

25 Chang Chung-yuan, *Creativity*, p. 218.

26 Munro, *Aesthetics*, p. 57.

27 Chang Chung-yuan, *Creativity*, p. 219.

28 A. E. Zucker, *Chinese Theater*, p. 196.

29 A. C. Scott, "Performance of Classical Theater," in Colin Mackerras, ed., *Chinese Theater: From its Origins to the Present Day* (Honolulu: University of Hawaii Press, 1983), p. 141.

30 A. E. Zucker offers an in-depth discussion of the analogy between the Elizabethan and traditional Chinese theater in *The Chinese Theater*, pp. 190-219.

31 Daisetz T. Suzuki, *Zen and Japanese Culture* (Princeton: Princeton University Press, 1973), p. 23.

[32] D. T. Suzuki, *An Introduction to Zen Buddhism* (New York: Grove Press, 1964), p. 61.

[33] Ibid., p. 35.

[34] Ibid., p. 64.

[35] Toshimitzu Hasumi, *Zen in Japanese Art* (London: Routledge and Kegan Paul, 1962), pp. ix-x.

[36] Hisamatsu, *Fine Arts*, pp. 30-34.

[37] Ibid., p. 21.

[38] Ibid., p. 31.

[39] Suzuki, *Japanese Culture*, p. 24.

[40] Ibid., p. 28.

[41] Toshimitzu Hasumi, *Japanese Art*, p. 81.

[42] Ibid., p. 82.

[43] Paul Reps, *Zen Flesh, Zen Bones* (New York: Doubleday, n.d.), pp. 150-151.

[44] Eugen Herrigel, *Zen in the Art of Archery* (New York: Vintage Books, 1971), p. 90.

[45] Jean Clay and editors of Realites, *Impressionism* (Secaucus, New Jersey: Chartwell Books, 1973), p. 56.

[46] Richard Illing, *The Art of Japanese Prints* (New York: Mayflower Books, 1980), p. 7.

[47] "Zingoro An Earnest Statue Maker, The Royalist or Kojima Takanori, The Geisha and the Knight—Plays in Japanese," *The New York Times*, March 2, 1900, p. 7.

[48] "Japan's Greatest Actress," *Harper's Bazaar* 33 (March 24, 1900), p. 251.

[49] Epes Sargent, "Dramatic Progress of the Japanese," *Metropolitan Magazine*, (May 1900), p. 501.

[50] Ibid., p. 503.

[51] Leonard Pronko, *Theater East and West* (Berkeley: University of California Press, 1967), p. 121.

[52] "Greatest Actress," p. 252.

[53] "Zingoro An Earnest Statue Maker," p. 7.

[54] Edward Braun, *The Theatre of Meyerhold* (New York: Drama Book Specialists, 1979), p. 48.

[55] Ibid., p. 56.

[56] Cheney, *The New Movement*, pp. 139-40.

[57] W. B. Yeats, "The Theater of Beauty," *Harper's Weekly* 55 (November 11, 1911), p. 11.

[58] Again I will use the Wade-Giles "Peking" instead of the Pinyin "Beijing," since the tradition, which dates back to the eighteenth century, has carried the name "Peking Opera" long before the adoption of the Pinyin system.

[59] David Wallace, "Writing a Chinese Play," *The New York Dramatic Mirror*, November 13, 1912, n.p.

[60] "Yellow Jacket," *The Theatre Magazine*, 41 (December 1912), p. 163.

[61] "The Yellow Jacket," *The New York Dramatic Mirror*, November 13, 1912, p. 7.

[62] *The Yellow Jacket* also was produced throughout Europe. It was presented in

London in 1913. Max Reinhardt produced it first in Berlin (in 1914) and later in Vienna and Budapest. Stanislavski did a production at the Moscow Art Theater. The play also appeared on stages in Spain, Italy, and France.

[63] Kenneth Macgowan and William Melnitz, *The Living Stage* (Englewood Cliffs: Prentice-Hall, 1955), p. 305.

[64] Sheldon Cheney, *The Theatre: Three Thousand Years of Drama, Acting and Stagecraft* (New York: Tudor Publishing Company, 1935), pp. 122-123.

[65] John Gielgud's introduction to Neilla Warren, *The Letters of Ruth Draper, 1920-1956* (New York: Charles Scribner's Sons, 1979), p. xi.

[66] Morton Dauwen Zabel, *The Art of Ruth Draper: Her Dramas and Characters* (Garden City, New York: Doubleday, 1960), pp. 33-34.

[67] Pronko, *East and West*, p. 96.

[68] Arthur Waley, *The No Plays of Japan*, (New York: Grove Press, 1920), p. 59.

[69] Donald Keene, *No: The Classical Theatre of Japan* (Tokyo: Kodansha International Ltd., 1973), p. 36.

[70] Quoted in Margot Berthold, *A History of World Theater* (New York: Frederick Ungar, 1972), p. 106.

[71] Pronko, *East and West*, pp. 76-77.

[72] Keene, *Classical Theatre*, p. 17.

[73] W. B. Yeats, "Introduction to Certain Noble Plays of Japan by Pound and Fenollosa," in Ezra Pound and Ernst Fenollosa, eds. *The Classic Noh Theatre of Japan* (New York: New Directions, 1959), p. 152.

[74] Ibid., p. 152.

[75] W. B. Yeats, "Instead of a Theatre," *Theatre Arts Magazine*, 3 (January 1919), pp. 35-36.

[76] Yeats, "Noble Plays," p. 152.

[77] Arthur Waley, *No Plays*, p. 46.

[78] Hermann Rosse, "Sketches of Oriental Theatres," *Theatre Arts Magazine*, 2 (Summer 1918), p. 142.

[79] Waley, *No Plays*, p. 31, and Pound and Fenollosa, *Classical Noh*, pp. 70-71.

[80] Waley, *No Plays*, p. 46.

[81] Pound and Fenollosa, *Classical Noh*, p. 5.

[82] Ibid., p. 159.

[83] Yeats, "Noble Plays," p. 152.

[84] Ibid., p. 153.

[85] Walter Prichard Eaton, "The Theatre: The Question of Scenery," *The American Magazine* 72 (July 1911), p. 384.

PART TWO:

LEADERS OF THE
NEW SIMPLE STAGE

4

Maurice Browne, Raymond Jonson, and the Chicago Little Theatre

The simple stage finds in "little theaters" the perfect home. Stage space is generally small, budgets are small, and so the producer must find ways to maximize imagination within minimal means. Thomas Dickinson, who ran the Wisconsin Dramatic Society, one of the first little theaters in the United States, defines the little theater in terms of simplification, reduction, and economy:

> The little theater is run upon the theory of absolute economy of management. Someone has called it a "complete theatre reduced from average dimensions." This reduction extends to all the factors of the theatre, the size of the audience, the number of performances, the code of production, the size of plays, and the budget sheet....Scenery is simple and made at home cheaply....The little theatre depends upon the reduction of all the factors of a production to the lowest terms....[1]

In some cases, little theaters were small in the way Dickinson describes only because they were not yet big: their directors aspired to do productions on a large scale, but could not attract the kind of subsidy necessary to achieve this. But in others, the leaders held to their modest and humble circumstances as a flag against the establishment theater that, to them, was either prostituting itself to entertain or smothered by the "little things" of mundane realism.

Among the first little theaters in the United States, one immediately came to be recognized as the leader not only in stripping the stage to essentials, but also in the little theater movement in general. The ideals and simplified images of Maurice Browne, its founder and artistic director, were heard and seen throughout the American theater through articles by and about him and his productions in magazines such as the *Theatre Arts Magazine, The Drama,* and *The Theatre*; through his national tour of *Trojan Women* in 1915; and his visits with other productions to theaters throughout the United States. Of the many little theaters that were born and died between 1912 and 1920, this one held most consistently to the goal of a simple stage and left an indelible imprint on the American *mise-en-scène*.

Not that Browne functioned alone in creating the Chicago Little Theatre's *mise-en-scènes*. His wife Ellen Van Volkenburg and stage designer Raymond Jonson (originally spelled "Johnson")[2] had input into those decisions, but the overall style, from the set, costume, and lighting design, to the actors's body positions and the handling of the script, all stemmed from or flowed through his artistic vision. And that vision reflected an aesthetic of simplicity.

In his autobiography, Browne reveals the principal influences on his work: the Irish Players, Craig's book *On the Art of the Theatre*, the team of Hellerau artists—Adolphe Appia, Emile Dalcroze, and Alexander von Salzmann—and East Asian art forms. Browne came to a simple stage via these routes.

In 1911, Browne and Volkenburg attended a performance by the Irish Players in Chicago. There they witnessed firsthand how much, in terms of atmosphere and suggestion, the Players were able to convey with fragmentary scenery and few lighting sources. They also observed the power of stillness. Browne relates the effect Sara Allgood's performance had on him as he and his wife watched her in Chicago:

> In *Cathleen Ni Hoolihan* she stood, a withered crone, against an open doorway and grew before my eyes from five foot-nothing till her head touched the stars. When I asked how she did it, she answered: '... I don't know; I suppose I just think of God and Ireland.' We asked where she and her fellow players had learned the deep and purposeful repose which was their hallmark... She said, "when we started we didn't know enough to move, so we stood still; now we know better than to move unless we must."[3]

Allgood's replies are revealing about Browne's perceptions of the Irish Players's acting style. Thinking intensely on stage can replace movement; watching stillness, the spectator can be moved.

Browne claims that Craig's *On the Art of the Theatre* was another important influence on his theater, referring to the book as his bible.[4] Theater scholars often trace the use of Craigian screens in the United States to the Chicago Little Theatre, even though Browne contends that he came upon the idea during a rehearsal in a studio which happened to have Japanese screens sitting around. But elsewhere, Browne acknowledges his debt to Craig in his company's use of screens and other semi-defined scenic elements in the cause of stage simplification: "We were the first in America to use Mr. Gordon Craig's ideas for scenery. We have screens and curtains, and allow nothing on the stage that has not a definite purpose."[5] Whether or not the screens came directly from Craig, Browne employed them in productions like *Delphine Declines* (1913), *Creditors* (1913), *Joint Owners in Spain* (1913), *The Philanderer* (1914), and *Four Plays of Today* (1916).

Like Craig, Browne also believed in the director as master of the whole *mise-en-scène*, as the conduit through which all creativity must flow. He shared Craig's assertion that the director must be an expert in all aspects of production.[6] Acknowledging Browne's mastery of the diverse aspects of production and his ability to use this knowledge to bring together all elements into one unified *mise-en-scène*, Cheney considers Browne one of the prime examples of the Craigian artist/director in the United States.[7]

In the summer of 1914, Browne and Volkenburg traveled to Europe where they were exposed to a new influx of simplifying influences which reinforced those from Craig and the Irish Players. The artists at Hellerau—Appia, Dalcroze, and Salzmann—made a lasting impression on Browne's style. Browne and Volkenberg visited Cologne and attended a "superb" exhibition of theatrical design, with one room set aside exclusively for the work of Adolphe Appia and his "rhythmic spaces"—only simple platforms, stairs, and light creating neutral spaces where the actor's art could thrive. Browne comments that Appia's designs left him and his wife "breathless."[8] Later they went to Hellerau where they saw for themselves the simple hall that Appia designed.[9] There they met Saltzmann, Appia's lighting designer, whom Browne calls the "master of us all."[10] From Appia and Saltzmann, Browne learned the potential of plasticity in stage imagery when suggestive sets and lighting are artfully blended.

Dalcroze and his system of eurhythmics, explored at Hellerau, had a profound impact on Browne's notion of the moving actor as an essential design variable of the *mise-en-scène*. Browne watched in awe at a demonstration of Dalcroze's rhythmically-moving performers, whose "hallmark was simplicity."[11] Later, Browne asked Dalcroze who in America taught his method the best and was told it was Lucy Duncan, who happened to be the woman training the actors at the Chicago Little Theatre. Thus, Dalcroze's method came to the Little Theatre's actors through the insights Browne gained during his 1914 visit and through Duncan's teaching.

Browne's tendency to utilize restraint and reduction also was fed by his exposure to East Asian arts. Browne claims he read everything in English on the

Noh theatre,[12] even though there was little available in English on the subject until Waley, Fenollosa, and Pound's essays were published. The Chicago Little Theatre closed in 1917; these works on the Noh came out between 1917 and 1920.

One can surmise that Browne was influenced as much by Japanese and Chinese art as he was by East Asian theater forms. Browne was introduced to the art of Japanese prints through his friend Arthur Ficke, who was a serious collector. At first they had little appeal to Browne, but Ficke persevered until Browne was won over by the "grave beauty of those craftsmen's restraint, austerity, power of elimination."[13] He and his wife became so intoxicated by them that they went out and bought Shunei prints.

The prints they purchased soon became the model for the theater's decor. Like the Shunei prints, the walls of the theater were stone and beige with olive touches. This restrained color scheme contributed to the theater's atmosphere, characterized by Browne himself as "austere stillness." The prints, which have been described as having human figures in the foreground costumed in the same neutral-toned colors as the background, hung on the walls of the Chicago Little Theatre. Browne considered them a symbol of the theater itself.[14]

Browne also created a tearoom off to one side of the auditorium. Decorated with Chinese tapestries and wood-carvings, this area contributed to the "simple, austere" atmosphere of the theater.[15] Surely Browne and his co-workers were inspired by the Japanese tearoom infused with the Zen values of simplicity, stillness, and tranquility.

East Asian motifs and color schemes contributed to the general ambiance on stage as well. Browne's production style, according to Browne himself, combined Craig and East Asian influences: "Our chief modification of Mr. Gordon Craig's ideas has been an attempt to introduce the principles of the Chinese and Japanese painters and color printers, whose work is remarkable for its simplicity and great economy of line and color."[16]

The artistic sensibilities of Browne and his two co-creators of the *mise-en-scène* were partially shaped by their experiences before working at the Chicago Little Theatre. In Great Britain, where he lived just prior to coming to Chicago, Browne wrote poetry, an art form whose first principle of technique, according to Browne, is elimination.[17] As for Ellen Van Volkenburg, she began as an actress. Before her engagement to Browne, she performed one-woman shows with no accessories but a single chair on an otherwise empty stage. Following in the long American tradition of "travesty" performance, she did comic imitations of famous actors and actresses in their most famous roles. Her experience in creating her own world without the aid of props, make-up, costumes, or scenery was surely useful at the Little Theatre to help mold the kind of acting style the performers needed on their simplified stages. The designer Raymond Jonson, who came to the Chicago Little Theatre, four months after it was founded, trained as a painter and therefore did not have to break out of shackles placed on him by the Italianate and naturalistic theater design traditions. The three co-creators came to the task of creating theater relatively fresh and unencumbered.

Browne and Volkenburg knew they wanted to start a theater almost from the beginning of their relationship. After witnessing the Irish Players, that idea became stronger. But the initial impetus for starting a small theater rather than a large one came from practical considerations: they had little money. When the owner of the Fine Arts Building offered them the Playhouse, a substantial space for their nascent company, they would have accepted but for the fact they knew they would not be able to support it. So they took instead a much smaller space on the fourth floor. That was within their budget. Thus, the decision to start a small theater came out of the "illusion" that "a small theater would cost less than a large one."[18]

But the decision was not solely an economic one, as evidenced by the following statement by Browne made several months before the theater's opening: "In staging, lighting, and the like our object will be to create dramatic illusion by the simplest means; there will be no attempt at the elaborate or the photographic."[19]

Four months after they began and had already produced several productions, their original designer, a painter named Bror Nordfeldt, decided to leave Chicago. He helped Browne find his replacement, recommending Raymond Jonson, who went on to become the principal stage designer for the Chicago Little Theatre until it closed in 1917.

THE THEORY OF RAYMOND JONSON

It is generally conceded that Jonson was not guided by the theory and work of others; he had never even heard of Craig when he began work at the Little Theatre. A practical man, he followed the principle that "the less you use, the better it is,"[20] not in emulation of others, but, according to Eunice Tietjens, in response to the budgetary and spatial limits of the Chicago Little Theatre and Browne's conceptual guidelines. Tietjens characterizes Jonson in terms of his pursuit of the economy principle, as a "master in the art of making much out of little."[21]

But it would be inaccurate to say that pragmatic issues preempted artistic ones. In an interview with the *Christian Science Monitor*, for instance, Jonson verifies this: "Simplicity is the keynote of little theater staging. This for the artistic reason, which I like to put first; and then for the more practical, the space."[22]

In interview after interview and essay after essay, Jonson propounds the notion that scenery is best when simplified or eliminated altogether. In the *Drama League Monthly*, he asks: Why shouldn't a stage be created that demanded very little scenery?

There usually is much, oh much too much, scenery and I believe the more we have the less illusion is possible. Light can do wonders, and if the proper equipment were used still less scenery would be necessary....We should get away from the scenery idea. Let us have a stage where no borders and no wings are necessary for masking....Let us have a simple, direct and significant backgrounds and against these put the important thing—the play, the play a work of art and nothing else.[23]

Like so many of his fellow simplifiers, Jonson's main target was the minute detail of illusionistic settings. This is not to say Jonson ignored or devalued detail; as he said in an interview with the *Christian Science Monitor*: "At the Chicago Little Theatre, we pay attention to the smallest details, down to the color of a necktie."[24] Even a cursory look at the CLT designs would confirm that this was true. But by having a bare minimum, the details chosen would "count," either in terms of the concept behind the design or for the actor.

In one interview, Jonson draws the connection between greater simplicity and increased freedom for the actor, the spectator, and ultimately, for the piece itself. If the designer would "let the piece have its way," argues Jonson, then it would "enforce on the designer simplicity of illustration."[25] These words imply that simplicity is not a conceptual imposition, but is inherent within the piece and that allowing the piece to express itself will reveal its own essence. Paring down allows the essential part of the piece to speak for itself.

One path to that essence is by way of the elements of the craft. Jonson argues that the designer will reach the essential—or what Jonson himself calls "significant form"—by returning to the basics of color, mass, and line and showing them in their elemental purity.

Jonson held not only to purity within his visual medium, but also purity of medium. In an essay written in 1919 for the *Theatre Arts Magazine*, Jonson declares that he and his fellow artists at the Chicago Little Theatre are attempting to create something that is pure theater: "We are trying to make the theatre an art, with a form that is of the theatre and not pieces of something else."[26]

THE THEORY OF MAURICE BROWNE

Browne was at least as persistent in his call for stage simplification as Jonson. Browne's most articulate statement promoting this ideal appeared in an essay he wrote during the summer of 1914, published in *The Drama* under the title "The New Rhythmic Drama." From this essay and his autobiography, written years later but based on diary entries made at the time he ran the Chicago

Little Theatre, we can construct a radical theory that fed and was fed by his work.

Simplicity lay at the heart of the Chicago Little Theatre's philosophy: "Simple things are the only ones that permanently satisfy the human soul, and the greatest master is he who uses one line where others use two. This is true of movement and light, no less than of language...."[27]

Browne's pragmatic philosophy of stage simplicity applies most obviously to sets and properties. Browne's policy toward stage accessories at the Chicago Little Theatre is stated as follows:

> No object was permitted on the stage unless it had dramatic purpose and at the same time unobtrusively satisfied the eye: a practice conditioned by our lack of space and commended by our poverty. Slowly we learned to use one vase, one table, one hanging in such a way that neither eye nor action needed more.[28]

In describing his philosophy of means, Browne invokes the less-is-more paradox:

> The farmer's business is to make two ears of wheat grow where one grew before, the artist's to make one line, one word, serve the purpose of two. We sought to make something out of—as nearly as possible—nothing: a wisp of cheese-cloth, a flower in a vase, a shaft of light.[29]

Browne expresses an equally strong commitment to essentiality in voice and movement: "The player... must eliminate every meaningless movement of body, voice and heart: the shifting of an eye, the unneeded inflection of a syllable, the moment of emotional self-indulgence."[30]

To Browne, economy is as valuable an asset in life as it is in art:

> Just as, in the practice of his art, the artist eliminates every word, every line, every tone that is not absolutely indispensable, and leaves only the simplest and therefore the most satisfying expression of his idea, so, in the conduct of his life, he would do well to eliminate wherever elimination is possible.[31]

These thoughts parallel those of Henry David Thoreau. The soul thrives on simplicity; economy has spiritual worth. Browne's pride in announcing that the first eighteen plays by the CLT were done for only $800 resembles Thoreau's that he built his house for $28 and change.

Like Thoreau, Browne believed that simplicity in life and work is the path to spiritual wealth. Browne maintains that the simplest methods in creating art will lead to a new rhythmic drama, wherein art will "cease to be a hobby and become a religion."[32] In his essay "The Temple of a Living Art," he refers to theater as a "temple," performance as a ritual. Many followers of the Chicago Little Theatre picked up this attitude, calling Browne's theater a "shrine" and performances there like "rituals."[33] But Browne goes a step further than positing a connection between art and religion. He goes so far as to say that without religious significance, there is no true art.[34]

The austerity that the spectators experienced in Browne's theater emerged from Browne's belief, not just in simplicity and essentiality, but also in the more spiritually-charged virtue of poverty: "Some men and women should formally dedicate themselves to the service of beauty and to poverty. Poverty, not merely simplicity!"[35] To answer this call, the artist must strip himself of everything except what is essential for his work and his life.

In his autobiography, Browne continually describes his struggles and setbacks over the five years the Chicago Little Theatre existed, referring often to the personal sacrifices he and his wife endured for their cause. At times, they literally could not afford a new pair of shoes; they even put their food money into their debt-ridden quest. And still their theater was often on the brink of bankruptcy. Browne admitted that the constraints of poverty were sometimes frustrating. He calls their tiny stage as "binding and as kindly as a coffin"[36] and confesses the "soul-sickness" of always having to make the best of nothing.[37] But in the final analysis, the constraints of poverty were, in Browne's worldview, the road to freedom. Browne touches on the paradox of freedom through limitation when he explains the liberating feeling one experiences as one strips down: "Anyone who has ever done such a thing, in however small a degree, is aware of that sense of liberty... that comes with each rejection."[38]

In expressing these ideas, Browne shows his spiritual kinship with two other directors: Jacques Copeau (who, when he met Browne in 1914, acknowledged that Browne's ideas and work influenced his own) and Jerzy Grotowski . The two European directors, from a spiritual vantage point, share Browne's commitment to an artistic asceticism, to "poor theaters" that make of the actor's preparation and performance a rite and a sacrifice. Like Browne, Copeau and Grotowki also have articulated their belief in material abnegation in one's life as well as in one's art. By anticipating the ideas of these two seminal figures of the twentieth century, Browne qualifies as a pioneer for a quintessential twentieth century theater aesthetic.

"The New Rhythmic Drama" reads almost like a manifesto for stage simplicity in a similar vein as Craig's *On the Art of the Theatre*. Both pieces call for radical simplification in all aspects of the *mise-en-scène*. Moreover, the two works similarly break down theater into its essential elements. Just as Craig reduces theater to action (the very spirit of acting), words (the body of the play), line and color (the very heart of the scene) and rhythm (very essence of dance), Browne breaks it down into movement, light, rhythm, and sound.[39]

This reductionist passion to return to basics and to eliminate inessentials, which Browne shared both with Craig and his collaborator Raymond Jonson, is fundamental to stage simplification. It also is interesting that Browne, unlike Jonson and Craig, leaves out color when delineating the fundamentals; color is viewed as an additive, not as an essential, a view that will be echoed by artists from Kasimir Malevich in the 1910s to Robert Morris in the 1960s.

THE *MISE-EN-SCÈNE* AT THE CHICAGO LITTLE THEATRE

Many critics and scholars confirm that Browne and Jonson's theoretical notions were reflected in their *mise-en-scènes*. Moderwell identifies Browne's overall directorial style as marked by "rigid simplification."[40] Krows characterizes Browne's entire *mise-en-scène* as "radical" in its simplicity of line and color.[41] Cheney writes how the settings at the Chicago Little Theatre were "simple to the absolute limit."[42] Daniel Reed, in an interview with Bernard F. Dukore, adds that Browne and Jonson's sets were even simpler than those of the other little theatres which followed their example.[43]

Critics and scholars also note the striking simplification in the acting. Charles Collins identifies the "Browne Method" as simple, devoid of exaggeration, and "not so much repression as quietism in acting."[44] Eric Delamarter describes his players' movement as devoid of "aimless 'crossing' of the stage" and that the acting "is in straight lines, without arabesque of gesture or stencil decoration of method. It is intimate, repressive, contemplative."[45] Ralph Roeder comments that the handling of language was always simple, relatively uninflected, and structural—never ornamental. Those who perceived this same trait negatively labeled it "grim monotone," "bleak and low tone severity" and "measured intoning."[46] Dukore contends that "the notion of 'effective scenes' was discarded in favor of simplicity."[47]

There is some dispute with regard to the degree of simplification in one element of the Browne *mise-en-scène*, and that is the lighting. On one side of the issue is O. L. Hall, who argues minimal lighting: "They use little light at the Little, but every ray of it goes effectively to the fulfillment of a definite design."[48] On the other side is Cloyd Head, who notes a tendency toward extravagant lighting with lots of color and many cues, especially in otherwise simplified productions like *Medea* and *King of the Jews*. Browne must have perceived himself as being too elaborate with his lighting because four years after the Chicago Little Theatre closed, he wrote an open letter to the *Theatre Arts Magazine*, confessing that he was overindulgent with the Little Theatre's lighting and warning others not to fall into the same trap.[49]

One of the root causes for the Little Theatre's need to simplify in all areas of production was its small theater space, its primitive equipment, and its modest budgets. The theater, located on the fourth floor of the Fine Arts Building in

Chicago, contained ninety-three seats, with a stage, according to Jonson, measuring fifteen feet across, eighteen feet deep and eleven feet, nine inches high (the height being the place where, according to Jonson, they were "pinched most"). Two three-foot square structural pillars were unavoidable factors in every set. One was located four-fifths of the way down on the stage left side, the other upstage right extending into the wings. This left about ten feet across in which to act.

In the last two seasons, Browne had access to a larger theater in the same building, the Playhouse, which, most importantly, gave the CLT added height. This allowed settings of some of his last productions to tower sixteen feet into the air and contributed significantly to a sense of monumentality in his last revival of Euripides's *Medea* and George Bernard Shaw's *Mrs. Warren's Profession* and *The Philanderer*.

The company's lighting equipment was elementary, except for a system of dimmers, rare in 1912, when the company first began operations. Because of the dimmers, the Chicago company could vary mood with a kind of precision uncommon in the American theater at that time. They had a switchboard with a bank of eight dimmers operating three-circuit strips. For floods, they used old dishpans, and for spotlights, they often resorted to tin funnels, bought at the local five-and-ten-cent store. Browne was one of the first in America to take the cue from Craig and dispense with footlights as permanent fixtures. He did eventually procure footlights which he could set up when they were artistically warranted, as for his production of *Grotesques* (1915).

Despite the modest circumstances of the Chicago Little Theatre, it is important to note that Browne's philosophy would not allow for the *mise-en-scène* to be haphazardly thrown together—even in the worst of financial straits. Practitioners from other little theaters freely admitted how they would throw together chairs and tables and focus on the acting and the script. Raymond Jonson's brother, who assembled a detailed account of Raymond Jonson's theater work, remarks that only once did the Chicago Little Theatre ever allow for a makeshift *mise-en-scène*, and that was when Browne had to reject Jonson's involved design plans for Yeats's *Deirdre* (to be performed only twice) since the company had no money for it. In this case alone did Browne resort to asking Jonson's assistant to cast about for whatever could be put together.[50] Otherwise, settings were carefully conceived and executed—in accordance with rigorous artistic standards.

As a visual context for Browne and Jonson's simplified production style, Browne made the theater itself quite spare. One supportive critic described it this way:

> The walls are in soft tones of gray and so is the upholstery. There are no plush, no gilt, no theatrical masks, no clutter, no curtains daubed with inane figures and no brass railings that look like

> plumbing. The curtain is drapery in the same tone as the walls
> and the permanent background of the stage continues the scheme
> of the auditorium. Against this background appropriate settings
> are placed for the plays.[51]

Within this aesthetically subdued theater and the ironclad limitations of
small budgets, tight space, and primitive lighting, Browne conceived many
different kinds of simplified productions. Some of the most salient examples will
be chosen from among the four major categories: (1) Greek revival permanent
settings; (2) simplified realism; (3) two-dimensional simplifications; and (4)
empty-space stages.

The 1913 production of Euripides' *The Trojan Women* (revived in 1914)
was CLT's first nationwide success. The methods of simplification employed in
this Greek revival were sustained throughout the *mise-en-scène*. Of the two most
famous Greek revivals at the CLT, *The Trojan Women*, the third show of their
first season, was the more simplified of the two. The production was so
successful that it was revived twice: first, in the Fine Arts Building in 1914, and
then again in 1915 when it toured America from coast to coast as part of the
pacifist movement of World War I. Although there were differences among the
three versions, most of its key features were similar enough for it to be discussed
as one production.

The original designer for *Trojan Women* was Jonson's predecessor, Bror
Nordfeldt, but Jonson refined his design, coming up with the setting that won
for *Trojan Women* its national acclaim. Browne and Jonson created a permanent
setting depicting the great wall of Troy with a large, jagged gap in the center
where the Greek army had seemingly broken through. The dimensionality of the
wall was actual not just painted; constructed out of wide-meshed burlap backed
with canvas, it was made to look very thick and massive.

The wall exemplified the quality of monumentality, even on the small Little
Theatre stage. This was accomplished by building the wall so its endpoints never
were seen; disappearing above the line of the proscenium arch and into the
wings, it seemed to be of infinite dimensions (photo 4.1). Jonson accentuated the
endless majesty of the wall by depicting it as a repeating pattern of enormous
cubic stones, set off from each other by purple tape for mortar. Each stone
seemed huge in proportion to the human beings before them. The monumentality
of the Trojan wall was even more pronounced when the production was
redesigned for higher stages on their national tour in 1915 (photo 4.2).

One critic described the overall impression the wall created as having
"much of the towering dignity we have admired in the sketches of Gordon Craig,
dwarfing the mortal figures until they seem but puppets in the hands of

4.1 Set for revival of *Trojan Women* (1914) at Chicago Little Theatre, designed by Raymond Jonson. Photo courtesy of the Jonson Gallery of the University Art Museum, University of New Mexico.

4.2 Touring set for Chicago Little Theatre production of *Trojan Women* (1915), directed by Maurice Browne and designed by Raymond Jonson. Photo courtesy of the Jonson Gallery of the University Art Museum, University of New Mexico.

destiny."[52] The seemingly endless height and breadth of the wall and the relatively small, powerless figures beneath de-individualized the Trojan women, making them seem like quintessential victims rather than particularized human beings.

By concentrating on and magnifying the wall in *Trojan Women* (and the palace doors later in their *Medea* production), Browne and Jonson raised this play somewhat out of its historical context so that it seemed to occur not only in Troy at the end of the Trojan War, but also in a symbolic neutral time and place. In this way the cracked wall becomes a symbol of violation of any people and any city.

Behind the constructed wall, visible through its gapping rent, Jonson hung a scrim on which his lights could shine different color washes to suggest a vast empty space beyond, to indicate the progression of the day from dawn to night and to convey the varying moods. Thus the lighting, like the wall, served realistic, symbolic, and formal functions. One reviewer summed up the impression created by the little piece of sky visible through the rent in the wall of Troy as "purplish, ominous, vast."[53]

The lighting for *Trojan Women* conspired with the monumental effect of the setting in reducing the characters to undifferentiated human shapes. Browne and Jonson employed a lot of backlighting, sometimes with little or no front light at all. One of his strongest images occurred when Hecuba stood silently "silhouetted against the dim light... filtering through the jagged walls of the captured city."[54] A commentator refers to another point in the play when the Chorus was backlit in such a way that the audience saw only the outlines of their raised arms and their heads bent low.[55] With the lights handled this way, characters became abstract, quasi-anonymous figures in a powerfully evocative atmosphere.

The costumes reduced the individuality of the characters. The tunics, loose-fitting and layered, hid the specific shapes of the characters' bodies, especially those of the Chorus. The tunics for the five chorus members were "somber-hued," blended together in a "low-keyed harmony."[56] Hecuba was robed in dull purple. The colors of the costumes and the walls were kept within a tightly controlled color range, unlike chorus costumes in the Anglin/Platt Greek productions.

As director, it was Browne's charge to bring these diverse scenic elements into unity. From the moment the production began to unfold, Browne integrated these visual elements with those of the blocking patterns and the voices of his actors. The curtains opened to reveal absolute darkness. Suddenly the audience heard the voice of a woman lamenting. Gradually faint streaks of light came up—the first rays of morning reflecting softly on a white arm of a woman crouching in what we later realize is the desolate field before Troy. At the moment when the light first came up, however, the woman the spectators saw was not yet Hecuba, the walls not yet Troy. She was all women, indeed all mankind, in a state of lamentation. Browne brought the chorus on slowly, one at a time, making the entrances as gradual as the ever-brightening glow of the early morning light.

The production ended using the same device in reverse. After the fire and the smoke and the final destruction of Troy, night comes slowly, gradually, and the characters are again reduced to anonymous shapes wandering off "in a midworld between earth and sky in the direction of the Greek trumpet and the ships."[57]

Browne read in Euripides' text a smooth, continuous, uninterrupted quality, which he then sought to carry into every part of the production plan—from the lighting cues to the movement and vocal inflections. In an unpublished essay, he describes the rhythm of this piece as "a slow and markedly continuous—a *legato*—movement, broken only at the rarest moments for the briefest space: an unending cry as it were, *crescendo, dimenuendo, crescendo...* an infinite thing, always continuing... a sense of unbroken movement into infinity."[58]

Evidently Browne succeeded in reinforcing the sense of uninterruptedness conveyed by the seemingly endless lines of the wall and the gradually transforming light in the way he choreographed the piece. Ellen Van Volkenburg described for Bernard F. Dukore how "Browne so related the actors to each other and the space that one seemed to see a limitless plane."[59] A contemporary account notes that the movement became "a majestic flowing rhythm held together in perfect unison."[60]

This treatment was especially evident in the blocking of the Chorus members. Here he combined *legato* movement with moments of stillness and silence, thus adding to the uniformity created by the traditionally identical costumes. Browne directed them to move in unison during the odes and freeze for up to fifteen minutes in poses and tableaux during the episodes. All movements and poses emphasized their similarities more than their differences. In a letter to Gilbert Murray, Browne referred to the Chorus as "statuary in motion."[61] Austere stillness, interspersed with hauntingly slow, swaying motions, were the movement patterns of the Chorus. One observer gave a vivid account: "the slow agony in movement, the sculptural silence and swaying of the shadow players in their groups and poses."[62]

The Choral odes were sometimes chanted, other times half sung. Barbara Winter describes the tempo of both the movement and the vocal rhythm as *legato* and explains that all voices were pitched between the notes D and F.[63] One disgruntled critic describes their vocal quality more pejoratively as "swamped in sing-song" with the effect of "deadly tedium."[64] The positive and negative comments reveal that Maurice Browne had succeeded in keeping the movement steady, flowing, and uninterrupted and the voices within a tightly restricted vocal range.

Browne accentuated the power of certain moments in the Euripides play through long periods of silence and stillness, not only among the Chorus members, but the characters, too. Browne himself describes how the quiet repose of Hecuba's presence contributed to the impact of the climactic moment:

> Hecuba slowly turned away, slowly walked up to the breach which the Greeks had battered in the wall of Troy, and stood there—it seemed for ever [sic]—with her back to the audience, gazing out over the ruined city. Then suddenly a little shiver ran through, her defeated body straightened, her head lifted and she turned around....[65]

Not only did Browne have Volkenburg hold in silent stillness, but he also closed her off from the spectator's view, emphasizing her abstract and symbolic traits over her individual ones.

One can immediately recognize the similarity between this moment with the eloquent silence in Sara Allgood's performance with the Irish Players, which so moved Browne and Volkenburg several years before. The power of silent stillness was reinforced when Browne—not long after he saw the Players in Chicago—watched another famous performer. At a performance of Winthrop Ames' Chicago tour of Schnitzler's *The Affairs of Anatol* in 1913, Browne saw John Barrymore stand in silence for seventeen minutes and thirty-nine seconds before picking up his cue, yet never losing his audience for a second. Therefore, by the time Browne did *The Trojan Women* later in 1913, he had witnessed two great feats of powerful stage silence and stillness.

Browne's casting reduced the traditional chorus of fifteen people down to four women plus a leader—a chorus of five. To create a Greek army, he had four or five soldiers carefully placed behind the wall to suggest a throng. Moreover, Browne cut Euripides' prologue between Athena and Poseidon, which he considered superfluous. In so doing, he saved himself two characters, and, in addition, focused more tightly on the plight of the Trojan women.

In looking at the production as a whole, commentators agree that it was simplified beyond any they had ever seen. Eloise Ramsey describes it, choosing the same words Moderwell uses in characterizing Browne's style in general: "rigid simplification." Like Moderwell, she recognizes that Browne not only simplified, but did so to a radical extreme—especially with *The Trojan Women*.

One aspect of the production that was not entirely simplified was the lighting. It is true that Browne and Jonson used it to suggest vast empty space and to reduce human beings to moving shapes, and, in these ways, they were employing it for purposes of detail reduction, but they also used a lot of color and many lighting changes. Viewing their dimmer board as analogous to a color organ, Browne and Jonson played it with less reserve than the other production factors. They also wanted to reflect emotional changes through lighting. As the mood or emotion of a key character or situation changed, so should the lights. A reviewer from Columbus, Ohio noted this when the Chicago Little Theatre brought the production to his town: "Every mood brought a new and strange light." As the crazed Cassandra entered, an angry red light filled the stage. Beautiful Helen's entrance was greeted by a burst of orange light, and as Troy burned, the stage turned a magnificent red, only to die away to a gray gloomy light as the women went to the waiting Greek ships.[66]

And yet the complex lighting scheme did not interfere with audience perceptions that *The Trojan Women* was a simplified production. Several commentators even observed restraint in the lighting. For example, Cloyd Head, who was the Little Theatre's advance man for the national tour of the play, refers to the lighting as "reticent,"[67] especially in comparison with some of Browne's other productions.

With *The Trojan Women* (and later with *Medea*), Browne found a way to project the grand spirit of Greek performance on a tiny stage, thereby opening many possibilities for producers and thus contributing enormously to the Greek revivalist movement sweeping the nation between 1904 and 1914. Browne proved the possibility of an approach different from the grand scale of the Anglin and Granville-Barker revivals. The isolated human figure on a small indoor stage, empty but for one salient element with lighting capable of suggesting an infinite space beyond, could convey a small-scale grandeur that presents, at once, the greatness of the Greek hero and his or her diminutive status vis-a-vis the gods and inexorable fate.

Any play in the realistic tradition at the CLT had to be presented according to simplified or suggestive realism. Most of the plays they did called for highly detailed, literal settings. Belascoism was impossible in their theater by virtue of cost and back- and on-stage space. Browne's antipathy toward painted scenery was legendary. He once told a reporter, with a bit of exaggeration, that painted scenery was unknown in his theater.[68] The only course, then, was to ignore most of the stage directions, choose only properties and settings absolutely needed by the actors and by the audience for getting a general sense of a time, place, or mood, and replace scenery with lighting wherever possible.

Taking the cue from the Irish Players, Browne inaugurated this style with the second production at the Chicago Little Theatre, Schnitzler's *Anatol* (1913). The settings for *Anatol* were significant more for their place as the first in a long line of Chicago Little Theatre productions to utilize simplified realism than for the quality of the sets themselves. The five scenes in which the comic repartee occurred were presented without walls—only hangings through which players entered and exited. Pieces of furniture and other scenic elements were introduced to distinguish one room from another. One room, for instance, had the hint of a fireplace, another the suggestion of a window, and all had a barest minimum of furniture. In the one outdoor scene, there was hardly even any suggestion; the actors stood before a big brown screen with only Anatol's umbrella and a call for a cab to convey the location.[69] Each of the five scenes were also distinguished from one another through different color lights on the same set of curtains that always remained.

In May 1913, Browne's company performed a double-bill: Oren Taft's *Delphine Declines* and Yeats' *The Shadowy Waters*. Dukore discusses how settings for the latter play "contained no more than the edge of a sail, a prow, the stump of a mast, and a low rail."[70] In the case of *Declines*, Browne and Jonson not only selected a few suggestive elements, but also imposed on themselves limits in their use of color. The action took place at a cafe overlooking a river at night. Browne suggested the embankment with a low, undyed sacking screen, the cafe with no more than two tables and four chairs. Behind everything stretched a dark blue curtain with a dim red light shining on it from below.[71] Browne further simplified the imagery by limiting the four characters to black and white costumes with only a touch of red: One woman wore a big red flower on her black dress. The resulting image was characterized as "a sort of Aubrey Beardsley design."[72] A reviewer from the *Chicago Daily Journal* commented that the "setting had more illusion to it than could have been created by a stageful of scenery."[73]

Browne's company performed Shaw's *Mrs. Warren's Profession* (1916) in a larger theater, the Playhouse. This enabled them to apply methods of simplified realism to a larger and higher stage. Jonson used the little money they had in the CLT coffers to create settings that were bold in their spare simplification. Browne wrote a note to Jonson after opening night, claiming that the "outstanding feature" in the production was his scenery.[74]

Shaw's play calls for four different settings, one for each act: Act One—summer afternoon in a cottage garden; Act Two—inside the cottage after nightfall; Act Three—In the rectory garden next morning; and Act Four—Honoria Fraser's chambers in Chancery Lane. Typical of plays from that period, Shaw's stage directions meticulously lay out each of the settings with innumerable properties and decorations, most of which Browne and Jonson simply disregarded.

The strategy they employed was to use panels that were sixteen feet high and to rearrange them from setting to setting, i.e., treating the pieces as adaptable units. The towering panels were a neutral, off-white, endowing them with surfaces responsive to the color of the lighting. The panels were lit differently from act to act to convey a different impression. At the same time, the fact that the settings were rearrangements of the same pieces and the outer frame was kept identical through the four acts enabled the setting to maintain a unified look—a sense of singleness.

The sixteen-foot panels served to make the eye of the spectator take in the vast space—in ways similar to the designs of Edward Gordon Craig. In the Act Four interior scene, Jonson made the doorways and back window especially high to further accentuate vast empty space (photo 4.3). In the Act One garden scene, a low fence extended across the stage, behind which was a plain backdrop (photo 4.4). The uncommonly low fence exaggerated the sense of the sky's expanse beyond it. The long monochromatic fence stretched across the stage, with only a brief interruption for a simple white gate in the center. The long horizontal line created by the fence and gate was reinforced by long benches before it. Thus, Browne and Jonson were able to create a sense of uninterruptedness in the dominant vertical and horizontal lines of the setting.

4.3 Chicago Little Theatre designer Raymond Jonson's sketch for act four of *Mrs. Warren's Profession* presented at the Chicago Little Theatre in 1917. Photo courtesy of the Jonson Gallery of the University Art Museum, University of New Mexico.

Jonson designed and built furniture exclusively for this production; Jonson describes how he would have "nothing to do with the post-Victorian and bulky Morris-inspired furniture which generally cluttered theater stages."[75] What he came up with instead was furniture with a hard-edged, simplified "modern" appearance, which, though it defied authenticity to period, suited the neutral look created by the high off-white panels.

The problem in the production came in the relationship between the set and the acting and costumes, which were left conventionally realistic. The disharmony between the sets and costumes is suggested in a review by Richard Henry Little: "the actors in their conventional everyday dress jar against it [the

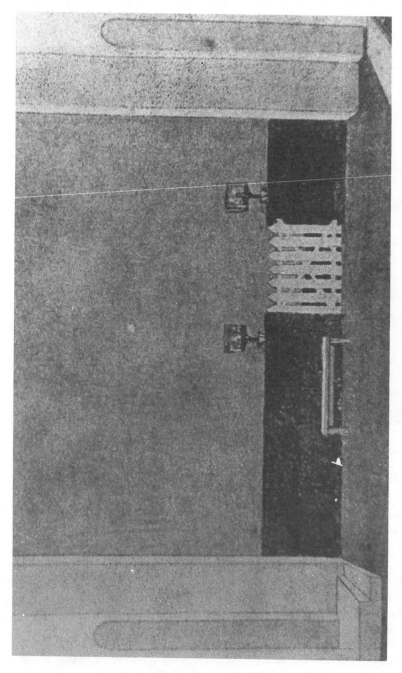

4.4 Raymond Jonson's sketch for act one of *Mrs. Warren's Profession* (garden scene) presented at Chicago Little Theatre in 1917. Photo courtesy of the Jonson Gallery of the University Art Museum, University of New Mexico.

scenery] as much as a monkey wrench on a plate of ice cream."[76] Cloyd Head, in his article "The Chicago Little Theatre," emphasized more the clash between the scenery and the acting. He acknowledges the scenery's simplification, noting the effective use of repeated motifs from scene to scene, but argues that the play failed on the grounds that the stylization of the scenery "divided the production into two parts—the acting and the *mise-en-scène*."[77] The message conveyed by these observations is that simplification and neutralization of settings demands like treatment of other aspects of the *mise-en-scène*.

The most notable productions in the third category of simple-stage, two-dimensional simplifications were *The Chicago Little Theatre Passion Play* (1913) and Cloyd Head's *Grotesques: A Decoration in Black and White* (1915). *The Chicago Little Theatre Passion Play*, or *Passion Play* as it came to be called, was performed around Christmas 1913. The show depicted episodes in the life of Christ in ten scenes. Most of the production was performed in pantomime, with the audience seeing it as a series of continuous tableaux in silhouette. Before each scene began, the audience listened, in complete darkness, to intoned readings from the Bible. Then the darkness slowly lifted to reveal the outline of characters silently re-enacting recognizable scenes in the life and death of Jesus Christ. Part of the experience of attending this production was exclusively visual, the other part, exclusively auditory. Browne was not mixing sensory impressions; he was expressing them in a purer way, one at a time.

Technically, Browne and Jonson's lighting—the key feature of this *mise-en-scène*—was used in such a way as to replace scenery, detailed costumes, and properties with a world of silhouettes and shadows. Browne describes how it worked: There was no front lighting at all. The only light that illuminated the actors was reflected off the plaster back wall, so only silhouetted figures were seen (photo 4.5). This was the furthest Browne and Jonson ever went in creating anonymous human figures. Browne was so successful in erasing his actors' individual features that no one in the audience guessed that the central figure of Christ was played by a woman.

Jonson also incorporated projections. At one point, a mighty cross filled the entire sky. This was done merely by drawing a tiny cross on a slide that was placed in front of a baby spotlight focused on the wall. The small cross on the slide became a huge cross when projected on the wall—another case of a big effect resulting from minimal means.

Moreover, the lights were designed in such a way as to accentuate large amounts of empty space. One critic applauds Browne and Jonson's lighting for creating the illusion of vast reaches of empty space by suggesting "the sense of a plain, of heights looking down upon it, of far reaches of a valley.... The mind leaps to spacious places...."[78] Another awed critic exclaimed: "Maurice Browne made his toy stage take on the appearance of the open world out upon which one looked through the doorlike proscenium"[79]—another image of anonymous human figures within suggested vastness.

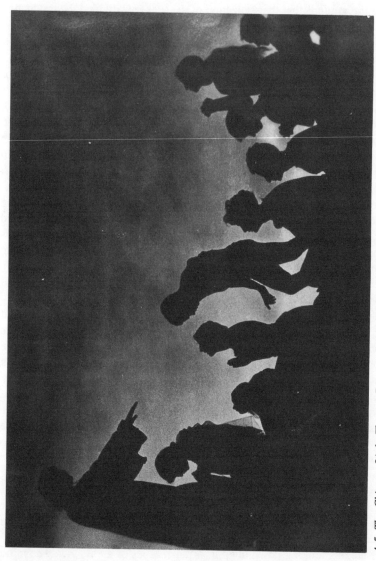

4.5 *The Chicago Little Theatre Passion Play* (1913), staged in silhouette by Maurice Browne in collaboration with the CLT cast and designed by Raymond Jonson. Photo courtesy of the Jonson Gallery of the University Art Museum, University of New Mexico.

As in *Trojan Women*, the movement and voice work by the actors stayed within strict boundaries. As they experimented, the Chicago players found that only large, slow, *legato* movements, such as the kind used in *Trojan Women*, created the kind of images they sought. Moreover, all movement had to parallel the lit back wall; otherwise, facial detail would be exposed and the imagery would be inconsistent. Thus, horizontal movement patterns in a tightly restricted space were necessary and a relief stage was created.[80] The woman who read from the Bible "intoned" it, i.e., she used an uninflected voice for her readings. Like the chants of the Trojan women, the voice stayed within a tightly restricted vocal range.

The actors employed another kind of restraint. In the course of rehearsals, they developed their own "inner monologue" to support the actions they were fulfilling. Browne relates how, in one rehearsal, they spoke their inner texts aloud. The unquestionable success of this exercise gave them a choice, but they unanimously decided to keep the enactments in pantomime, never revealing in performance their inner script. By choosing silence over language—after they realized that adding the language was effective—the actors were employing another self-imposed constraint.

In November 1915, the Chicago Little Theatre produced *Grotesques*, a poetic play subtitled a "Decoration in Black and White." This landmark play has stage simplification built into the text and stage directions. It is difficult to know how much the production molded the style of the play and how much the play governed the production choices, but it is clear that the text as it appeared in *Poetry Magazine* contained aspects calling for a simple stage.

Raymond Jonson, who often referred to his design for this play as his finest achievement, carried a black-and-white idiom into all aspects of the production. Even though the company had come close two years before with *Delphine Declines*, this marked the furthest Browne and Jonson had ever gone in limiting stage color. The dominant element of the set was a black picture frame with a black platform within it. Along with side panels, these elements made up a miniature proscenium frame. Against the black background were white decorations of meager delicacy, capturing the shapes and rhythms of certain Japanese prints. The decorations were as simplified as possible without sacrificing recognizability. Stylized trees, brook, moon, stars, and owl were placed against the black background (photo 4.6).

Only Capulchard had realistic makeup. The Grotesques' faces were chalk white and their hair, eyebrows, eyelashes, nostrils, lips, and fingernails were black; the rest of their bodies were white. Most costumes, including the stockings and clothes were white, with black decorations, while others were black with white trappings.

The decorative features in the set were all minimal and suggestive. For instance, instead of a night full of stars, three, painted close together, were enough. The white trees were thin and bare, with only a white leaf here and a

4.6 Cloyd Head's *Grotesques* (1915), staged by Maurice Browne and designed by Raymond Jonson. Photo courtesy of the Jonson Gallery of the University Art Museum, University of New Mexico.

white branch there. The brook, suggested merely by jagged white and black lines, stretched across the tiny inner stage. The white owl was portrayed with two white circles for eyes and one half of the owl's outline; the audience could fill in the rest. With this incomplete line-drawing of an owl, Browne and Jonson were borrowing from the art of the Japanese screen painter.

Everything in the *mise-en-scène* conspired to flatten out every aspect of the stage picture, except for one—Capulchard. For this production, Browne set up borderlights and footlights for the very reason that he dispensed with them in his other productions—their tendency to eliminate dimensionality and facial detail. Moreover, the lights were left untinted so that the black and white motif could be retained. Dukore explains that light in *Grotesques* was used "not as an active, but as a static element. The effect was not of movement, but of movement constrained."[81]

The color scheme also helped maintain the two-dimensional stage picture. Since no shades of gray were used, there was no molding or highlighting of features to give depth, nor was there perspective to make the spectator's eye move back in space and hence register depth. Moreover, the white chalk on the faces flattened facial features, making the face look two-dimensional.

In terms of movement, the Grotesques, until the end, stayed confined within the three-foot deep picture-frame. Not only did they have to move within constricted space, but also along a horizontal plane; they only moved from side to side, never forward or back. Having learned how to move parallel to the back wall in *Passion Play*, the actors playing the Grotesques were prepared for the extreme "relief" stage within which Capulchard (and Browne) kept them prisoner.

Head also calls for the actors to use pantomime throughout. For instance, the Sprite, one of the Grotesques, at one point does a shadow-dance and the Girl-Motive enters in silence in an exaggerated, idyllic manner. Tietjens astutely remarked how the production presented "almost a pantomime on the surface of which the words float, like corks on a stream."[82]

At various points in the play, Capulard struck characters motionless or rendered them inactive, making them sink down inert. At others, Head called on them to speak in slow, monotonous voices or intone their lines. Capulchard, on the other hand, is written to be outside the play's design and is as active and vocal as the grotesques are inert. His features molded, his costume and makeup realistic, he is allowed to move in and out of the tight proscenium at his own free will (but within Browne's will). He is a three-dimensional creature in a two-dimensional world.

The chalk on the faces of the Grotesques, the footlights, and the black-and-white costumes all conspired to blot out individualizing detail. In *Passion Play* Browne attained stage anonymity through the silhouetting device; in this play, it was done in these other ways. But the effect was the same; people became not so much people as elements in a design.

At the very end of the play, Capulchard first takes down the moon, then the stars, and finally tears away the background, leaving the "stage a void filled by a strange diminishing light... an emptiness in which the Grotesques... move vaguely."[83] Built into the play, then, is a breaking out of two-dimensions into a three-dimensional void—from one kind of simplification to another.

This play is a study in negational elements. The empty space at the end becomes a factor only after the audience has been placed within a world with minimal color, minimal dimensionality, minimal kinetic activity, and minimal sound (or minimally differentiated sound). Silence, stillness, emptiness, colorlessness, and dimensionlessness together create a universe of negative aesthetics. Until Samuel Beckett's first plays, no major Western play would go as far as this in weaving negational elements into the theatrical fabric of a play.

Both in form and content, this play features an exploration of the paradoxes of freedom within constraint, which receives primary attention for most of the play, and slavery in freedom, which surfaces at the end when the Grotesques wander through the void. Thus the production manifests the essential paradox behind the aesthetics of simplicity: the connection between nothingness and infinity.

The last group of productions are those featuring empty space as a predominant part of the visual picture. As already shown, this approach was taken in productions of other categories, such as the light beyond the wall of Troy; the high vertical lines of the panels in *Mrs. Warren's Profession* which made the eye attentive to a large volume of empty space; and the void presented at the end of *Grotesques*.

From their own experimentation, Browne and Jonson discovered how a bit of sky, properly lit, could create a sense of limitless expanse, whereas a larger sky painted always looked painted. In one production, explains a commentator, that patch was no bigger than a dinner plate and yet it created an "amazing illusion of depth."[84] Eloise Ramsey of the Children's Theatre of Detroit observed how, in set after set, Jonson lit a piece of sky "to suggest limitless space" and "miles and miles of depth," so frequently in fact that she concluded that "the note of infinite space [is] as essentially a part of the Jonson setting as is the profuse color a part of the Bakst setting."[85]

Some productions featured empty space as the prominent design element, including an early CLT production of Yeats's *The Shadowy Waters*, in which empty space and a carefully lit cyclorama, together with suggestive properties and scenic pieces, helped convey a ship's desolation in an endless sea and sky— no mean task in the diminutive Little Theater. With the implication of how much was created with so little, the reviewer from the *Chicago Daily Journal* described the setting for the Yeats play: "The edge of a golden sail, a high-lifting prow, the stump of a mast, a low rail—that was all the stage held but the mystery of the sea and the wonder of the darkling air were in the picture."[86]

In the next season, Browne and Jonson did a production of Arkell's

Colombine along similar lines, only this time they attempted to use empty space not as sea and sky, but as a "wild, mysterious, desolate plain," somewhere at "the top of the world." One critic gave this a detailed account of the impression created by the *mise-en-scène*:

> When the curtains of the tiny stage parted, darkness and the very faint outlines of a high place were disclosed in the foreground; in the far background a dull, rose-hued glow. It looked like miles of moorland. As a landscape it was as big as Salisbury plain.[87]

Browne contributed to this feeling of desolation by putting into this rose-hued glow a slender faun piping from the rim of the world at dawn. Browne sustained the sense of endless expanse by having the actors make their entrance onto the stage by crouching down at the back and entering by slowly rising as though their heads were just appearing over the crest, using a technique for which French mime Marcel Marceau has become famous.

Bennett, invoking the less-is-more paradox, twice uses this production to support the contention that New-Stagecraft simplicity is preferrable to naturalistic production techniques:

> he [Browne] proved more in his quiet way with a backdrop and the adroit distribution of light than David Belasco with all his clutter ever proves....As a stage production it was as big in the effect it produced as that vista of English landscape Irving used to fling across the stage in "Becket"....[88]

In the five years that the Chicago Little Theatre existed, Browne and Jonson persisted in finding different ways to simplify their stages. Because of this, Maurice Browne is not only the "father" of the little theater movement, but can also be considered the "father" of the American simplified *mise-en-scène*. And one can count among his progeny directors and designers of other little theaters born in the United States between 1912 and 1918, each making their own individual contributions to a simpler stage.

NOTES

[1] Thomas Dickinson, *The Insurgent Theatre* (New York: B.W. Huebsch, 1917), p. 77.

[2] According to Jonson's brother, C. Raymond Johnson changed his last name from Johnson to Jonson and dropped the C. in 1920. In this book, Jonson's name will be spelled as he later chose, although citations from the time he was working at CLT (1912-1917), which use the other spelling, will not be changed.

[3] Maurice Browne, *Too Late to Lament* (London: Victor Gollancz Ltd., 1955), p.

116.

[4] Ibid., p. 172.

[5] "Chicago's Little Theatre," *Literary Digest*, 47 (August 23, 1913), p. 287.

[6] Bernard F. Dukore, "Maurice Browne and the Chicago Little Theatre," *Theatre Survey*, Vol. 3, 1962, p. 70. Dukore's essay provides an excellent summary of the work of the Chicago Little Theatre, including the acting, directing, and lighting and set design.

[7] Sheldon Cheney, *The Art Theatre* (New York: Alfred A. Knopf, 1917), p. 118.

[8] Browne, *Lament*, p. 166.

[9] Ibid., p. 158.

[10] Maurice Browne, "Lonely Places," *Theatre Arts Magazine*, 5 (July 1921), p. 210.

[11] Browne, *Lament*, p. 168.

[12] Ibid., p. 186.

[13] Ibid., p. 113.

[14] Ibid., p. 114.

[15] Ibid., p. 121.

[16] "Chicago's Little Theater," *Literary Digest*, p. 287.

[17] Maurice Browne, "The New Rhythmic Drama," *The Drama*, 4 (November 1914), p. 629.

[18] Browne, *Lament*, p. 111.

[19] "Plan 'Little Theater'," *Chicago Daily News*, February 25, 1912, p. 15.

[20] "Drama League to Examine Little Theater Exhibit," *The Christian Science Monitor*, April 15, 1916, p. 8.

[21] Eunice Tietjens, "The Work of C. Raymond Johnson," *Theatre Arts Monthly*, 4 (July 1920), p. 229.

[22] "Drama League," p. 8.

[23] Extract from letter by Raymond Jonson, reprinted in *The Drama League Monthly*, 3 (February 1919), p. 8.

[24] "Drama League," p. 8.

[25] O. L. Hall, "Company; Scenic Artist States His Faith; Stage Gossip," *Chicago Daily Journal*, December 15, 1915, n.p.

[26] C. Raymond Johnson, "The New Stage Designing," *Theatre Arts Magazine* (August 1919), p. 121.

[27] Maurice Browne, "The New Rhythmic Drama," *The Drama*, 4 (November 1914), pp. 629-630.

[28] Browne, *Lament*, p. 153.

[29] Ibid., p. 158.

[30] Ibid., p. 154.

[31] Browne, "Rhythmic Drama," p. 152.

[32] Ibid., p. 630.

[33] Dukore, "Maurice Browne and the Chicago Little Theatre," *Theatre Survey*, p. 67.

[34] Browne, "Rhythmic Drama," p. 146.

[35] Ibid., p. 154.

[36] Browne, *Lament*, p. 124.

[37] Maurice Browne, "The Temple of a Living Art," *The Drama*, 3 (November 1913), p. 176.

[38] Browne, "Rhythmic Drama," (February 1915), p. 155.

[39] Craig, *On the Art of the Theatre*, p. 138, and Browne, "Rhythmic Drama," (November 1914), p. 617.

[40] Hiram Moderwell, *The Theatre of To-day* (New York: John Lane Co., 1914), p. 145.

[41] Arthur Krows, *Play Production in America*, p. 163.

[42] Cheney, *The Art Theatre*, p. 119.

[43] Bernard F. Dukore, "Maurice Browne and the Chicago Little Theatre," (Diss., University of Illinois at Urbana-Champaign, 1957), p. 70. Dukore's dissertation contains many useful observations of Browne's productions made by Midwestern critics.

[44] Ibid., p. 56.

[45] Ibid., p. 57.

[46] Ibid., p. 58.

[47] Dukore, "Maurice Browne," *Theatre Survey*, p. 69.

[48] O. L. Hall, "Three Little Plays by Mrs. Havelock Ellis are Staged by Maurice Browne," *Chicago Daily Journal*, February 3, 1915, p. 6.

[49] Maurice Browne, "Lonely Places," *Theatre Arts Magazine*, 5 (July 1921), p. 210.

[50] Arthur Johnson, "The Theatre of Raymond Jonson," p. 6. An unpublished manuscript housed in the Jonson Gallery at the University of New Mexico, Albuquerque.

[51] James O'Donnell Bennett, "Getting at the Meaning of the Experiments of Worthy Amateurs," *The Sunday Record-Herald*, November 17, 1912, Part II, p. 2.

[52] "'Trojan Women' Stirs Large Audience Profoundly," *Indianapolis News*, May 19, 1915, p. 9.

[53] James O'Donnell Bennett, "On a Little Stage Mr. Browne Does Big Work," *The Sunday Record-Herald*, February 2, 1913, Part II, p. 7.

[54] "*Trojan Women*," *Columbus Citizen*, May 11, 1915, in Maurice Browne file, Billy Rose Theatre Collection.

[55] Bennett, "Big Work," p. 7.

[56] Tietjens, "Raymond Johnson," p. 230.

[57] "Large Audience Profoundly," p. 9.

[58] Maurice Browne, "Inspiration and Rhythm 1914-1916," p. 33. Unpublished manuscript in the Maurice Browne/Ellen Van Volkenburg Collection in the Department of Rare Books and Special Collections, Harlan Hatcher Graduate Library, University Library, University of Michigan.

[59] Dukore, "Maurice Browne," (Diss.), p. 80.

[60] Eloise Ramsey, quoted in Arthur Johnson, "Theatre of Raymond Jonson," p. 40.

[61] Quoted in Dukore, "Maurice Browne," (Diss.), p. 94.

[62] Amy Leslie, "The Trojan Women At Little Theater," *The Chicago Daily News*, March 19, 1914, p. 7.

[63] Browne, *Lament*, p. 384.

[64] James O'Donnell Bennett, "Art of Stage Management Versus Millinery," *The*

Sunday Record-Herald, March 22, 1914, Part II, pp. 1-2.

65 Browne, *Lament*, p. 182.

66 "Trojan Women Comes to Columbus," *Columbus Citizen*, May 11, 1915, n.p.

67 Cloyd Head, "The Chicago Little Theatre," *Theatre Arts Magazine*, 1 (May 1917), p. 111.

68 "Chicago Little Theater Works on Unity Basis," *Christian Science Monitor*, November 2, 1915, n.p.

69 Bernard Dukore, "Maurice Browne," (Diss.), p. 74.

70 Dukore, "Maurice Browne," *Theatre Survey*, p. 72.

71 "Chicago's Little Theatre," *Literary Digest*, p. 287.

72 Ibid., p. 287.

73 "News and Gossip of the Theatre," *The Chicago Daily Journal*, May 15, 1913, p. 6.

74 Letter from Maurice Browne to Raymond Jonson, dated November 16, 1916—on file in the Jonson Gallery at the University of New Mexico, Albuquerque.

75 From "Remarks by Raymond Jonson Concerning Some of His Stage Designs," in Arthur Johnson's "The Theatre of Raymond Jonson," p. 24.

76 Dukore, "Maurice Browne," (Diss.), p. 77.

77 Cloyd Head, "The Chicago Little Theatre," p. 116.

78 Quoted in Browne, *Lament*, p. 381.

79 O. L. Hall, "Little Theatre Offers 'Happy Prince' and Biblical Pantomime," *The Chicago Daily Journal*, December 27, 1913, p. 7.

80 Browne, *Lament*, p. 202.

81 Dukore, "Maurice Browne," (Diss.), p. 106.

82 Tietjens, "Forward," vi, quoted in Dukore, "Maurice Browne," (diss.), p. 102.

83 Cloyd Head, *Grotesques*, in *Poetry: A Magazine of Verse*, (October 1916), p. 30.

84 Eunice Tietjens, "The Work of C. Raymond Johnson," p. 229.

85 Untitled manuscript by Eloise Ramsey apparently written in 1918, included in Arthur Johnson's "The Theater of Raymond Jonson," pp. 50 and 51.

86 "News and Gossip of the Theaters," *The Chicago Daily Journal*, May 15, 1913, p. 6.

87 James O'Donnell Bennett, "Pretty Toys at the Little Theater," *The Chicago Record-Herald*, October 23, 1913, p. 6.

88 Ibid., p. 6.

5

Browne's Legacy: Contributions From Other Little Theaters

While Browne's Chicago Little Theatre went further than any other "little theater" in simplifying the *mise-en-scène*, among the many that followed in its wake, several made especially significant contributions.[1] Some of these can be traced directly to the pioneering work of Browne and Jonson; others resulted from the influences all the little theaters shared, primarily from ideas and images of the European New Stagecraft, which, by 1915, were flowing into the United States in a steady stream. Another reason for simpler stages was the fact that financial and logistical constraints were at least as much factors in the productions of the Boston Toy Theatre, the Provincetown Players, and the Arts and Crafts Theatre of Detroit as in those presented at the the Chicago Little Theatre. Certain directors, producers, and designers in these theaters, which were arguably the most visible and influential little theaters outside the Chicago Little Theatre, took the crucial additional step of happily embracing simplification as their *modus operandi*.

THE BOSTON TOY THEATRE

Even though Lyman Gale founded the Boston Toy Theatre eleven months before Browne founded the Chicago Little Theatre, the accomplishments in Chicago surpassed and overshadowed those in Boston. In fact, the evidence seems to indicate that Browne and Jonson's CLT productions had considerably more influence on the older sibling than the other way around. The CLT impressed The Toy Theatre and their audiences when the Chicago company visited the Toy with *Trojan Women* during the CLT's first season (two years before the national tour of that same play as part of the World War I peace effort) and Wilde's *The Happy Prince* during the CLT's second season. Browne notes that Boston audiences hailed his company as "argonauts, crusaders,"[2] but Browne never had the chance to host the Toy in Chicago, so there was no opportunity for a reciprocal reaction.

Like the CLT, the Toy faced harsh material limitations from the start. The founder, Mrs. Lyman Gale, created the original Toy by converting a stable into a theater in the Back Bay section of Boston. Her stage was small but relatively deep: fifteen feet wide and twenty-three feet to the back wall.[3] Seating only a hundred and twenty-seven people, the theater could not generate enough income for elaborate productions, especially since Gale could only get her company of amateurs to perform thirty-two times a year.

Gale and her associates did not view these restraints as detrimental, because they believed that "elaborate staging... is not essential to a satisfactory production of a play...."[4] According to Dickinson, Gale wanted her little theater "to be simple, honest, a return to the rudimentary principles of stage practice."[5] Gale's "back-to-basics" philosophy was an attempt to place emphasis not on superfluities, but where it "belonged": on the acting and the plays themselves.[6]

The simplicity and economy that characterized Toy productions also stemmed from a transcendentalist philosophy similar to the one that captivated Browne. A strain of Emersonian self-reliance and Thoreauvian thrift underscores the company's reason for being, as evident in these words from Lyman Gale: "Toys that people make themselves, toys made of string and wood, and anything that comes to hand, mean more to the children, and are far more valuable, both in educating and amusing their owners, than the finest ready-made toys the shops afford."[7]

Although the Toy was most famous for simplifications in stage design, the role of the director was key in this process. Although there is little mention of that fact, Cheney does note how the the Toy's directors exhibited "reticence of touch" and "concentration of effect."[8]

But the stage simplifier who gave the Toy recognition on a national scale was Gale's chief stage designer, Livingston Platt, who would later go on to become Margaret Anglin's chief designer for her Greek and Shakespeare revivals (see Chapter One). When Lyman Gale hired him, Platt already had toured Belgium and become influenced by the new simplicity appearing on European stages. This experience made him an ideal choice for directing and designing productions on the Toy's diminutive stage.

In the four years of the Toy's life, Platt designed thirty-four plays as well as several dances and pantomimes. Hunter praises Platt for having "worked miracles" on that stage. Writing in 1914, Moderwell was so impressed with Platt's designs that he referred to him as "the most able of the young American designers."[9]

Simplification and suggestion were the prominent qualities in Platt's designs, which matched the traits of the Toy Theatre itself. Like those of the Chicago Little Theatre, the walls in Gale's theater were gray and unadorned, with the stage a basic oblong box at one end. Platt's settings were usually pale monotones, lit by diffused lights.[10] Moderwell characterizes the Platt set as having simple, straight, and uninterrupted lines and masses with flat and "discreet" color schemes. From his "radical methods of simplification and suggestion"[11] and his double role as both director and designer (in the Craig tradition), Platt created *mise-en-scènes* in which he succeeded at "omitting detail except where... specifically demanded."[12] Cheney identifies Platt's chief objective as designer for the Toy: "to build up unobtrusive backgrounds, gaining atmospheric effects by simple suggestion rather than by elaborate detail."[13]

When Platt was brought into the professional theater world, he took with him the lessons of simplification he learned at the Toy. Producer John Craig commissioned him to do sets for two Shakespeare plays, first for *Comedy of Errors* and then for *Julius Caesar* at Boston's Castle Square Theatre during the 1913-1914 season. Many of the typical traits of a Platt design can be seen in this watercolor of a scene from the *Comedy of Errors* production (see photo 1.6 on page 22). The simple, uninterrupted lines and masses and the minimal detail are all evident in this rendering. Cheney praises Platt's clever use of simple combinations of hangings and columns in both of these Shakespearean productions. One member of his *Comedy of Errors* audience was crucial to his career after he left the Toy. As we have already seen, Margaret Anglin was so impressed with Platt's work that she made him her chief designer for her subsequent Greek and Elizabethan revival productions.

After launching Platt, the Toy did not last much longer. It closed in 1916 after moving from its small theater on Lime Street to a medium-size (600 seat) theater in Copley Square. Dickinson interprets the change in theater as symptomatic of change in company attitude. In going from Lime Street to Copley Square, the company went from trying to represent ideals to a "frantic effort to pay the rent."[14] Cheney pins the blame of the Toy's demise on the fact that "its ambitions outgrew its wisdom."[15] But through Livingston Platt, the Toy Theatre contributed significantly to stage simplification in the American theater.

THE PROVINCETOWN PLAYERS

While it is difficult to trace any influence between Lyman Gale and Livingston Platt and the other little theaters, plenty of evidence exists attesting to Browne's influence on the Provincetown Players. In *Too Late to Lament*, Maurice Browne disclaims the distinction of being the "father of the little theater in America," but he does acknowledge paternity in the case of two: the Provincetown Players and the Washington Square Players.[16] Direct lines of influence between Browne's Chicago Little Theatre and the Provincetown Players can easily be identified. Browne was close friends in Chicago with George Cram Cook, the founder and spiritual leader of the Provincetown Players, and Cook frequently attended performances at his friend's theater. C. W. E. Bigsby contends that Maurice Browne's Little Theater also seized the imagination of Cook's wife, playwright Susan Glaspell, when she was in Chicago.[17]

Browne also had strong connections to Floyd Dell, who helped found the Provincetown Players and wrote and directed several of its plays. Moreover, Floyd Dell praised much of the Little Theatre's work in his capacity as reviewer for the *Chicago Evening Post*, a position which he later passed to his friend, George Cram Cook. Bror Nordfeldt, who was with the Players from its inception, was the original designer for Browne's production of *Trojan Women*. Besides helping to convert Lewis Wharf into the Provincetowner's first theater, Nordfeldt also designed a few Provincetown productions—some in Cape Cod, some in New York—and wrote *Joined Together*, produced by the Provincetowners in December 1916. Elaine Hyman (later known as Kirah Markham) was an actress, first with the Chicago Little Theatre and later with the Provincetown Players.[18] Many thinkers and artists who fed the communal spirit of the Players in one way or other—such as Emma Goldman, Francis Buzzell, Florence Kiper Frank, Theodore Dreiser, and Cloyd Head—were first introduced to Cook through Browne in Chicago. With all these ties, Browne surely had a right to identify his dramatic blood in the veins of the Provincetowners.

Some parallels in philosophy and practice between the CLT and Cook's Provincetowners resulted not from direct influence but by exposure to similar models—positive and negative. For example, Cook, Glaspell, Dell, and the most famous Provincetown playwright, Eugene O'Neill, all marveled at the Irish Players when they toured the United States in 1911. In fact, Dell and Glaspell both claim in their autobiographies that there would not have been a Provincetown Players at all if not for the Irish Players.[19] The founders of both companies also reacted negatively to the Broadway productions which, Glaspell complained, "didn't ask much of you," that "having paid for your seat, the thing was all done for you, and your mind came out where it went in, only tireder."[20] These words could just as easily have come from Maurice Browne.

East Asian influences trickled into the Provincetown pool of creative ideas through Floyd Dell. He did a production with New York's Liberal Club in 1913 that planted the seeds of rebellion, which the Provincetowners would later harvest when they moved to New York. Possibly responding directly or indirectly to the *The Yellow Jacket* production the year before, Dell presented a play "in the Chinese manner" without scenery and with a Propertyman who suggested changes in location and moved around what few properties they did have. Dell later praised this production as having a "fine careless rapture" that was subsequently lost after the Liberal Club acquired lots of scenery, costumes, a curtain, and footlights.[21] Dell had learned the lessons of less-is-more through his work with Chinese theater conventions and carried those lessons into his work with the Provincetowners.

Despite the influx of ideas and images of stage simplicity, the Provincetown Players did not go as far in this direction as the Chicago Little Theatre. First, they did not have one stage director for any length of time. Committed to new plays by American playwrights, the Provincetowners had a policy whereby playwrights typically served as their own directors. Since they produced plays by over forty-seven different authors—each with his own style and approach—a wide variety of *mise-en-scènes* were displayed. Second, their spiritual leader, George Cram Cook, nurtured the ideal of collective creation under the supervision of the playwright. It is more difficult to maintain a single vision of simplicity in all aspects of production when many imaginations are involved in a project, although the Chicago Little Theatre did accomplish this with their *Passion Play* silhouette production. And third, Cook imbued the company with two other ideals in conflict with stage simplicity: spontaneity and Dionysian intoxication and abandon which would more likely lead to aesthetic abandon and indulgence than aesthetic restraint.

But Cook did bring to the Provincetown Players certain tendencies that would lead them toward stage simplification. Born into a wealthy Iowa family, Cook turned his back on his family's fortune to become a subsistence farmer. By so doing, he was proving himself to be what Bigsby called a "Midwestern Thoreau."[22] Susan Glaspell lends credence to this image by explaining that she and Cook were labeled radical bohemians but were actually "particularly simple people... needing each other as protection against complexities," with "an instinct for the old, old things, to have a garden, and neighbors, to keep up the fire and let the cat in at night."[23]

Accordingly, the principles of stage simplification guided the minds of the company's founders from the beginning, as evidenced by their statement of purpose which accompanied the announcement of their first New York season: "to afford an opportunity for actors, producers, scenic and costume designers to experiment with a stage of extremely simple resources—it being the idea of the

Players that elaborate settings are unnecessary to bring out the essential qualities of a good play."[24] Unlike the Chicago Little Theatre, the emphasis was on plays, not the *mise-en-scène*. Still, the intent was clear: Production factors should be kept auxiliary, so that focus remains on the literary qualities of a given work.

Susan Glaspell, in *The Road to the Temple*, discusses Cook's commitment to stage simplification. She describes her husband's desire to keep sets minimal: "He liked to remember *The Knight and the Burning Pestle* they gave at Leland Stanford, where a book could indicate one house and a bottle another. Sometimes the audience liked to make its own set."[25]

Practical considerations reinforced their commitment to simplifying stage production. The two principal theaters in which they performed had small stages and hence imposed severe limitations on what the creators could do. With the Lewis Wharf Theatre in Provincetown, the artists were confined by a ten-by-twelve foot stage; in their first Macdougal Street theater in New York, they had a stage measuring fourteen-by-ten-and-a-half feet with virtually no space for shifting scenery; and in their second New York theater, they had a proscenium twenty-six-feet wide, but with insufficient depth for flexibility. And these limitations were a source of pride for the Provincetowners. Deutsch and Hanau discuss how Cook's group, throughout the life of their company, "made a virtue of the simplicity which the limited area and proscenium height imposed upon them."[26]

The financial support for the theater, both in Provincetown and New York, was very limited, and thus the financial health of the theater—except when the Stage Society of New York had all its members buy subscription tickets—was usually very poor. Production costs always had to be kept down. The most expensive production at the Wharf Theater cost only thirteen dollars; playwright Alfred Kreymborg put up his play *Lima Beans* (1916) for a mere $2.31.[27]

The combination of small stages, limited budgets, and the realistic style in which most of the plays were written, encouraged productions that were generally in the manner of simplified realism. Some individual productions went further than others in production simplicity. Among the sets employing some kind of simplified realism were those for O'Neill plays such as *Thirst* (1916), *Fog* (1917), and *The Long Voyage Home* (1917) as well as Susan Glaspell's *Trifles* (1916) and *Bernice* (1919).[28]

The Provincetowners often used light to depersonalize the human figure, although never to the extreme of some of their little theater colleagues. In Steele's *Contemporaries* (1915) at the Lewis Wharf Theatre, the action began on a stage dark but for indirect candlelight, which, according to Robert Sarlos, was "apparently rendered by the ocean's reflected light through the open roll-away door of the fishhouse."[29] Most of the play was performed in this negligible

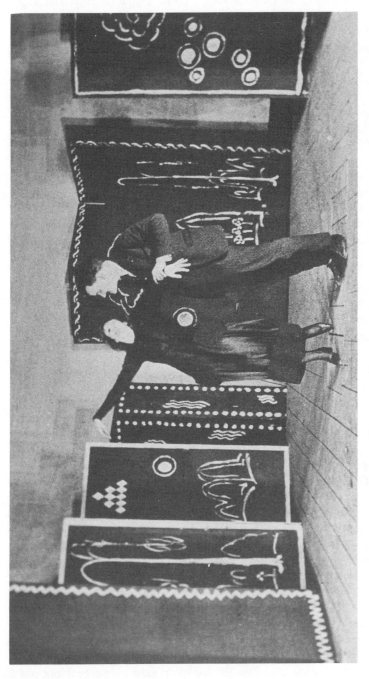

5.1 Settings for *Aria da Capo* by Edna St. Vincent Millay. Actors Norma Millay and Harrison Dowd in rehearsal without costumes or sets in place. Reprinted with permission of Macmillan Publishing Company from *The Provincetown: A Story of the Theatre* by Helen Deutsch and Stella Bloch Hanau. Copyright 1931 H. Deutsch and Stella Hanau; copyright renewed 1959 Helen Deutsch and Stella Hanau. (Reissued by Russell & Russell Publishers, New York, 1972).

light, with the identity of the characters and their location a mystery. The stage became light only at the end, revealing the characters in Roman costumes and their location as Jerusalem. James Oppenheim's *Night* (1917) used light and settings to deliteralize the stage. The set consisted merely of an unspecified simple mound and the suggestion of a hilltop, while lights were used to erase the features of the actors, who were presented in silhouette before a lighted blue screen. The first part of Wallace Stevens's *Three Travelers Watch a Sunrise* (1920) was presented entirely in shadow play; the play ended with a sunrise in which one then saw colorful costumes in the brightening light.[30]

Even in these cases, the Provincetown Players did not seem to carry stage simplification as far as their counterparts in Chicago. This led to frustration for participants like Floyd Dell who came into their own aesthetic consciousness under the influence of the Chicago Little Theatre. The following comment by Dell on the Players' production of his own *Sweet and Twenty* (1918), for instance, simultaneously reveals the simplicity employed in his production, how it is representative of Dell's own aesthetic preferences, and his discontent with the typical Provincetown *mise-en-scène*:

> A single cherry-bough with blossoms painted on a flat blue-green backdrop, with the same branch repeated on the two blue-green screens that masked the sides of the scene, composed the cherry-orchard, in the center of which there was a bench; its simplicity, after the incredible fussiness into which the Provincetown Players had descended, made it very beautiful indeed.[31]

The Provincetowners, like the Chicago Little Theatre, also experimented with black-and-white design motifs. For Edna St. Vincent Millay's *Aria da Capo* (1919), the group employed settings consisting of black screens (some six feet high, others ten feet high) with white borders and white quasi-abstract decorations painted on them (photo 5.1), and no more than a small table and chairs with thin legs and high narrow backs—as called for in Millay's stage directions. The black-and-white screens were similar to, but more elaborately decorative than, the white-on-black backdrop in Browne's production of *Grotesques* at the Chicago Little Theatre. The costumes for *Aria da Capo*, however, were not in black and white as were those for *Grotesques*; instead, the costumes were brightly colored in the Commedia dell' Arte tradition, from which the Millay piece draws heavily.

The Players also revived Cloyd Head's *Grotesques* (1921). They used the black-and-white motif that the playwright designates for both sets and costumes and placed the action on a shallow relief stage. One can see the difference between the more extreme simplicity of productions at the Chicago Little Theatre and those of the Provincetown Players merely by looking at the two designs of this same play. The flats and backdrop used by the Provincetown

5.2 Cloyd Head's *Grotesques*, performed by the Provincetown Players, 1921. Reprinted with permission of Macmillan Publishing Company from *The Provincetown: A Story of the Theatre* by Helen Deutsch and Stella Bloch Hanau. Copyright 1931 H. Deutsch and Stella Hanau; copyright renewed 1959 Helen Deutsch and Stella Hanau. (Reissued by Russell & Russell Publishers, New York, 1972).

Players were busier and more detailed than the more essentialized one in the Chicago production (compare photo 5.2 with photo 4.6 on page 100).

5.3 Chain-gang episode (scene four) from Eugene O'Neill's *The Emperor Jones* (1920), directed by George Cram Cook and designed by Cleon Throckmorton. Photo courtesy of the Billy Rose Theatre Collection, The New York Public Library at Lincoln Center, Astor, Lenox, and Tilden Foundations.

   While the Provincetowners demonstrated their willingness to experiment with shallow stages and relief blocking in productions like *Grotesques*, they more often went in the opposite direction of a simple stage: toward an exploration of a sense of spaciousness on their small stages. When they did O'Neill's *The Fog* (1917), for instance, the post-impressionist painter Nordfeldt tried to create the illusion of a "broad expanse of sea."[32] Apparently more successful was the deep blue light on the backdrop for Oppenheim's *Night*. Rebecca Drucker's review in the *New York Tribune* cites how "The effect of depth and of expanse is finely attained on the tiny stage."[33]
   But the Provincetowners did not yet have a designer committed to space-stage aesthetics, despite the occasional appearance of this kind of image. The

breakthrough occurred in 1920 when Jig Cook took on the role of director for O'Neill's *The Emperor Jones* and decided that the play could not be done without a permanent concrete-and-iron dome (modeled after the German *kuppelhorizont*). By creating a permanent cyclorama designed as a constant curve in every direction, Cook wanted to fulfill his "vision of pure space on a tiny stage," and create "the effect of infinite and intangible distance,"[34] or, as Sarlos explains it, "nothing... but infinity and the stage."[35] At first it seemed that this feature was destined to become just another of Cook's unrealized dreams. Charles Ellis, the original designer, could not utilize the newly installed feature. After the O'Neill play opened, Cook replaced Ellis with Cleon Throckmorton, who managed to make "a virtue of the simplicity which the limited area and proscenium height imposed."[36]

5.4 Scene seven. Jones in foreground with witch doctor and crocodile in background. *The Emperor Jones* by O'Neill (1920). Directed by George Cram Cook and designed by Cleon Throckmorton. Photo courtesy of the Billy Rose Theatre Collection, The New York Public Library at Lincoln Center, Astor, Lenox, and Tilden Foundations.

Throckmorton's setting was one of the most spectacular yet one of the simplest settings presented on the Provincetown stage. The forest scenes were depicted through silhouetted drops and hanging canvas tree forms, against the dome where, as Glaspell quotes Cook, "ten feet can give you infinity."[37] Among the most memorable sequences in the production were two scenes performed in partial silhouette, with strong back- and side-lighting—Scene Four in which Emperor Jones, fleeing through the forest, relives his experience on a chain gang (photo 5.3) and Scene Seven, in which Emperor Jones confronts a witch doctor and crocodile, personifications of his own primordial fears (photo 5.4). As the photographs indicate, Throckmorton erased detail, transforming people and objects into deliteralized shapes of the unconscious. The dome allowed these images to stand out against a background suggesting great expanse.

Other aspects of *The Emperor Jones* script and production contributed to an impression of singleness and sameness. Ronald Wainscott points out the "relentless focus on a single character... a virtual mono-performance,"[38] which invites comparison with O'Neill's *Before Breakfast* (1916). And whereas the acting of Charles Gilpin as Jones was in no way simplified (in fact, it was noteworthy for his vicissitudinal emotional display and fully individualized characterization), O'Neill's script led director Jig Cook to treat many of the other characters, especially the figures from Jones's memory/imagination, as dumb-show silhouettes, automatons, hazy unindividualized figures, and multiple characters that moved and looked alike.

In general, the acting at the Provincetown Playhouse was stylistically as diverse as the plays themselves. Without one consistent director and with Cook's own eclectic proclivities, the company did not develop a unified acting style. Since most of the plays were realistic and the sets had to be simplified due to space and budget restrictions, most of the acting tended toward a modified, simplified realism. But some individuals, on their own, went further toward simplicity. When Jacques Copeau went to visit the Provincetown company, he was especially impressed with Susan Glaspell. Robert Sarlos describes how Copeau marvelled at "'the simplicity of her presence'."[39]

Many of the plays chosen for production by the Provincetown Players call for a simpler stage than that dictated by the current fashion. Like most little theaters, they preferred one-act to full-length productions. In fact, all but a handful of the almost one hundred plays presented by the Players from 1915 to 1922 were one-act plays. Some of the plays manifested special additional constraints. Eugene O'Neill's *Before Breakfast* (1916) can be viewed as an experiment in certain aspects of stage simplification. O'Neill wrote it under the influence of August Strindberg's *The Stronger*, written to be performed in the Intimate Theatre in Stockholm. In Strindberg's very short play, Mrs. X comes to the realization that Miss Y has been having an affair with her husband, but this is accomplished by the self-imposed constraint of having Miss Y never speak.

O'Neill takes the decision to keep one character silent one step further and has a wife tormenting a husband who not only never speaks, but is also placed offstage. His arm reaches on the stage once, but that is nearly our only acquaintance with the husband whose suicide closes the piece. This play—along with the prototype by Strindberg—prefigures an extreme simplicity later to be seen in the works of Samuel Beckett.

Before Breakfast did not simplify all aspects of the *mise-en-scène*. Just as *The Stronger* calls for a realistically rendered ladies' café, the stage directions for *Before Breakfast* ask for all the paraphernalia of a realistic kitchen setting. But it was paired with *Lima Beans*, the Kreymborg piece with a $2.31 set and characters acting, moving, and speaking like puppets. The two plays on this third bill of the 1916-1917 season offered a common style around self-imposed limitation.

Obviously, the kind of concentration and simplification in these two productions was not necessarily typical for the Provincetowners. But certain kinds of concentration were regular features, necessitated by the austere budgets within which they had to function. The company regularly did plays with two and three characters, and each actor would often play two or three roles in pieces with many characters. Generally, the shortest, most concentrated works were those submitted by the company's poets: Alfred Kreymborg, Edna St. Vincent Millay, and William Zorach. As poets of a modernist sensibility, these three writers were accustomed to thinking in less-is-more terms. They were drawn to theatrical forms of expression like pantomime, puppet work, and mono- and duologues. In their interest in these non-realistic artforms, they were at odds with the Provincetown established aesthetic. The three dramatists soon found themselves a dissenting minority amid the Provincetowners.

After a while, their differences prompted them to rebel and form their own little company. Even though their company—called the Other Players— produced only one bill, they tried to carry their aesthetic further than they could with the Provincetown Players. They simplified to a much greater degree than the typical products of their mother company, especially in the acting and directing. Their four pieces, presented at the Playwright's Theatre between the fifth and sixth bills in the 1917-1918 season, were short, aesthetically economic, and called for a performance style requiring physical and vocal restraint.

The Other Players' opening piece, *Manikin and Minikin* by Kreymborg, was described by its author as a static "duologue in Bisque." The characters were two bisques by a fireplace who spoke in puppet fashion and never moved. An ancient clock's metronomic ticking accompanied their interactions. One reviewer commented on the actors' use of monotonous chattering, giving evidence that variety in speech and movement was put aside in favor of stillness, stiffness, and repetitiveness.

The second piece on the bill was a dance form distinctive for another kind of self-imposed limitation. Rihani described it in a letter to Robert Sarlos:

I can't remember who invented the name of "static dances," possibly I did.... I never moved from one spot, all the movement was for the head, torso, arms and hands, as in certain Persian dances. In one dance, the Sphynx, I started standing and finished on the floor in the attitude of the title. At other times I began on the floor and rose to my knees or to my feet.[40]

Some dances also occurred with Rihani squatting on a couch, as pointed out by a critic from the *Theatre Magazine*. The same reviewer also noted how Rihani, in her short piece called *The Slave*, turned "divan-posturing to a fine art."[41]

Next on the bill was Millay's *Two Slatterns and a King*, followed by Kreymborg's playlet *Jack's House*. Both pieces were very short. In Sarlos's *Jig Cook and the Provincetowners*, Millay describes her piece as "very light and slender,"[42] and how the character, Chance, intones the Prologue. For the second piece, Rihani performed much of the role of Jack in pantomime, with Millay playing Jack's wife. In Kreymborg's autobiography, the two characters are described as having looked and acted like puppets, Jack's gestures characterized as large, dreamy, *legato*, and kept to a bare minimum.[43]

In their one and only bill, the Other Players applied extreme simplification to almost every aspect of every piece. They did not, however, have the opportunity to develop further their aesthetic of simplicity beyond this first performance series. They were not well-received; perhaps audiences were not yet ready for so radical a simplification.

THE ARTS AND CRAFTS THEATRE OF DETROIT

When one looks at the major contributions of little-theater directors and designers to simplifying the *mise-en-scène*, one cannot overestimate the importance of Samuel Hume and his Arts and Crafts Theatre of Detroit (1916-1918). As producer, director, set, lighting, and costume designer, and sometime actor, Hume was in the position to carry simplification into all aspects of production. Hume embodied Craig's ideal of the omnipotent artist/director. He also shared Craig's interest in simplified imagery and economic use of few stage elements.

More than any other American director and designer, Hume was the direct recipient of Craig's doctrine. As the only American designer to apprentice with Craig, he had a first-row view of the master's ideas and their applications. He worked under Craig between 1908 and 1912 and was involved in many of Craig's most influential projects. For instance, Hume reputedly constructed for Craig the models for Yeats's screen set at the Abbey Theatre in 1910 and for the Moscow Art Theatre's famous *Hamlet* production in 1911. From these and other experiences, Hume learned the value of economy and the potential for atmospheric variety by rearranging into different mass relationships the same few monochromatic, neutral-toned scenic elements.

His philosophy of suggestion echoes Craig's. Like Craig, he rejected the premises behind literalism, arguing that "Illusion is a thing of the imagination and can be achieved only by suggestion, never by statement."[44] Hume's philosophy—at least the one expounded early in his career—also parallels Craig's in supporting severe simpification. Dickinson explains how Hume "holds strictly to the idea of the reduction of factors to their simplest terms."[45] Moderwell admires Hume for his ability to get "the most nicely... adjusted effect with the simplest means,"[46] and Bolin points out that Hume and Craig both had a taste for the austere and the high vertical line.[47]

There are several places of intersection between Hume's career and the Chicago Little Theatre. Although Browne does not list Hume as one of the direct heirs to his aesthetic, there is no doubt that they knew each other's work. In his autobiography Browne comments that Hume "began to dream dreams akin to ours and gave us courage."[48] Like Lyman Gale, Hume invited Browne and the Chicago Little Theatre to perform at his own theater. This enabled Hume's company to learn from a group that had already ventured where they wanted to go. Hume had been a strong advocate of Browne's work years before Browne's Detroit visit; Hume had included Raymond Jonson's CLT designs in his celebrated New Stagecraft Exhibition.

If Hume had never been hired by the Arts and Crafts Theatre of Detroit, his contribution to stage simplification in the United States would still be significant based on this Exhibition and its extensive dissemination of the ideas and images of stage simplicity. Hume's New Stagecraft Exhibition began in Cambridge and then traveled to New York, Chicago, and Detroit between October 1914 and May 1915. The Exhibition presented to the theater community the designs and production ideas not only of European designers and directors like Craig, Reinhardt, and Bakst, but also the earliest American proponents of a simplified stage. The earliest designs of Raymond Jonson, Livingston Platt, Robert Edmond Jones, and Hume himself were seen and praised throughout the theater community, receiving attention from several national magazines and many local newspapers.

The power of stage simplicity was one of the overriding themes of this influential exhibition and, in supporting this theme, he drew not only from the European New Stagecraft and the modern American simple stage, but also from past conventions as well. In New York, for instance, he added to his exhibition models of the Hearst Greek Theater in Berkeley and the traditional neutral stage of Peking Opera.[49]

Hume also displayed technical advances that could help directors and designers achieve a sense of limitless depth. In New York, with the help of Robert Edmond Jones, Hume demonstrated the skydome wherein a quarter-sphere of concrete at the back of stage, serving as a reflector of light, creates—as one observer noted—"a sense of distance and of a horizon infinitely remote and serene."[50] The Neighborhood Playhouse, the Provincetown Players, and Hume's own Arts and Crafts Theatre of Detroit adapted this idea to fit their own intimate theaters.

Among the scholar/critics who attended this exhibition were Hiram Moderwell, Sheldon Cheney, and Kenneth Macgowan and they, in turn, used it as a basis for their theoretical conclusions about the new aesthetic that was taking over the American stage. Macgowan saw the exhibition first in Boston, then in New York. He noticed Craig's "gray masses" there but was more impressed with two of Hume's models of unit settings, which "utilized tall pillars of white, with dark hangings—for all the infinite moods of poetic drama, from an open palace courtyard to a delicately shaded bedroom, this with a mere shifting of the same pillars."[51]

A reporter for the *Christian Science Monitor* also recognized the positive attributes of Hume's first steps toward an adaptable setting, although he was not yet able to distinguish between Craig's and Hume's contributions to the idea:

> Mr. Hume has two models showing the flexibility of the Craig system of stage settings founded on the use of folding screens and in built-up units. Until these elements have been pointed out, it is quite impossible to identify the same materials in the two studies for poetic drama.[52]

What both of these commentators were noticing was the beginning of Hume's idea for a unit setting that would reach its final form two years later in Detroit. Unquestionably the primary source of this scheme derives from Edward Gordon Craig. But Hume's method for adaptable scenery did not just transplant Craig's ideas into American soil unaltered. He was skeptical about some aspects of Craig's screens. By nature more practically inclined than his mentor, Hume devised screens that were more easily adjustable than Craig's unwieldy creations. He rejected Craig's mobile, freestanding screens, preferring his own adaptation of the same basic idea.[53]

Hume, who was hired to run the Arts and Crafts Theatre of Detroit in part due to the success of the Exhibition, had the chance to try out his scheme and prove its efficacy. Not only did it work, but the idea spread rapidly. Hume's adaptable settings caught the attention of Sheldon Cheney, the editor of a newly formed journal based in Detroit. Through publication in the *Theatre Arts Magazine*, Hume's plan had almost immediate and repeated exposure in the theater world. Hume's scheme, designed for permanently based companies, answered the needs of most theaters, especially academic and community theaters. Consequently, as Cheney reports, "Hume's adaptable setting was copied on stages all over the country."[54]

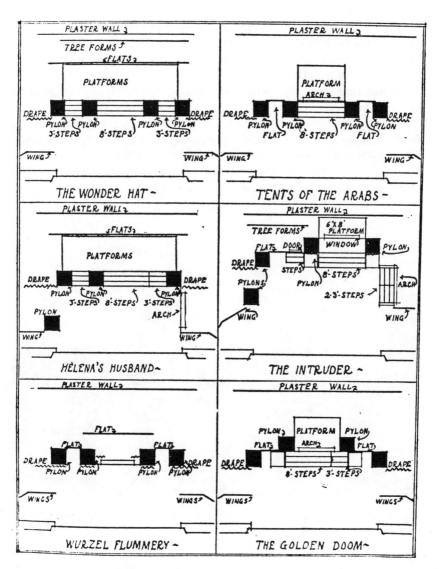

5.5 Diagram of six arrangements for Sam Hume's adaptable settings at the Arts and Crafts Theatre of Detroit—1916-1917.

Hume implemented his scheme for purposes of both financial and aesthetic economy. He achieved both ends. The great majority of the nearly fifty works (mostly one-acts) were presented out of combinations of the same relatively few scenic elements. And Hume therefore was able to keep his costs down. The figures tell all. Where the average cost of one Hume production was $800, the average cost for a Washington Square Players' production was around $1500. The Arts and Crafts Theatre was one of the few little theaters to emerge from its first season with a profit.

In his first season in Detroit, Hume produced nineteen plays requiring twenty scenes, eleven of which were done with only minor rearrangements of the same scenic units. One of Hume's great admirers, Sheldon Cheney, described the wide range of locales achieved principally from the modular pieces used during Hume's first season: "the interior of a medieval chateau for *The Intruder*, the Gates of Thalanna for *The Tents of the Arabs*, the wall of Heaven for *The Glittering Gate*, and a Spartan palace for *Helena's Husband*."[55]

5.6 *The Wonder Hat*, presented in 1916 at the Arts and Crafts Theatre of Detroit. Directed and designed by Sam Hume.

To create these and many other settings, Hume used different combinations of the following units: four eighteen-foot pylons (made of canvas stretched on wood frames); two canvas flats; three step-units (two short and one long); three platforms of the same height but differing lengths; dark green hangings the length of the pylons; two folding screens used for masking and covered with cloth which matched the hangings as high as the pylons; and two irregular freestanding shapes resembling trees.[56] Many productions were done with only these units; for others, Hume added a window, arch, decorative frame, or other elements demanded by the specific play's action. For example, whereas nothing new was added to *The Wonder Hat* to create the setting for *Tents of the Arabs*, *Helena's Husband* required the addition of two decorated curtains and *Abraham and Isaac* called for a large Gothic window piece.

Hume's diagram for six arrangements of the same step units, flats, and pylons, reproduced in the book *Theater and School*, show some of the ways he applied his economic system at the Arts and Crafts Theatre (photo 5.5). A similar diagram circulated widely around the theater community since it was displayed in one of the earliest issues of *Theatre Arts Magazine*. Photographs of some of the productions presented in the two seasons in Detroit reveal the enormous variety in mood and location that Hume achieved with neutral units and the addition of only a few suggestive properties (photos 5.6 to 5.9).

5.7 Lord Dunsany's *Tents of the Arabs* (1916), directed and designed by Sam Hume for the Arts and Crafts Theatre of Detroit.

5.8 *The Doorway*, directed and designed by Sam Hume of the Arts and Crafts Theatre of Detroit.

5.9 *Dr. Faustus* by Christopher Marlowe, adapted by Samuel Elliot, directed and designed by Sam Hume at the Arts and Crafts Theatre of Detroit (1917).

Among the almost fifty productions presented with Hume's adaptable settings, some were simpler than others. Hume was not afraid to add color, and sometimes his costumes and lighting effects became very complex and detailed. With other sets, he added so many decorative curtains and furniture that simplicity and economy were sacrificed in favor of visual variety. But still the overall scheme epitomizes the principle of aesthetic economy, and enough of the particular settings showed sufficient restraint to prompt Allard to label Hume's settings as "unusually subdued."[57]

Besides the overall idea, there were several productions during the two seasons which can be seen as high points from the perspective of stage simplicity. The simplest, most basic arrangement of pylons, step units, and platforms was used for *The Wonder Hat* (photo 5.6). In *A Doctor in Spite of*

Himself, Hume utilized only curtains. He threw strong emphasis on the high vertical lines in the *Tents of the Arabs* set, juxtaposing them with the loosely cloaked, dwarfed figures of the characters below (photo 5.7). He focused attention on the eighteen-foot pylons and draperies in some of the other sets, especially the austere setting for *The Doorway* (photo 5.8). With *The Chinese Lantern*, Hume borrowed both simplified and decorative qualities from the traditional Chinese theater. On one hand, he put together a shallow relief stage, spare translucent screens (backlit at times to produce two-dimensional outlines), and actors' movements reduced to those of shadow puppets and, on the other, highly decorative costumes, a vivid red and green set, and a rectangular red-orange frame bearing Chinese characters. For *Dr. Faustus*, Hume again emphasized the high vertical lines through his lighting (photo 5.9), but an overall feeling of simplicity was facilitated by Samuel Eliot's highly condensed version of the Marlowe text. Besides extensively cutting, Eliot reworked the play so that the action took place entirely in and around Faustus's study. While not a blatantly simplified *mise-en-scène*, Eliot's *Dr. Faustus* is simple relative to how Marlowe's plays would generally be performed in the first decades of the twentieth century.

Hume's system of lighting added to the attributes of the settings to allow for different types of simplified *mise-en-scènes*. The Arts and Crafts Theatre built for Hume a plaster back wall, which enabled him to create that sense of infinite space. Although not visible in all productions and not always lit for spaciousness even when it was visible, the plaster wall often created an aura of vast emptiness within which people and objects seemed small and isolated. Since the Arts and Crafts Theatre was also equipped with footlights, Hume also could go in another direction of simplicity and flatten out the features of the actors or the scenic elements if he wanted instead a shallow, two-dimensional stage, as he did with *The Chinese Lantern.*

Surely Hume's directorial style and his actors' movement contributed to the overall feeling of a simple stage at the Arts and Crafts Theatre. Unfortunately, we have few records of the acting and directing at Hume's theater. Cheney indirectly gives us some indication that Hume's directing matched the simplification of the settings: "He... helped to develop, by individual training, every actor. And he rehearsed every play, looking after all those matters of movement, gesture and coordination of action which, while not noticeable to the audience, are important aids to synthetic effect."[58] If Hume was coordinating the movement and gesture and creating a synthesis with the highly simplified settings, then we can only surmise that the acting style and the blocking were as simplified and restrained as the settings.

After finishing his tenure at the Arts and Crafts Theatre, Hume went on to direct and design all over the United States. Through his book *Theater and School* and his national circuit of lectures, Hume's ideas for adaptable settings were disseminated throughout the country. He did not, however, make major contributions to the professional theater, except through his work at the Arts and Crafts Theatre and his New Stagecraft Exhibition.

One of the key—albeit indirect—ways the Exhibition contributed to the development of the simple stage was by bringing Robert Edmond Jones to the attention of the New York Stage Society which, indirectly, gave Jones the break he needed to enter into the mainstream professional theater. It was Jones who led in taking stage simplification into this larger, more visible arena.

NOTES

[1] To detail all the important little theaters that effectively utilized simplified means in productions would go beyond the scope of this book. Some other companies that made significant contributions not fully covered in this study are: the Washington Square Players (especially the designs of Rollo Peters), the Portmanteau Players (Stuart Walker, the Artistic Director, devised an ingeniously economic and attractive unit setting for his company's tours), and the Neighborhood Playhouse. For information on the work of these companies, see Constance Mackay's *The Little Theatre in the United States*.

[2] Maurice Browne, *Too Late to Lament*, p. 130.

[3] Homer Howard, "The Toy Theatre of Boston," *The Drama*, 4 (May 1914), p. 266.

[4] Ibid., p. 267.

[5] Dickinson, *The Insurgent Theatre*, pp. 133-134.

[6] Ibid., p. 268.

[7] Quoted in Lauriston Bullard, "Boston's Toy Theatre," *The Theatre*, 15 (March 1912), p. 84.

[8] Cheney, *The New Movement*, p. 169.

[9] Moderwell, *Theatre of To-day*, p. 140.

[10] Krows, *Play Production in America*, pp. 183-184.

[11] Moderwell, *To-day*, p. 189.

[12] Ibid., p. 139.

[13] Cheney, *The New Movement*, p. 168.

[14] Dickinson, *Insurgent Theatre*, p. 138.

[15] Cheney, *The Art Theatre* (New York: Alfred A. Knopf, 1917), p. 65.

[16] Browne, *Lament*, p. 200.

[17] C. W. E. Bigsby, ed., *Plays by Susan Glaspell* (New York: Cambridge University Press, 1987), p. 5.

[18] Robert Sarlos, *Jig Cook and the Provincetowners: Theatre in Ferment* (Boston: University of Massachusetts Press, 1982), p. 10.

[19] Floyd Dell, *Homecoming* (New York: Farrar and Rinehart, 1933), p. 208, and Susan Glaspell, *The Road to the Temple* (New York: Frederick A. Stokes, 1927), p. 218.

[20] Glaspell, *The Road to the Temple*, p. 248.

[21] Sarlos, *Jig Cook*, pp. 11-12.

[22] Bigsby, *Susan Glaspell*, p. 3.

[23] Susan Glaspell, *Temple*, p. 235.

[24] Oliver Sayler, *Our American Theatre* (New York: Brentano's, 1923), p. 91.

25 Glaspell, *Temple*, p. 255.

26 Helen Deutsch and Stella Hanau, *The Provincetown: A Story of the Theatre* (New York: Farrar & Rinehart, 1931), p. 62.

27 Deutsch, *The Provincetown*, p. 31.

28 Sarlos, *Jig Cook, passim.*

29 Ibid., p. 19.

30 Ibid., pp. 114-115.

31 Floyd Dell, *Homecoming*, p. 299, as quoted in Sarlos, *Jig Cook*, p. 86.

32 Constance D'arcy MacKay, *The Little Theater in the United States* (New York: Henry Holt & Co., 1917), p. 53.

33 Rebecca Drucker, *New York Tribune*, quoted in William Vilhauer, "A History and Evaluation of the Provincetown Players,"(Diss., U. of Iowa, 1965), p. 280.

34 Sheldon Cheney, *The New Movement*, p. 133.

35 Sarlos, *Jig Cook*, p. 123.

36 Deutsch, *The Provincetown*, p. 62.

37 Glaspell, *The Road to the Temple*, p. 290.

38 Ronald Wainscott, *Staging O'Neill: The Experimental Years, 1920- 1934* (New Haven: Yale University Press, 1988), p. 44.

39 Sarlos, *Jig Cook*, p. 49.

40 Sarlos, *Jig Cook*, pp. 88-89. Sarlos, in general, gives a vivid account of the short-lived Other Players.

41 "The Other Players," *Theatre Magazine*, 27 (May 1918), p. 288.

42 Sarlos, *Jig Cook*, p. 89.

43 Alfred Kreymborg, *Troubadour, An Autobiography* (New York: Boni and Liveright, 1925), p. 316, as quoted in Sarlos, *Jig Cook*, p. 89.

44 Sam Hume, "The Use and Abuse of the Greek Theatre," *Sunset*, 29 (August 1912), p. 203.

45 Dickinson, *The Insurgent Theatre*, p. 203.

46 Moderwell, *To-day*, p. 144.

47 John Seelye Bolin, "Samuel Hume: Artist and Exponent of the American Art Theatre," (Diss., University of Michigan, 1970), p. 183.

48 Browne, *Lament*, p. 131.

49 John Seelye Bolin, "Samuel Hume," p. 69.

50 *New York Times*, November 10, 1914, p. 11, in Bolin, p. 70.

51 Kenneth Macgowan, "America's First Exhibition of the New Stagecraft," *The Theatre*, 21 (January 1915), p. 28.

52 *The Christian Science Monitor*, October 6, 1914, n. p., quoted in Bolin, "Hume," p. 66.

53 Bolin, "Samuel Hume," p. 51.

54 Cheney, *The Art Theatre*, p. 125.

55 Sheldon Cheney, "Sam Hume's Adaptable Settings," *Theatre Arts Magazine*, 1 (May 1917), p. 120.

56 Ibid., p. 120.

[57] Stephen Allard, "The Art Societies and Theatre Art," *Theatre Arts Magazine*, 1 (February 1917), p. 31.

[58] Cheney, *The Art Theatre*, p. 123.

6

Robert Edmond Jones
and Arthur Hopkins

Director Arthur Hopkins and designer Robert Edmond Jones collaborated in bringing the simple stage not only to the mainstream professional theater, but also to Broadway, where they presented an alternative to conventional stage decoration. Their most influential collaborations occurred between 1915, when they joined forces to do Edith Ellis's stage adaptation of *The Devil's Garden*, and 1922, the year of their legendary *Hamlet* production with John Barrymore playing the title role.

Examining Jones's design work from the earliest years of his career to the end of 1915 reveals how much he was already influenced by the European New Stagecraft movement, even before meeting Hopkins. Jones's first acquaintance with the principles of stage simplification came when he read Edward Gordon Craig's *On the Art of the Theatre* while at Harvard. He graduated in 1910, but stayed on another two years as an art instructor. During that time, he had the opportunity to witness the first American tour of the Irish Players. Describing one of their *mise-en-scènes* in *The Dramatic Imagination*, Jones underlines the importance this first experience with a severely simplified realism was to his artistic sensibilities:

The setting was very simple....Neutral-tinted walls, a fireplace, a

door, a window, a table, a few chairs, the red homespun skirts and
bare feet of the peasant girls. A fisher's net, perhaps. Nothing
more. But through the little window at the back one saw a sky of
enchantment. All the poetry of Ireland shone in that little square
of light, moody, haunting, full of dreams, calling us to follow on,
follow on....By this one gesture of excelling simplicity the setting
was enlarged into the region of great theatre art.[1]

Jones saw that set in 1911. He left Cambridge the next year, worked as a
costume designer in New York City, and then traveled to Europe to experience
the New Stagecraft firsthand. In the summer of 1913, he went to Florence to try
to study with Craig. When he was denied an audience, Jones went instead to the
Deutsches Theatre in Berlin and served as a kind of apprentice under Max
Reinhardt and his designers Ernst Stern and Emil Orlik.

At the Deutsches Theatre, Jones was exposed to simplified, evocative stage
pictures. One key scene from Ernst Stern's *Sumurun* showed Jones the potential
of working on a shallow "relief" stage and the visual impact of a white
background. He saw Reinhardt's stark production of *Hamlet* and the German
director's *Faust*, which was dominated by a single high church pillar in the
tradition of Craigian design. Jones did a sketch of one scene from this
production, reproduced in *Theatre of Tomorrow*. Ruth Gottholdt, in an article
written soon after Jones returned to America, explains how, at the Deutsches
Theater, he learned to pound away at a single visual motif, "by word, by gesture,
light, sound, color, until the audience was fairly intoxicated with its
overwhelming intensity."[2] From reading Craig and becoming directly exposed
to Reinhardt's work at the Deutsches, Jones became schooled in the art of single-
gesture design.

During this trip to Europe, Jones, like Browne and Van Volkenburg, also
visited Hellerau, where he encountered the stark ramps and stairs of Adolphe
Appia's "rhythmic spaces" and the empty room where Dalcroze conducted
classes in eurythmics. Gottholdt quotes Jones's description of the performance
space used by Dalcroze's students:

The most perfect representations I ever witnessed... were given
in Dalcroze's school....Imagine a hall with white walls, entirely
without windows. A long box of a place it is, with a queer glossy
floor....There is no stage, only a space for the actors; and a piano
at the side. Here, then, is a room stripped of every possible
superfluity which might detract from the completeness of the
emotional appeal.[3]

Jones goes on to describe the "magic" created by the actors' rhythmic
movements and the improvised spotlighting of Alexander von Salzmann. By

seeing this demonstration in Hellerau, reading Craig at Harvard, and observing Reinhardt's staging, Jones learned thrice over that suggestive lighting on semi-defined, three-dimensional bodies and shapes, placed before bare surfaces or in a void, could produce powerful stage effects. This kind of lighting for mysterious moods and plasticity would become a key feature of Jones's stagecraft.

Jones returned to the United States in the fall of 1914, his trip cut short by the outbreak of World War I. He returned to a New York theater milieu virtually identical to the one he left and a bold contrast to what he saw in Berlin and Hellerau. Scenery on the New York stage fit into one of two categories: three-dimensional box-set realism and the "trompe l'oeil illusion of painted flat scenery."[4] But Jones came back with many new ideas and images with which he would help change the face of America's theater scenography.

At about the same time as Jones, director Arthur Hopkins traveled through Europe, mesmerized by Max Reinhardt's productions. What impressed him most about these productions was how much Reinhardt was able to convey with so little. In "Hearing a Play with My Eyes," an essay Hopkins wrote soon after returning from Europe, he expresses his admiration for how much Continental directors and designers were able to convey with minimal means. For instance, he tells about a production at the Comédie Française, in which a factory was suggested by a single huge steel crane. "That crane told the whole story of the size and importance of this factory... [better]... than thousands of whirring wheels."[5] In another article written about his trip, he describes Reinhardt's use of suggestion in his *Faust* production, wherein so little "conveyed volumes": "With very little structure and almost no painting, it proved a picture never to be forgotten. It was a perfect example of scenic suggestion."[6]

The Reinhardt productions he witnessed were not only simplified in their sets, but also in their acting and directing style. One of Reinhardt's actors, Alexander Moissi, inspired Hopkins in how he "eliminated the man and left only the disembodied character."[7] Moissi accomplished this feat by staying "completely free from...personal emphasis and exaggeration...."[8] According to Hopkins, this actor has "reduced simplification and elimination to its seeming last analysis."[9]

Another production provided a model for directing. Hopkins describes a performance of Schnitzler's *Dr. Bernardi* as a "breathless rendition without movement or action."[10] What impressed him was the potential of directorial restraint.

Both Jones and Hopkins were also influenced by examples from pre-Italianate stages and East Asian art forms, even if the European New Stagecraft was their chief model. Jones contends that the great stages of the past—the Greek, the Medieval *platea*, the Elizabethan—all were virtually scenery-less. Only in lifeless theatrical periods, he contends, does emphasis lie on spectacular sets. So, conversely, to revitalize a theater encumbered by things, we can begin, argues Jones, by stripping it bare:

the best thing that could happen to our theater at this moment
would be for playwrights and actors and directors to be handed a
bare stage on which no scenery could be placed, and then told
that they must write and act and direct for this stage. In no time
we should have the most exciting theatre in the world.[11]

Asian arts also figured into the molding of their artistic preferences. In
How's Your Second Act?, Hopkins prefers the Chinese reliance on the
imagination of actor and spectator in dramas wherein "palaces, forests, legions
and hordes were summoned by the wave of a propertyman's bamboo stick."[12]
And Jones was deeply impressed by the fragile, spare qualities that he noticed in
Japanese prints, as indicated in his description of how they influenced his
settings for *The Claw* (1921):

the profoundly quiet, pale, melancholy light of early winter
filtering through high windows—the light seen and recorded in
the poignant prints of Hiroshige and Hokusai where knots of
people come out to view the first snowfall. A cool delicate touch
of light like a gentle hand on a fevered brow.[13]

From these influences and their own practical experiences before and after
they began collaborating, Jones and Hopkins put their ideas to paper, coming up
with a respectable body of theory supporting their efforts. Their attack against
the detailed "prosaic" stage of compulsively literal realists and for a stage
stripped to essential images was spread out through many books and articles that
came out during their lifetimes, but their ideas are most summarily and
persuasively set forth in what came to be their most influential books: Jones's
The Dramatic Imagination (published in 1941, but based on lectures given at
University of California, Berkeley in 1927) and Hopkins's *How is Your Second
Act?* (1918).

Throughout *The Dramatic Imagination*, Jones repeatedly affirms the need
for stage simplicity. Jones begins his chapter "To a Young Stage Designer" with
Michelangelo's words: "Beauty is the purgation of superfluities."[14] Jones
considers the stage designer a poet in that his job is not to detail the surface of a
situation, but give "expression to the essential quality of a play."[15] Jones's
design strategy is to eliminate down to the essential line and shape, the single
gesture revealing the "soul" of a play.

As an example of how an actor's choice can follow this single-gesture
philosophy, Jones discusses an actress from a D'Annunzio novel, *La Foscarina*,
modeled after Eleanora Duse. Jones relates how La Foscarina played Juliet with
a bunch of white roses as one prop, her single ornament for the play: "I mingled
them with my words, with my gestures, with each attitude of mine. I let one fall

at the feet of Romeo when we first met; I strewed the leaves of another on his head from the balcony; and I covered his body with the whole of them in the tomb."[16] Jones exuberantly praises this "one gesture of excelling simplicity" for its power to unify and exalt the human tragedy of romantic passion.

Realistic detail was the chief target of their attack. Jones argues that the ideal set should "give expression to the essential quality of a play rather than to its outward characteristics,"[17] that the artist should "omit the details, the prose of nature and give us only the spirit and splendour."[18] Hopkins uses sterner language: "Detail has been the boon [sic] of the American theatre for twenty years, detestable, irritating detail, designed for people with no imagination."[19]

Because they want to mobilize the imaginations of their audience, both Jones and Hopkins prefer suggestion to depiction. Jones looks forward to a future stage that will be "distinguished, austere, sparing in detail, rich in suggestion."[20] Hopkins proposes that the only mission of settings is to "suggest place and mood, and once that is established let the play go on...."[21] Hopkins names Jones as the personification of this selfless ideal.

To correct the theater's indulgent use of literal detail, Jones and Hopkins took measures in their productions to strip their stages of everything extraneous. Jones credits Madame Freisinger with having shown him the way toward simplified costumes: "I learned from her not to torture materials into meaningless folds, but to preserve the long flowing line, the noble sweep."[22] As a consequence his costumes were noted for their simple lines: "Many of the costumes I design are intentionally somewhat indefinite and abstract. A color, a shimmer, a richness, a sweep—and the actor's presence."[23]

Hopkins views directing as a stripping-away process. Since he propounds the aesthetic idea that, in the creation of art, the artist reveals only what is already there,[24] Hopkins concludes that the artist's main purpose is to cut away rather than add on. The ideal director, then, must act not as a contributor, but rather as a censor, eliminating any movement, gesture, or inflection that does not add to the desired impression:

> I eliminate all gesture that is not absolutely needed, all unnecessary inflection and intonings: the tossing of heads, the flickering of fans and kerchiefs, the tapping of feet, drumming of fingers, swinging of legs, pressing of brows, holding of hearts, curling of moustaches, stroking of beards and all the million and one tricks that have crept into the actor's bag.[25]

Hopkins recognizes how the simplified set demands a simplified acting style, for, after all, once the set became simplified, the acting had to follow suit: "With the introduction of the plain background it became imperative that the entire action and movement of the play be simplified since every movement was instantly thrown forward in much bolder relief."[26] When a simplified setting was paired with conventionally busy realistic acting, as was the case with Gordon Craig's setting and Robert Mantell's acting, Hopkins notes that it led to a distinct and shrieking clash.[27]

Jones and Hopkins share belief in the notion of "unconscious projection," though Hopkins was the one to name and define the concept. This idea is the antithesis of Bertolt Brecht's notion of alienation, which favors a continuous conscious involvement in a play. Hopkins and Jones preferred the bypassing of the conscious mind, to absorb the audience on an unconscious level. Thus, both artists reject anything in the *mise-en-scène* that engages the conscious mind and distracts the unconscious which wants to merge with the theatrical event. Any busy details—any embroidery on a set or costume, or extraneous movement by an actor—obstructs the spectator's entrance into the play. Any conscious awareness of settings or direction disrupts the flow of involvement between auditorium and stage. Thus, the simplicity of unobtrusive images is necessary for an audience to become fully connected to the action and meaning of a play.

Hopkins explains the relation between "unconscious projection" and stage simplicity in *How's Your Second Act?*:

> Extreme simplification—that is what I strive for incessantly—not because I like simplicity.... it is a working out of the method of Unconscious Projection. It is the elimination of all the non-essentials, because they arouse the conscious mind and break the spell I am trying to weave over the unconscious mind.... I want the unconscious of the actors talking to the unconscious of the audience, and I strive to eliminate every obstacle to that.[28]

Jones echoes this idea in *The Dramatic Imagination*, though he never uses Hopkins's phrase. He describes the best set as one that does not interfere with the inner connection between actor and audience: "The actor enters. If the designer's work has been good, it disappears from our consciousness at that moment. We do not notice it any more."[29]

By coming to a simple stage via the notion of unconscious projection, Jones and Hopkins do not accept all simplified endeavors. Jones explains how some forms of simplification engage the conscious mind of the spectator and hence prevent unconscious involvement:

> When I go to the theater I want to get an eyeful. Why not? I do not want to have to look at one of the so-called "suggestive" settings, in which a single Gothic column is made to do duty for a cathedral....I do not want to see any more "skeleton stages" in which a few architectural elements are combined and re-combined for the various scenes of a play.... No, I don't like these clever, falsely economical contraptions....[30]

For Jones (and Hopkins would probably agree), sets that call attention to their own clever economy break the spell Hopkins and Jones are attempting to cast because the spectator is made to admire the designer's ingenuity or wonder how one set piece will transform later in the production.

Hopkins and Jones argue so vehemently the superiority of a minimally detailed stage that they even posit the empty stage as a kind of ideal. Ironically, Jones characterizes the stage of his dreams, the future stage of America, as a bare one, asserting that the ideal stage is empty but for actors and light:

> What we need in the theatre is a space for actors to act in, a space reserved for them where they may practice their immemorial art.... They will be able to move with ease to and from this space, they will be able to make their appropriate exits and entrances. We shall find a way to bathe these actors in expressive and dramatic light. And that is all.[31]

Hopkins also came to the bare stage ideal based on models from his own theater practice. He realized how the empty stage is a normal part of every rehearsal period. In *Reference Point*, he concludes that the empty rehearsal room is the place where theater can reach its purest and most perfect state, a "perfection never... recovered" once the production moves into the theater and becomes burdened by settings and properties.[32]

The empty stage ideal, which looks ahead to the plays of Thornton Wilder in the 1930s, is linked to the less-is-more paradox. Jones's theory is replete with stated or implied references to this paradox. He begins the second chapter of *The Dramatic Imagination* with a quotation from Ralph Waldo Emerson: "Art... teaches to convey a larger sense by simpler symbols,"[33] thus positing a connection between simple symbols and large meanings. Upon remembering the Irish Players, he marvels how a "little square of light" can evoke "all the poetry of Ireland" and "one gesture" can be "enlarged" into "great art."[34] Ultimately, to Jones, a good set is one that "says nothing, but... gives everything."[35]

Undoubtedly, the Jones/Hopkins collaborations supported their theoretical pronouncements. Critics continually noted the simplification not only in their settings, but also in their entire *mise-en-scènes*. For example, in writing about Jones in 1917, Hiram Moderwell notes Jones's tendency to simplify.[36] As late as 1930, John Mason Brown describes Jones's settings as "backgrounds of life that are simplified into significance."[37] Brown goes on to say the semblance of reality is strong, but "stripped of its details, relieved of its distractions, magnified in its essentials."[38] These words apply equally well to Hopkins's directing.

This is not to say that all aspects of all their productions were spare and minimal. Jones showed remarkable fluency in the language of abstract decoration, even if this was not his primary artistic tendency. The most renown example was his design for *Til Eulenspiegel* (1916), which he did for Serge Diaghilev's *Ballets Russes*. His complex arrangement of swirling lines and pointed, Gothic rooftops proved that Jones could conform to the ornate tastes of the company that epitomized the decorative strain of the New Stagecraft.

Throughout his career, Jones's costumes were not simplified in terms of restraint in color. Jones never lost his taste for bright and primary colors, even when his sets were austere and neutral-toned. But even when Jones's costumes were at their most colorful, he still chose simple materials, long-flowing lines, and undetailed patterns. As Arthur Krows phrases it, Jones typically reduced his costumes to their lowest possible terms.[39]

From reviews and photographs, it is easy to prove that Jones simplified sets and costumes in many different ways. It is more difficult to detect directorial simplification from these sources. Hopkins scholar Delmar Hansen questioned several actors who worked with Hopkins to ascertain from them Hopkins's contributions in simplifying the *mise-en-scène*. Hansen recounts the following story from an interview with Jacob Ben Ami: "Hopkins once asked an actor to eliminate several gestures when he felt they meant little to the play. The actor, on asking Hopkins what he should do instead, was answered with one word— 'nothing'."[40] More evidence that Hopkins successfully translated his theory into practice comes from the following quotation from actor Henry Daniell who performed for Hopkins in several productions in the 1920s: "Unlike most directors of that period, he was not obsessed by the urge for movement. If a scene held and was intelligently played, he preferred it to play itself and did not introduce movements for the sake of movements."[41]

Both Jones and Hopkins came back from their European sojourns eager to translate what they learned into actual simplified stages. Jones had already begun to experiment with models and sketches in Europe. He brought these home and exhibited them, to much acclaim. His drawings for *Merchant of Venice* were placed in an exhibition sponsored by the Stage Society of New York. Two drawings caught the attention of theater scholar Hiram Moderwell, who recorded Jones's own descriptions of the images. The first design depicted Belmont for Act One Scene Two. Moderwell described it this way:

> Here you see the sky—and little else. A shallow flight of steps,
> leading up to a great round window. Curtains at each side, some
> red and black cushions. Renaissance chairs. Portia and Nerissa in
> rose and silver, the servant in black. The curtains in this design
> are ivory.[42]

In a few strokes, Jones captured what he saw as the essence of Belmont—its comfortable aristocracy with the whole world in its reach (photo 6.1). How much more than the Renaissance chairs were needed to establish period? From

Jones's vantage point, to have everything on stage following period would be redundant; the chairs were sufficient. And what besides the cushions were necessary to project aristocratic idleness? The key feature—the round window opening to a seemingly limitless sky—captured an essential aspect of Belmont without a lot of literal detail. Moreover, Jones placed this image on a shallow stage, thus restricting his performance area. He boasted about all he managed to represent with a sky "and little else."

6.1 Sketch for act one, scene two of Shakespeare's *Merchant of Venice*, designed by Robert Edmond Jones and appearing in Sam Hume's Exhibition of New Stagecraft.

In the exhibition, Jones also described his sketch depicting Shylock's walk home after the trial. This lonely walk had become a traditional part of the play's performance history and was included in many famous productions from the eighteenth century to World War I. Prior to Jones's, however, presentations had been literal, showing true-to-life bridges and walks to a facsimile door of Shylock's facsimile house. Jones's design concentrated more on suggestion and mood as evidenced by his description of the image:

The curtain rises on... the silhouette of a great bridge along which Shylock passes from right to left, black against a dull red sky, till he is lost to sight in the tangle of masts and ropes. I want this scene to hit your eye, bang! like an enormous poster, and to last but a moment.[43]

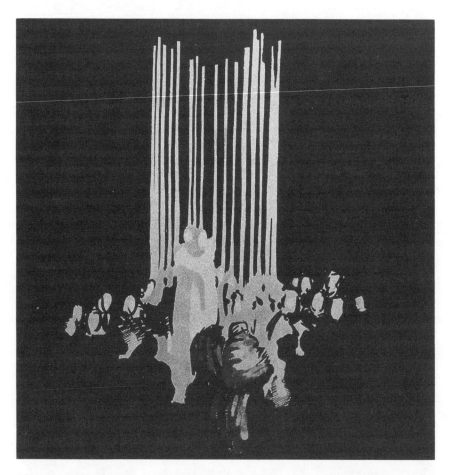

6.2 Robert Edmond Jones's sketch for *The Cenci*, act v, scene iv—Hall of the Prison. Project for Arena Staging, 1913. By permission of the publisher, Routledge, Chapman & Hall, Inc.

Jones opted for an evocative image and compelling mood rather than a literal representation. He chose to suggest the bridge, not depict it, and the striking contrasts of red and black were aimed directly at the viewer's emotions. By presenting a symbol of Shylock's isolation and his ongoing entanglement with a hostile society, Jones intended his scenic image to work not as a narrative sequence, but like a poster—as a single impression.

Jones also brought back designs for Shelley's *The Cenci*, which manifested other aspects of stage simplification. Jones conceived of the play taking place on a raised boxing ring lit from above with harsh white light and surrounded by the dark figures of the audience. Most of the scenography would be created by strange, menacing movements of a silent chorus carrying long spears and banquet trays, or wearing helmets glowing in the dark (photo 6.2). The costumes would be black, gray, and white, except for occasional streaks of screaming red. The overall atmosphere, then, would be stark and severe, the actors shining from the surrounding blackness as "through the eye of an X-ray."[44]

With this project, Jones intended to present an empty stage on which deep emotional states could be evoked through the interplay of movement and light, the same combination that excited him at Hellerau. His *Cenci* designs, with the violent contrasts of red, black, and white amid amorphous shapes in a black void, are prototypes for the "space stage," which would later become emblematic of expressionist scenography in the United States and Europe during the 1920s and serve as preliminaries for Jones's own *Macbeth* designs.

Even before embarking on his professional career, Jones had succeeded—at least on paper—in stripping the stage to bare essentials in two very different ways. With *Merchant*, he had struck a balance between the literal and the abstract; with *Cenci*, he had gone toward extreme abstraction. He had conceived *Merchant* on a shallow, two-dimensional stage; with *Cenci* he found ways to emphasize a stark three-dimensionality. *Merchant* was colorful with undetailed surfaces; *Cenci* employed a limited palette with no solid surfaces at all, except the moving shapes of the actors and the still shapes of the spectators. And while *Merchant* used a bare minimum to suggest literal realities, *Cenci*, with a bare minimum, suggested deep psychological states. With these two projects, Jones built two corners of a foundation on which his future simplified set designs could rest.

Jones's next challenge was to make his designs work on a living stage. It did not take him long. Soon after his return from Europe, Albert Boni asked him to help the Liberal Club by creating a set for a modest production of Lord Dunsany's *The Glittering Gate*. Jones agreed and put together a simple set.

The production took place in the back room of the Washington Square Book Shop on a raised platform placed amid the bookshelves. The settings were created from found objects. Jones made two columns from ten feet of wrapping paper and "eternity's walls out of window curtains."[45] Besides some sheets, the only other accessories were the few candles, by which Jones lit the makeshift set.

In the summer of 1915, Jones arranged sets for another influential little theater, the Provincetown Players. To mount the Provincetown Players' first two one-acts in the Hutchins Hapgood house, Jones chose to use the house's veranda backed by the Atlantic Ocean for the first play and then had the spectators turn their chairs around to face a broad doorway for the second. In so doing, Jones used the environment of the house itself to create the appropriate moods for the two plays. Rather than add objects to change scenes, Jones rearranged audience perspective within the environment, a decision which enabled him to have a new image without additional properties or set pieces. He also employed minimal lighting. Glaspell remembers that the entire lighting was done with just "a candle here and a lamp there."[46]

As with the Washington Square Book Shop experience, his work at the Hapgood home taught him how scant funds can stimulate ingenuity with little. The lessons of how to work within the financial limitations of American little theaters were reinforcing the aesthetic values Jones learned in Europe. These early experiences conspired in teaching Jones the power of stage simplicity.

Between the two little theater debuts, Jones designed his first Broadway production. Late in 1914, Emily Hapgood, President of the Stage Society of New York (the same organization that sponsored the exhibition which showed Jones's *Merchant* designs), asked him to create the setting for *The Man Who Married a Dumb Wife* by Anatole France. That production was never realized under those auspicies, but visiting English director Granville-Barker, who needed a curtain-raiser for Shaw's *Androcles and the Lion*, watched a rehearsal of the ill-fated Hapgood production and decided to resurrect it with himself as director and Jones as designer.

On January 27, 1915, the play opened at Wallack's Theatre, displaying the first American-designed, Broadway presentation of the New Stagecraft. For many audiences, it was an entirely new look. Surely some spectators had seen something like it in Europe, where simple stages had appeared in intimate theaters in Germany, France, and Sweden. Or perhaps they had witnessed a production at the Chicago Little Theatre or the Boston Toy Theatre. Some also may have remembered Reinhardt's New York production of *Sumurun*, presented three years before or looked in wonderment at Craig's monumental but depersonalized sketches in *On the Art of the Theatre*. But for many this was a new look. This was not the highly detailed naturalistic stage of David Belasco, nor was it the spectacular flats and drops of the Shuberts's plush extravaganzas, neither was it the ornate abstraction created by Diaghilev's designers or the American designer, Joseph Urban. Suddenly an American designer had made a Broadway stage strikingly simple and spare, a precedent that would be followed intermittently for the next seven years.

6.3 Set for Anatole France's *The Man Who Married a Dumb Wife*, designed by Robert Edmond Jones. Presented at Wallack's Theatre in 1915 under the direction of Harley Granville-Barker. Photo courtesy of the Billy Rose Theatre Collection, The New York Public Library at Lincoln Center, Astor, Lenox, and Tilden Foundations.

According to a story related by Arthur Krows, Granville-Barker planted the seed for the play's simple design by telling Jones he only wanted a door, two windows, and a room.[47] Not concerned with presenting an authentic Medieval scene, the English director wanted only the bare essentials for making the farce work. In the final set design, Jones incorporated his director's wishes, but in such a way as to present an aura of fanciful Medievalism. As with his *Merchant* designs, Jones selected scenic elements cautiously to avoid redundancy and superfluity. Since the costumes were Medieval, the set could convey something else.

So instead of making the set Medieval, Jones utilized the farcical possibilities of the Roman stage. He and Granville-Barker presented not just a large room as Anatole France designates in his stage directions, but rather a street backed by a house façade with a large window through which a large part of the room could be seen (photo 6.3). The window, which acted as a kind of second proscenium, and the street appeared like a simplified *scaenae frons*. For Granville-Barker, the farce could move fast on Jones's set, with the action jumping from inside the house to outside in the street. By turning France's locale inside out, Jones created both a private and public sphere for the play's action and combined two sets in one. Moreover, through the twelve-foot square window, only a few essential properties were visible, including a bookcase, writing table, stepladder, and bench—far less than the number France designates in his stage directions.

Like Reinhardt's *Sumurun* designed by Ernst Stern, Jones put *The Man Who Married a Dumb Wife* on a shallow stage and arranged the house façade parallel to the proscenium line, which has become characteristic of the "relief stage." He emphasized the uninterrupted horizontality of the set by including two long steps leading to the house and by emphasizing the line across the top of the house façade which extended uninterruptedly the width of the stage. To echo these horizontal lines, Jones added a long bench beneath the window and a balcony railing just outside the window frame. Two other factors accentuated the flat horizontality of the stage picture. Jones scholar Eugene Black points out how the arrangement of rectangles, with their dark outlines standing out from the lighter-toned wall, gave an overall effect of flatness. The lighting contributed to this feeling by being "unvaried, plain, and uniform" throughout the production.[48]

The colors in the set, as in Stern's *Sumurun* design, stayed predominantly within the black-to-white spectrum. The windows, balcony, and door, outlined in black, stood out from the house's stippled gray wall. The only bold colors were touches of red that accented the stepladder in front of the stark white bookcase inside the house and a colorfully patterned piece of material draped over the stage left section of the balcony railing. Typically for Jones, the costumes showed no restraint in color; they were in dazzling purples, oranges, yellows, and reds.

6.4 Robert Edmond Jones's act one set for Edith Ellis's *The Devil's Garden*, directed by Arthur Hopkins.

Like the *Merchant* designs, *The Man Who Married a Dumb Wife* set struck a balance between the literal and the abstract. The rectangles on the façade were recognizable as windows and a door, but, at the same time, they called attention to themselves as an abstract arrangement of shapes. The simplicity of the stage added to this abstract impression. By being stripped of all but the most essential elements, the stage became as much a resonant symbol as an actual place in an actual time.

Thus, before Jones even began working with Hopkins, he had learned and applied the principles of stage simplification, so that experience was supporting theory and theory was generating a certain kind of experience. Arthur Hopkins returned from Europe, also eager to apply the lessons of simplification to his practical theater work. He, too, did not have to wait long. When he returned to the United States, he discarded the elaborate models for his *Evangeline* production and reconceived it along simpler and more unified lines. He borrowed from Reinhardt the idea of an adjustable proscenium, which enabled him to restrict the size of the proscenium opening. Commenting on the use of an adjustable proscenium in Berlin, Hopkins noted how "the smallness of the scenes... resulted in an intimacy in the action that contributed greatly to its dramatic force."[49] Hopkins achieved a similar effect when he applied it to *Evangeline*. The results did not go unnoticed; writing in 1914, Cheney expressed his opinion that four of the ten settings in *Evangeline* were "as finely simple and suggestive as anything in the European theatre."[50]

COLLABORATIONS BETWEEN JONES AND HOPKINS

Hopkins and Jones had learned a great deal on their own; now they were ready to pool their talents and simplify the New York professional stage together. Two years after his *Evangeline* production, Hopkins teamed up with Jones in doing Edith Ellis's dramatization of W. B. Maxwell's *The Devil's Garden*, which opened in December 1915, at the Harris Theatre. During this production—and confirmed over and over through future productions—Hopkins (and Jones) had found what Brooks Atkinson would later call a perfect "spiritual collaborator."

One can trace the origins of simplified realism in the American professional theater to this production. The three settings were noteworthy for their minimal detail, especially when compared to the typical realistic settings of the time. Walls were bare, furniture was kept to a minimum, and the color range was held in check.

The first-act setting was the most radically simplified; indeed, it may have been the sparest *mise-en-scène* yet seen on the American professional stage (photo 6.4) and caught the attention of several critics. The site of the action was an anteroom in a general post office. Hopkins and Jones opted to put it on a

shallow stage, a mere ten feet deep. The walls were dull gray with the back wall
set parallel to the proscenium line. The only object on the wall was a buff-toned
map placed directly behind the stage right table, surrounded by three chairs. Two
identical doors, placed symmetrically in the side walls, faced each other across
the room.

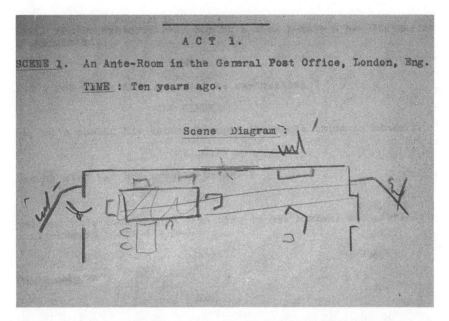

6.5 Scene diagram out of what seems to be an assistant stage manager's typescript for act
one of Ellis's *The Devil's Garden*. Photo courtesy of the Billy Rose Theatre Collection,
The New York Public Library at Lincoln Center, Astor, Lenox, and Tilden Foundations.

In the stage directions, Edith Ellis designated a fourth chair to be included
with the other chairs and table, but Hopkins and Jones decided to separate this
chair from the other furniture by putting it far stage left. They defied the stage
directions by placing the three table chairs so they faced each other around the
table, thereby isolating the fourth chair even more.

The stark image that confronted the audience when the curtain rose was one
of isolation and cold bureaucratic insensitivity. It was a clear choice of mood
over detailed representation. Jones could have strewn the set with bags of mail
and other post office paraphernalia to indicate the scene's location. He chose
instead to leave the room spare and hence abstracted, to some degree, out of time
and place. In *Theatre of Tomorrow*, Macgowan labeled the Act One set a
"perfect piece of realism, and a perfect piece of abstraction besides."[51] Hopkins

and Jones had succeeded in balancing the literal and the abstract, as Jones had done with Granville-Barker in *The Man Who Married a Dumb Wife* set.

How Hopkins and Jones came up with this innovative design is difficult to determine precisely. A penciled sketch from an assistant stage manager's promptbook seems to indicate that the decision evolved during rehearsals. The sketch shows two arrangements of furniture, one crossed out, a new one sketched in (photo 6.5). The crossed-out sketch closely follows Ellis's stage directions, while the new one is very close to the final design appearing in production photographs. Evidently, sometime during rehearsals, Hopkins and Jones realized the effectiveness of isolating one chair and closing off the other three. That decision was key to the evolution of simplified realism and the synthesis between abstract and realistic set design.

The lighting and costume design, both by Jones, contributed to the set's bleak, cold atmosphere. The bureaucratic officials wore gray and black, and the lighting was harsh, cold, and unrelieved. Macgowan summarizes the scene's mood, commenting that it "breathed bureaucracy, the thing that was about to grip the clerk,"[52] the protagonist who sat in the isolated chair, far stage left of the other on-stage characters.

Although not as extreme, the production's other settings were simplified beyond what audiences were accustomed to in 1915. The second act, which takes place in a cheap hotel, featured garish red wallpaper and drab furniture. Jones allowed himself bolder colors and more furniture than in Act One, but still used far less to create a tawdry atmosphere than the standard naturalistic set. In the sets used in Acts Three and Four, Jones presented a sitting room tailored to convey a single impression, described by Eugene Black as "tasteful conventionality."[53] In the sets for all three acts, but primarily for the one in Act One, Hopkins and Jones selected a few essential details to establish time and place but subordinated both considerations to a predominant mood, thereby aiming at the spectator's unconscious, not the eye roaming through details.

The next year, Hopkins and Jones applied the principles of simplified realism and suggestion to Clare Kummer's *Good Gracious Annabelle* (October 1916), at the Republic Theatre. In *Good Gracious Annabelle*, the first setting was placed on a relief stage and featured high vertical lines towering over relatively small human figures. This dwarfing of actors, presented somewhat abstractly, has its origin in Appia's forests and Craig's palaces and would become standard in Jones's later sets.

In this opening set, Jones portrayed the Waldorf's Peacock Alley, familiar to many in the audience, but instead of trying to reproduce it accurately as Belasco did with Childs Restaurant, another familiar site, Jones presented only the Alley's most prominent features: its tall French windows (photo 6.6). Hopkins remembers this stripped-to-essentials stage design years later in *Reference Point*: "a shallow set, one long flat with three curtained French windows, two plain settees, two chairs, all with summer covers."[54] As of May 1917, Jones considered the Act One set for *Annabelle* his most personally satisfying achievement.

6.6 Sketch by Robert Edmond Jones for act one (Waldorf's Peacock Alley) of *Good Gracious Annabelle* (1916). Photo courtesy of the Billy Rose Theatre Collection, The New York Public Library at Lincoln Center, Astor, Lenox, and Tilden Foundations.

One observant critic from the *Boston Transcript* described the production's *mise-en-scène* in terms that have become standard for simplified realism: the shallow stage; the "clear, straight lines" in all the sets; "the plain, bare surfaces"; the "intelligent selection of means" and the "just proportion in the distribution of them."[55] To match these plain settings, Hopkins had to keep his directing simple—even with a farce—a form traditionally "smothered with elaboration."[56] Looking back at this production in 1948, Hopkins felt he accomplished this.

For the years after *Annabelle*, Hopkins and Jones clung tightly to their goal of simplicity, as evidenced by observations from the critics. For instance, *Redemption* in 1918 was praised for its "utmost simplicity in line and color,"[57] and the next year Jones was praised for the way he "remarkably suggested" the medieval atmosphere in *The Jest*.[58] But their reputations soared when they applied principles of stage simplification to their Shakespeare collaborations in the early 1920s. Hopkins and Jones broke new ground in the professional New York theater with their quasi-permanent set productions of *Richard III* and *Hamlet* and their "space stage," expressionist *Macbeth* production in between. The stages they created afforded them the means to capture the Elizabethan spirit of doing plays swiftly and sparely, for which they received considerable critical and scholarly acclaim.

The Tragedy of Richard III, the first of these collaborations, opened at the Plymouth Theatre in March 1920 and featured John Barrymore in the title role. Behind him and the rest of the cast stood the menacing Tower of London. To create this set, Jones went to England to study the Tower. He spent hours watching the massive gray structure, noticing how natural light, at different times of day, subtly changed the mood it evoked. At the Plymouth, Jones sought to reproduce not its authenticity but its essential features. The stone entranceway with its heavy iron-bar gate dominated the center of the stage, and massive walls curved into the wings, creating an enveloping quality (photo 6.7). Kenneth Macgowan called Jones's Tower a "moldering gray threat" that "stood like the empty skull of Richard with the hideous drama within it."[59] The main character's inner state of being informed the choice of the central stage image. Hopkins and Jones were treating *Richard III* as a monodrama, as Craig did eight years before in his Moscow Art Theatre *Hamlet*.

The Tower functioned as a kind of permanent set, lurking ominously behind the action through most of the production. Several times the Tower disappeared from view, which somewhat compromised the permanent set idea. For example, the spectator's view of the Tower was completely blocked when a large arras was strung across the stage for some scenes and when a large gibbet was wheeled on for the final scene. The permanent set idea was again compromised on Bosworth Field when the light from a high source produced a small pool of light around Richmond and left the Tower in total darkness. Except in these cases, at least a piece of the Tower could be detected throughout the production.

According to Macgowan, Jones wanted the Tower to be present throughout the production, but Hopkins chose to block it out at times. For instance, Jones wanted the final scene to feature the gibbet outlined in silhouette against a flaming red Tower. Hopkins vetoed that idea, and the Tower was completely blocked from view. In *Theatre of Tomorrow*, Macgowan expresses his dismay at the final decision; Macgowan supported Jones's inclination to maintain the tower as a visual motif throughout.

6.7 Hopkins/Jones 1920 production of Shakespeare's *Richard III* (act four, scene four). Queen Margaret, Duchess of York and Queen Elizabeth as they appear before the Tower of London quasi-permanent setting. Photo courtesy of the Billy Rose Theatre Collection, The New York Public Library at Lincoln Center, Astor, Lenox, and Tilden Foundations.

When the Tower was visible, Jones found many ways to change the mood and suggest different locales, thereby creating variety with this one setting. Thrones, jail cells, Henry VI's hearse, and other simple set pieces were enough to establish where the action was taking place. Jones also created various moods by chiaroscuro lighting of the Tower and whatever was in front of it. Jones experimented with shadows and silhouettes by using side- and backlighting, as well as different washes on the Tower itself. In this way, Jones used lighting to erase detail and communicate one overall austere mood.

The lighting and the costuming also de-emphasized the traits that distinguished the characters from each other. The people on the stage were treated both as individual characters as well as semi-defined shapes. Hopkins and Jones lit these shapes from behind or from the side; Hopkins directed the actors to move slowly and ominously around the stage (photo 6.8). And by backlighting Richard III's throne, he created a second menacing feature to echo the qualities of the Tower. The shadows and silhouettes obscured detail, but accentuated the essential mood.

6.8 The shape of Richard III's throne, side-lit, with palace gate of Tower of London behind. Designed by Robert Edmond Jones and directed by Arthur Hopkins. Photo courtesy of the Billy Rose Theatre Collection, The New York Public Library at Lincoln Center, Astor, Lenox, and Tilden Foundations.

The Tower enabled Jones to strike yet another compromise between the literal and the abstract. In some scenes, the Tower functioned merely as itself, with characters conversing before it as if they were standing on a London street. When a scenic element was placed before it, changing the location, the Tower functioned as a symbolic reminder of Richard III's evil domination and as a mood-evoking dark mass.

Hopkins and Jones returned to the idea of a modified permanent set when they did *Hamlet* two years later. This time the dominant image was a spacious "Great Hall" with a Romanesque arch rear center and stairs leading up to it (photo 6.9). The arch was massive, stretching twenty-five feet high, with an additional ten feet to the top of the set. Jones emphasized its verticality by placing lamps above the balcony and employing a lot of side- and backlighting.

Using the same design strategy as for *Richard III*, Jones kept at least part of the vast arch in view through most of the scenes and maintained variety by flying in decorative curtains (which in some scenes completely blocked out the arch as the arras did in *Richard III*), by lighting scenic elements differently, and by introducing properties. A bare minimum was used to establish location. Thus, a throne was enough to create a palace, a single grave a graveyard.

Once again, the common scenic element—the arch—played both a literal and abstract function. When Ophelia's funeral occurred before the same arch which was background to the court scenes, it created some confusion with those not accustomed to the concept of a permanent setting as a symbol. One critic, for instance, confused the literal and abstract functions of the arch, complaining that Ophelia was "buried in the parlor."[60]

Hopkins and Jones also created King Hamlet's ghost in a very simple way when they chose to represent him merely as a green shape and beam of bright light. In Act One, Scenes Four and Five, they depicted the ghost as light streaming onto the stage from behind the stage right arch. The bright light on John Barrymore's face created a ghost through reflection rather than literal embodiment.

From Edward Gordon Craig, Jones had learned the power of a high vertical structure juxtaposed with a relatively small, schematized figure of a person. He touched on this principle in his Act-One set for *Good Gracious Annabelle* and carried it even further with his Shakespeare sets. The arch in *Hamlet*, as with the London Tower in *Richard III*, allowed majestic architectural forms to dwarf the human figures below, transforming the characters in the play to relatively small, abstract figures moving through a vast emptiness.

The *Hamlet* set contained stairs, another design element often used on the stripped stage. When Jones first went to Europe, he saw Appia's experiments with step units at different angles on a bare stage. Just before he designed *Hamlet*, he and Macgowan witnessed Leopold Jessner's production of *Richard III* with its famous flight of stairs. These examples demonstrated for Jones how steps can exercise a rhythmical control on moving actors. Thus, the vast empty space defined by the arch and the world outside it, and the steps leading in three different directions, conspired to abstract the actor, transforming him into a rhythmically moving being in a semi-defined space as well as an individualized character in the play's situational context.

Hopkins and Jones sustained this quality through lighting. Jones lit the scrim behind the arch so as to emphasize a vastness outside the palace, just as

6.9 Foreground, John Barrymore as Hamlet in the Hopkins/Jones 1922 production. In the background, the great arch which served as a quasi-permanent element in the production. Photo courtesy of the Billy Rose Theatre Collection, The New York Public Library at Lincoln Center, Astor, Lenox, and Tilden Foundations.

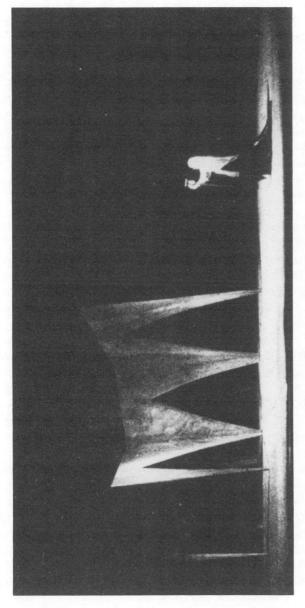

6.10 The Lady Macbeth letter scene (act one, scene five) from 1921 Hopkins/Jones production of Shakespeare's *Macbeth*, February 1921. Photo courtesy of the Billy Rose Theatre Collection, The New York Public Library at Lincoln Center, Astor, Lenox, and Tilden Foundations.

Jones's *Merchant of Venice* window made us conscious of a large, empty world outside the room. By contrasting the small schematized human being with a vast emptiness beyond, Jones's design variables were presenting the image of a little man in a large but empty world.

Between working on *Richard III* and *Hamlet*, Hopkins and Jones presented *Macbeth* at the Apollo Theatre in 1921. The space stage they chose to employ was an extension of what Hopkins and Jones did with the *Richard III* production the year before. The design strategy again was to highlight as much empty space as possible and thereby suspend the actor in a surrounding void. In *Richard III* and *Hamlet*, Hopkins and Jones did it with large architectural structures and light; in *Macbeth* they took away the permanent structures and instead created a black void with lights highlighting a few semi-defined human shapes and freestanding arches. A comment from one reviewer attests to how much Hopkins and Jones accomplished with little: "With two sets of staggered arches, Mr. Jones has achieved moving drama, which two carloads of naturalistic scenery could never achieve."[61]

All the essential features of the expressionist "space stage" were present in the Hopkins-Jones *Macbeth*: the deep stage space, black hangings, black floor, and high light sources. American audiences had not yet seen this combination of design variables in their own professional theater. Hints of the space stage were evident already in *Richard III* when toplighting picked out Richmond from surrounding darkness on Bosworth Field. Not until *Macbeth* in 1921, however, did Jones or any other Broadway designer employ the space stage throughout a production.

This kind of stage suited the production concept. Since they interpreted the play as the story of all-powerful evil forces of the unconscious, Hopkins and Jones needed a landscape that reflected the vast and mysterious human psyche. They had no use for a literal setting, as Hopkins explained in an article that came out in *The New York Times* on the eve of their production: "To us it is not a play of Scotland or warring Kings or of any time or place or people. It is a play of all times and all people. We care nothing about how Inverness may have looked...."[62]

Floating in the black void of Jones's space stage were scenic elements with skewed conical shapes. The same basic shape took different forms at different times in the production. In Lady Macbeth's letter scene (Act One, Scene Five), two sets of Gothic arches, strongly askew, created a kind of maze through which she slowly moved (photo 6.10), whereas in her sleep-walking scene, Jones used freestanding conical shapes reminiscent of Gothic stained-glass windows, without the glass. (The vituperative critic Alexander Woollcott likened the shapes to "giant snowshoes battered by storm."[63]) The same shape was repeated in the properties. Shields, helmets, and spears were variations on the same visual theme. Jones indicated the mental deterioration of the main characters by making the arches and other conical shapes more and more skewed and fewer in number as the play progressed. By the end of the show, only one grotesquely skewed arch remained.

Another unifying image in Jones's design was a set of three giant silver masks suspended above the play's action. During the witch scenes, sharp lights burned through the eyes of the masks and illuminated the similarly masked, red-clad witches below (photo 6.11). Jones kept the masks visible during most of the play, providing a symbol to help hold the abstract production together, as the Tower and arch did in *Richard III* and *Hamlet*.

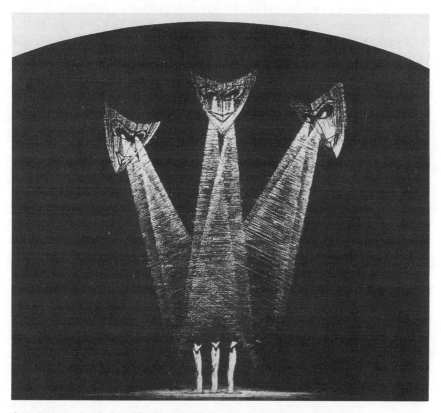

6.11 Jones's sketch for 1921 Hopkins/Jones *Macbeth*. Three witches in act one, scene one. By permission of the publisher, Routledge, Chapman & Hall, Inc.

In the banquet scene (Act Three, Scene Four), Jones projected Macbeth's unstable mind onto the stage. The throne tottered, and on two shaky banquet tables Jones placed candles set askew. All scenic elements were gray but for red touches such as Lady Macbeth's costume and the throne's backing.

Jones's use of color in his *Macbeth* production recalls its use in *The Man*

Who Married a Dumb Wife: a severely limited palette in the set and a much wider range in the costumes. The *Macbeth* sets were predominantly light gray scenic elements floating in blackness. The costumes were mostly in primary colors. The costumes were simplified; each one was a uniform color with simple flowing lines. Moreover, the costumes were made of the "simplest materials"[64] and hung loose on the actor's bodies so as not to emphasize the differences in their body shapes.

As in their other simplified productions, Hopkins and Jones straddled the literal and the abstract. At times, the lighting, the spacing, and the movement patterns of the actors and the set pieces played down their individualizing traits, so that their presence read more as shapes than individuals. In the banquet scene, for instance, Macgowan described Macbeth's visitors as "brooding and malignant shapes."[65] Stark Young described how Lady Macbeth, in her long flowing white robe, slowly moved in the shadows before her entrance in the sleepwalking scene.[66] Jones's models and sketches demonstrate Jones's artistic intention of transforming actors into moving figures as well as specific human beings in the specific circumstances of the play. Hopkins and Jones had succeeded at turning empty space into a symbol of psychological isolation and metaphysical alienation.

Some of the simplifications were not accepted by the critics. Kenneth Macgowan faulted the directing for being "too slow a pace and too static a treatment of the people on the stage."[67] Macgowan also criticized Lionel Barrymore's delivery, accusing him of plodding "heavily through the long play, dwelling endlessly on every vowel."[68] Macgowan laments that Macbeth's moments of terror and anguish were no more than "heavier accents of a slow and laboriously rumbling beat of the voice."[69] In fact, the critical response in general was mixed; perhaps audiences and critics were not ready for so extreme an abstraction. But scholarly interest in this production has endured, probably for its groundbreaking use of expressionist stagecraft. Following in its wake were many expressionist space stages designed by Lee Simonson at the Theatre Guild and, finally, the most simplified professional production to date: the Komisarjevsky/Simonson production of Claudel's *The Tidings Brought to Mary*, which opened on Christmas Eve, 1922.

NOTES

[1] Robert Edmond Jones, *The Dramatic Imagination* (New York: Duell, Sloan & Pearce, 1941), p. 75.

[2] Ruth Gottholdt, "New Scenic Art of the Theatre," *Theatre Magazine*, (May 1915), p. 137.

[3] Ibid., p. 138.

[4] Eugene Robert Black, "Robert Edmond Jones: Poetic Artist of the New

Stagecraft," (Diss., U. of Wisconsin, 1955), p. 13.

5 Arthur Hopkins, "Hearing a Play With My Eyes," *Harper's Weekly*, 50 (August 23, 1913), p. 13.

6 Arthur Hopkins, "Brain Plays in Germany," *Harper's Weekly*, 58 (September 13, 1913), p. 25.

7 Arthur Hopkins, *To a Lonely Boy* (Garden City, New York: Doubleday, Doran & Co., 1937), p. 150.

8 Arthur Hopkins, *How's Your Second Act?*, (New York: Alfred A. Knopf, 1918), p. 53.

9 Ibid., p. 55.

10 Hopkins, *Lonely Boy*, p. 150.

11 Jones, *Dramatic Imagination*, p. 135.

12 Hopkins, *Second Act?*, p. 48.

13 Oliver Sayler, *Our American Theatre* (New York: Brentano's, 1923), p. 158.

14 Jones, *Dramatic Imagination*, p. 69.

15 Ibid., p. 78.

16 Robert Edmond Jones, "The Artist's Approach to the Theatre," *Theatre Arts Monthly*, 12 (September 1928), pp. 633-634.

17 Jones, *Dramatic Imagination*, p. 78.

18 Ibid., p. 82.

19 Hopkins, *Second Act?*, pp. 47-48.

20 Jones, *Dramatic Imagination*, p. 144.

21 Arthur Hopkins, *Second Act?*, pp. 48-49.

22 Jones, *Dramatic Imagination*, p. 34.

23 Ibid., p. 35.

24 Arthur Hopkins, *Reference Point*, (New York: Samuel French, 1948), p. 50.

25 Hopkins, *Second Act?*, p. 31.

26 Ibid., pp. 51-52.

27 Ibid., p. 52.

28 Ibid., p. 33.

29 Jones, *Dramatic Imagination*, p. 27.

30 Ibid., pp. 24-25.

31 Ibid., pp. 143-144.

32 Hopkins, *Reference Point*, p. 124.

33 Jones, *Dramatic Imagination*, p. 23.

34 Ibid., p. 75.

35 Ibid., p. 26.

36 Hiram Kelley Moderwell, "The Art of Robert Edmond Jones," *Theatre Arts Magazine*, 2 (February 1917), p. 61.

37 John Mason Brown, *Upstage* (New York: W. W. Norton, 1930), p. 158.

38 Ibid., p. 160.

39 Krows, *Play Production in America*, p. 199.

40 Delmar Hansen, "The Directing Theory and Practice of Arthur Hopkins," (Diss.,

U. of Iowa, 1961), p. 176.

[41] Hansen, "Arthur Hopkins," p. 202.

[42] Moderwell, *To-day*, p. 143.

[43] Ibid., p. 143.

[44] Robert Edmond Jones, *Drawings for the Theatre* (New York: Theatre Arts, Inc., 1970), p. 15.

[45] Sayler, *Our American Theatre*, p. 78.

[46] Susan Glaspell, *The Road to the Temple*, p. 251.

[47] Krows, *Play Production*, p. 137.

[48] Black, "Robert Edmond Jones," p. 23.

[49] Hopkins, "Brain Plays," p. 25.

[50] Cheney, *The New Movement*, p. 171.

[51] Macgowan, *Theatre of Tomorrow*, p. 25.

[52] Ibid., p. 24.

[53] Black, "Robert Edmond Jones," p. 35.

[54] Hopkins, *Reference Point*, p. 98.

[55] "Round Boston Stages," *Boston Transcript*, October 27, 1916, n. p., found in Jones file in Billy Rose Collection.

[56] Hopkins, *Reference Point*, p. 98.

[57] Hansen, "Arthur Hopkins," p. 139.

[58] Hansen, "Arthur Hopkins," p. 139.

[59] Macgowan, *Theatre of Tomorrow*, p. 132.

[60] Jones, *Drawings*, p. 14.

[61] Quoted in Hansen, "Arthur Hopkins," p. 141.

[62] Arthur Hopkins, "The Approaching Macbeth," *New York Times*, February 6, 1921, section 6, p.1.

[63] Alexander Woollcott, "A Rebellion Against the Emperor Jones," *The New York Times*, February 27, 1921, sec. 6, p. 1.

[64] Kenneth Macgowan, "The Jones-Barrymore-Hopkins Macbeth" in Montrose Moses and John Mason Brown, *American Theatre As Seen By its Critics, 1752-1934* (New York: W. W. Norton and Co., 1934), p. 204.

[65] Ibid., p. 204.

[66] Ralph Pendleton, *The Theatre of Robert Edmond Jones* (Middletown, CT: Wesleyan University Press, 1958), pp. 5-6.

[67] Macgowan in Moses, *American Critics*, p. 205.

[68] Ibid., p. 205.

[69] Ibid., p. 205.

7

Lee Simonson, Theodore Komisarjevsky, and *The Tidings Brought to Mary*

When American designer Lee Simonson and visiting Russian director Theodore Komisarjevsky presented *The Tidings Brought to Mary* at the Theatre Guild in December 1922, they reached an important landmark on the road to the neutral empty stages of playwright Thornton Wilder in the 1930s. The set and production concept was radical in its simplicity, combining the ideas of a permanent set and the bare stage as neutral space. One can look at the theory expressed in their writings and their earlier work as preparing them for the task of creating this boldly simplified production and opening the way for future endeavors in this aesthetic direction.

LEE SIMONSON

Simonson was the principal designer for the Washington Square Players and, when some of its founders retrenched to create the Theatre Guild, Simonson continued as a key player in the new enterprise. His bent toward essentials in stage design characterized his work with the Players and the Guild.

Like Jones, Simonson's first inspirations to simplify the stage can be traced to a trip to Europe in 1909, even though he had not yet designed a set. He saw

performances of the Ballets Russes in Paris, where he was awed by the
possibilities of vivid color. He also went to the Munich Art Theatre, where he
marveled at the use of a shallow "relief" stage,[1] both aspects appearing in some
of his early designs. Among his most vivid experiences as a spectator were
occasions when stages were left nearly bare. He relates how he saw Isadora
Duncan dancing Iphigenia to Gluck's score. He describes her as a "limpid grace
dominating a vast empty stage, backed by a single billowing sackcloth curtain."[2]
At the Karlsruhe Theatre, Simonson attended visiting director Lugne-Poe's
production of Andreyev's *Life of Man* with severely skeletal settings against
black curtains.[3]

In his early practice, Simonson kept his stages to a bare minimum. His sets
for the Players featured bare wall surfaces; a few well-spaced pieces of furniture;
long, uninterrupted lines and masses; and static picturizations that lacked
perspective. Moderwell characterizes Simonson's designs with the Players as an
"abstraction from reality, a selection and intensification" and as lacking motion.
Moderwell observes that they have a stillness about them, that "they are meant
to stay put."[4] Moderwell identified in Simonson's earliest stage designs a visual
stasis.

But Simonson's early work tended to be vividly colorful. His Washington
Square Players's designs had, in his own words, a "posterlike brilliance."[5] His
passion for color drove him to a one-man crusade against the "great American
God—Grey."[6] Extravagance in color, however, did not deter him from severely
limiting stage detail. Tired of the "dingy detailed stage settings of the day,"[7]
Simonson vowed to cut out of his stage picture all but the barest essentials. His
philosophy of simplification revolves around the principle of aesthetic economy:

> The problem has been summarized in Degas' dictum: You make a
> crowd with five people not with fifty: the problem of the
> suppression of unnecessary detail which any art student learns at
> his first life [drawing] class....The basic principle of scenic
> design is the truism... : the more one shows the less one reveals.[8]

This "truism" is a restatement of the less-is-more and more-is-less paradoxes.
Simonson continues:

> Only elimination can produce expressive design whatever the
> scale of design be, within the borders of a rug, a picture frame or
> the frame of a stage itself. Even for a realistic script, Flaubert's
> advice to Maupassant holds good: one must note not all the
> documentary details, but the one significant detail....[9]

But when Simonson did his very first stage design at the Bandbox Theatre,
simplicity was more a function of practicality than philosophy. The ironclad

limitations of working in a small theater for a company with little money commanded artistic restraint. Simonson describes how the Players's circumstances forced him to utilize maximum imagination with minimal resources: "I walked on to the diminutive stage of the Band Box and found that the problem... was a pragmatic one and not a matter of dogma.... I faced the necessity as a craftsman, of meeting a concrete predicament with as much imagination as possible."[10] Surely Simonson was referring to the practical necessities behind his earliest settings when, in his autobiography, he writes fondly of the "esthetic virtue that is often bred by necessity."[11] He did finally embrace simplicity for its aesthetic merits as well.

Simonson's first assignment was to design a set for Andreyev's *Love of One's Neighbor* (1915). At first he had to accomplish this task with only two pieces of scenery; he managed to get permission for a third piece along the way. With the first piece, a red cliff, he unabashedly borrowed from Hokusai's waterfall prints. The only other things on the stage were a fence and a cutout of cloud shapes placed before a lemon-colored horizon.

While vivid color became the hallmark of a Lee Simonson set during his Washington Square days, there were exceptions. One was his set for *A Miracle of St. Anthony* (1915). According to MacKay, Simonson produced an austere, neutral-colored setting. In the playscript, Maeterlinck designates two different locations. Simonson and his director, Philip Moeller, condensed the set needs by putting both scenes in the same interior. In this setting, the walls were off-white, and even though Maeterlinck's stage directions call for a clothes rack with all kinds of hats, capes, and wraps, Moeller and Simonson opted instead for a row of identical, wide-rimmed black hats. This decision to reject a realistic clothes rack in favor of multiple uniformity evidences a tendency toward simple-stage thinking. Nordvoldt notes in the photographs for this production the typical qualities of Simonson's work: "bare walls graced with a minimum of details that, in their striking simplicity, are at once artistic and appropriate."[12] Simonson hints at these qualities when he uses this set as an example—along with his *Sea Gull* setting (1916)—of "realistic sobriety"[13] in the midst of the "decorative excesses" of his other Washington Square sets.

In between *St. Anthony* and *The Sea Gull*, Simonson designed a show which, though polychromatic, did employ other kinds of simplification. In *The Farce of Pierre Patelin* (1916) Simonson chose the primary colors common in fairy tale illustrations. He acknowledges for this set the influence of European color poster-making techniques, in which bold and colorful simplicity is the prominent quality.

More significantly, Simonson's *Pierre Patelin* set showcased an idea that was seen as a breakthrough in aesthetic economy. He devised an ingenious scheme to telescope the seven scenes called for by the play's action. Simonson utilized maximum economy with few scenic elements by having a stage frame (a second proscenium) and a backdrop, both of which served double purposes. On the frame Simonson painted two exteriors, thereby creating a multiple stage setting. Since the frame was always visible, it acted as a permanent setting and thus provided pictorial unity. The curtain served both as scenery (on it was painted a street scene) and as a concealing curtain before which action could be played while the more elaborate inner scenes were being changed. By combinations of these elements, Simonson was able to go from a street to the interior of Patelin's house, to a draper's shop, back to the street, then again to Patelin's house interior, and finally to a marketplace. This technique intrigued Hiram Moderwell, who announced that Simonson's "big idea" had pointed the way toward more efficient use of settings on our stages.[14]

When the Theatre Guild was created in 1919, the founders were very careful not to make the same mistakes that sank the Washington Square Players. So they decided to procure a large theater, one that could pay for itself. A theater holding less than 300, or even 600, would not suffice. They chose to take over the Garrick Theatre, which had just become vacated by Copeau's Vieux Colombier. Experience had also shown the founders that the one-act play—the staple of the Washington Square Players—did not satisfy audiences the way longer plays did. So the new theater severed its little-theater roots and offered full-length works to help achieve success as a professional art theater.

But the founders did not want to abandon totally the positive lessons and the aesthetic values that guided their little-theater experiences. They believed in stage simplification, for economic reasons if not for aesthetic ones. By 1919 when the Guild was founded, simplified settings no longer involved great risks, as they did five years earlier when the spare look first began to appear on American stages. So their new practicality did not force them to abandon the aesthetic ideal of stage simplification.

To be sure, not all Guild productions featured simplified settings. Their more detailed sets—such as those for *John Ferguson, Heartbreak House,* and *R.U.R.*—were not much different from the lesser detailed sets shown by Belasco and other Broadway directors and producers. And once the Guild moved from the Garrick to their own Broadway house in 1925, elaborate display became more and more common.

As the Theatre Guild's resident stage designer, Simonson was the one most responsible for simplified stages. His designs executed in the early years of the Guild actually were simpler than his creations with the Washington Square Players. Saylor hints at this when he recognizes "greater aesthetic economy and poise" in Simonson's settings at the Garrick than at the Bandbox and the Comedy[15]—the two theaters in which the Washington Square Players performed.

One factor contributing to this impression was his change in attitude toward color. He claims the turning point was his set design for John Masefield's *The Faithful* (1919). New York audiences, thinking they knew Simonson's work, expected a feast for their color appetites when this play about Medieval Japan came to the Garrick. But Simonson surprised everyone. Instead of displaying bright and varied colors, he followed the spare aesthetics of Japanese printmaker Hiroshige and painted the set in combinations of red cedar, cream, silver-gray, and ruddy gold, a far more limited palette than was his usual. A reviewer from the *New York Tribune* noticed the change: "Mr. Simonson, who has been known for his daring use of brilliant colors, has departed from his former method to achieve the quieter but richer harmonies of a Japanese color scheme."[16]

The choice of greater restraint in color turned out to be more than just a temporary detour. It actually signaled a transformation in his taste and style. In discussing the decision in his autobiography, Simonson suggests that *The Faithful* represented a maturing in his attitude toward color and a veritable turning point in his use of it:

> Conceptions of one's art often mature, like wine, in some cool, well-aired but dark cellar of the mind. I had not consciously reconsidered any of my theories of stage design when I found, in doing *The Faithful*, that a brilliant parade of color no longer seemed of primary importance. I accepted the subdued hues of the samurai palace and welcomed the cool grey and white patterns of the scene in the snow gorge that I took from Hiroshige's color print.[17]

Thus Simonson's color campaign was abandoned—or at least moderated. In his autobiography *Part of a Lifetime*, he acknowledges how he finally rejected colorfulness, succumbing "to the monochrome schemes of modern interior architecture."[18] He writes off his Washington Square designs as guilty of "decorative excess."[19]

The Faithful is an important juncture on the way toward *The Tidings Brought to Mary* production in other ways, too. For the exterior scenes, Simonson designed two sets of folding screens—one a snow gorge, the other a forest scene with the outline of jagged mountains above it. He arranged them on a flat, horizontal plane, which established a shallow relief stage. Simonson kept the space in front of the screens fairly empty, except for a single property here or there on which an actor could sit or kneel (photo 7.1). The Japanese prints had shown him the way toward a self-imposed restraint not present during his Washington Square years.

7.1 Exterior, Masefield's *The Faithful*, Lee Simonson, designer, and Augustin Duncan, director. Performed at the Theatre Guild, May 1919. Photo courtesy of the Billy Rose Theatre Collection, The New York Public Library at Lincoln Center, Astor, Lenox, and Tilden Foundations.

7.2 March of the Ronin in silhouette. Masefield's *The Faithful* designed by Lee Simonson and directed by Augustin Duncan. Theatre Guild, May 1919. Photo courtesy of the Billy Rose Theatre Collection, The New York Public Library at Lincoln Center, Astor, Lenox, and Tilden Foundations.

During the March of the Ronin scene, director Augustin Duncan had his actors march in back of the forest scene, lit from behind. Their silhouetted figures, banners, and weapons appeared on the screens as shadows (photo 7.2), creating an effect reminiscent of Browne and Jonson's *Passion Play* pantomime. For the interior scenes, Simonson created a spare Japanese palace room that resembled the one designed by Japanese director/dancer Michio Ito years before in the Washington Square Players's production of *Bushido*, seen only three years earlier. The walls were free of ornament, but for "a length of delicate fretwork, a single flowering branch and a large round window above which sits the household god...."[20] Again the floor space defined by the two side walls set at right angles to the back wall, was very shallow, with virtually no furnishings (photo 7.3).

But there was another important lesson still ahead for him, one that he would need to learn before he could design his *Tidings* production in the manner

7.3 Interior scene from Masefield's *The Faithful*, designed by Lee Simonson and directed by Augustin Duncan. Theatre Guild, May 1919. Photo courtesy of the Billy Rose Theatre Collection, The New York Public Library at Lincoln Center, Astor, Lenox, and Tilden Foundations.

that he did. Before Simonson went to Europe in 1921, scenic design revolved first and foremost around scenery. After seeing Jessner/Pirchan's *Richard III* and Fehling and Strohbach's production of Toller's *Man and the Masses* at the Volksbuhne in Berlin, he realized that the moving figure of the actor on a virtually empty stage could serve as the most important element in the stage picture and even replace scenery altogether. Simonson's most highly acclaimed simplified *mise-en-scènes* after his trip to Europe were variations on the "space stage."

From the two German director/designer teams of Fehling and Strohbach and Jessner and Pirchan, Simonson learned how black draperies, stairs, and platforms can create a void in which patterns of actors in motion can be the principal pictorial element in a performance. Simonson saw this idea as capable of revolutionizing the *mise-en-scène*:

> Within the last decade a few directors and designers have begun to create the only art of the theatre which has any right to call itself modern, precisely because it abolishes the scenery as painted decoration altogether and destroys the stage picture in every sense that it has been known for two centuries. The setting becomes nothing more than the actors themselves, its design is the patterns they make, the rhythm of their movements; its form is simply the shifting groups that build into masses and disintegrate again.[21]

Upon Simonson's return from Europe, he wrote passionately about these new images. Simonson was barely off the boat from Europe when an article appeared in the *Boston Evening Transcript* in which he articulated his new insights and praised the Fehling/Strohbach *Man and the Masses mise-en-scène*. He also freely credited Jones for having initiated the execution of these principles in the United States, probably remembering the Hopkins/Jones *Macbeth*, which he saw just before leaving on his trip:

> That is the sort of thing that Robert Edmond Jones has been talking about here and that perhaps we haven't understood too well. It is the business of... designing your play with people; and this production is to me a sign of how tremendous, how tense and how extremely beautiful that sort of thing should be.[22]

He hammers away at the same idea in the April 1922 issue of *Theatre Arts Magazine*, arguing the need for suppressing scenery and replacing it with patterned movement and posings of actors.

This new insight translated itself into several production ideas both before and after *Tidings* was presented. He eliminated all but the essential properties, often skewed the scenic pieces he did include, and then concentrated on the figure of the sculpted figure of the actor isolated in and moving through space. He employed this kind of expressionist "space stage" in his designs for Georg Kaiser's *From Morn to Midnight* (1922); Elmer Rice's *The Adding Machine* (1923); and Ernst Toller's *Man and the Masses* (1924). In this last play, he virtually reconstructed the Fehling/Strobach *Man and the Masses* he saw in Berlin, with actors' movements on steps in a black void as the main design feature.

During his years with the Theatre Guild, Simonson also became famous for what has come to be known as simplified, selective, symbolic, or suggestive realism. One of the variants of this style was a combination of the space stage and realism, wherein fragments of a room are presented floating in a black void. In Lenormand's *The Failures* (1924) and Werfel's *Goat Song* (1926), Simonson stripped a room down to its essentials; in *The Failures* a room was represented by two adjoining walls, a mere corner, before which floated minimal furnishings. Simonson also worked within a variation of selective realism more like the Hopkins/Jones *The Devil's Garden* Act One set, with bare surfaces, long uninterrupted horizontal or vertical lines, and few decorative features. Several of his O'Neill settings for the Guild in the late 1920s featured scenes in this mode.

THEODORE KOMISARJEVSKY

Most of the plays Simonson designed at the Theatre Guild were directed by Philip Moeller. Simonson himself directed *Man and the Masses*. But Simonson's most neutral and elemental production resulted from a fruitful collaboration with a visiting director, Theodore Komisarjevsky. Not only did he encourage Simonson to simplify the design far beyond even the most simplified Guild productions, but he also thoroughly applied these aesthetic principles to the production's directing style. Theodore Komisarjevsky proved to be Simonson's ideal complement in creating a simple stage for *The Tidings Brought to Mary*.

Komisarjevsky had been exposed to some of the most radical experiments in stage simplicity when he served as technical director under Vsevolod Meyerhold at Vera Kommissarjevskaya's little theater in St. Petersburg from 1906 to 1907. In that capacity, Komisarjevsky helped his sister by designing and overseeing the execution of designs for Meyerhold's simplified symbolist productions.

Three of Meyerhold's productions at Vera Kommissarjevskaya's Dramatic Theatre—Ibsen's *Hedda Gabler* (1906), Maeterlinck's *Sister Beatrice* (1906), and Andreyev's *Life of Man* (1907)—featured stripped-to-bare-essential stages as well as actors who moved and talked in repetitive, minimal, or economic ways. With *Hedda Gabler* and *Sister Beatrice*, Komisarjevsky observed Meyerhold's use of relief staging with flat settings, one-directional straight-on lighting from overhead battons and footlights, and horizontal actor movements.

He also watched as Meyerhold had his actors take lengthy pauses and assume poses, exhibiting the traits of a Maeterlinckian "static theater." For Andreyev's *The Life of Man* (1907), Komisarjevsky designed Meyerhold's space stage, which featured isolated characters and properties in a vast empty space with black draperies and, in one scene, single-source high-angle lighting. In *Sister Beatrice* and *Life of Man*, Meyerhold utilized multiple uniformity techniques, having characters who looked, moved, and talked alike. Komisarjevsky himself designed the dresses for the identically-clad nuns in the former play.

What ultimately alienated Vera Kommissarjevskaya from Meyerhold was his tendency to depersonalize the actor in every way. In all three productions, Meyerhold did everything he could to make the actors anonymous figures moving through space and to confine them within tight limits. He clothed them in the same colors as those on the backdrop; he put on their bodies shapeless, neutral-toned garments; he lit them in ways to blur and dim their features; he limited the range in the actors' vocal pitch and forced them into repetitive, non-literal movement patterns. These tendencies culminated in his production of *Pelleas and Melisande*, where he had the actors move and speak like puppets. According to Komisarjevsky, his sister had to dismiss Meyerhold when this production made her realize fully "how he cramped and limited the actors with his methods...."[23] So Meyerhold was forced to leave the Dramatic Theatre in 1908, before Remizov's *The Devil's Show* opened, and his replacement was Theodore Komisarjevsky, who was then given his first directing assignment.

As short-lived as Meyerhold's tenure was at the Dramatic Theatre, his productions had considerable impact. And even though Komisarjevsky, like his sister, rejected Meyerhold's rigid confinement and defigurization of the actor, Meyerhold's influence can be detected in Komisarjevsky's productions, especially in *Tidings*.

Admittedly, Komisarjevsky's theory and practice does not exclusively point him toward a simple stage. On the contrary, his advocacy of "the universal actor," a "synthetic theater" (cf. Wagner's *gesamtkunstwerk*), "dynamic decor," and "psychologized decor"[24] often placed his productions on the more decorative side of New Stagecraft aesthetics. But he did show sympathies toward stage simplification. In his autobiography, *Myself and the Theatre*, Komisarjevsky states: "It needs much more brain and art to interpret a deep feeling at a simple, unobtrusive moment than to present sensational sets and costumes, women's bodies, horses, crowds of supers, and all the rest of the paraphernalia of a big show."[25] When presenting plays on a proscenium, Komisarjevsky argues, "the best possible 'decor' is a high plain screen or wall at the back and sides of the stage and a floor, the levels of which can be changed."[26] In terms of actual production, Komisarjevsky claims to have been the first to use a totally bare stage when, in 1912 at the Nezlobin Theatre in Russia, he did a dramatic adaptation of Dostoyevsky's novel, *The Idiot*.

Lawrence Langner, the director of the Theatre Guild Board, brought

Komisarjevsky from England to the United States originally to direct *Man and the Masses*. This assignment was later changed, the Toller play given instead to Simonson. Komisarjevsky ended up directing three plays for the company's fifth season (1922-1923): *The Lucky One* by A. A. Milne, *The Tidings Brought to Mary* by Claudel, and *Peer Gynt* by Ibsen. Although *Tidings* was withdrawn after only 33 performances (compared to 121 performances for *Peer Gynt*), it represents a landmark production in taking simplicity to a logical extreme.

THE TIDINGS BROUGHT TO MARY

Even though *The Tidings Brought to Mary* received a lukewarm response from critics and audiences, it was widely viewed as a success in its *mise-en-scène*. One commentator expressed his preference for the simplicity of this production over the complexity of others with the following oxymorons: "And we wondered what one of Mr. Ziegfield's Follies might become if only it were done with the same glory of simplicity and lavishness of suggestion."[27]

The overall concept for the set design, said to have been Komisarjevsky's brainchild, was to create a quasi-abstract space composed of a large Gothic-styled arch, a central platform with a plain rectangular block in the center, a wide staircase leading to that block, and neutral hangings in the rear. The color of the setting was the stone gray of a Gothic church. Facing the audience on either side of the proscenium façade were the two doorways that Jacques Copeau had left behind. The doors called to mind church portals, and the main arch, with high pillars supporting it, suggested a cathedral, the block an altar. This set remained constant throughout the production, acting as a unifying permanent setting from scene to scene with changes in scenes coming only from variations in the properties, the lighting, and the body positions of actors. Thus, even though Simonson did not use a standard space stage as he did for *Man and the Masses*, he did utilize some of its corollary principles in relying heavily on actor movement and flexible lighting as primary elements in the design.

On the eve of *The Tidings Brought to Mary* production, Simonson announced his design strategy in an article in the *New York Tribune*: "The characters and their shifting groups, the costumes, and the lights are the scenes....There is to be nothing actual; we suggest."[28] It is interesting that for the Hopkins/Jones *Macbeth* and the Komisarjevsky/Simonson *Tidings*, it was thought necessary to educate the public beforehand as to the purposes behind the *mise-en-scènes*. The fact that Hopkins wrote an article in the newspaper just before his *Macbeth* and Simonson wrote this article in the *Tribune* shows how uncertain they were in presenting these productions to mainstream New York audiences. Considering the responses from most reviewers and the public, their concerns were well-founded.

In placing the action on a permanent, quasi-abstract set, Komisarjevsky and

Simonson were ignoring the realistic, elaborately literal stage directions indicated for each scene in Claudel's script. As playwright, Claudel did not take the initiative toward simplification that Masefield did in his stage directions for *The Faithful*, which called for an almost bare stage. Nor does Claudel's script encourage a director or designer to depersonalize the actor by using generic character names as do many symbolist plays by Andreyev or Maeterlinck and expressionist plays by Kaiser or Toller. If individualizing features of *Tidings* were to be shorn away resulting in more neutral elements, it had to be done through the director and designer's self-initiated constraints.

7.4 Claudel's experimental theater at Hellerau for production of his own *The Tidings Brought to Mary*, October 1913. Sheldon Cheney and Kenneth Macgowan attribute set to Adolphe Appia.

To be sure, there were precedents for this kind of strategy in doing the Claudel play. In 1912, Lugne-Poe did a somewhat simplified version, benefitting from Claudel's direct input during the rehearsal process.[29] But it was Claudel himself as director who, the very next year, took the most radical measures in simplifying the play's *mise-en-scène*. Defying his own stage directions, Claudel, possibly with the help of designer Adolphe Appia, staged *Tidings* at Hellerau in 1913 with a permanent setting very similar to the one utilized by Komisarjevsky and Simonson. At Hellerau, they presented the entire play on three levels and implemented Claudel's theory of "permanent actors," i.e., having certain properties so constantly visible on stage that they took on the status of actors. In the *Tidings* production, the hearth, door and table were "permanent actors." (photo 7.4). Komisarjevsky and Simonson employed the same idea, but they chose to have only one: a single rectangular block, with stairs leading to it and a Gothic arch framing it (photo 7.5).

7.5 Bread defining block as dinner table in Claudel's *The Tidings Brought to Mary* presented at the Theatre Guild in December 1922. Directed by Theodore Komisarjevsky and designed by Lee Simonson. Gothic arch functions as a permanent unit and central block as different realities as determined by how actors handle it. Photo courtesy of the Billy Rose Theatre Collection, The New York Public Library at Lincoln Center, Astor, Lenox, and Tilden Foundations.

It is unclear from the evidence whether Simonson or Komisarjevsky saw the Hellerau production, but it only takes a brief glance at Claudel's setting to see the influence on the Simonson set. Step-units and platforms were dominant elements for both settings, enabling the action to be broken up and performed on different levels. Both had dignified, high columns, which, in combination with the steps, suggested a cathedral (compare photos 7.4 and 7.5).

But Simonson's set was even simpler than Claudel's. The Hellerau setting had more columns and a more complex arrangement of stairs. Claudel's step-units went off in several different directions, creating more broken surfaces and forcing the eye along a windy path. Simonson's steps, in contrast, led upward very smoothly toward center, with no detours for the spectator's eye path. Thus, even though both sets were symmetric and permanent, Simonson's was simpler, sparer, less detailed, and smoother to the movement of the eye.

Still, the sets resemble each other enough to suggest some kind of influence. It is possible that Claudel had a direct influence on their production, whether or not Komisarjevsky and Simonson saw the Hellerau production. A letter from Claudel may have provided Komisarjevsky the impetus for the Guild production's permanent set. In *Claudel on the Theatre*, Petit and Kempf cite information that proves Claudel's input in a production of the play, and we can only assume by the similarities between suggestion and *mise-en-scène* that it was Komisarjevsky and Simonson's production: "For *Tidings Brought to Mary* he [Claudel] advised a producer to have no scenery at all and a few days later sent him photographs of stained-glass windows and a cathedral porch to give him ideas."[30]

Even a cursory look at the Komisarjevsky/Simonson production photographs suggest that the central images were those of a Medieval cathedral and a stained-glass window. The main Gothic arch, the side portals, the pillars, the steps, the rectangular block, the continual presence of eight nuns, and the general spareness of the stage picture all helped to convey the aura of a cathedral. Remarks from critics verify this impression. James Craig of the *New York Mail* explains how the action of the play "takes place in a single setting, something like the interior of a church."[31] *The Evening Post* concurred, describing how the set "remotely resembled a cathedral interior."[32] But Simonson avoided making it only a church interior; he wanted to keep the stage neutral enough so that it could become other locations, depending on how the actors related to the space and the few properties.

Some especially perceptive reviewers also noticed the stained-glass imagery in the *mise-en-scène*. Percy Hammond, for instance, explained how the production looked like a "Medieval, painted window,"[33] and the reviewer from *The Nation* remarked that "the pictures are like the most precious stained-glass of the best period."[34] Eaton remembered the production this way: "The long flowing costumes, the soft play of tinted lights, and the groupings under this pointed arch, gave... the effect of a stained-glass cathedral window come to life in three dimensions—an effect, of course, peculiarly in harmony with the drama."[35]

Thus, the cathedral and stained-glass imagery worked together to create an overriding atmosphere of faith and religiosity. Instead of trying to depict the Medieval period literally with all the paraphernalia of facsimile interiors, Komisarjevsky and Simonson chose instead to convey the spirit of the period through these central images and a dominant ecclesiastic atmosphere. They conveyed the essence of the period through repetitions of the same scenic and movement motifs and thereby created more out of less.

Komisarjevsky and Simonson took other measures to evoke a sacred place of worship rather than a theater. They opted not to use a front curtain; beginnings and ends of scenes and acts were designated only through lighting changes. And Komisarjevsky directed the actors to move slowly and solemnly, as though walking through a cathedral, during the action or when moving properties between scenes.

The Gothic arch that contained the play's action served several functions. First of all, the arch, like the jetting platform and lack of curtain, diverted attention from the piece's theatricality and emphasized more its aura of sacredness. Second, it functioned as a second or false proscenium. Like Simonson's earlier set for *Pierre Patelin*, a proscenium within a proscenium was used as a device to simplify changes in the stage picture. And third, the arch—like the Tower of London in the Hopkins/Jones *Richard III* and the arch and stairs in their *Hamlet*—served to unify the play by being a permanent presence throughout.

Simonson and Komisarjevsky also contributed to the feeling of spareness by endowing the arch and stairs with long horizontal and vertical uninterrupted lines. The director/designer team gave themselves an extra six feet of playing space by building out a platform over the first seats of the Garrick Theatre. This not only brought the action closer to the audience, but also provided more room around the isolated cloaked figures, expressing a greater sense of sparseness.

Since the set never changed, it became necessary for Komisarjevsky and Simonson to find ways to create as much visual variety as possible within their self-imposed fixities. They also had to discover imaginative ways to indicate changes in location. Like the Medieval *platea*, the Elizabethan platform, and the Noh and Peking Opera stages, the stage for *Tidings* was as much a neutral place as it was a cathedral. The lights, costumes, properties, as well as the actors' movements and gestures, could define time, location, mood, and circumstance.

The lights ended up taking on the primary responsibility for changing scenes and establishing visual variety. Many of his lighting transformations, however, were done not only for the sake of visual variety but also, in tune with Komisarjevsky's notion of "psychologized decor," to reflect changes in the psychological states of principal characters on stage—just as Browne and Jonson did for their *Trojan Women* and *Medea* productions at the Chicago Little Theatre. This principle worked against the severe restraint exercised in other areas.

But in other ways the lighting did contribute to an overall simplicity. Although lighting changes were happening constantly, an observant critic noted how they were always in "simple gradations."[36] This created an unbroken, smooth *legato* rhythm in how the visual picture transformed. Perhaps this accounts for Percy Hammond's observation that the lights sustained an hypnotic effect.[37] The lighting also helped give a visual context of infinity. Like Browne and Jonson's success with light on a cyclorama and Cook and Hume's light on plaster domes, the lighting on the cyclorama in *Tidings* evidently contributed to a feeling of "great spaciousness,"[38] a background "shimmering with eternity."[39] The accents of light on the vertical lines of the pillars also added to a feeling of vastness. In addition, at several moments through the production only side- and backlighting were used, so that characters were presented as shadows and silhouettes or otherwise lit so as to appear more as moving shapes than as specific people (photo 7.6).

7.6 Theatre Guild production of *The Tidings Brought to Mary*. Side- and back-lighting to eliminate surface detail. Photo courtesy of the Billy Rose Theatre Collection, The New York Public Library at Lincoln Center, Astor, Lenox, and Tilden Foundations.

The use of sound in the production helped replace what could have been actualized onstage. Broun describes how a cavalcade on the march was suggested without visual representation, just the offstage sounds of distant bells and trumpets seemingly coming nearer and nearer, and, "strangest of all, we saw them, horse and foot, because they swept before our mind without the inadequacy of visual appearance."[40]

While Komisarjevsky and Simonson did not entirely foreswear the use of bright colors in their costuming, they took other measures to simplify them. The peasant garb that the principal characters wore, for example, stayed within the limited, neutral palette of the settings, and the "long, flowing" costumes[41] were loose-fitting in conformity with the style of the period. By having these qualities, the garb was vague in defining the individual body shapes of the characters, making them, in coordination with the higher vertical lines of the arch, as much semi-defined shapes as individuals. The "flowing" quality that Eaton attributes to the costumes also added to the production's other smooth and lulling traits. The costumes for the nuns supplied color to the production, but even here the choices were toward single primary colors. Each nun wore a robe that was uniformly red, blue, or yellow. Introduced for the sake of visual variety and to emphasize the vitality of religiosity in the Middle Ages, these costumes stood out boldly from the neutral-toned, permanent set. This, along with the vast cyclorama lit in a series of bright colors from scene to scene, added to the stained-glass-window image Komisarjevsky and Simonson wanted to create.

Komisarjevsky also chose to have few properties, so stage business was by necessity kept to a minimum. By having the kitchen scene presented on a bare stage with only bread on the ever-present rectangular block, the bread took on the resonances of a religious symbol, rather than part of a detailed picture. It was aspects like these that justify John Corbin's description of the stage as manifesting an "austere symbolism."[42] What few properties Komisarjevsky did have he used economically, endowing them not only with maximum symbolic significance but also with the kind of transformability which typified Peking Opera and Noh theater and Sam Hume's adaptable settings in Detroit. One object which took on multiple functions was the cloth. The same material that served as a tablecloth in an early scene was recognizable as Violaine's winding sheet at the play's end.

But the prime example, of course, was Komisarjevsky's use of the rectangular block, which took on different meanings through the production according to how the actors behaved in relation to it. When the nuns prayed before the block, it became an altar. When they put a cloth on it and took out chairs from within its hollow structure and then placed them around, it magically became a dinner table. At one point in the production, the Mayor sat on it, transforming it into a roadside bench, and in the orchard scene it served as a rock. At the end of the play when the dying Violaine was placed on it, it became her deathbed (photo 7.7), and, after she died, the eight nuns prayed before her prostrate body, transforming the block into a bier (photo 7.8).

Other directing decisions supported the simplicity of the settings and how they were utilized. Komisarjevsky enforced an overall acting style summed up by one unhappy reviewer as "something of that catalepsy of self-hypnosis which our players usually succumb to only in giving Maeterlinck."[43] One commentator made the analogy not with symbolist but with Medieval aesthetics, writing that the production "narrates in slow-moving Medieval style."[44] Both critics were noticing the slow, *legato* movement of the actors which promoted an atmosphere of sacredness and religious rite.

7.7 The death of Violaine from *The Tidings Brought to Mary* at the Theatre Guild, with block as deathbed. Photo courtesy of the Billy Rose Theatre Collection, The New York Public Library at Lincoln Center, Astor, Lenox, and Tilden Foundations.

Whether the actors were able to maintain this style throughout and in all aspects of the performance is another question. Some comments suggest that they could not. For instance, Lee Simonson, looking back several years after the production, blamed the show's failure on the actors who "were unable to sustain the mood of austere formalism... that Komisarjevsky had conceived."[45] In fact, the most frequent criticism directed at the production was the dull, montonous intonations of the actors (Percy Hammond described the phenomenon as "desert vocalism"). Perhaps this followed the director's intention, representing another aspect of "austere formalism." Maybe the voices were hushed and unvaried to lull audiences into the hypnotic state which the slowly evolving lights, solemn physical movement, and unchanging neutral sets and hangings were helping to create.

Central to Komisarjevsky's stylistic intent of austere formalism was his treatment of the nuns, who unified the production by being a constant and mono-lithic presence on stage. Like the rectangular block, they were, in a sense, "permanent actors." Always moving solemnly as if in a cathedral, the eight nuns were handled as one entity, with every aspect of their appearance and behavior designed to emphasize their similarities and erase their differences (photos 7.8 and 7.9). Thus they moved as one, were dressed alike, and at times chanted in unison. By staging the nuns in conformity with the principle of multiple uniformity, Komisarjevsky was closely following Meyerhold's treatment of the sisters in his production of *Sister Beatrice*.

7.8 Block as bier in Theatre Guild production of *The Tidings Brought to Mary*. Courtesy of the Collection of American Literature, Beinecke Rare Book and Manuscript Collection, Yale University.

The activities of the nuns substituted for scenery and properties by con- tinually redefining a scene's time, place, and mood. To set the atmosphere for Act One Scene One, in which a main character announces he wants to make a religious pilgrimage, for instance, the nuns entered from the portals before the scene began, lit candles, and then prayed before the block, which was now an al- tar. For another scene, they set the dinner table and thus became servants while still retaining their identity as nuns. They even became trees in the orchard scene, not by trying to disguise themselves as illusionary trees but rather by merely standing still throughout the scene and holding in their hands branches of gold, silver, and coral (photo 7.10). In the final scene, they carried off Violaine's dead body, thus suddenly becoming her pallbearers—an image closely parallel-ing the death scene from Meyerhold's *Sister Beatrice* production.

7.9 Chorus of nuns transform rectangular box into altar and permanent set into a cathe-dral in *The Tidings Brought to Mary*. Courtesy of the Collection of American Literature, Beinecke Rare Book and Manuscript Collection, Yale University.

By so transforming the nuns, Komisarjevsky achieved the same kind of aesthetic economy as with the block and cloth; through an imaginative ma-nipulation of a few people or things on a quasi-neutral stage, he was able to suggest many stage realities without depending on lots of scenery or properties, and this attests to influence from East Asian production conventions. Besides the transformability of objects and people that characterizes the Noh, this production also manifested the influence of Peking Opera, in which a propertyman changes and evokes diverse settings. New York audiences, who had seen this device in the 1912 production of *The Yellow Jacket*, were now seeing its application with a Chorus of characters rather than the single propertyman of the Winthrop Ames production.

Claudel's script in no way indicates that the nuns should be used in this manner. In fact the text does not call for nuns at all. By adding this element, Komisarjevsky was reducing the need for a lot of scenery and stage properties.

The nuns provided a unifying element and were handled as a single element by their uniform appearance, smooth and unbroken movement and vocal patterns, and economy in conveying different realities. They also reinforced the central image/concept of the production: a church interior and the scenes as stained-glass images coming to life.

7.10 Nuns representing forest setting on permanent stage in *The Tidings Brought to Mary* at the Theatre Guild. Courtesy of the Collection of American Literature, Beinecke Rare Book and Manuscript Collection, Yale University.

The Tidings Brought to Mary production at the Theatre Guild can be viewed as a grand summation of all the theory and practice Simonson and Komisarjevsky had developed up to that point. The permanent setting featured the bare surfaces, high vertical lines, and minimal furniture that characterized most Simonson scenery, from his Washington Square years onwards. The sets and hangings were all a neutral-toned gray, following the lessons of color control Simonson learned from *The Faithful*, and, in imitation of productions seen during his 1921 European trip, Simonson (with the help of director Komisarjevsky) made the groupings and movement of actors the central aspect of the overall *mise-en-scène*. The austere formalism of the acting style—the hushed voices and restricted movement—evinced directorial restraint, just as the permanent setting revealed a self-imposed restriction on Simonson's part.

Reduction, too, was a key factor. Komisarjevsky and Simonson reduced each aspect of the *mise-en-scène* to a bare minimum and stripped the overall image to the essentials of a dignified cathedral, while maintaining enough neutrality so that the stage could become a forest, a cave, and the interior of a house. Indeed, minimal materiality defined so many of their decisions, especially their utilization of a wide-open arch and a single bare block, with a mere few properties added to redefine it from scene to scene. Vast volumes of empty space continually confronted the spectator's eye due to the constant presence of that high vaulted arch and its supporting columns, with just enough light added to accent their towering vertical lines. Aesthetic economy was evident in the multiple uses of the one block and nuns to define the various times, locales, and moods. One critic realized that this production was unprecedented in its simplicity: "Never has a more sumptuous effect been achieved by simpler means."[46] Komisarjevsky applied the principle of sameness by treating the nuns as a single entity, and Simonson did his share by designing a stage dominated by the uninterrupted horizontal lines of the stairs and the vertical lines of the columns as well as the solid, undifferentiated masses of the backdrop, the platforms, and the arch itself.

Clearly, *The Tidings Brought to Mary* in 1922 went about as far with stage simplicity as Belasco's *The Governor's Lady* in 1912 did with facsimile realism. And, as with the Belasco production, by going so far, a retreat would inevitably occur—at least until a new participant in the creative process could revive the cause in a new way. Simonson viewed the *Tidings* set as a potential turning point in the evolution of the American *mise-en-scène*; to his chagrin, it did not prove to be so. In *The Stage is Set* written in 1932, Simonson laments how the *Tidings* set elicited "no outspoken recognition that stage setting had found the clue to its proper development."[47] Simonson blamed the playwright for not having picked up on the initiative taken by the designers. Simonson vents his frustration in *The Stage is Set*:

> the most persistent efforts to reduce settings to a bare minimum, to formalize them almost out of existence, to make the group movements of the actors the only pictorial element of a performance, have been made by the scene-designers themselves. But they have failed to establish a successful tradition in this country because playwrights would not join the movement.[48]

Simonson was so incensed by the situation he even wrote an open letter to Robert Littell, the drama critic of the *New York World*, challenging any American playwright to "write a play in which lines and business are so independent of scenery that it can be played on a bare stage."[49]

Almost as Simonson wrote these words, Thornton Wilder was working on a series of one-act plays that would do just that. As if heeding Simonson's call,

Thornton Wilder wrote plays with bare and neutral stages, building stage simplicity into the plays themselves.

NOTES

[1] Lee Simonson, *Part of a Lifetime* (New York: Duell, Sloan and Pearce, 1943), p. 23.

[2] Ibid., p. 24.

[3] Ibid., p. 26.

[4] Hiram Kelley Moderwell, "A Note about Lee Simonson," *Theatre Arts Magazine*, 2 (December 1917), p. 17.

[5] Lee Simonson, *Lifetime*, p. 29.

[6] Lee Simonson, "The Painter and the Stage," *Theatre Arts Magazine*, 2 (December 1917), p. 10.

[7] Simonson, *Lifetime*, p. 29.

[8] Walter Prichard Eaton, *The Theatre Guild: The First Ten Years* (New York: Brentano's, 1929), p. 189.

[9] Eaton, *Theatre Guild*, p. 189.

[10] Ibid., p. 186.

[11] Simonson, *Lifetime*, pp. 70-71.

[12] Robert Nordvoldt, "Showcase for the New Stagecraft: The Scenic Designs of the Washington Square Players and the Theatre Guild," (Diss., Indiana University, 1973), pp. 56-57.

[13] Simonson, *Lifetime*, p. 28.

[14] Hiram Moderwell, "Mr. Simonson's Big Idea," *The New York Times*, June 18, 1916, p. 6.

[15] Sayler, *Our American Theatre*, p. 160.

[16] *New York Tribune*, October 5, 1919, cited in Simonson, *The Stage is Set* (New York: Harcourt, Brace and Co., 1932), p. 124.

[17] Simonson, *Lifetime*, p. 47.

[18] Ibid., p. 30.

[19] Ibid., p. 28.

[20] Zack York, "Lee Simonson: Artist/Craftsman of the Theatre," Diss., U. of Wisconsin, 1951, p. 187.

[21] Lee Simonson, "Men as Stage Scenery Walking," *New York Times*, May 25, 1924, p. 8.

[22] Lee Simonson, "New Ways, New Means, New Outcome as European States Now Yield Them," *Boston Evening Transcript*, December 17, 1921, n.p.

[23] Theodore Komisarjevsky, *Myself and the Theatre* (New York: E.P. Dutton and Company, 1930), p. 79.

[24] Ibid., *passim*.

[25] Ibid., p. 165.

[26] Ibid., p. 150.

[27] Heywood Broun, "At the Garrick Theatre," *New York World*, December 25, 1922, n. p.

[28] Lee Simonson, "A New Guild Play," *New York Tribune* December 24, 1922, as quoted in Nordvoldt, p. 252.

[29] Paul Claudel, *Claudel on the Theatre*, trans. Christine Trollope, (Coral Gables, FL, 1972), pp. 10-16.

[30] Ibid., p. xv.

[31] James Craig, "The Tidings Brought to Mary," *New York Mail*, December 27, 1922, n. p., in *Tidings Brought to Mary* file, Billy Rose Collection, Lincoln Center.

[32] *The New York Evening Post*, December 26, 1922, n. p., in *Tidings* file, Billy Rose Collection.

[33] Percy Hammond, "Oddments and Remainders," *New York Tribune*, January 8, 1923, p. 6.

[34] *The Nation*, 116 (Jan. 24, 1923), p. 102.

[35] Eaton, *Theatre Guild*, p. 67.

[36] Cuthbert Wright, "The Theatre," *The Freeman*, 6 (January 24, 1923), p. 473.

[37] Hammond, "Oddments," *New York Tribune*, p. 6.

[38] Broun, "At the Garrick Theatre," *New York World*, p. 9.

[39] *The Nation*, 116 (January 24, 1923), p. 102.

[40] Broun, "At the Garrick Theatre," p. 4.

[41] Eaton, *Theatre Guild*, p. 67.

[42] John Corbin, *New York Times*, December 25, 1922, p. 20.

[43] Alexander Woollcott, "Claudel in Thirty-Fifth Street," *New York Herald*, December 25, 1922, n. p., in *Tidings* file, Billy Rose Collection.

[44] "Tidings Brought to Mary," *Theatre Magazine*, 37 (March 1923), p. 20.

[45] Eaton, *Theatre Guild*, p. 192.

[46] Cuthbert Wright, "The Theatre," p. 473.

[47] Simonson, *Stage is Set*, p. 123.

[48] Ibid., p. 122.

[49] Ibid., p. 124.

8

Thornton Wilder and the Playwright's Initiative

Before Thornton Wilder's one-act plays were published in 1931, no major American playwright had consistently built into his or her playwriting the necessity for a simplified stage. From 1912 to 1928, the initiative clearly belonged to director/designer teams like Browne and Jonson, Hopkins and Jones, and Komisarjevsky and Simonson. This fact was noticed before Lee Simonson in the early 1930s. In 1919 Samuel Eliot, in discussing Jacques Copeau's program for stage simplification at the Garrick Theatre, observed that his simplified presentational method had not yet been adopted by playwrights, despite Copeau's encouragement.[1] Three years later Kenneth Macgowan made it clear that the situation had not yet changed, that contemporary playwrights—with the exception of British playwright/poet John Masefield in his Japanese tragedy, *The Faithful*—were not finding clever ways to construct plays in such a way that directors and designers *had* to simplify the stage.[2]

This is not to say that there were not scenes or even full plays written before Wilder calling for stage simplicity either in stage directions or required by the dialogue. We have already looked at some plays with severe self-imposed limitations: Cloyd Head's *Grotesques* (1915) which called for a black-and-white relief stage; Eugene O'Neill's *Before Breakfast* (1916-1917) and its offstage non-speaking second character; and playlets written by poets Edna St. Vincent

Millay and Alfred Kreymborg for the short-lived Other Players (1917-1918). There were scenes from American plays generally classified as expressionist that called for the utilization of empty-space aesthetics, multiple characters that walked, talked, and looked alike, and other kinds of stage simplification, plays like Elmer Rice's *The Adding Machine* as well as O'Neill's *Emperor Jones* (1920) and *The Hairy Ape* (1921). But despite a play or a scene here or there, no major playwright evinced an aesthetic commitment to a near-empty stage and bare essentials in multiple aspects of the *mise-en-scène*.

From his earliest efforts in playwriting until *Our Town* in 1938, Wilder sought various ways to create more with less, limiting himself severely in certain aspects of his craft to expand the imaginative scope of his work. His preliminary efforts along this line were his so-called three-minute playlets (the first ones dating back to 1915) anthologized under the title *The Angel That Troubled the Waters and Other Plays*, published in 1928. He found another, more successful and producible, way of creating more with less in his next series of one-acts, especially with *The Long Christmas Dinner, Pullman Car Hiawatha*, and *The Happy Journey to Trenton and Camden* published in 1931. This use of a bare stage on which to create an imaginative fullness climaxed in 1938 in *Our Town*, a play that fulfills an aesthetic impulse in the American theater begun around 1912.

Wilder's playwriting career did not end with *Our Town*. He went on to write plays that did not call for a simple stage. For instance, in 1938 he also wrote *Merchant of Yonkers* (later retitled *The Matchmaker*), a period farce requiring all the bric-a-brac that usually accompanies that form. Four years later, *The Skin of Our Teeth* was produced, which, though utilizing some neutral properties of the stage, went more in a showy theatrical direction. It featured a flashy carnival-like style, layered anachronisms, and a complex matrix of superimposed realities with characters simultaneously functioning on multiple planes of reality. To express this, he employed a busy, active, and colorful stage, the theatrical complexities of which contradicted the simplifying qualities associated with stage neutrality.

Yet Wilder had not left stage simplicity behind entirely. He would return to it, most obviously in the early 1960s, with his so-called *Plays for Bleecker Street*, a triple bill of one-acts written to be produced on a bare thrust stage requiring only a few chairs and other assorted properties. Even though some of the pronouncements around the time these plays were presented at the Circle-in-the-Square Theatre echoed sentiments expressed twenty-five years earlier,[3] in reality these one-acts added little to the ideals exhibited in Wilder's plays of the 1930s.

Wilder's 1930s one-acts and *Our Town* manifest an aesthetic inclination toward simplification, restraint, and self-imposed limitation. Many years after the successful production of *Our Town*, Brooks Atkinson wrote how Wilder was constantly setting technical limits for himself to keep his writing under control.[4]

Wilder's writing career, as he himself freely admits in his introduction to his three-minute plays, reflects a "passion for compression."[5]

Many scholars and critics have alluded to Wilder's tendency to simplify and condense. Malcolm Cowley, in an article written for the *Saturday Review* in 1956, commented on how Wilder holds to "the classical ideals of measure and decorum."[6] Tyrone Guthrie admires Wilder for his "utmost economy of means,"[7] including a symbolism which is "extremely simple" and a sense of humor which is "dry and rather Puritan."[8] Malcolm Goldstein, in his *The Art of Thornton Wilder*, comments on Wilder's simplification not only of the stage[9], but also of character[10], gesture,[11] and dialogue[12]. When *Our Town* came out in 1938, a review in the *Theatre Arts Monthly* identified as prominent traits of Wilder's writing his simplicity and his sense of moderation.[13]

Wilder admired writers who associated simplicity of means with higher metaphysical concerns. Wilder can even be viewed as a descendant of certain writers and philosophers in the Anglo-American literary tradition who make that connection. He ascribes the greatness of Jane Austen, for instance, to "her perfections in the small" which "implies her comprehension of the large."[14] In this association between the simple and the transcendent, one can also chart Wilder's spiritual lineage from American Puritanism in which austerity in everyday living manifests spiritual purity, and from Transcendentalism, especially the Thoreauvian vein, in which simplicity and economy open the way for communion with Nature in all of her grandness. Tyrone Guthrie recognizes Wilder's Puritan traits and origins; Malcolm Cowley calls Wilder "heir to the Transcendentalists."[15]

Wilder's specific interest in simplicity and aesthetic economy also reflects a worldview partly shaped by other modernist artists. With their guidance, Wilder plays out his own thoughts about the paradoxes of time, identity, and the relationship between the infinite and the momentary here-and-now. Wilder focuses on, as Goldstein phrases it, "moments of eternity singled out of our attention and played against the panorama of infinity."[16]

Wilder's notion of infinte time and everywhere predisposes him to a neutral stage where temporal vagaries and contradictions can rein freely and not be tied down as they would on the illusionistic stage. The neutral stage allows him to place the individual in relation to infinity, an idea that he ascribes to James Joyce. Wilder calls Joyce:

> the novelist who has most succeeded in placing man in an immense field of reference, among all the people who have lived and died, in all the periods of time, all the geography of the world, all the races, all the catastrophes of history. And he is also the one who has most dramatically engaged in a search for the validity of the individual as an absolute.[17]

Wilder's plays of the 1930s, especially *Pullman Car Hiawatha* and *Our Town* (and later *The Skin of Our Teeth*[18] in the 1940s) translate what Joyce did into dramatic form. The neutral stage gave Wilder a vehicle for theatricalizing the individual as an absolute in an immense field of reference.

Gertrude Stein had a more direct impact on Wilder. Having brought Stein to the University of Chicago where he was teaching in the mid-1930s, Wilder promoted her art and thought, wrote introductions to several of her books, and remained one of her faithful advocates throughout his career.

One can draw a clear parallel between Gertrude Stein's notion of a "continuous present" in which the "present is in continual flux"[19] and Wilder's "perpetual present"—the notion he uses to explain the fundamental difference between plays and novels. To Wilder, plays exist in a "perpetual present time" whereas novels exist only in the past.[20] It follows, then, that the theater is best served with a stage that is perpetually neutral and without commitment to one time and place. If the stage is too rooted in a context, then its action seems to have already happened, rather than to be playing itself out in the present.

Stein's view of the influence of geography on intellect and art parallels Wilder's own. Stein believes that the art and thought of continental countries like the United States reflect a sense of infinite time and space and therefore limitless movement potential. Wilder assumes Stein's idea in "Towards an American Language" when he explains the crisis in our national character: that Americans, especially those in this century, live with a constant awareness of limitlessness. Because of this, they tend to have no home, no identity, no connectedness—only a relationship "to everywhere, to everybody, and to always."[21] Here again is Wilder's notion of the individual in relation to an "immense field of reference." A relatively neutral and bare stage allows Wilder to express both fluid rootlessness and momentary rootedness in a specific time and place.

Gertrude Stein distinguishes between Human Nature and the Human Mind, the former a clinging to identity and location in time and space, the latter an ascension to non-identity, a hovering within a state of pure existing and pure creating. In his plays, Wilder seems to bridge these two states, to present Human Nature in all its specificity and rootedness to the here-and-now, while keeping stage and drama sufficiently neutral to take the human imagination wherever it wants—any time, space, or situation.

Goldstein argues that life's experience reinforced Wilder's philosophical understanding of the paradoxical nature of time when he participated in an archaeological dig in 1920-1921 outside Rome and helped unearth an ancient Etruscan street.[22] This brought him in touch with the simultaneous feeling for infinite fluid time and the fixed present moment. And what he sensed about time was paralleled later in the realm of space by his experience as an inveterate traveler. Wilder lived for extended periods of time in many different countries on different continents as well as in various states in the United States. Thus, personal experience of travel through space and imaginatively back through time helped solidify the double sense of the particular and the universal that he was absorbing and synthesizing from the thought and art of Joyce and Stein.

From his earliest plays on, Wilder attempted to express infinity by way of self-imposed limitation. His first approach was to write three-minute plays, as if by severely limiting play length, he, like Austen, could imply his comprehension of the large through perfections in the small. The discipline of trying to express vast themes in three minutes of stage time constitutes one strategy for creating more with less. But the *mise-en-scènes* he writes into his stage directions are complex and would be prohibitively expensive and inefficient to realize in three-minute plays. He had not yet fully comprehended the potential of a neutral bare stage.

At some point between 1928 and 1931, Wilder discovered the feasibility of using an empty or near-empty neutral stage—a zero-place in a zero-time—that would begin and remain undefined until someone (a character or narrator) designated time and place through dialogue or stage activity. Once done, it could be redefined at will; time and space could remain as fluid as the human imagination itself.

During this interval, Wilder came to some basic realizations. First of all, he recognized that the empty stage by itself is an immediate metaphor for the infinite. As he expressed it years later in his preface to *Our Town*, with a lighted space at one end of an otherwise darkened auditorium, "things seem to be half caught up into generality already," and that the stage itself "cries aloud its mission to represent the Act in Eternity."[23]

The neutrality of an empty stage was not a new idea and Wilder was perfectly aware of that. Like other theater artists of the simple stage, such as Jacques Copeau and Maurice Browne, Wilder's model for this kind of stage is a three-way synthesis between past uses in Western theater history, especially in the Ancient Greek, Elizabethan, and Spanish Golden Age performance traditions; East Asian models; and the use of the simple stage by contemporary (mostly European) stage artists. One must also factor in his protest against the illusionistic stage, both the painterly Italianate or naturalistic box-set varieties— a dissatisfaction that he shared with the other theater artists.

In his preface to *Our Town* and his introduction to *Three Plays*, Wilder freely admits that, by stripping the stage of all bric-a-brac, he is not an innovator but a "rediscoverer of forgotten goods"[24] and in its "healthiest ages the theater has always exhibited the least scenery."[25] Wilder was well-versed in the operations of the Greek stage and its lack of scenery. Isabel Wilder, Thornton's sister, relates how, as a boy of nine or ten, her brother participated in many Greek plays presented in the spare but vast Hearst Theater on the University of California's Berkeley campus. As a college student, Wilder voraciously read the Greek dramatists and studied Greek plays and production with Professor Charles Wager at Oberlin. He taps into this background when he reminds us that, in

Aristophanes's *The Clouds*, all we see are two beds, with Strepsiades asleep on one. When he crosses the stage, he is at Socrates' "Thinkery." This exemplifies how even the Greeks (despite the biased view of the French Neo-Classicists) did not always make the stage a single rooted time and place as became standard in the Italianate and naturalist stage traditions; it, too, was open to redefinitions of time and space.

Wilder was also well aware of the even more neutral properties of the Golden Age and Elizabethan public stage. He became acquainted with Lope de Vega and Golden Age Theater at least by the early 1920s.[26] He went on to become a recognized expert in this period of theater history, spending many years researching methods of dating Lope de Vega's early plays. Wilder had Lope de Vega's neutral stage in mind when he tells how, in one of Lope's plays, a rug is to be placed in the middle of the stage to represent a raft in the middle of the ocean bearing a castaway. As for the similar Elizabethan performance tradition, he notes how Shakespeare and his fellow Elizabethans used the stage in ways that parallel those by the Golden Age playwrights.[27] Wilder's familiarity with Shakespeare and the Elizabethan performance tradition dates back at least to 1916 when he was a college student. Gilbert Harrison contends that the primary influence on Wilder's neutral stage was the simple public stages used during the Elizabethan and Golden Age periods.[28]

Wilder was also knowledgeable about the East Asian aesthetic traditions, specifically the use of a neutral stage in Chinese and Japanese theater. He spent many of his early years in China and Japan, even though his sister has said he never actually saw a Chinese or Japanese play while he was there. She contends his knowledge of Eastern theater traditions can be attributed to his extensive reading on the subject.[29] However he learned about them, his preface to *Three Plays* reveals his understanding of how the Chinese and Japanese can utilize a neutral stage to traverse great expanses of time and place and activity with suggestive properties as a shorthand of communication to the audience:

> In Chinese drama a character, by straddling a stick, conveys to us
> that he is on horseback. In almost every Noh play of the Japanese
> an actor makes a tour of the stage and we know that he is making
> a long journey.[30]

The fact that he had this tradition in mind when writing his one-act plays and *Our Town* is clear from a postcard sent to his lifelong friend, Amy Wertheimer, dated November 14, 1937, in which he relates how he read *Our Town* to Jed Harris, identifying the new play as a "New Hampshire village!! explored by the technique of Chinese Drama and of *Pullman Car Hiawatha*."[31]

In looking for a more immediate source for Wilder's stage, one can find it in contemporary productions of classical and contemporary plays he attended between 1915 and 1930, the year he wrote his one-acts. Richard Goldstone states that Wilder was well-acquainted with Jacques Copeau's architectural stage, having attended productions of the Vieux Colombier in New York City during its 1917-1918 and 1918-1919 seasons.[32] In an interview in 1935 Wilder named Copeau's production of *Twelfth Night* on a simple *treteau* as one of his all-time favorite productions.

The catalyst for endowing his stage with neutrality may have come from Copeau's nephew, Michel Saint-Denis, who carried his uncle's aesthetic ideals into the operations of his Compagnie des Quinze. As a director, Saint-Denis went even further than Copeau in stripping his stage to bare essentials, coming up with an architectural stage even purer and barer than Copeau's and experimenting extensively with neutral and minimal suggestive properties. Among Saint-Denis's most highly celebrated accomplishments were his productions of the plays of Andre Obey.[33] Wilder had read about Saint-Denis's stagings of Obey's plays and was especially interested in Saint-Denis's decision to have commentators on the stage shepherding the audience through imaginative realities and to include a character on the stage who prowled "through a house by merely walking between posts set up on the stage...."[34]

On the same list of favorite productions on which Copeau's *Twelfth Night* appears, Wilder included as his number-one favorite production Brock Pemberton's Broadway production of *Six Characters in Search of an Author*[35] which he saw the year after attending (and loving) the original production of the play in Rome under the direction of Dario Niccodemi. These productions gave Wilder a firsthand and immediate acquaintanceship with Pirandello's themes which influenced his own, encouraged Wilder in the feasibility of placing his characters on a bare and neutral stage, and guided him toward a "liberation from the box set and the use of theater aisles and lobbies as settings."[36] In these productions of the Pirandello play, he saw how an empty stage—with a frank recognition of a stage as stage—could present a convincing and flexible reality for an audience.

Wilder's protest against the box set and the naturalist stagecraft in general also informed his decision to adopt a bare stage. Long after *Our Town*, Wilder argued that eliminating scenery encourages truth: "The less seen, the more heard" and "the eye is the enemy of the ear in real drama."[37] He goes so far as to portray the box set and all its paraphernalia as a nineteenth-century mistake continued into the twentieth.[38]

The neutral near-empty stage, then, reappropriated from theater history to fit his own modernist philosophy, provided Wilder with a practical way to use theatrical space to convey multiple, specific here-and-nows within fluid time while maintaining an immense field of reference. The empty stage endowed him with a dynamic paradoxical metaphor for all-and-nothing: infinity and the infinite combinations of specifics on one hand and a neutral no time/no place on the other. The empty stage also presented him with a laboratory in which Wilder's penchant for conciseness could be applied.

The six Wilder one-acts written in 1930 and published in 1931 constitute the laboratory for this experimentation. In *Love and How to Cure It*, Wilder sets the action on an empty stage, but not as a neutral, imaginatively fluid place for action to occur, but rather as an actual site. Indeed, the near-empty stage is the only trait in the work that at all smacks of bare-stage aesthetics. The action takes place on the stage of the Tivoli Palace of Music in Soho, London, in April 1895. The stage directions designate that the stage is empty but for a table and an oil lamp. The rest of the stage is "bare, dark, dusty and cold."[39]

Everything that happens here is realistically rendered and entirely literal. Wilder never asks us to leave the Tivoli Palace nor move ahead or back in time, except through expositional dialogue. We are always firmly rooted in one context. It seems that Wilder places the action here for no other reason than to see how the empty stage itself can affect how we experience a situation. Wilder seems to choose an empty stage, almost as a control to the other one-acts published in the same volume. Putting one unhappy man's story on a vast empty stage underscores his loneliness and isolation since we witness a private grief enacted in a public place, now empty. Wilder will depend on this and other connotative values of the empty stage in his other one-acts in which he carries principles of simplicity much further.

With *The Long Christmas Dinner*, *Pullman Car Hiawatha*, and *The Happy Journey to Trenton and Camden* Wilder breaks new ground on the road leading to *Our Town*. Wilder applied the neutral properties of the stage to these three plays and thus found a far more practical and therefore more producible way of creating more with less than his 1928 three-minute plays or a literal bare stage. The neutral stage enabled him to make realities appear and disappear or be stretched out or compressed.

The strategies built into the one-acts are similar in that each calls for a stage with neutral attributes and presents changes in reality through economic means, but they differ in terms of which dimensions are explored: *The Long Christmas Dinner* uses the neutral stage to explore fluidity in time and keeps place constant, while the other two concentrate less on the properties of fluid time and more on changes in space.

The Long Christmas Dinner depicts many years in dramatic time, in a relatively short actual or performance time. The place remains constant throughout; we see the same dinner table at selected eventful or typical Christmas dinners over a ninety-year period in a play that would run approximately thirty minutes.[40] Wilder effected the accelerated motion through time with minimal technical help. There are no scene or lighting changes indicated to guide the viewer. The actors fluidly age before our eyes. Wilder employs as technical aids a few properties and costume pieces to project the passage of the years. At certain designated times, some of the characters, in full view of the audience, put on white wigs as they grow old. Wilder's stage direction to the actor is to carry out this task "simply and without comment."[41]

Actresses are asked to draw shawls about their shoulders as they grow older. Thus, even when technical aids are called for, they are used not to obscure the actor's craft, but to help illustrate it in the most concise ways.

Where other playwrights might have depended on properties and scenic and lighting changes, Wilder simplifies by choosing only the most crucial elements to communicate the one place and the flow of time. To represent the Bayard dining room, Wilder's stage directions includes only the perennial turkey and the long dining table "handsomely spread" for Christmas dinner.[42] This is the bare minimum to denote the central constant occasion of the play. Wilder leaves out many possible room decorations and unnecessary furniture altogether and calls on the actors to suggest others through pantomime activities. Thus, throughout the play characters eat imaginary food with imaginary forks and knives.

Since the interactions that take place in the Bayard dining room are a distillation of ninety years, what we do see stands as synecdoche for the whole lives of each of the characters, indeed of the entire family history. Entrance into the dining room is a literal coming to the dinner table as well as a birth; correspondingly, an exit can mean either a departure from the table, house and family or, more broadly, a representation of death. To focus attention on metaphors for life's entrances and exits, Wilder calls for two portals, one decorated in flowers and fruits for birth and the other in black velvet for death. Thus, these minimal elements call attention to a broader metaphysical plane.

Since time is in constant flux, costumes and other elements of the *mise-en-scène* cannot be so tied to a specific period that they detract from our sense of time passing and a changing in styles. In the opening stage directions, Wilder designates "inconspicuous clothes" for the actors.[43] By keeping the attire relatively neutral, the clothing stays appropriate despite the style changes that would be occuriring over the ninety years.

In *The Long Christmas Dinner*, Wilder proved himself the master of what might be called single-gesture characterizations. Characters have to make themselves known to us in the space of a short scene lasting two to four pages; there is little opportunity for representing complex or subtextual relationships or other kinds of detailed or multi-layered portraiture. The characters need to do no more than present a basic attitude, serve a simple function, or embody a single need or drive. And the situations in which these characters are caught—going off to war, breaking out from paternal influence, bringing a new child into the family, or coping with a recent death—have to be depicted through bare, essential dialogue and gesture, since it must be clear and universal (yet specific) in minimal stage time.

In *The Long Christmas Dinner*, simplicity of dialogue reinforces other aspects of stage simplification. Wilder foreswears not only the ornate and emotionally extravagant writing associated with the Romantic and Victorian literary traditions of the former century, but also the more recent energized dialogue from expressionism. He chooses cooler, more neutral words, charged not by the character's intensity from a wrenching situation, but by plain and direct utterances suited to these archetypal situations. By attempting this, he also rejects the legacy of naturalist writing and its individualizing dialects and idiosyncratic speech common in the American theater since O'Neill's early plays.

Malcolm Goldstein recognizes the interconnection between the bare stage, the simplified characters, and the spare dialogue in this and the other one-acts. After explaining how the bare stage "stunningly sets off each phrase"[44] of these plays, Goldstein illustrates this feature with Genevieve's response to the death of her mother in *The Long Christmas Dinner*: "I never told her how wonderful she was. We all treated her as though she were just a friend in the house. I thought she'd be here forever."[45] He posits that this line becomes "the cry of everyone in grief" and that it is given its "full value" on the nearly empty stage.[46]

Goldstein is making an important correlation between these simple, resonant words of regret that speak to a time that is forever past and passing and the empty stage on which these words are spoken. The words have space within which to resonate, and they call attention to swiftly passing time. Thus these characters are isolated, portrayed as mere specks in vast time and space, but with their own integrity and significance in the fleeting moment. Empty space and spare but resonating dialogue reinforce one another.

Certain lines are repeated throughout the work in order to indicate how various realities stay the same and yet change over the years. Four times in the play characters refer to the splendid Christmas sermons (the preachers' names keep changing) which made them weep;[47] several times they comment on the twigs wrapped in ice.[48] The play is brimming with references to time as seeming to move so quickly or so slowly, depending on the perspective of the speaker. It shows how certain perceptions of the characters stay the same from generation to generation, and yet each repetition carries with it its own particular quality, since the theatrical context (from our point of view) and the historical context (from theirs) changes from one generation to the next.

There are also repetitions in stage actions; again and again, babies are wheeled in through the portal, kisses are exchanged, glasses are raised, wigs go on, characters die by exiting through the dark portal, and the surviving family members sadly respond—all "as though life were one long happy Christmas dinner." Goldstein goes so far as to claim that this repetition is the meaning of the play. The same names being used for different characters—we have three different Mother Bayards, for instance—reinforce this sense of repetition, all of which highlights the paradoxical quality of time and identity as simultaneously in the moment and in an ever-changing eternity.

The other two one-acts in Wilder's 1931 anthology emphasize movement through space more than through time, and to do this on a fixed stage without major scene and lighting changes, Wilder utilizes a narrator figure he calls the "Stage Manager." This figure is the perfect mate for the near-empty, neutral stage. There his narrations, interactions with other characters, and activities can simply shift time, place, action, and perspective. He proves a great asset for Wilder in reaching his goal of a theatrically feasible way to present the particular in relation to the eternal.

It is difficult to pinpoint a single precedent for this figure; many currents actually converge in the Stage Manager's sudden appearance in 1931. His ancestors include the Greek Chorus, the Narrator in Medieval Morality Plays, and the characters like "Chorus" from Shakespeare's *Henry V.* Wilder would have been familiar with all of these progenitors. And then there were the Saint-Denis productions of Obey's plays at the Compagnie de Quinze, previously described, which, Harrison notes, had two onstage commentators.[49]

But the most obvious precedent is the Propertyman—sometimes even called the Stage Manager—from Peking Opera. It is clear Wilder had this traditional figure foremost in mind when he strategically placed him in the two one-acts and later in *Our Town.* As we have seen, the Chinese Propertyman moves furniture and provides the actors with properties and, in other ways, serves as a kind of bridge, albeit an understated self-effacing one, between them and the audience. Wilder used him as a model, but molded this figure to his own specific needs.

In *Pullman Car Hiawatha*, the Stage Manager takes on a more active and intrusive position than his traditional Chinese counterpart. Actually he fills many different functions. First of all, he is an omniscient narrator, directly addressing the audience. In this capacity, he helps us jump from one time and place to another without our needing additional technical support. Second, in nimble Pirandellian fashion, he interacts with the other people onstage, either in their roles as characters or outside their roles as actors. To do so, he is given license to interrupt the action or leave one action line and initiate another. Third, he takes over several minor roles. And fourth, he openly moves furniture on- and offstage, serving as a surrogate stagehand. In carrying out these multiple functions, he is the key to aesthetic economy in this play.

Pullman Car Hiawatha presents a train ride on a literal and metaphorical plane. Literally, it is a trip from New York to Chicago, symbolically a life journey. Throughout the play the characters, a cross-section of society, occupy and remain in berths that the Stage Manager indicates in chalk on the stage floor. In the course of the trip, one traveler dies and archangels come down to escort her heavenward. Suddenly we are on an interplanetary trip through eternity, with the Stage Manager leading the way. But then we are back on the literal level, being on a train just arriving in Chicago.

For this play, Wilder has retained the near-empty stage but does not treat it literally as in *Love and How to Cure It*, but rather as a neutral space awaiting definition by the Stage Manager. Wilder's stage directions call for a balcony or bridge leading into the wings in both directions. Like Raymond Jonson's Trojan Wall, this is one way of suggesting the infinite. Wilder then asks for two flights of stairs descending to the stage, followed by the directive: "There is no further scenery."[50] We are on the way toward an empty stage.

In the beginning of the play, soon after the Stage Manager has defined the outline of the performance space on the bare stage floor, the actors enter with two chairs apiece. They set them across from one another within the boundaries, thereby making them represent beds. Chairs then are neutral scenic units, defined as berths by the activities of the actors and the dialogue of the Stage Manager.

Indeed the script calls for few properties, the assumption being that the actors are to mime many of the activities indicated in the stage directions. To an even greater extent than in *The Long Christmas Dinner*, Wilder wants his actors to use pantomime, enabling everyday activities on the Pullman Car—turning on and off berth lights, heads appearing through curtains, the knitting of stockings, and foreheads leaning against what is to us a nonexistent windowpane—to be executed without the aid of physical properties.

To economize on people as well as things, the Stage Manager plays several secondary roles such as characters who call out from the train berths. Wilder allows the Stage Manager time only to suggest these characters with a single line and, for a woman, a falsetto voice. The other characters are also written as single-gesture characterizations; no depth is intended or achieved. They are reduced to a single need and function, a mere moving point strung on an elemental plotline.

The actors themselves are asked to be more than their characters; for instance, they are surrogate stagehands when they bring out the chairs at the top of the show. A bit later, on the Stage Manager's cue, the actors create the sound of their characters thinking with a "murmuring-swishing noise,"[51] repeated still later to simulate the thinking sounds of the whole earth.[52] They also mark changes in time and place by constantly telling each other the hour of day or location of the train. Instead of scenery showing the places that pass by their "windows," the actors look out above the audience and describe what they see. Thus, the characters, along with the Stage Manager, lead our imaginations through accelerated time and space, with the essentials of dialogue, gesture, and movement to replace supernumeraries, stagehands and scenery, as well as lighting and sound effects.

Wilder takes us from the microcosm in the train to the macrocosm through minimal technical means. The Stage Manager employs dialogue and synecdochic symbols to provide a kind of aerial view, with a near-empty stage behind him to help. To provide a wide context "geographically, meteorologically, astronomically, theologically",[53] the omnipotent Stage Manager has a single child step forward to signify all of Grover's Corners, Ohio, an old farmer's wife to embody the 2604 souls of Parksburg, Ohio. Another single character emerges from the wings to represent the field through which the train is passing with all its millions of insects and other inhabitants from the animal kingdom. A parade of other characters address the audience in ways that help us maintain the long view, including a ghost of a German workman killed in building the trestle for the train, a mechanic giving a nationwide weather report, beautiful girls as philosphers personifying the hours.

All this builds to the longest view of all. The theological perspective is reached as the archangels come down for Harriet, who dies on the train. The play draws to a close with the Stage Manager calling out the entire universe on the stage (at least its representatives), recreating the music of the spheres by having everybody hum their sound as Harriet enters Heaven and the train arrives in South Chicago. In this way he merges different planes of reality.

Wilder has found a way to make a few people and things stand for bigger and more plentiful realities. When one person on stage stands for millions of insects, or a few people on stage are the entire solar system, much is represented by relatively little. On the theatrical plane, a similar economy exists with one character (the Stage Manager) playing many roles and few words doing service for what could be literally truckloads worth of scenery, properties, and lighting equipment.

But we have to qualify the conclusion that Wilder is employing simple-stage aesthetics. After all, he presents us with a stage filled with actors—women holding Roman numerals, archangels, whirring planets, passengers in berths. And even if the lone individual on a seemingly infinite empty stage is there, it can be viewed as subordinated to a theatricalist allegory, which contradicts the spare imagery created by the simple and the few on a stage dominated by emptiness, silence, and stillness. And yet, when the stage is cleared at the end and the cleaning ladies come on stage to wash off the chalk marks indicating the berths, we are left with an acute awareness of the vast empty space. Relative to what this play could require, the production called for by Wilder's stage directions shows restraint and economy—simplification relative to the demands of what he is trying to portray.

No qualifications are necessary in discussing the simplicity of the next one-act, *The Happy Journey to Trenton and Camden*. Of all Wilder's one-acts, it is the most consistent and thorough in its simplification of set, properties, costumes, lighting, use of characters—their language and stage activity. As with *Hiawatha*, Wilder foreshortens time and space in this one-act with the understated aid of the Stage Manager. The action begins in Newark where the Kirbys live, and a car trip takes them through New Jersey while we watch them sitting on four chairs that serve as a car. They remain in the same area of the stage, while the progress of their ride is announced by the characters who tell each other (and therefore us) when they are in Elizabeth, New Brunswick, Laurenceville, Trenton, and finally in Camden—their destination. Twenty minutes of stage time and virtually no movement in stage space carries us through many hours on the road, a long journey through New Jersey, and an even longer emotional and symbolic journey into the life of an essential American family.

And this is done with minimal scenic support. The opening stage direction sets it all up: "No scenery is required for this play."[54] Wilder wants neutrality, a "zero place" from which a lot could be suggested. Thus in the Samuel French edition of the play, Wilder—after explaining that no scenery is required—states: "The idea is that no place is being represented. This may be achieved by a gray curtain back-drop with no side-pieces; a cylorama; or the empty bare stage."[55] In other words, the bare stage is only one among several options to denote empty space; his first priority seems to be to create a neutrality from which to conjure a story from the imagination; having a stage that looks like a stage is secondary.

In this neutral space, the Stage Manager places minimal properties to suggest much more, as is standard fare in Japanese and Chinese theater forms. Thus, four chairs become the all-important car, a bed is brought out when the family arrives at its destination to suggest a room in a house. The imagination of the spectator is asked to fill in where the actors and properties leave off. In addition, the world of the play is created through verbal or gestural suggestion. As the Kirbys drive from their home in Newark to Camden to visit their oldest daughter Beulah, they describe what they see, prodding the imaginations of the audience to picture it all with them. There are no panoramas being unscrolled, no film or slides to help out. Even scenic suggestions are omitted. The actors merely look out over the audience or to the wings and describe open fields, billboards, funeral processions, stores, a bridge, a collie dog, whatever. One is reminded of the motto of the first symbolist theater, the Theatre d'Art: "The word creates the decor."

To further his goal, Wilder designates that most objects are mimed. To present everyday activities without scenery and extraneous properties, a clear choice is for the actors to use pantomime. Wilder relishes this necessity since, as he states in his preface to *Our Town* years later, a stage devoid of accessories forces the spectator into the role of co-creator, that "by lending his imagination to the action, [he] restages it inside his own head."[56] We have observed the call for mime in *The Long Christmas Dinner* with the silverware and food; it is implied that the actors would mime the activities the script requires of them in *Pullman Car Hiawatha*; but in *Happy Journey* Wilder explicitly and extensively calls for the actors to pantomime realities. Arthur is to mime his marbles and the frankfurters he brings to his family; Ma Kirby her hat that she puts on in front of an imaginary mirror; and Pa Kirby his car and its steering wheel and gearshift.

As with the bare stage and the Stage Manager figure, the incorporation of mime into a performance does not begin with Thornton Wilder. Indeed one can go back to Ancient Greece where Chorus members may have mimed activities narrated by a character or other members of the Chorus. Mime constituted a part of Roman comedy as well as Medieval and Elizabethan dumb-show traditions. But Goldstone proposes two more immediate influences on Wilder's decision to incorporate mime, Harrison another. Goldstone notes that Wilder was deeply impressed by the Chinese actor Mei Lan-Fang, whom he saw perform in New York in 1930, especially his "effective use of pantomime."[57] Goldstone mentions the influence of director Richard Boleslavsky whom Wilder observed using mime with his actors in rehearsal for Wilder's early play *The Trumpet Shall Sound* in 1926.[58] And finally, Harrison relates how Wilder read everything he could about the French playwright Obey, especially admiring his biblical play, *Noah*, in which actors mime animal roles.[59]

But pantomime does not always have to be simple and economic, even though it does supplant the need for lots of things. The kind Wilder calls for in *The Happy Journey*, however, does, since it is reduced to only the most essential actions. This becomes especially clear when his stage directions are compared with those added by the first director of the play, Alexander Dean. The first Samuel French edition of the play uses Dean's stage directions while the other published versions contain Wilder's own directions. When the Kirbys are about to embark on their journey, for instance, Dean directs the actor playing Ma Kirby to complete every action she tells Mrs. Schwartz she is to do before leaving the house. So Dean has her locking the door and putting the imaginary key behind the imaginary icebox and then going out the door. Wilder does not feel so obliged and, in the edition without Dean's stage directions, merely has the characters going directly to the imaginary stairs and walking into the street. If time is being condensed, all actions do not need to be slavishly demonstrated. Wilder wants the actors to mime only the crucial activities—even if it means missing a literal step or two.

Wilder takes additional measures toward aesthetic economy in this play. He calls for a small cast: only the Stage Manager and the five Kirbys. But as is the case with *Pullman Car Hiawatha*, Wilder writes in more roles than actors; at the beginning of the play, the Stage Manager stands in for all the Kirbys' neighbors and later performs more fully the role of the gas station attendant. He also serves as a surrogate stagehand, setting up and taking away the chairs that represent the car and the bed in Beulah's house.

But with these two functions, his similarity to the Stage Manager in *Pullman Car Hiawatha* ceases. The *Happy Journey* Stage Manager does not narrate nor does he converse with the people on stage as actors, only as characters when he himself is also playing a role. Therefore he does not interrupt the flow of the action. Because of this, the Stage Manager from *The Happy Journey* is closer in spirit to the unobtrusive Propertyman of Chinese Opera than the Stage Manager of *Pullman Car Hiawatha* or his direct descendant, the Stage Manager in *Our Town*.

The Stage Manager in *Happy Journey* is also unlike the other two in that he does not blatantly provide the long view. Since he does not address the audience at all, he can never explain the action from a meteorological, geographical, or theological point of view. But he does subtly influence the field of reference by the very nature of his role as outsider, as objective observer of the action. When he is not actively playing a role, he leans against the proscenium, smoking a cigarette as he contemplates the action. In so doing, he serves a similar function as the Propertyman; he provides ballast to the action and the emotions generated by the scene, being a somewhat distant but involved representative of the audience.

One can guess at Wilder's thought process in creating the Stage Manager by tracing the process he underwent in coming up with him in his final form. In an earlier, handwritten draft of *Happy Journey*, Wilder calls the Stage Manager "Author" and, on several occasions, has him addressing the audience directly. When Wilder conceived him as the Author, he provides the long view in a blatant fashion. Thus, for example, at one point on their car trip he tells the audience: "Now they are fallen silent. They're looking at a sunset. You know how nice driving can be in that last hour of the afternoon.—There are 126 million Americans."[60]

In the final draft, however, he no longer narrates, and the long view is given to the characters themselves. Arthur inquires about the population of the United States. The father answers, "126 million."[61] This is a more subtle way of making us see the small (the Kirby family) in relation to the large field of reference (all the families in the United States). When the Kirbys stop their car to allow a funeral to pass, Ma Kirby, after a pause, says: "Well, we'll all hold up the traffic for a few minutes some day."[62] Later on Caroline sees her first star and implores everyone in the car to make a wish,[63] subtly placing this family in relation to the cosmos. And the final moments open the action up in a similar fashion, as Ma absent-mindedly sings the following words:

> There were ninety and nine that safely lay
> In the shelter of the fold,
> But one was out on the hills away,
> Far off from the gates of gold.[64]

These subtle references to the vast infinity stand in juxtaposition to the everyday actions of the play.

In taking the long view from the Stage Manager and giving it to the characters, Wilder is moving toward neutrality. By changing his name to Stage Manager, he is opting for a separation of himself from this character, as if he wants the character's attitude to be more removed than a raisonneur figure, less personal than the work's own author could ever be. Wilder is seeking an impersonal style. By reducing emotion and personal involvement, he makes the Stage Manager more neutral, like the empty stage itself. And Wilder goes even further in this direction by calling for the Stage Manager not to act. Wilder instructs the Stage Manager to play the family's neighbors by holding a script and reading their lines with "little attempt at characterization," scarcely altering his voice.[65] He is asking the Stage Manager to be like a rehearsal stage manager stepping in for an absent actor who usually is instructed not to act but rather just to deliver the cues for the actors present on stage. This neutral delivery style is what Michael Kirby, in his seminal essay "On Acting and Non-Acting,"[66] has defined as non-matrixed presentation and is akin to how the Propertyman is traditionally employed in the Peking Opera.

In calling for minimal characterization, Wilder has taken a step beyond *The Long Christmas Dinner* and *Pullman Car Hiawatha* toward stage simplification by extending his use of stage neutrality. In *Christmas Dinner* he calls for concise "single-gesture" characters asked to show their characters in five minutes of stage time. The Stage Manager impersonates other characters by changing his voice and giving a few lines of dialogue in that new voice. By taking out all vestiges of characterization and calling for a neutral delivery in *Happy Journey*, Wilder eliminates characterization altogether, marking an additional step in the stripping-away process.

But towards the end of the family's journey, the Stage Manager actively takes on a role. Wilder directs the Stage Manager to put down his script and fully play out the role of the gas station attendant. Wilder created the Stage Manager so that he grows into characterization, in a way, gathers theatrical life as he goes along, and thereby parallels what should be the audience's growing involvement in the play. The play grows from an empty stage and neutral delivery to stage and characters brimming with imaginative vitality.

Except for Ma Kirby, the Kirbys are schematically drawn. They are not stereotypes but single-gesture characters, with one basic trait or type of relationship to the other members of the family. They are no more complexly drawn than the Bayards or the characters occupying the berths in *Pullman Car Hiawatha*. There is a purity in their own personal traits as well as in how they commingle with those of the other family members. Wilder has created characters and relationships of essentials.

Wilder asks for multi-dimensionality only in Ma Kirby; unquestionably this is her play. In fact, Wilder originally subtitled the play *Portrait of a Lady*. At the same time that she is portrayed as having rock-solid (albeit somewhat idiosyncratic) values and principles, she is also shown as capable of developing "a fancy" for a gas station attendant. Thus, she can be both a righteous and loyal wife and mother and still be attracted to another man. Sometimes she is ice-cold as, for instance, when Arthur inadvertently makes light of her relationship with the Lord; at other times, she is warm and tender, as when she forgives Arthur or comforts Beulah, who has been shaken by the trauma of having lost a child at childbirth. The strategy Wilder employs, then, is to set off her complex, multi-sided nature from the schematic, essentialized characterizations of her family and gas station attendant and the neutral presentations of the neighbors.

Another aspect of his artistic intent is that, by stripping down to essentials, he can make the simplest words and gestures resonate that much more and carry strong emotional impact. Some of the most moving sections of the play are restrained, even understated. When they arrive in Camden to comfort Beulah on her loss, Wilder generates a lot of audience emotion from only the most essential

lines and gestures. The following brief exchange between father and daughter
after he gives her a present is a case in point:

> BEULAH: Crazy old pa, goin' buyin' things! It's me that ought to
> be buyin' things for you, pa.
> ELMER: Oh, no! There's only one Loolie in the world.
> BEULAH: (whispering as her eyes fill with tears) Are you
> glad I'm still alive, pa?[67]

Wilder does not then linger on the emotion. He cuts short the interchange by
adding the following stage direction: "She kisses him abruptly and goes back to
the house steps." This attenuated exchange contains strong emotional
reverberation, especially on an empty stage.

Wilder is even more economic in the following passage in which he
sketches a scene from the past with only enough of an image for an audience to
fill in the rest. Ma Kirby looks at Beulah and recalls the last time she saw her
daughter:

> MA: Well, well, when I last saw you, you didn't know
> me. You kep' saying: When's mama comin'? When's
> mama comin'? But the doctor sent me away.[68]

Writers less prone to a concise writing style might have used this opportunity for
a monologue. But with just a few words, we are given enough to visualize a
whole, deeply moving scene.

Wilder informs us twice in the course of the play that Beulah had been sick
and that is why the family has embarked on this journey, but we do not know the
full story. Now, after the mother recounts her last visit, the whole picture is
completed with the following lines from Beulah, eliciting comfort and wisdom
from her mother:

> BEULAH: It was awful, mama. It was awful. She didn't even live
> a few minutes, mama. It was awful.
> MA (Looking far away): God thought best, dear. God thought
> best. We don't understand why. We just go on, honey, doin' our
> business.
> (Then almost abruptly—passing the back of her hand across her
> cheek.)
> Well, now, what are we giving the men to eat tonight?[69]

We now know that Beulah's sickness was related in some way to the death
of her baby, about which she tells us indirectly. Wilder holds back on this last
piece of exposition until now, allowing these words to have maximal emotional

impact. Beulah's lines combine many aspects of theatrical simplicity: telegraphic conciseness, revelation through suggestion, and a powerful use of repetition. And her mother's response utilizes repetition and features a personal philosophy that puts this specific incident into a large field of reference, followed by a warm but simple gesture. Wilder does not milk the moment; he cuts it short as they both return to everyday concerns.

Wilder's attitude, as evidenced by his own notes, is that the most effective way to fulfill the aesthetic requirements of his plays is to say the lines and execute business with simplicity. He realizes that the more restrained the external, the deeper and broader the potential emotional resonance. Sentimentality would detract from the economy of his writing. This is why Wilder prefaced the Samuel French edition of *Happy Journey* with the following note to the producer: "The atmosphere, comedy and characterization of this play are most effective when they are handled with great simplicity and evenness."[70]

Looking at this little play in terms of what it achieves on an emotional and psychological level despite (or partly because of) its minimal means, one can understand why, in 1941, Wilder listed it as his best play.[71] But if number of productions and critical response is the criterion, one can think of all the 1931 one-acts as finger exercises in preparation for Wilder's three-act masterpiece, *Our Town*, written in 1938.

Before turning to this play, it is important to make note of a powerful one-act by another important playwright who utilized a bare stage, a play written and performed between Wilder's one-acts in 1931 and *Our Town* in 1938. In January 1935, the Group Theatre presented *Waiting for Lefty* by Clifford Odets at the Civic Repertory Theatre. Its instant success made it reach a far bigger audience than the initial performances of Wilder's early one-acts. The bare stage in this Odets play functions in two ways: (1) as a union hall where members of a taxi-driver union are meeting to discuss whether or not they should go out on strike (with the audience implicitly defined as members of the union watching the proceedings); and (2) as a neutral space in which the characters replay scenes from their recent past in order to sway the audience that a strike is necessary. The neutral space undergoes several transformations in time and place as the different characters leave their chairs (arranged in semi-circle) and recreate scenes from their pasts. After *Waiting for Lefty*, Odets never again wrote for a bare stage, but this very successful production, remembered mostly for its political content, also set a precedent in the mainstream professional theater for the neutral bare stage of Wilder's *Our Town*.

The first sentence in *Our Town* is "No curtain," which already distinguishes it from *Happy Journey*, *Pullman Car Hiawatha*, and *Waiting for Lefty*. The second is the stage direction, "No scenery," followed with the words: "The audience, arriving, sees an empty stage in half-light."[72] Thus, Wilder has taken an additional step in shedding pretense. Wilder initially does not define the stage as anything but an empty stage (no implied union hall, as in the Odets play).

There is no permanent set or property to locate place, like the dinnertable in *Long Christmas Dinner*. There is "no balcony or bridge or runway leading out of sight in both directions," as in *Pullman Car Hiawatha*. The Stage Manager addresses us as an audience here and now. The stage is neutral in every way, awaiting definition of time, place, and circumstance by the Stage Manager and the other characters.

The empty stage is built into the play itself. The Stage Manager spends the first five or ten minutes of playing time describing where everything is on the empty stage. And his elaborate description of all the buildings, streets, and other details of the town make violating Wilder's no-scenery stage direction not only impractical and needlessly expensive, but also aesthetically redundant. The original production, directed by Jed Harris, did not even employ a set designer.

Writing to Gertrude Stein in October 1937, Wilder called *Our Town* a "little play," but "with all the big subjects in it"[73] (again, the paradox of less-is-more). He had tried to cover the "big" subjects with his three-minute plays in 1928 and, more successfully, with the 1931 one-acts, but with *Our Town* in 1938, he adopts the three-act form to achieve the large picture with minimal means; this time he pursues a different kind of stripping down than overall length.

Our Town differs from the Odets play by virtue of its blatant avoidance of the controversial political issues of the 1930s in favor of metaphysical ones for all time; in fact, the bare neutral stage, with all of its infinite potential for creating realities, is treated as a metaphor for the eternal itself. Wilder's artistic strategy was, in his own words, "to set the village against the largest dimensions of time and place,"[74] or, more poetically stated, to portray "the life of a village against the life of the stars."[75] On the naked stage, he could place two lovers in two neighboring families in one small village in relation "to everywhere, to everybody and to always."[76] He states in his preface to *Our Town* that, in taking this tack, he is borrowing from the archaeologist's approach, combining the "view of the telescope with the view of the microscope," to "reconstruct the very distant with the help of the very small."[77]

The very small is Grover's Corners, New Hampshire. It is the coming together of Emily and George, their marriage, Emily's death in childbirth, and her attempt to retrieve something from her life through a posthumous return to her family on her twelfth birthday. But the empty stage provides a large canvas for this examination.

Once again, Wilder engages an omniscient Stage Manager, who, more like his progenitor in *Hiawatha* than in *Happy Journey*, is a god-figure endowed with the ability to take us through time and space, both human and celestial. He allows us, at the threshold of Emily's wedding, to flash back to the first time George and Emily met; he also has the power to take Emily back to her childhood, to her twelfth birthday and, afterward, to return her, disillusioned, back to her place among the dead. He helps us traverse infinite time and space, so we can view the individual in relation to the coordinates of eternity. Thus, as in *Pullman Car Hiawatha*, Wilder enlists the Stage Manager to establish a broad field of reference. Accordingly, the Stage Manager stops the action and introduces characters who either step out from the play's action or come from outside it and address the audience directly. For example, he first invites onto the stage Professor Willard from the University, who has nothing to do with the play's internal action; later Mr. Webb talks directly to the audience. Cued by the Stage Manager, these characters help supply what Wilder himself calls the "great perspectives of time, social history and current religious ideas."[78]

One can view this as a far more simple and direct use of the epic theater devices being employed by the Federal Theatre Project's Living Newspaper productions at about the same time as the original production of Wilder's *Our Town*. Whereas Living-Newspaper productions between 1936 and 1939 were using short film sequences, cartoons, slide projections of maps and charts, and off-stage loudspeakers to provide the larger context for the stage action, Wilder provides the larger picture in *Our Town* (as he does earlier in *Pullman Car Hiawatha*) with characters coming out and presenting information to the audience through direct address.

In *Our Town* Wilder allows other characters to contribute to the presentation of the big picture. He sustains it within the play's internal story by having characters in Grover's Corners make countless reference to the stars, the planets, the sun, and the moon; to events that reach far back in American and World history; to time passing; and to the immensity of the human population, the earth, and the universe. In allowing the large context to be presented through the internal dialogue, Wilder is returning to the method he employs in *Happy Journey*.

As in *The Long Christmas Dinner*, Wilder speeds up and collapses time. In *Our Town*, this process is facilitated by the Stage Manager. As we watch Joe Crowell, the newspaper boy, talk with Dr. Gibbs, the Stage Manager informs us that he will die in France years later in World War I.[79] As the Stage Manager readies us for George and Emily's wedding in Act Two, he compresses time, in this play using words rather than stage action (as he does in *Christmas Dinner*):

> You know how it is: you're twenty-one or twenty-two and you
> make some decisions; then whisssh! you're seventy: you've been
> a lawyer for fifty years, and that white-haired lady at your side
> has eaten over fifty thousand meals with you.[80]

The Stage Manager again races through time, narrating the journey from marriage to death, at George and Emily's wedding: "The cottage, the go-cart, the Sunday-afternoon drives in the Ford, the first rheumatism, the grandchildren, the second rheumatism, the deathbed, the reading of the will."[81] A few essential events stand for a long life.

In general, the characters are more in the single-gesture style of the one-acts. Missing are contradictions in personality and complexity in interrelationships, even in and among the Webbs and the Gibbs' who occupy the center of the play's action. What character details Wilder does provide, such as Dr. Gibbs's fascination with the Civil War or Mr. Webb's with Napoleon, make the people of Grover's Corners specific enough to be definite points in time and space so they are not totally depersonalized, but never as complex and detailed as, say, the Mother in *Happy Journey*. Wilder also utilizes some of the principles of neutral acting. Besides being the narrator, the Stage Manager also is neutral enough to assume the roles of other characters within the action of the play, including the soda jerk who bears witness to the drug-store meeting that brings Emily and George together and the minister who finally marries them.

Wilder depersonalizes many of the characters through various physical and vocal stage directions. At George and Emily's wedding in Act Two, Wilder has the congregation facing the back wall. In Act Three, the stoic dead, arranged in ten or twelve chairs in three evenly-spaced rows, look straight ahead and deliver their lines in matter-of-fact style,[82] reminiscent of the Stage Manager's delivery of the neighbors' lines in *Happy Journey*. At Emily's funeral, most of the mourners come on the stage behind identical wet umbrellas so we can not discern individual features. The repetitive image of the umbrellas and the blank, uniform expressions of the dead can be seen in the original stage production directed by Jed Harris (photo 8.1). These choices present us with a portrait of the living who are as undifferentiated as the dead.

Wilder simplifies his *mise-en-scène* further by eliminating the need for properties. As in his earlier one-acts, the play calls for the actors to mime their character's daily activities, such as grinding coffee, opening windows, and drinking ice-cream sodas. Only the most essential properties are present on stage, only the bare minimum of furniture. Just as two chairs facing each other depict berths in *Hiawatha* and four chairs do service for a car in *Happy Journey*, so, at the beginning of *Our Town*, the Stage Manager sets up a table and three chairs stage right to represent the Gibbs' house and a low bench stage left to suggest the Webbs'. Later on George and Emily's interaction from their upstairs rooms in their adjacent houses are simplified to the two of them on ladders talking across an empty stage.

The manipulation of stage silence is a key element in the artistry of *Our Town*. At several key points in his stage directions, Wilder writes in or implies pauses. He does this, for instance, when he wants to underscore individuals in relation to vastness such as when the Stage Manager looks at the morning star in the beginning of the play or when Mrs. Gibbs and Mrs. Soames gaze up at the moon later in the act. This gesture, repeated later when the Gibbs children peer up at the moon and realize that the moon is probably also shining at that very second on South America, Canada, and half the whole world,[83] a realization

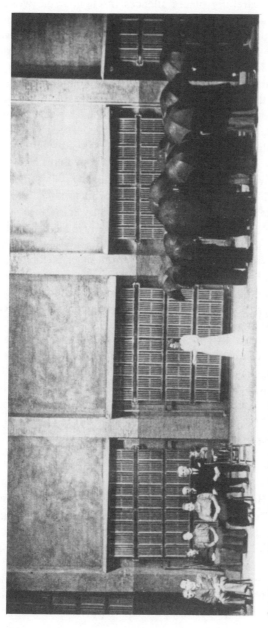

8.1 Graveyard scene from final act of original production of *Our Town*, 1938. Directed by Jed Harris. Photo courtesy of the Billy Rose Theatre Collection, The New York Public Library at Lincoln Center, Astor, Lenox, and Tilden Foundations.

that is again answered by stage silence. Wilder is creating a sense of awe and wonder at the vastness of time and space beside the momentary here and now.

Indeed, Wilder carefully places silences throughout the work, thereby creating auditory space around lines of dialogue to parallel visual empty space. He provides a kind of imaginative space in which certain lines can resonate and travel beyond themselves, at once through time and space and through the potentially infinite imagination of the spectator. In some cases stage silence accentuates certain lines; in others it highlights man's solitude in time and space, his vulnerability to the great expanse. This is especially true in silences after a character ponders something far out in the firmament. This device will become increasingly a part of modern dramaturgy after Wilder, especially in the plays of Samuel Beckett, a playwright whom Wilder admired greatly.[84]

Before *Our Town* was produced, Wilder sent a copy to his Oberlin Classics professor, Charles Wager. Writing back a letter glowing with pride and praise, Wager made special note of Wilder's skillful use of silence: "Your 'Aeschylean silences'—'They are silent,' 'Mrs. Gibbs does not answer,' 'Pause'—what must they be like on the stage when they move me so deeply in the book?"[85]

Wager realized that the silences would have immense theatrical value. But their value in *Our Town* cannot be separated from other factors. The silences work so well in part because they are supported by empty space surrounding the characters; the essentialized nature of the characterizations themselves; the presentation of a stage stripped of virtually everything; and Wilder's concept of the life of a village juxtaposed to the life of the stars.

There are moments in *Our Town* when all factors work together so seamlessly that one can hardly separate where language, *mise-en-scène*, or the central theme of the play begins and where the other factors end. It is at these places in the text where Wilder shows himself to be so in control of his medium that he only needs a director and actors to follow faithfully the implied or explicit directions in the text.

One of these moments is at the end of Act One when Rebecca is speaking with her brother George late at night. She relates how a letter was addressed to Jane Crofut from her minister: "Jane Crofut; The Crofut Farm; Grover's Corners; Sutton County; New Hampshire; United States of America; Continent of North America; Western Hemisphere; the Earth; the Solar System; the Universe; the Mind of God."[86] The words draw a simple line between an individual and the universal, a line that is reinforced by the visual line created by the high ladder on which she stands. George is on the ladder, too, listening to her story. They both are suspended in a void, each on a rung—just as Jane Crofut is a rung—on a ladder leading outward toward the Mind of God. By writing into the play the tall vertical lines of ladders and the image of suspended figures in a pool of light high up in nighttime darkness, Wilder provides a visual companion for his words and their meaning.

In this final image of Act One, we have all negations reinforcing each other.

Rebecca and George are standing as if floating in empty space; they are perfectly still (their positions on the ladder keep them still), and they are silent in wonder at the fact that the postman delivered the postcard anyway. And the simple, gradual opening from the particular to the generality, from the single individual to the vast mind of God, reverberates in the silent, empty stillness onstage.

And Wilder's Act Three finale, when Emily revisits her family on her twelfth birthday, also thrives on the simple stage. Recalling Molière's famous dictum that all one needs to make theater is a platform and a passion, Wilder expresses his pride that the climax of *Our Town* does not require a lot of scenery, but merely "five square feet of boarding and the passion to know what life means to us."[87]

Wilder succeeds, then, in answering the challenges of Samuel Eliot, Kenneth Macgowan, and Lee Simonson who called for the playwright's participation in simplifying the stage. As did playwrights in theater's distant past (especially the Greeks and the Elizabethans), Wilder constructs plays so that they utilize the power of stage as stage. He calls for high vertical lines in George and Rebecca's ladders (in the tradition of Edward Gordon Craig); he creates characters that require line-drawing acting (in the tradition of Jacques Copeau) and essentialized, non-busy staging (in the tradition of Arthur Hopkins); at times he calls for the neutral acting we see in several East Asian theater traditions; he allows his characters to traverse vast time and space as they occasionally do in the Japanese Noh and the traditional Chinese theater; he borrows the idea of a narrator figure from Shakespeare and Obey to guide his audience through different contexts; and, learning from Boleslavsky and others, he uses mime to reduce the need for physical properties and to apply a metaphysical cast to the characters and their activities. He links the simple stage to the larger metaphysical ideas of James Joyce and Gertrude Stein. Even though his ideas for stage simplicity are all borrowed, they blend into a simplicity that is radical, unique, and innovative.

NOTES

[1] Samuel A. Eliot, Jr., "Le Theatre du Vieux Colombier," *Theatre Arts Magazine*, (February 1919), p. 30.

[2] Kenneth Macgowan, *Theater of Tomorrow*, p. 131.

[3] For example, in Joseph Morgenstern, "The Demons Sit on His Shoulder," *New York Herald Tribune*, January 7, 1962, p. 5, Wilder says the following: "When I wrote *Our Town*, I got rid of the picture, but I began to realize the stage should be sparer yet, clean as a hound's tooth....The principal law on which this all hangs is this: when the eye is overfed, the ear cannot hear. Strip the stage of clutter and a word gains new vitality."

[4] Brooks Atkinson, "Critic at Large: Thornton Wilder, at 65, Full of Energy, Enthusiasim and a Thirst for Learning," *New York Times*, February 13, 1962, n.p.

[5] Thornton Wilder, *The Angel that Troubled the Waters* (New York: Coward-McCann, 1928), p. xiii.

[6] Malcolm Cowley, "The Man Who Abolished Time," *Saturday Review*, October 6, 1956, p. 14.

[7] Tyrone Guthrie, "The World of Thornton Wilder," *The New York Times Magazine*, November 27, 1955, p. 27.

[8] Ibid., p. 26.

[9] Malcolm Goldstein, *The Art of Thornton Wilder* (Lincoln: University of Nebraska Press, 1965), pp. 78-79.

[10] Ibid., p. 77.

[11] Ibid., p. 78.

[12] Ibid., p. 81.

[13] Edith Isaacs, "Who Killed Cock Robin?", *Theatre Arts Monthly*, (March 1938), p. 172.

[14] Donald Gallup, ed. *The Journals of Thornton Wilder, 1939-1961*, (New Haven: Yale University Press, 1985), p. 5.

[15] Malcolm Cowley, "Abolished Time," p. 52.

[16] Goldstein, *Thornton Wilder*, p. 102.

[17] Thornton Wilder, "James Joyce: 1882-1941," *Poetry*, March 1941; reprinted in Wilder, *American Characteristics and Other Essays* (New York: Harper and Row, 1979), p. 176.

[18] Thornton Wilder was accused of having plagiarized Joyce's *Finnegans Wake* in *Skin of Our Teeth*. Wilder denied the charge but freely acknowledged Joyce's influence, both specifically in this play and in his work and thought in general.

[19] Robert Bartlett Haas, ed. *A Primer for the Gradual Understanding of Gertrude Stein* (Los Angeles: Black Sparrow Press, 1971), p. 49.

[20] Thornton Wilder, "Some Thoughts on Playwriting," in Toby Cole, ed., *Playwrights on Playwriting* (New York: Hill and Wang, 1960), p. 114.

[21] Wilder, "Towards an American Language," *American Characteristics*, p. 15.

[22] Goldstein, *Thornton Wilder*, p. 1.

[23] Thornton Wilder, "A Preface for *Our Town*," in Wilder, *American Characteristics*, p. 101.

[24] Wilder, *Three Plays* (New York: Avon Books, 1957), intro., p. xii.

[25] Wilder, *American Characteristics*, p. 101.

[26] Gilbert Harrison, *The Enthusiast: A Life of Thornton Wilder* (New Haven: Ticknor and Fields, 1983), p. 78.

[27] Wilder, *American Characteristics*, p. 102.

[28] Harrison, *The Enthusiast*, p. 186.

[29] Letter from Donald Gallup, Wilder's literary executor, to the author, dated March 9, 1988.

[30] Wilder, Preface to *Three Plays*, p. xi.

[31] Wilder collection, Beinecke Library, Yale University.

[32] Richard Goldstone, *Thornton Wilder: An Intimate Portrait* (New York: E. P. Dutton, 1975), p. 119.

[33] Wilder later translated and adapted one of Obey's plays, *Le Viol de Lucrece*, which was presented in New York in 1932, with Robert Edmond Jones designing sets and costumes.

[34] Harrison, *The Enthusiast*, p. 152.

[35] *New York Sun*, February 1935, n.p.

[36] Harrison, *Enthusiast*, p. 186.

[37] Arthur Gelb, "Thornton Wilder, 63, Sums Up," *The New York Times*, November 6, 1961, p. 74.

[38] Ibid., p. 74.

[39] Thornton Wilder, *The Long Christmas Dinner and Other Plays In One Act* (New York: Harper Colophon, 1963), p. 71.

[40] This kind of elliptical writing was not new; almost twenty years before Wilder's one-acts the Italian futurists wrote *sintesi* like *Sempronio's Lunch* by Corra and Settimelli and *Education* by Rognoni in which whole lifetimes were compressed into less than two minutes of stage time (see Michael Kirby's *Futurist Performance*). One can say Wilder renovated these techniques for the American theater.

[41] Wilder, *Long Christmas Dinner*, p. 1.

[42] Ibid., p. 1.

[43] Ibid., p. 1.

[44] Goldstein, *Thornton Wilder*, p. 78.

[45] Wilder, *Long Christmas Dinner*, p. 16.

[46] Goldstein, *The Art of Thornton Wilder*, p. 79.

[47] Wilder, *Long Christmas Dinner*, pp. 3, 7, 10, and 17.

[48] Ibid., pp. 3, 13, and 25.

[49] Harrison, *Enthusiast*, p. 152.

[50] Wilder, *Christmas Dinner*, p. 49.

[51] Ibid., p. 52.

[52] Ibid., p. 64.

[53] Ibid., p. 58.

[54] Ibid., p. 89.

[55] Thornton Wilder, *The Happy Journey* (New York: Samuel French, 1931), p. 3.

[56] Wilder, Preface to *Our Town*, in *American Characteristics*, p. 101.

[57] Goldstone, *Thornton Wilder*, p. 119.

[58] Ibid., p. 119.

[59] Harrison, *Enthusiast*, p. 155.

[60] Thornton Wilder, handwritten manuscript of "Happy Journey," dated by author, July 1931, in Beinecke Library, Yale University, (ZaWilder43).

[61] Wilder, *Christmas Dinner*, p. 104.

[62] Ibid., p. 95.

[63] Ibid., p. 105.

[64] Ibid., p. 110.

[65] Ibid., p. 89.

[66] Michael Kirby, "On Acting and Non-Acting," *The Drama Review*, T-53 (March

1972), pp. 3-15.

67 Wilder, *Christmas Dinner*, p. 108.

68 Ibid., p. 109.

69 Ibid., p. 109.

70 Wilder, *Happy Journey*, p. 4.

71 Goldstone, *Thornton Wilder*, p. 86.

72 Wilder, *Three Plays*, p. 5.

73 Harrison, *The Enthusiast*, p. 177.

74 Wilder, *Three Plays*, p. xi.

75 Wilder, Preface to *Our Town*, in *American Characteristics*, p. 102.

76 Wilder, "Towards an American Language," in *American Characteristics*, p. 15.

77 Wilder, Preface to *Our Town*, p. 100.

78 Wilder, Preface to *Our Town*, in *American Characteristics*, pp. 100-101.

79 Wilder, *Three Plays*, p. 8.

80 Wilder, *Our Town*, in *Three Plays*, p. 38.

81 Ibid., p. 49.

82 Ibid., p. 50.

83 Wilder, *Three Plays*, p. 27.

84 According to Alan Schneider, Wilder considered *Waiting for Godot* one of the two greatest modern plays. See Alan Schneider, *Entrances* (New York: Viking Penguin, 1986), p. 222.

85 Quoted in Harrison, *Enthusiast*, p. 180.

86 Wilder, *Three Plays*, p. 28.

87 Wilder, Preface to *Three Plays*, p. xi.

CONCLUSION

The modern simple-stage tradition began developing at the turn of the century as a protest against the elaborate illusionism that characterized the Italianate and, more immediately, the naturalistic *mise-en-scène*. The rebellion took the form of either reviving simple stages prevalent before the Italianate stage began its hegemony over Western theater practice or developing new simple stages, aided by the new capabilities of indoor lighting. Between 1900 and 1920, the Greek and Elizabethan revival movements and the new interest in non-Western forms of expression led directors and designers to experiment with modern versions of the ancient Greek theater, the Elizabethan public stage, and the production techniques of East Asian theater forms, especially Peking Opera and the Japanese Noh. At the turn of the century, Kawakami Otojiro and Sadda Yakko toured the United States, exhibiting a more simplified acting style than what American audiences had been used to. Over a decade later, the neutral stage conventions of Chinese theater were seen in the Benrimo/Hazelton production of *The Yellow Jacket*. In the 1910s, Margaret Anglin and Livingston Platt reestablished the elegant simplicities of the Ancient Greek theater and the Elizabethan public stage in California, New York, and Boston.

Between 1912 and 1925, the most influential models for a new simplified stage came to the American theater via Edward Gordon Craig's *On the Art of the Theatre*, Max Reinhardt's production of *Sumurun*, the 1911-1912 tour of the Irish Players, Jacques Copeau's two seasons at the Garrick Theatre (1917-1918 and 1918-1919), and expressionist productions of plays like Toller's *Man and the Masses* and Shakespeare's *Richard III* viewed by American directors and designers traveling abroad in the 1920s.

The simple stage began to appear in American little theaters in 1912 when Lyman Gale in Boston and Maurice Browne in Chicago sought different ways to strip the stage to bare essentials in their intimate theaters. For the next eight years, those and other little theaters would showcase various ways of creating more with less, most notably at Samuel Hume's Arts and Crafts Theatre of Detroit and George Cram Cook's Provincetown Players in Massachusetts and New York.

Some of the highlights of less-is-more thinking among artists in American little theaters between 1912 and 1920 were: *Trojan Women* at the Chicago Little Theatre, where Jonson created a sense of monumentality on a diminutive scale and made a single rent in the Trojan wall become a large statement about the destructiveness of war; Browne and Jonson's relief-stage, black-and-white *mise-en-scène* for Cloyd Head's *Grotesques*, in which different levels of reality—including an empty void—were gradually revealed; the collaborative silhouette creation of *Passion Play* by the members of the Chicago Little Theatre; Samuel Hume's two seasons of plays using recombinations of the same modular units at the Arts and Crafts Theatre of Detroit; and George Cram Cook and Cleon Throckmorton's production of Eugene O'Neill's *The Emperor Jones*, which, with the help of Cook's plaster dome and Cleon Throckmorton's dangling black shapes, took its audience through a primordial forest amid vast emptiness into ever deeper levels of the main character's own personal, racial, and collective unconscious.

Between 1915 and 1922, the highlights in the professional theater were: the relief-stage, monochromatic setting of the Jones/Granville-Barker *The Man Who Married a Dumb Wife*; the realism of the Hopkins/Jones production of Ellis's *The Devil's Garden* which, in the case of Act One, was simplified almost to the point of formal abstraction; the Hopkins/Jones permanent-set productions of *Richard III* and *Hamlet* in which the Tower of London and a grand arch, respectively, became symbols for forces looming over and within the main characters; the Hopkins/Jones space-stage, expressionist landscape of *Macbeth*; and the Komisarjevsky-Simonson presentation of Claudel's *The Tidings Brought to Mary*, which combined the simplicities of the permanent and neutral stage, repetitive visual and auditory elements, and continually transforming properties and characters.

The playwright's contribution to the simple stage mostly came in the 1930s, although O'Neill's *Before Breakfast* and Head's *Grotesques* helped pave the way in the 1910s. In the 1920s, plays like O'Neill's *The Emperor Jones* and *The Hairy Ape* were written to take place within vast empty space and incorporated repetitive elements, like characters moving, talking, and looking like. With the one-act plays of Thornton Wilder—especially *The Long Christmas Dinner*, *Pullman Car Hiawatha*, and *The Happy Journey to Trenton and Camden*— Thornton Wilder, borrowing from theater conventions of the past, investigated different ways to use a neutral stage while wresting it away from director/designer teams into the hands of the playwright. After Clifford Odets presented a bare stage which was transformed by the actors from a union hall to various homes and workplaces of the main characters in *Waiting for Lefty*, the bare and neutral stage made its most lasting impression in Wilder's *Our Town*.

The simple stage had now become a metaphor for all time and all place, a neutral space in which reality could be continually reshaped into diverse times and places with the aid of a bare minimum of language, gestures, and stage accessories.

Paralleling these theatrical explorations are writings by the artists themselves and their scholar/critic supporters which explain, justify, and document uses of the simple stage. Some of the most salient works by the American simple-stage artists are: "The New Rhythmic Drama" by Maurice Browne, *How's Your Second Act?* by Arthur Hopkins, *The Dramatic Imagination* by Robert Edmond Jones, *The Stage is Set* by Lee Simonson, and Thornton Wilder's "Preface to *Our Town*" and "Preface to *Three Plays*." Works by the contemporary scholar/critics providing theoretical and critical support for simple-stage work include: Sheldon Cheney's *The Art Theatre, The New Movement in the Theatre,* and *The Open-Air Theatre*; Kenneth Macgowan's *The Theatre of Tomorrow*; Walter Prichard Eaton's article, "The Theatre: A Question of Scenery"; Arthur Krow's *Play Production in America*; Hiram Moderwell's *Theatre of To-day*; and Clayton Hamilton's essay, "The New Art of Stage Direction." Taken together, these works compose a significant body of aesthetic theory for simplicity in stage practice.

It may be argued that simplified realism has remained the major stage-design style in the United States, after its beginnings in the little theaters and the amateur and professional work of Robert Edmond Jones and Lee Simonson between 1912 and 1924. This style continued under the leadership of Jo Mielziner (who apprenticed with Jones) in the 1940s and 1950s, most memorably in Mielziner's celebrated settings for *Glass Menagerie* (1945), *A Streetcar Named Desire* (1947), *Death of a Salesman* (1949), and *Cat on a Hot Tin Roof* (1955). It is in one or another hybrid form of simplified realism—somewhere between Wilder's bare stage and Belasco's elaborately detailed realism—that the simple stage is most consistently preserved in today's mainstream professional theater.

Simple stages also are standard fare in academic, community, and amateur performances. Many academic institutions have some form of "black-box" theater equipped with some combination of neutral screens, platforms, step-units, and adaptable seating to allow for simplified productions at minimum cost. The ubiquitous presence of these theaters and their neutral, economic properties are indebted to the ingenious designs of Samuel Hume and those who followed his example.

The stage as a neutral space in which a performer can create multiple realities with the help of a few properties and costume pieces has endured on the American stage, too. Some of the most prominent examples have been homegrown, others imported from Europe. Inspired by *The Yellow Jacket*, Ruth Draper created one-woman shows between 1912 and 1956 (the year she died), featuring short plays, performed by herself alone on a near-empty stage with minimal properties and costume pieces. In these pieces she evoked a whole society of characters in a wide variety of imagined times and settings. At about the time of Draper's death, French mime Marcel Marceau began touring his popular one-man performances throughout the United States. His artistic heritage can be traced to Jacques Copeau's acting school and mime Etienne Decroux, who was Marceau's teacher and Copeau's student. From the mid-1950s to the mid-1980s, Marceau has shown American audiences how much a lone performer can evoke on an empty stage lit by untinted light, with white-face makeup, a neutral costume, and no more than a single hat or property.

The plays of Samuel Beckett first came to the United States in the mid-1950s—about the same time as Marceau began to tour—in productions directed by Alan Schneider. Beckett took the next major playwriting step after Wilder in creating the stage as void. Beckett takes us into a fragmented world where stage emptiness expresses not a fluid space in which multiple realities are created, but one constant malignant void. *Waiting for Godot,* for example, presents an exterior wasteland, *Endgame,* an interior one. Since the writing of these plays, Beckett has given us stripped stages dominated by figures in urns, sand, or left off-stage, condemned to silence, stillness, existence in empty space. In *Not I,* for instance, he reduces the human figure to lips and a mere shadow existing in blackness. From the 1950s through the 1980s, Beckett's stark landscapes would mesmerize American theater artists like Wilder, playwright Edward Albee, and director Joseph Chaikin. For these artists and others, Beckett's plays were a beacon leading them toward a deeper, darker simplicity than the kind offered by modernist simple-stage artists like Jones and Wilder.

The next wave of influence came in the 1960s through the "poor theater" of Polish director Jerzy Grotowski . His approach in stripping the stage of all but essentials recalls the simplifiers working earlier in the century, especially Jacques Copeau and Maurice Browne. Grotowski's ideas, transmitted to the American theater community through his book *Towards a Poor Theatre* and his frequent visits to the United States, have had a tremendous impact on experimental American directors and designers who have studied with him. The influence is especially noticeable in the work of director Richard Schechner, designers Jerry Rojo and Jim Clayburgh, and their work with the Performance Group, and the Open Theatre's founder, Joseph Chaikin. Not all, but many productions by these theater artists since the late 1960s, have put focus on "poor" actors unencumbered by things. Examples include Schechner's productions of *Dionysus in 69* (1968), where actors in plain minimal costumes performed in a bare space between and within rough-wood platform towers, and Seneca's *Oedipus* (1977) performed in a pit of dirt surrounded by coliseum-style seating in miniature. Chaikin utilized distilled, spare imagery in productions such as *The Serpent* (1968), *Terminal* (1969), and *Antigone* (1982). Chaikin, collaborating with Sam Shepard, built simplicity into every aspect of the text and indicated *mise-en-scène* in their play, *Tongues* (1979). In it, a single actor, with a simple Indian blanket on his lap, sits without moving on a bare stage, back-to-back with a nonspeaking percussionist and embarks on an imaginative journey through the lives and souls of many people as well as his own.

Two theater simplifiers from England, a playwright and a director, have shown significant impact on the American theater. Harold Pinter's pared-down dialogue and abundant silences to suggest internal and external mysteries within and between characters sustained a legacy harking back to the writings of Maurice Maeterlinck and August Strindberg early in the century. One can trace the influence of Pinter's sparse dialogue on the hard-hitting, concise, and unembroidered directness of the language used in plays by American playwrights Sam Shepard and David Mamet, two of the most influential contemporary dramatists writing "serious drama" today.

American audiences have also been exposed to bare-stage aesthetics through major contributions by English director Peter Brook, who himself was influenced by Jerzy Grotowski . Brook presents classic plays and adaptations on material from non-Western cultures in stripped-bare environments that call attention to the performer in empty space. Not only do his ideals of simplification permeate his books *The Empty Space* (1968) and *The Shifting Point* (1987), which have been widely read throughout the American theater community, but also were incorporated in memorable productions which toured the United States, including his groundbreaking white-box *A Midsummer Night's Dream* (1970), followed by two productions taking place in a pit of sand, *The Ik* (1975) and *Carmen* (1983). Brook's version of Bizet's opera proved how cutting an opera down to its very bones could breathe new life into the piece itself as well as the medium in general. His production of Chekhov's *The Cherry Orchard* (1988) featured only a few pieces of furniture laid out on a large Persian carpet.

The primary reasons why twentieth-century theater artists have gone the way of simplicity have been aesthetic: to each of them, for their own reasons, less can be more. But the simple stage also has proved financially economical. Since there has been little consistent and reliable government subsidizing of the American professional theater (except between 1935 and 1939, the years of the Federal Theatre Project), it has had to exist mostly in accordance with the whims of the marketplace. Productions in intimate theaters with small audiences or productions that take risks and initially appeal more to the few than the many, by necessity, have had to be kept simple. Financial necessity and aesthetic appreciation of the simple things are forever coming together in the simple stage.

Aesthetically, the simple stage has allowed directors, designers, and playwrights to flow in and out of multiple levels of reality and varied contexts with relative ease. The neutral simple stage is supple and transformable; it is not weighted down by any one specific time and place. This suits it well for theater artists who want to make their own statements about the multi-layered nature of modern-day reality. The simple stage is fit for theatrical explorations into the layers of the unconscious, into the fluid and relative qualities of time and space, into the dark mysteries of metaphysical realms, into the act of performance itself—and into the interpenetration of these planes of existence. A bare stage can also make a statement when kept fixed. The expressionists in the 1920s and Samuel Beckett from the 1950s through the 1980s have turned the simple stage into a constant void that suggests desolation and alienation, a stark landscape stripped of meaning and interpersonal connection. Whether the simple stage is employed as fluid and neutral or as unchanging void, it is an emblem for modern times.

Kenneth Clark, in his book *Civilization*, has shown how a great painting, a piece of sculpture, even a bridge can tell the story of an era. So can a stage. The multiple-angled perspectives of Bibienas's stages reflected Baroque consciousness of infinity. The naturalistic stages of David Belasco told of a materialistic age and an Industrial Revolution capable of producing objects in what seemed like an endless volume, objects calling for our constant attention, sometimes determining our behavior, even our fate. The bare stage is a suitable emblem for modern consciousness because it can so readily be shaped into a symbol for infinite time and place, the endless human imagination, the vast unconscious. It can also connote empty meaningless lives, the illusory value of material things, feelings of alienation and solitude, an existence without God, or the haunting image of world's end. The simple stage has evolved into the empty stage, which has become the very picture of this century's collective encounter with Nothingness.

BIBLIOGRAPHY

A. BOOKS

Belasco, David. *The Theatre Through Its Stage Door*. New York: Harper and Brothers, 1919.

Bentley, Eric. *In Search of Theater*. New York: Vintage Books, 1955.

Bigsby, C. W. E. ed. *Plays by Susan Glaspell.* New York: Cambridge University Press, 1987.

Brockett, Oscar, and Robert Finlay. *Century of Innovation: A History of European and American Theater and Drama Since 1870*. Englewood Cliffs: Prentice-Hall, 1973.

Brown, Frederick. *Theater and Revolution*. New York: Vintage Books, 1989.

Brown, John Mason. *Upstage*. New York: W. W. Norton, 1930.

Browne, Maurice. *Too Late to Lament*. London: Victor Gollancz Ltd., 1955.

Burbank, Rex. *Thornton Wilder*. Boston: Twayne Publishers, 1978.

Burdick, Elizabeth, et al. *Contemporary Stage Design U.S.A.* Middletown, CT: International Theatre Institute of the United States, 1974.

Capra, Fritjof. *The Tao of Physics*. New York: Bantam Books, 1988.

Carter, Huntly. *The New Spirit in Drama and Art*. New York: Mitchell Kennerley, 1913.

— *The Theatre of Max Reinhardt*. New York: Mitchell Kennerley, 1914.

Chang, Chung-yuan. *Creativity and Taoism*. New York: Harper Colophon Books, 1963.

Cheney, Sheldon. *The Art Theatre*. New York: Alfred A. Knopf, 1917.

— *The New Movement in the Theatre*. New York: Mitchell Kennerley, 1914.

— *The Open-Air Theatre*. New York: Mitchell Kennerley, 1971.

— *Stage Decoration*. New York: Benjamin Bloom, 1966.

Chuang Tsu. *Inner Chapters*. Trans. Gia-Fu Feng and Jane English. New York: Vintage Books, 1974.

Claudel, Paul *Claudel on the Theatre*. Trans. Christine Trollope. Coral Gables, FL: University of Miami Press, 1972.

Cole, Toby, and Helen Chinoy. *Actors on Acting*. New York: Crown Publishers, 1970.

— *Directors on Directing.* New York: Bobbs-Merrill, 1963.

Craig, Edward Gordon. *On the Art of the Theatre.* Chicago: Browne's Bookstore, 1911.

De Bary, Theodore, ed. *The Buddhist Tradition in India, China and Japan.* New York: The Modern Library, 1969.

Dell, Floyd. *Homecoming, An Autobiography.* New York: Farrar and Rinehart, 1933.

Deutsch, Helen, and Stella Hanau. *The Provincetown: A Story of the Theatre.* New York: Farrar & Rinehart, 1931.

Dickinson, Thomas. *The Insurgent Theatre.* New York: B. W. Huebsch, 1917.

Eaton, Walter Prichard. *At the New Theatre and Others.* Boston: Small, Maynard & Co., 1910.

— *Plays and Players: Leaves from A Critic's Notebook.* New York, Appleton, 1916.

— *The Theatre Guild: The First Ten Years.* New York: Brentano's, 1929.

Fuerst, Walter, and Samuel Hume. *Twentieth Century Stage Decoration, Vols. 1 and 2.* London: Alfred A. Knopf, 1928.

Gallup, Donald, ed. *The Journals of Thornton Wilder 1939-1961.* New Haven: Yale University Press, 1985.

Garman, Ed. *The Art of Raymond Jonson: Painter.* Albuquerque: University of New Mexico Press, 1976.

Gassner, John. *Directions in Modern Theater and Drama.* New York: Holt, Rinehart & Winston, 1967.

Gelb, Arthur and Barbara Gelb. *O'Neill.* New York: Harper and Row, 1973.

Glaspell, Susan. *The Road to the Temple.* New York: Frederick A. Stokes Company, 1927.

Goldstein, Malcolm. *The Art of Thornton Wilder.* Lincoln: University of Nebraska Press, 1965.

Goldstone, Richard. *Thornton Wilder: An Intimate Portrait.* New York: E. P. Dutton, 1975.

Harrison, Gilbert A. *The Enthusiast: A Life of Thornton Wilder.* New Haven: Ticknor and Fields, 1983.

Hasumi, Toshimitsu. *Zen in Japanese Art.* Trans. from the German by John Petrie. London: Routledge & Kegan Paul, 1962.

Herrigel, Eugen. *Zen in the Art of Archery.* New York: Vintage Books, 1971.

Hisamatsu, H. S. *Zen and the Fine Arts.* Trans. Gishin Tokiwa. Kyoto, Japan: Kodansha International Ltd., 1971.

Hoover, Marjorie. *Meyerhold: The Art of Conscious Theater.* Amherst, Mass.: University of Massachusetts Press, 1974.

Hopkins, Arthur. *How's Your Second Act?* New York: Samuel French, 1931.

— *To a Lonely Boy.* Garden City, New York: Doubleday, Doran & Co., 1937.

— *Reference Point.* New York: Samuel French, 1948.

Hume, Samuel, and Lois Foster. *Theater and School.* New York: Samuel French, 1932.

Illing, Richard. *The Art of Japanese Prints.* New York: Mayflower Books, 1980.

Jones, Robert Edmond. *The Dramatic Imagination.* New York: Duell, Sloan & Pearce, 1941.

— *Drawings for the Theatre.* New York: Theatre Arts, 1925.

Keene, Donald. *No: The Classical Theatre of Japan.* Tokyo: Kodansha International Ltd., 1973.

Knapp, Bettina Liebowitz. *Louis Jouvet: Man of the Theatre.* New York: Columbia University Press, 1957.

— *The Reign of the Theatrical Director: French Theatre, 1887-1924*. Troy, NY: Whitston Publishing Co., 1988.

Komisarjevsky, Theodore. *Myself and the Theater*. New York: E. P. Dutton and Company, 1930.

—and Lee Simonson. *Settings and Costumes of the Modern Stage*. New York: Benjamin Bloom, 1966.

Kreymborg, Alfred. *Troubadour, An Autobiography*. New York: Boni and Liveright, 1925.

Krows, Arthur Edwin. *Play Production in America*. New York: Henry Holt and Company, 1916.

Kuner, M. C. *Thornton Wilder: The Bright and the Dark*. New York: Thomas Y. Crowell, 1972.

Lao Tsu. *Tao Te Ching*. Trans. Gia-Gu Feng and Jane English. New York: Vintage Books, 1972.

Latourette, Kenneth Scott. *The Chinese: Their History and Culture*. New York: Macmillan, 1946.

Leabhart, Thomas. *Modern and Post-Modern Mime*. New York: St. Martin's Press, 1989.

Macgowan, Kenneth. *The Theatre of Tomorrow*. New York: Boni and Liveright, 1921.

Macgowan, Kenneth, and Robert Edmond Jones. *Continental Stagecraft*. New York: Harcourt, Brace and Co., 1922.

Macgowan, Kenneth, and William Melnitz. *The Living Stage*. Englewood Cliffs, NJ: Prentice Hall, 1955.

MacKay, Constance D'arcy. *The Little Theater in the United States*. New York: Henry Holt & Co., 1917.

Marker, Lise-Lone. *David Belasco: Naturalism in the American Theatre*. Princeton, NJ: Princeton University Press, 1975.

Marshall, Norman. *The Producer and the Play*. London: MacDonald and Company, 1957.

Moderwell, Hiram K. *Theatre of To-day*. New York: John Lane Co., 1914.

Moses, Montrose and John Mason Brown. *American Theatre as Seen by its Critics, 1752-1934*. W. W. Norton and Co., New York, 1934.

Munro, Thomas. *Oriental Aesthetics*. Cleveland: The Press of Western Reserve University, 1965.

Nadel, Norman. *A Pictorial History of the Theatre Guild*. New York: Crown Publishers, 1969.

Pendleton, Ralph. *The Theatre of Robert Edmond Jones*. Middletown, CT: Wesleyan University Press, 1958.

Plugge, Domis. *History of Greek Play Production*. New York: Bureau of Publications, Columbia University Teacher's College, 1938.

Pound, Ezra, and Ernest Fenollosa, eds. *The Classic Noh Theater of Japan*. New York: New Directions Publishing Co., 1959.

Pronko, Leonard. *Theater East and West*. Berkeley: University of California Press, 1967.

Purdom, C. B. *Harley Granville Barker: Man of the Theater, Dramatist, and Scholar*. Cambridge, MA: Harvard University Press, 1956.

Reps, Paul. *Zen Flesh, Zen Bones*. New York: Anchor Books, n.d.

Rudlin, John. *Jacques Copeau*. New York: Cambridge University Press, 1986.

Saint-Denis, Michel. *Theatre: The Rediscovery of Style*. New York: Theatre Arts Books, 1960.

Sarlos, Robert. *Jig Cook and the Provincetown Players: Theatre in Ferment*. Boston: University of Massachusetts Press, 1982.

Sayler, Oliver. *Our American Theatre*. New York: Brentano's, 1923.

Scott, A. C. *The Theatre of Asia*. New York: Macmillan, 1972.

Simonson, Lee. *Part of a Lifetime*. New York: Duell, Sloan and Pearce, 1943.

— *The Stage is Set*. New York: Harcourt, Brace and Co., 1932.

Speaight, Robert. *William Poel and the Elizabethan Revival*Cambridge, MA: Harvard University Press, 1954.

Stage Society of New York. *The Art of the Theatre: An Exhibition, November 1914*. New York: 1914.

Stern, Ernst. *My Life My Stage*. London: Victor Gollancz Ltd., 1951.

Styan, J. L. *Max Reinhardt*. New York: Cambridge University Press, 1982.

Suzuki, D. T. *An Introduction to Zen Buddhism*. New York: Grove Press, 1964.

— *Zen and Japanese Culture*. Princeton: Princeton University Press, 1973.

Timberlake, Craig. *The Life and Work of David Belasco, the Bishop of Broadway*. New York: Library Publishers, 1954.

Waley, Arthur. *The No Plays of Japan*. New York: Grove Press, 1920.

Warren, Neilla. *The Letters of Ruth Draper, 1920-1956*. New York: Charles Scribner's Sons, 1979.

Watts, Alan. *The Way of Zen*. New York: Vintage Books, 1957.

Wilder, Thornton. *American Characteristics and Other Essays*. New York: Harper & Row, 1979.

— *The Angel That Troubled the Waters*. New York: Coward-McCann, 1928.

— *The Happy Journey*. New York: Samuel French, 1931.

— *The Long Christmas Dinner and Other Plays In One Act*. New York: Harper Colophon Books, 1963.

— "Some Thoughts on Playwriting (1941)." in Toby Cole, ed. *Playwrights on Playwriting*. New York: Hill and Wang, 1960.

— *Three Plays*. New York: Avon Books, 1957.

Wilson, Garff. *Three Hundred Years of American Drama and Theatre*. Englewood Cliffs, NJ: Prentice-Hall, 1973.

Young, William. *Documents of American Theater History, Vol. 2*. Chicago: American Library Association, 1973.

Zabel, Morton Dauwen. *The Art of Ruth Draper: Her Dramas and Characters*. Garden City, NY: Doubleday and Company, 1960.

Zucker, A. E. *The Chinese Theater*. Boston: Little, Brown and Company, 1925.

B. MAGAZINES

Allard, Stephen. "The Art Societies and Theatre Art." *Theatre Arts Magazine*, 1 (February 1917), p. 31.

Belasco, David. "How I Stage My Plays." *Theatre Magazine*, 2 (December, 1902), pp. 31-32.

— "Why I Believe in the Little Things." *The Ladies Home Journal*, 28 (September, 1911), pp. 15, 73.

Browne, Maurice. "Lonely Places." *Theatre Arts Magazine*, 5 (July 1921), pp. 207-215.

— "The New Rhythmic Drama." *The Drama*, 4 (November 1914), pp. 616-630; 5 (February 1915), pp. 146-160.

— "The Temple of a Living Art." *The Drama*, 3 (November 1913), pp. 160-178.

Bullard, F. Lauriston. "Boston's Toy Theatre." *The Theatre*, 15 (March 1912), pp. 84-86.

Cheney, Sheldon. "The American Artist and the Stage." *International Studio*, 74 (December 1921), pp. 150-157.

— "Answering Mr. Simonson." *Theatre Arts Monthly*, 6 (July 1922), pp. 231-232.

— "Cloyd Head's Grotesques." *Theatre Arts Magazine*, 1 (November 1916), pp. 13-20.

— "The Exhibition of American Stage Designs at the Bourgeois Galleries." *Theatre Arts Magazine*, 3 (April 1919), p. 83.

— "The International Exhibition in Amsterdam." *Theatre Arts Monthly*, 6 (July 1922), pp. 140-146.

— "The International Theatre Exposition." *Theatre Arts*, 10 (March 1926), pp. 204-206.

— "The Most Important Thing in the Theater." *Theatre Arts Monthly*, 1 (August 1917), pp. 167-171.

— "The New Interior," *Theatre Arts Magazine*, 1 (May 1917), p. 84.

— "New York's Best Season." *Theatre Arts*, 1 (February 1917), p. 67.

— "The Painter in the Theater." *Theatre Arts Monthly*, 6 (July 1922), pp. 191-199.

— "Sam Hume's Adaptable Settings." *Theatre Arts Magazine*, 1 (May 1917), pp. 119-127.

— "The Space Stage." *Theatre Arts*, 11 (October 1927), pp. 762-772.

— "What We Stand For." *Theatre Arts Magazine*, 1 (August 1917), p. 149.

"Chicago's Little Theatre." *Literary Digest*, 47 (August 23, 1913), p. 287.

Copeau, Jacques. "The New School of Stage Scenery." *Vanity Fair*, (June 1917), pp. 36, 114.

— "The Theatre Du Vieux-Colombier." *The Drama*, 29 (February 1918), pp. 69-75.

— "The True Spirit of the Art of the Stage." *Vanity Fair*, (April 1917), in Billy Rose Collection, Lincoln Center, Robinson Locke Collection, vol. 84, p. 155.

Cowley, Malcolm. "The Man Who Abolished Time." *Saturday Review*, October 6, 1956, pp. 13-14, 50-52.

Dukore, Bernard F. "Maurice Browne and the Chicago Little Theatre." *Theatre Survey*, vol. 3, 1962, pp. 59-78.

Eaton, Walter Prichard. "Acting and the New Stagecraft." *Theatre Arts Monthly*, 1 (January 1916), pp. 9-12.

— "Arthur Hopkins." *Theatre Arts*, 5 (July 1921), pp. 230-236.

— "The New Stagecraft." *American Magazine*, 74 (May 1912), pp. 104-113.

— "The Significance of the Theatre Guild." *The Theatre*, 42 (July 1925), p. 12.

— "The Theatre: A Question of Scenery." *American Magazine*, 72 (July 1911), pp. 374-384.

Eliot, Samuel A. "Le Theatre du Vieux Colombier." *Theatre Arts Magazine*, 3 (January 1919), pp. 25-30.

Feinsod, Arthur. "Arthur Feinsod Replies." *The Drama Review*, T112 (Winter 1986), pp. 10-11.

— "Stage Designs of a Single Gesture: The Early Work of Robert Edmond Jones." *The Drama Review*, T102 (Summer 1984), pp. 102-120.

Gottholdt, Ruth. "New Scenic Art of the Theatre." *Theatre Magazine*, (May 1915), p. 137.

Guthrie, Tyrone. "The World of Thornton Wilder." *New York Times Magazine*,

November 27, 1955, pp. 26-27, 64.

Hamilton, Clayton. "Belasco and the Independent Theatre." *Bookman*, 45 (March 1917), pp. 8-12.

— "The Decorative Drama," *The Bookman*, 35 (April 1912), p. 168.

— "The New Art of Stage Direction." *The Bookman*, 35 (July 1912), pp. 481-488.

— "The 'New' Stagecraft Ceases to be New and is Immediate and Necessary." *Vogue*, 47 (February 15, 1916) pp. 118, 120.

— "Scenic Settings in America." *The Bookman*, 43 (March 1916), pp. 20-29.

— "Seen on the Stage." *Vogue*, (January 1, 1916), p. 33.

— "Seen on the Stage." *Vogue*, (June 15, 1917), p. 60.

— "Seen on the Stage." *Vogue*, (December 1, 1918), n.p.

Head, Cloyd. "The Chicago Little Theatre." *Theatre Arts Magazine*, 1 (May 1917), pp. 110-116.

— *Grotesques.* in *Poetry: A Magazine of Verse*, October 1916.

Hewitt, Barnard. "Thornton Wilder Says 'Yes'." *Tulane Drama Review*, December 1959, pp. 110-120.

Hopkins, Arthur. "Brain Plays in Germany," *Harper's Weekly*, 58 (September 13, 1913), p. 25.

— "Hearing a Play with My Eyes," *Harper's Weekly*, 50 (August 23, 1913), p. 13.

— "Our Unreasonable Theatre," *Theatre Arts*, 2 (February 1918), pp. 79-84.

Hornblow, Arthur. "Mr. Hornblow Goes to the Play." *Theatre Magazine*. 27 (January 1918), p. 21.

Howard, Homer. "The Toy Theatre of Boston." *The Drama*, 4 (May 1914), pp. 264-269.

Hume, Samuel. "The New Stage-craft," *The Cornhill Booklet*, 4 (December 1914), pp. 72-75.

— "A Permanent Set for the School Stage." *Theatre and School*, 7 (October 1928), pp. 14-19.

— "A Permanent Set for the School Stage." *Theatre and School*, 11 (October 1932), pp. 8-12.

— "The Use and Abuse of the Greek Theatre." *Sunset*, 29 (August 1912), p. 203.

Issac, Edith, "Who Killed Cock Robin?" *Theatre Arts Monthly*, (March 1938), pp. 172-173.

"Jacques Copeau and his Theatre." *Theatre Magazine*, 26 (December 1917), p. 342.

"Japan's Greatest Actress." *Harper's Bazaar*, 33 (March 24, 1900), pp. 249, 251-252.

Johnson, C. Raymond. "The New Stage Designing." *Theatre Arts Magazine*, 3 (August 1919), p. 121.

Jones, Robert Edmond. "The Future of Decorative Art of the Theatre." *Theatre Magazine*, 15 (May 1917), p. 266.

— "Notes on the Theatre." *Theatre Arts*, 8 (May 1924), pp. 323-325.

— "Six Drawings for The Cenci." *Theatre Arts*, 8 (June 1924), pp. 408-431.

— "The Artist's Approach to the Theatre," *Theatre Arts Monthly*, 12 (September 1928) pp. 633-634.

Katz, Albert. "Copeau as Regisseur: An Analysis." *Educational Theatre Journal*, 25 (May 1973), pp. 160-172.

— "Jacques Copeau: The American Reaction." *Players Magazine*, (February 1970), pp. 133-143.

Komisarjevsky, Theodore. "The Producer in the Theatre." *The Drama*, 13 (October 1934), pp. 19-22.

Larson, Orville. "A Note on the New Stagecraft in America." *Educational Theatre Journal*, 13 (December 1961), pp. 278-279.

Larson, Orville. "To The Editor." *The Drama Review*, T112 (Winter 1986), pp. 9-10.

"Le Vieux Colombier," *Vogue*, (February 15, 1918), p. 53.

"The Limits of Stage Illusion." *The Living Age*, 268 (December 3, 1910), p. 589.

Macgowan, Kenneth. "And Again Repertory," *Theatre Arts Magazine*, 7 (April 1923), pp. 98-108.

—— "America's Best Season in the Theatre." *Theatre Arts*, 4 (April 1920), pp. 91-104.

—— "America's First Exhibition of the New Stagecraft." *Theatre Magazine*, 21 (January 1915), p. 28.

—— "Broadway at the Spring." *Theatre Arts*, 6 (July 1922), pp. 179-90.

—— "The New Season." *Theatre Arts*, 5 (January 1921), pp. 3-14.

—— "The New Stagecraft in America." *Century*, 87 (January 1914), pp. 416-421.

—— "Portrait of a Season." *Theatre Arts*, 6 (April 1922), pp. 91-106.

—— "Robert Edmond Jones." *Theater Arts*, 9 (November 1925), pp. 720-726.

—— "Ten Years of the New Stagecraft." *Vanity Fair*, 18 (February 1922), pp. 47, 82-86.

—— "Year's End." *Theatre Arts*, 6 (January 1922), pp. 3-14.

Meyer, Annie Nathan. "The Vanishing Actor: And After." *Atlantic Monthly*, 113 (January 1914), pp. 89-90.

Moderwell, Hiram Kelley. "The Art of Robert Edmond Jones." *Theatre Arts*, 1 (1916-1917), pp. 50-61.

—— "The Cenci." *Theatre Arts*, 1 (February 1917), p. 61.

—— "A Note about Lee Simonson." *Theatre Arts*. 2 (December 1917), pp. 12-17.

—— "Scenery that Helps the Actor." *Theatre Magazine*, 24 (September 1916), p. 128.

—— "Stage Scenery in the Making." *The Theatre*, 2 (July 1916), p. 33.

"An Obliging Man." *Time Magazine*, 61 (January 12, 1953), pp. 45-47.

"The Other Players." *Theatre Magazine*, 27 (May 1918), p. 288.

Peters, Rollo. "To Jacques Copeau." *Theatre Arts Magazine*, 2 (February 1918), p. 84.

Raymond, Antonin. "The Theatre Du Vieux-Colombier." *Journal of the American Institute of Architects*, 5 (August 1917) pp. 384-387.

Rosse, Hermann. "Sketches of Oriental Theatres." *Theatre Arts Magazine*, 2 (Summer 1918), pp. 140-143.

Sargent, Epes. "Dramatic Progress of the Japanese." *Metropolitan Magazine*, (May 1900), pp. 497-503.

Sergeant, Elizabeth Shepley. "A New French Theatre," *The New Republic*, X (April 21, 1917), pp. 350-352.

Simonson, Lee. "Answering Mr. Cheney," *Theater Arts Monthly*, 6 (July 1922), pp. 226-230.

—— "The Case of Gordon Craig." *Theater Guild Magazine*, 8 (February 1931), pp. 18-23.

—— "The Function of the Setting." *The Arts*, 3 (January 1923), pp. 50-52.

—— "Historic Impressions." *New Republic*, 2 (March 1915), pp. 207-208.

—— "A Lesson in Stagecraft." *The Drama*, 14 (January 1924), pp. 133-137.

—— "The Necessary Illusion." *Theatre Arts Monthly*, 3 (April 1919), pp. 91-92.

—— "The Painter and the Stage." *Theatre Arts Monthly*, 2 (December 1917), pp. 3-12.

"Staging Shakespeare." *The Nation*, 82 (March 8, 1906), p. 193.

"The Theater of the 'Old Dove-Cote'." *Literary Digest*, (December 15, 1917), pp. 26-27.

"Tidings Brought to Mary." *The Dial*, 74 (February 1923), 216.

"Tidings Brought to Mary." *Theatre Magazine*, 37 (March 1923), p. 20.

Tietjens, Eunice. "The Work of C. Raymond Johnson." *Theatre Arts Magazine*, 4 (July 1920), pp. 227-237.

"'Twelfth Night' in French." *Vanity Fair*, (June 1919), n.p.

Volbach, Walther R. "Jacques Copeau, Appia's Finest Disciple." *Educational Theatre Journal*, 7 (October 1965), pp. 206-214.

Wright, Cuthbert. "Tidings." *The Freeman*, 6 (January 24, 1923), p. 473.

Yeats, W.B. "Instead of a Theatre." *Theatre Arts Magazine*, 3 (January 1919), pp. 35-37.

— "The Theater of Beauty," *Harper's Weekly*, 55 (November 11, 1911), p. 11.

"Yellow Jacket." *The Theatre Magazine*, 41 (December 1912), p. 163.

C. NEWSPAPERS

Atkinson, Brooks. "Critic at Large: Thornton Wilder, at 65, Full of Energy, Enthusiasm and a Thirst for Learning." *New York Times*, February 13, 1962, n.p.

Barnes, Djuna. "Introducing Monseur Copeau." *Evening Telegraph*, June 3, 1917, n.p., in Billy Rose Collection, Lincoln Center, Robinson Locke Collection, vol. 84, pp. 156-157.

Belasco, David. "David Belasco Sees A Menace to True Art in Toy Playhouses and Little Repertory Theatres," *New York Herald*, January 7, 1917, Drama Section, p. 1.

Bennett, James O'Donnell. "Art of Stage Management Versus Millinery." *The Sunday Record-Herald*, March 22, 1914, Part II, pp. 1-2.

— "Getting at the Meaning of the Experiments of Worthy Amateurs." *The Sunday Record-Herald*, November 17, 1912, Part II, p. 2.

— "On a Little Stage Mr. Browne Does Big Work." *The Sunday Record-Herald*, February 2, 1913, Part II, p. 7.

— "Pretty Toys at the Little Theater." *The Chicago Record-Herald*, October 23, 1913, p. 6.

Bonner, Geraldine. "M. Copeau's Players." *New York Times*, March 17, 1918, n.p., in Billy Rose Collection, Robinson Locke Collection, vol. 347, p. 131.

Broun, Heywood. "At the Garrick Theatre." *New York World*, December 25, 1922.

Castellun, Maida. "In the World of the Theatre." *New York Call*, June 4, 1922.

"Chicago Little Theater Works on Unity Basis." *Christian Science Monitor*, November 2, 1915, n. p.

Copeau, Jacques. "To Bring Back Actors to Fervor." *Boston Transcript*, December 19, 1917, p. 11.

Corbin, John. "Tidings Brought to Mary." *New York Times*, December 25, 1922, p. 20.

Craig, James. "The Tidings Brought to Mary." *New York Mail*, December 27, 1922, n. p., in *The Tidings Brought to Mary* file, Billy Rose Collection.

"Drama League to Examine Little Theater Exhibit." *The Christian Science Monitor*, April 15, 1916, p. 8.

Gelb, Arthur. "Thornton Wilder, 63, Sums Up." *New York Times*, November 6, 1961, p. 74.

Hall, O. L. "Company; Scenic Artist States His Faith; Stage Gossip." *Chicago Daily Journal*, December 15, 1915, n. p.

— "Little Theatre Offers 'The Happy Prince' and Biblical Pantomime." *The Chicago Daily Journal*, December 27, 1913, p. 7.

— "Three Little Plays by Mrs. Havelock Ellis are Staged by Maurice Browne." *Chicago Daily Journal*, February 3, 1915, p. 6.

Hammond, Percy. "Oddments and Remainders," *New York Tribune*, January 8, 1922, p. 6.

Hopkins, Arthur. "The Approaching Macbeth." *New York Times*, February 6, 1921, section 6, p. 1.

"Ibsen Played in French." *New York World*, December 3, 1918, p. 11.

"Japanese Tragedy Admirably Staged." *New York Times*, November 14, 1916, n. p., Washington Square Players file, Billy Rose Collection.

Jones, Robert Edmond. "The Decorator." *New York Times*, December 10, 1916, section 2, p. 2.

Leslie, Amy. "The Trojan Women At Little Theater." *The Chicago Daily News*, March 19, 1914, p. 7, in Maurice Browne file, Billy Rose Collection.

"Little Plays Again at the Bandbox." *New York Times*, March 27, 1915, n. p., in Washington Square Players file, Billy Rose Collection.

Moderwell, Hiram Kelley. "Mr. Simonson's Big Idea." *New York Times*, June 18, 1916, section 2, p. 6.

Morgenstern, Joseph. "The Demons Sit on His Shoulder." *New York Herald Tribune*. January 7, 1962, p. 5.

Nathan, George Jean. "New York Letter." *Chicago Herald*, December 16, 1917, n. p., in Billy Rose Collection, Lincoln Center, Robinson Locke Collection, vol. 347, p. 102.

"News and Gossip of the Theatre." *The Chicago Daily Journal*, May 15, 1913, p. 6.

Noguchi, Yone. "Sada Yacco." *New York Dramatic Mirror*, February 17, 1906, p. 11.

"Plan 'Little Theater'." *Chicago Daily News*, February 25, 1912, p. 15.

Porter, Russell Bryan. "Copeau Says No 'Highbrow Ideas' Rule Vieux Colombier." *New York World*, January 13, 1918, n. p. in Billy Rose Collection, Lincoln Center, Robinson Locke Collection, vol. 347, p. 129.

Roche, Henri Pierre. "Arch Rebel of French Theatre Coming Here." *New York Times*, January 28, 1917, n. p. in Billy Rose Collection, Lincoln Center, Stead Collection Scrapbook, p. 3.

"Round Boston Stages." *Boston Transcript*, October 27, 1916, n. p., in Robert Edmond Jones file, Billy Rose Collection.

Simonson, Lee. "Men as Stage Scenery Walking." *New York Times*, May 25, 1924, section 4, p. 8.

— "New Ways, New Means, New Outcome as European States Now Yield Them." *Boston Evening Transcript*, December 17, 1921.

"Stagecraft at the Chicago Little Theatre." *Christian Science Monitor*, November 2, 1915, n. p., in Maurice Browne file, Lincoln Center's Billy Rose Collection.

Taubman, Howard. "Theatre—Three Wilder Plays." *New York Times*, January 12, 1962, n. p.

"Trojan Women Comes to Columbus." *Columbus Citizen*, May 11, 1915, n. p., Maurice Browne file, Billy Rose Collection, Lincoln Center, New York.

"'Trojan Women' Stirs Large Audience Profoundly." *Indianapolis News*, May 19, 1915, p. 9.

Wallace, David. "Writing a Chinese Play." *The New York Dramatic Mirror*, November 13, 1912, n. p.

Woollcott, Alexander. "Claudel in Thirty-Fifth Street." *New York Herald*, December 25,

1922, n. p.

"The Yellow Jacket." *The New York Dramatic Mirror*, November 13, 1912, p. 7.

"Zingoro An Earnest Statue Maker, The Royalist or Kojima Takanori, The Geisha and the Knight—Plays in Japanese." *New York Times*, March 2, 1900, p. 7.

D. DISSERTATIONS

Black, Eugene Robert. "Robert Edmond Jones: Poetic Artist of the New Stagecraft." Diss., University of Wisconsin, 1955.

Bolin, John Seelye. "Samuel Hume: Artist and Exponent of the American Art Theater." Diss., University of Michigan, 1970.

Bradley, Robert Harlow. "Proposals for the Reform of the Art of the Theatre as Expressed in General American Periodicals, 1900-1915." Diss., University of Illinois, 1964.

Dukore, Bernard F. "Maurice Browne and the Chicago Little Theater." Diss., U. of Illinois at Urbana-Champaign, 1957.

Feinsod, Arthur. "The Origins of the Minimalist *Mise-en-Scène* in the United States." Diss., New York University, 1986.

Katz, Albert. "A Historical Study of Jacques Copeau and the Vieux-Colombier Company at the Garrick Theater in New York City." Diss., University of Michigan, 1966.

Handly, John Guy. "A History of the *Theatre Arts Magazine*: 1916-1948." Diss., Louisiana State University, 1960.

Hansen, Delmar. "The Directing Theory and Practice of Arthur Hopkins." Diss., University of Iowa, 1961.

Johnson, Gordon Arnold. "The Greek Productions of Margaret Anglin." Diss., Case Western Reserve University, 1971.

Nordvold, Robert O. "Showcase for the New Stagecraft: The Scenic Designs of the Washington Square Players and the Theatre Guild." Diss., Indiana University, 1973.

Vilhauer, William. "A History and Evaluation of the Provincetown Players." Diss., University of Iowa, 1965.

Wank, Eugene. "The Washington Square Players: Experiment Toward Professionalism." Diss., University of Oregon, 1973.

York, Zack. "Lee Simonson: Artist-Craftsman of the Theatre." Diss., University of Wisconsin, 1951.

E. PROGRAMS, YEARBOOKS, EPHEMERA AND UNPUBLISHED DOCUMENTS

Browne, Maurice. "Inspiration and Rhythm 1914-1916." Unpublished manuscript in Maurice Browne collection at University of Michigan Special Collections Library, p. 33.

Letter from Maurice Browne to Raymond Jonson, dated November 16, 1916—on file in the Jonson Gallery at the University of New Mexico, Albuquerque.

Hume, Sam. Program for "Exhibition of New Stagecraft." Detroit Museum of Art, April

22-May 13, 1915.

Johnson, Arthur. "The Theatre of Raymond Jonson." In Jonson Gallery, University of Mexico, Albuquerque.

Jonson, Raymond, part of letter reprinted in *The Drama League Monthly*, 3 (February 1919), p. 8.

Moderwell, Hiram Kelley. "The Modern Stage Movement in Europe and America." In *Drama League of America Yearbook—* 1915-1916, p. 71.

"The Theatre du Vieux-Colombier: Paris—October, 1913 to May, 1914." Essay in Program for Jacques Copeau's first season at Garrick Theatre, in Billy Rose Collection, Lincoln Center Library of the Performing Arts.

INDEX

ABOUT THE AUTHOR

ARTHUR FEINSOD is Director of Theater in the Theater and Dance Department at Trinity College, Hartford, Connecticut. He has written essays and reviews appearing in *The Drama Review* and *Theatre Journal* and co-edited a book of plays by his playwriting students, *Strawberries, Potatoes and Other Fantasies*, with an introduction by Edward Albee. Recently he has been the recipient of a National Endowment for the Humanities grant. Feinsod is also a playwright and director.